BLOOD, RUST, AND STEEL

By Stuart MacBride

THE LOGAN MCRAE BOOKS

Cold Granite

Dying Light

Broken Skin

Flesh House

Blind Eye

Dark Blood

Shatter the Bones

Close to the Bone

22 Dead Little Bodies

The Missing and the Dead

In the Cold Dark Ground

The Blood Road

All That's Dead

This House of Burning Bones

STEEL & TUFTY BOOKS

Now We Are Dead (fits here in the timeline: after *In the Cold Dark Ground*)

And the Corpse Wore Tartan (fits here in the timeline: after *All That's Dead*)

Blood, Rust, and Steel (fits here in the timeline: after *This House of Burning Bones*)

THE ASH HENDERSON BOOKS

Birthdays for the Dead

A Song for the Dying

The Coffinmaker's Garden

THE OLDCASTLE BOOKS

A Dark So Deadly (fits here in the timeline: after *A Song for the Dying*)

No Less the Devil (fits here in the timeline: after *The Coffinmaker's Garden*)

In a Place of Darkness (fits here in the timeline: after *The Coffinmaker's Garden*)

STANDALONE

The Dead of Winter

OTHER WORKS

Sawbones (a novella)

12 Days of Winter (a short-story collection)

Partners in Crime (two Logan and Steel short stories)

The 45% Hangover (a Logan and Steel novella)

The Completely Wholesome Adventures of Skeleton Bob (a picture book)

WRITING AS STUART B. MACBRIDE

Halfhead

BLOOD, RUST, AND STEEL

Stuart MacBride

MACMILLAN

First published 2026 by Macmillan
an imprint of Pan Macmillan
The Smithson, 6 Briset Street, London EC1M 5NR
EU representative: Macmillan Publishers Ireland Ltd, 1st Floor,
The Liffey Trust Centre, 117–126 Sheriff Street Upper,
Dublin 1 D01 YC43
Associated companies throughout the world

ISBN 978-1-0350-6498-4 HB
ISBN 978-1-0350-6499-1 TPB

1 3 5 7 9 8 6 4 2

A CIP catalogue record for this book is available from the British Library.

Typeset by Palimpsest Book Production Ltd, Falkirk, Stirlingshire
Printed and bound in the UK using 100% Renewable Electricity by
CPI Group (UK) Ltd

FSC www.fsc.org MIX Paper | Supporting responsible forestry FSC® C116313

In Chapter 2.14, Davey recites part of the Police Act 1996, Section 90(1). He does it again in Chapter 2.16, and Pine joins in too. This is public sector information licensed under the Open Government Licence v3.0.

In Chapter 2.16 Naomi butchers 'With Cat-Like Tread' from The Pirates of Penzance (or The Slave of Duty) by W.S. Gilbert and Arthur Sullivan, first produced at the Royal Bijou Theatre in Paignton, Devon, 30 December 1879. She makes a much better job of it in Chapter 3.01.

For my grandfather,
William 'Bill' MacBride,
26 Jan 1915 – 27 May 1984
who enlisted at the start of WWII,
joined the Highland Light Infantry,
then transferred from there to the 24th Lancers –
driving tanks in Holland, France, and Germany,
fighting Nazis.

He would be appalled by the rising tide of fascism,
ignorance, and hate that's sweeping around the world today.

— warning —

the following is NOT based on a true story
and anyone who says otherwise is lying

carrion, crows

it begins with a scream...

Alice glared at him from the passenger seat. 'I don't care: pull over.'

Scott forced a smile. Pregnancy hormones were supposed to make people all maternal and loving and caring, but Alice had turned into a proper jet-propelled—

'*Pull over!* PULL OVER!' Her face went the same shade of beetroot that had preceded every explosion for the last eight-and-a-bit months, turning her freckles so dark they were nearly as black as the shapeless summer dress that made her look a *teeny* bit like she was wearing a bin-bag.

Scott did *not* sigh. Because that just hastened an impending detonation. Instead, he peered out through the gritty windscreen: fog. Nothing but sodding fog since the Aberdeen bypass. A velvet-grey shroud that smothered the life out of everything.

Should've made good time, but not in this.

Could barely do thirty. Too risky. What if they rammed into the back of something? Even this early in the morning. And Alice was angry enough already.

She jabbed a finger at the fog. 'There!'

A sign glowed blue at the side of the road: a capital 'P' for parking. But just beyond it lay a line of gloomy orange cones, with reflective stripes, flanked by 'NO ENTRY' and 'WORK ACCESS ONLY', blocking off the lay-by. So that was a non-starter.

'Maybe if we—'

'PULL OVER RIGHT BLOODY *NOW*!' Eyes clenched, teeth bared, spittle flecking the dashboard.

So he did.

Hitting the brakes, swerving between the cones … only maybe not one hundred percent successfully, because a horrible *scraiking* noise grated out from the front of the car. Then the nose dipped as they hit a pothole the size of Belgium, and the cone they were pushing must've tipped over, because that grinding gravelly sound worked its way from beneath the bonnet to under his feet, then the box-laden back seat, and finally the boot. Each *crunk* and *scrrrrrrrrrrrit* like tinfoil on a filling.

Then it was gone.

Hopefully not taking anything with it.

He steered through the minefield of ruts, dips, scars, holes, and dents, past a dark mound of gravel and another of macadam, then a pair of black wheelie bins, before coming to a halt.

Scott killed the engine.

Huffed out a breath as Alice struggled with her seatbelt.

Checked the rear-view mirror for evidence of the cone's flattened corpse. But the boxes, piled up in the back, blocked everything. Two whole lives, packed into a beige Citroën C1.

Well, *three* now.

Which was a thought…

The car's dipped headlights still made the fog glow, picking out the curve of the lay-by, the semicircle of grass between them and the A96, and the angry-pink spikes of fireweed with a dark mass of woodland beyond.

'There we go. Pulled over.' He turned off the lights.

Gloom swamped the lay-by. Like someone had just shut the lid of his coffin.

He turned the lights back on again.

'Bastard thing!' Alice wrestled the clippy end free and hauled off her seatbelt. Snarling out her cruellest impersonation of him: 'Oh no, I can't be arsed stopping for *you*, Alice. You're not *important* enough.'

'I didn't say that. I just said you might be more comfortable if—'

'*You* try being "*comfortable*" with a foot in your bloody bladder!' She shoved the passenger door open. 'This whole thing was a stupid idea! I should've sodding *known*!'

Difficult to tell if she meant the trip, the new job, the baby, or them...

Alice squeezed and wriggled, trying to birth herself through the car's door. 'Oh for *God's* sake!'

He clambered out into the fog – so thick you could chew mouthfuls of it, heavy with that fusty soil smell, tainted with something rank and slithery. Cold enough to raise goose-pimples on his bare arms as he hurried around to her side, ready to help. 'Here, let me—'

'Get off!' She slapped his hand away. 'I can do it myself.'

A septic glow bloomed in the fog, curving closer, then thundered by on the main road, hauling an articulated lorry behind it. The huge machine was only visible for a moment, before the grey world swallowed it again, leaving nothing but the bitter blue taint of diesel.

Scott reached for her again. 'I was only trying to—'

'I can *do* it!' It took a lot of huffing and puffing and panting and wriggling, but eventually she levered herself out into the murk. Glaring at Scott till he retreated.

'I'm sorry, I'm sorry. We'll be there soon. Promise.' He checked his watch: 06:41. 'Twenty minutes, tops.'

But Alice wasn't listening, she was wading out into the fireweed that teemed along the lay-by's edge. She was stopped by a waist-high chain-link fence – where she turned her back on the looming woods, hitched-up her dress, dropped her massive blue pants, then squatted down to pee. 'Told you to stop in Inver-sodding-rurie.' A wobble, and she steadied herself against the fence. 'Whose *bloody* stupid idea was it to leave at three in the morning?'

Scott looked out into the fog. Away. Anywhere but at the grown woman peeing in the weeds at the side of a lay-by. Because even after six years together *some* things were not meant to be shared. 'We didn't want to be late for the movers, did we? No. Of course not. It's just a little—'

'Should *never* have listened to you. I had a perfectly good job in Dundee!'

Because everything always had to be *his* fault, didn't it.

A car grumbled by, taking with it the sickly glow of head-lights – arcing through the fog.

Then silence.

Except for Alice's … *widdling*.

Two crows cawed their way out of the woods, like ragged scraps of black plastic caught on the non-existent breeze. They settled on top of the wheelie bins. And stared at him.

He cleared his throat.

Shuffled his feet.

Fiddled with the tatty collection of friendship bracelets that dangled from his left wrist.

And Alice was *still* going.

Should've put the car radio on. At least that would mask the—

A snap rang out, sharp and jagged, in the woods behind the lay-by.

Scott whirled around. Staring at the out-of-focus grey mass of trunks and branches. 'Hello?' Backing away a pace. 'Did you hear that?' He swallowed. Pulled his chin up. 'Hell-oh-oh? Anyone there?'

Silence.

Then another *crack*.

His bladder clenched.

He retreated a little further. 'There's *definitely* someone out there.'

More silence.

'Oh, for God's sake. It was a badger, or a fox, or a … *whatever*. Grow up. You're such a baby.'

But what if it wasn't?

What if *someone* was out there?

Scott went up on his tiptoes, ears straining to pick out the telltale sounds of a pervert or murderer, creeping through the woods towards them.

Nothing, just the horrible sound of Alice—

Another ghostly artic roared past, and Scott flinched hard enough to leave the ground for a second – a startled squeal shrieking free as the lorry's frosted headlights swept across the lay-by.

He spun around just in time to catch the HGV disappearing back into the fog. Yeah. That was…

Gave himself a little shake. 'Just … caught me by surprise, that's all.' Nothing wrong with that. He was on high alert, protecting his family. Like a ninja. Scott cleared his throat. 'Look: the satnav said we passed a sort of bus-that's-a-diner thing just back there. The Pitstop?' Pointing away into the gloomy grey murk. 'Think they might be open yet? You know, for bacon butties and things? Maybe you'd feel better with—'

'Tissue.'

Bit random. 'What?'

'TISSUE!' She waved a hand at him. 'I need a tissue. You buried the bloody toilet paper at the bottom of the boot, didn't you. Because you *always* know best.'

How was that fair?

He was the one who packed everything. *He* was the one who put it all in the car. And *he*'d be the one unpacking it all again when they finally got to the new house.

Scott blinked. 'I was only trying to…' What was the point? He sagged: giving up. Again. Because it was easier than fighting. 'Yes. No. You're right. Sorry. Sorry.' Scurrying back to the car. 'Have we still got paper towels in the glove compartment?' Going in for a rummage. 'Right. Here we go.'

He carried his fistful of McDonald's napkins back to the mother of his child – holding them out to her, with his head facing the road. Not looking. Because … *urgh*.

She snatched them from his hand, without so much as a thank-you. Leaving him standing there while she did whatever it was she had to do. Then: 'Well? Don't just stand there: help me!'

Scott risked a look, and there she was, hauling her pants up with one hand, the other outstretched towards him. 'Oh, erm… Yes. OK…' He rubbed his fingertips together. 'Only you haven't washed your hands or anything and—'

'SCOTT WILLIAM BAIRD, you *will* help me out of these *bloody* weeds, or I swear to *Christ* I'm going to cut your *bloody* knob off and feed it to those *bloody* crows!'

At which point, one of the dark feathery bastards opened its beak wide, like it was ready to feast.

OK.

Right.

Scott buried a grimace and helped Alice to her feet. 'There: all better. And—'

She slapped a wodge of damp napkins into his open palm.

Oh God…

They were still warm.

'It's only *pee*!' She pointed at the wheelie bins. 'Honestly, how are you going to cope with shit-filled nappies if you can't handle a little pee?'

A full-on shudder stampeded down his spine. 'It... I... Urgh...' He stuck his arm straight out, away from his body, to minimise contamination, as he headed for the twin bins with a clenched-buttock shuffle.

The bins were boxed in with a few bars of thin rusty metal, presumably there to stop them from blowing away in a strong wind. And the closer he got, the louder this strange *buzzing* sound grew. It was coming from inside the nearest bin – low and sleepy, like someone had thrown away a phone on vibrate. Or a sex toy that was running out of batteries.

Both crows pop-hopped onto the other bin's lid. Watching. Heads cocked. A hungry look in their shiny black-button eyes.

And it wasn't just the weird buzzing that was getting louder, there was a smell that went with it. That sour, manky, slithery stench swelled with every step. Till it was strong enough to make his chin pull in and his eyes blink, like he'd walked into something solid.

'Urgh... Bloody hell...'

'IT'S ONLY PEE!'

He turned. 'No, it's not that, it's—'

'Hoy!' Alice tapped an invisible watch. 'Twenty minutes, you said!'

'All right, all right, I'm sorry. Coming.'

He reached out with his other hand. Took a deep breath – which was a mistake, given the smell – and slid a single fingertip in beneath one of the handles on the bin's lid. Because it was probably *crawling* with bacteria and viruses and mould and all sorts. Every bit as germ-laden as the piddle-wipe napkins, if not worse.

Out on the road, what had to be a tractor growled past. Slow-moving and huge, with spotlights on the roof that made the fog glow a bright alien-abduction white.

OK.

Scott flipped the lid open and dropped the soggy napkins inside.

They landed with a *slap*, and a cloud of thrumming bluebottles erupted from the wheelie bin, riding a tidal wave of stench so foul that even a dozen feet away, Alice gagged.

The two crows flapped into the air, cawing, spiralling away from the smell.

And Scott *ran* – getting away from the stinking bin, knees high, back hunched, waving his hands over his head to ward off the flies. Eyes screwed shut, shrieking like a startled child.

Alice retched. Coughed. 'CLOSE THE LID! CLOSE THE LID!'

He staggered to a halt, and turned.

The tractor's lights and howling engine faded away into the fog, leaving the lay-by shrouded in gloom and silence once more. Well, except for the flies.

Alice had one hand clamped over her nose, the other waving at the bins. 'CLOSE THE BLOODY LID!'

Scott bit his bottom lip, clenched his shaking hands, and crept back to the bin, holding his breath till his lungs *burned.* Grabbed the lid and whacked it shut. Eyes watering as his stomach clenched and roiled.

He backed away, blotting the tears with the back of his sleeves. Blinking at the buzzing bin. Grimacing.

Wait... Was that...?

The crows settled onto the other wheelie bin.

No. Couldn't be.

One black-feathered fiend hopped onto the stinking bin, cocking its head at Scott, then rapping its beak on the now-closed lid. As if trying to explain something horrible to a very stupid child.

He must've imagined it.

Scott's insides curdled.

But what if he *hadn't*?

Alice escaped to the other side of the car, putting the thing between her and the rancid stink. Still covering her mouth and nose, even though she hadn't washed her hands.

What if he'd seen what *really* lurked deep inside that bin's putrid plastic depths?

Oh God...

He wiped his palms on his trouser legs.

The wheelie bins loomed in the fog like twin tombstones, topped with carrion crows – all set to a theme tune of trapped buzzing.

Some weird *ping-pyong-twang*ing noises joined in. Getting louder. And louder.

Alice peered at him. 'What?'

Only one way to be sure.

Scott crept forward again, holding his breath as he lifted the lid to peek inside – properly this time.

Without the tractor's spotlights, it was hard to see anything. What with the fog shutting out the morning sun and everything. Now all that remained were some vague rounded shapes lying deep within, wrapped in that putrid stench.

And that's when the *ping*ing *twang*ing noises turned into a diesel roar as a blue-white-and-yellow train rattled past in the fog, heading north. Lights blazed from the carriage windows – sweeping the lay-by with their greasy tallow glow.

The beams flickered through the line of trees that stood guard between the fireweed and the tracks, sending shadows to whirl around Scott and Alice like dancing monsters.

Casting more than enough light to make out what stared back at Scott from deep inside the bin.

He screamed, jerking back from the horrible sight, but his collection of shabby friendship bracelets caught on the lid's handle – binding him to the stinking black-plastic nightmare.

Scott yanked and tugged, wrenching his wrist from side to side, struggling to free himself as the smell grew fangs.

'SHUT THE BLOODY LID, YOU MORON!'

He heaved his whole body sideways, pulling the bin with him hard enough to snap one sidebar from the rusty metal frame.

The bin timbered down, *booonnnng*ing against the gritty tarmac, and almost taking him with it.

When it hit the deck, the contents burst free in a stinking clatter of yuck and explosion of foetid bin juice.

The last bar of carriage-window light streaked across the potholed tarmac, illuminating the slimy jumble of bones and sludge. Making the jawless skull glimmer.

Which is when Scott's legs gave up, depositing him on his backside in the dew-damp grass, staring back at those empty sockets as reeking bin juice spread out like a wave on the beach, leaving a high-tide mark of maggots to wriggle and flail.

The train thundered away into the fog, taking its light and snarling engine with it, leaving the lay-by smothered in gloom and silence once more. Until Alice produced her phone and, calm as you like, called 999.

And Scott had a damn good go at vomiting out every single one of his internal organs.

10

Want to know how you could tell God was an utter bastard? Hangovers. No beneficent all-powerful deity would *ever* have plagued womankind with sodding hangovers. And they especially wouldn't inflict them on paragons of virtue like Roberta Steel, who'd done *nothing at all* to deserve the mariachi band of hobnail-booted scumbags currently fiesta-ing it up inside her skull.

Who weren't even keeping time with whatever crap was currently yodelling out from the car radio. Which made Roberta's stomach dance to a tune of its own.

She was sunk down in the passenger seat of her bright-red MX-5 as the little sports car crawled through fog – thick and grey as porridge.

Could've been at *home*, slobbing about in her jammies, instead of out here, nursing a bandaged left hand and bruised knuckles. Wearing sunglasses and her all-black Police Scotland get-up: clingy T-shirt, itchy trousers, peaked cap, Doc Martens, and the kind of scowl that could kill a detective sergeant at twenty paces.

Just a shame it didn't work on pointy-nosed wee detective *constables*.

DC Quirrel – AKA: The Wee Loon, AKA: Captain Bumlumps, AKA: The Massive Pain In Her Hoop, AKA: *Tufty* – sat behind the wheel, nodding his stupid pointy little head along to the radio. His hair was cropped to the bone, like a half-arsed Irn-Bru-coloured velvet. One of his watery blue eyes was bloodshot, the skin beneath it lined with purple and green, another bruise riding high on one cheek. He was in the full Police Scotland black too, but he'd accessorised with a stabproof vest, high-vis waistcoat, and every item of kit known to man – attached to his utility belt and various clippy bits.

Because he was an idiot.

He kept the MX-5 at a safe-ish distance, following the tail end of a teeny police convoy: consisting of one patrol car, a police van – complete with riot grille – and a Scenes Transit that had seen better days. But not the soggy slap of a soapy sponge. At least, not *this* side of the millennium.

The front pair of vehicles were little more than muffled shapes in the gloom as their miserable cavalcade crept its way along the A96, with only the occasional hatchback and four-by-four coming the other way to break the whispered monotony.

Still, at least the lead patrol car had its lights on, flickering away in blue-and-white. About as festive as a mortuary Christmas tree. Decorated with post-mortem leftovers.

The 'musical' interlude came to a halt, and the tossers on the radio started singing again.

The tosser in the driver's seat joined in:

'And everyone-nun-nun is made of plas-ta-sceeeene!
And everyone-nun-nun has got an augh-ber-geeeeeen!
And evvvvvery-onnnnnne can—'

Roberta thumped him.

'Ow!' Tufty rubbed at his arm. 'No hitting the driver!'

'No annoying the detective inspector!' Waving her thumping hand in threat. 'And stop being so spudging *cheerful*. No' even singing the proper words.'

'Not *my* fault you had a bucket yesterday, Guv.'

She hit him again.

'Ow! Stop it!'

The horrible song on the horrible radio clattered to a horrible halt, followed by a horribly upbeat tit of a man:

'There you go, told you it was fun.' Comedy honking noise. *'It's twenty-five to eight, and we're breaking with tradition here to have a wee bitty of a phone-in! So: after the Union Street Riot this weekend, we want to know your—'*

Roberta switched the radio off, then sat there, massaging her throbbing forehead, trying to stop her whole cranium from falling apart as the mariachi bastards really got into the swing of things.

Another couple of cars growled past on the other side of the road, emerging from the fog then vanishing again. Then another, and another, as rush hour began to build. Not that there would be much rushing going on with visibility down to a dozen feet.

Tufty gave her the side-eye. 'Do you even remember going home from the barbecue last night?'

'Shut up.'

'How about falling off the climbing frame and breaking the Sarge's bird table?'

'Hmmmph!' She folded her arms and turned the scowl up a notch.

'See: people think you soon-to-be-retired types is all full of sensibleness and The Wisdom Of The Ancients and stuff, but you is *totally* rejecting that stereotype.'

'Should've let Harmsworth drive. You're a *crap* sidekick.'

A grin. 'Nah: I'm a spudging delight.'

The wee shite reached for the radio, but she slapped his hand away.

'Ow! No hitting the *driver*!'

Roberta was about to give him another wallop when her Airwave handset bleeped three times, announcing an incoming call.

Lund's voice crackled out into the foggy morning: *'Acting Guv: safe to talk?'*

'Only if you're no' calling to wind me up, Veronica, cos I'm a sodding danger to shipping!'

'We roused the head of Road Maintenance from his scratcher.' A sniff. *'Wasn't very happy about it.'*

Ahead, another set of flickering lights bloomed in the fog, faint and far away, but growing brighter and flashier as the convoy got nearer.

Roberta went back to squeezing her cranium again. 'And are you planning on *telling* me what he said, or do you want me to hunt you down and stuff my boot so far up your—'

'They've got loads of people off with the lurgy, so nearly every bit of roadworks in Aberdeenshire is going absolutely nowhere. Normally, it's budgetary restrictions – you know, robbing Peterhead to pay Portsoy – but—'

'Swear to Christ: I'll no' even lube it first. And I'm wearing my *big* boots the day!'

Lund groaned. *'All right, all right. Flipping heck... Your lay-by's been coned-off since the twenty-fifth of April. Chuckies and the like were dumped there: morning of the twenty-eighth. And no one's done a stroke of work on it since.'*

Oh for God's sake.

'Well, that's a whole heap of sod-all-help, isn't it. You've narrowed down the window of deposition to forty-nine snidging days!' Idiots. 'Put Davey on.'

'His highness, Acting *Detective Sergeant Barrett is currently indisposed. Coughing and spluttering, trying to kid on he's got the plague.'*

She sat up. 'He better no' have!'

'It's not the snottery virus he's suffering from, it's,' Lund's voice jumped a couple of decibels, *'too much vodka and pickled onions, yesterday! ... Yes,* you*: with your face like a puckered frog's bumhole!'* Then the sound went all muffled, as Lund presumably pressed the handset to her ample bosom. *'It's herself. Wants to talk to you.'*

'No' if he's infectious, I don't.' Cos it was bad enough with half the division off sick and another third crippled after Saturday's protest-cum-riot... Mind you, calling it a 'protest-cum-riot' made it sound a *lot* more fun than it was. Stickier too.

Anyway, where was she?

Ah yes: motivating her team of halfwits and ne'er-do-wells. 'And to be frank, DC Lund, I expected better of you! Letting Barrett get that blootered, at a family barbecue, on a *Sunday* night; what were you thinking?'

'Supposed to be a rest day, today! And how is he my *responsibility? You were the one screaming* "Dos mezcales más, por favor!"*, clicking your fingers, and dancing round DCI McRae's garden like a—'*

'Unlubricated, size six, bovver boots – express delivered to your flipping colon!'

There was a decidedly chilly pause, then: *'Oh go ... poop in your sombrero.'*

And with that, Lund ended the call.

The police convoy had slowed to a crawl, and now the lead patrol car's blue-and-whites took a left, leaving the main road.

Roberta turned her scowl on Tufty again, cos the judgemental wee sod was staring at her. '*What?*'

'Didn't say anything, Guv. Did I say anything? Cos I don't remember saying anything. Not a word.'

'Shut up.'

The police van pulled in too, followed by the arse-end of

that filthy Scenes Transit, exposing the entrance to a coned-off lay-by, complete with 'KEEP OUT' signs.

'Here we go.' The wee loon brought up the rear, and the MX-5 lurched as one of its front wheels disappeared into a pothole – pulling a gravelled *scrrrrrrr*aping noise from the undercarriage.

'Watch it!'

He winced. 'Oops.'

Give *him* something to wince about.

'OW! Stop *hitting* me!'

She pointed. 'Park, you idiot.'

And, soon as he did, she lowered her sunglasses an inch and gave him the kind of bloodshot glare that had him shrinking back in his seat.

Should think so too.

Roberta poked her glasses into place again and climbed out into the … flipping heck. There was a decided whiff to the air. As if the fog was three weeks past its sell-by date and hadn't been too fresh to start with.

A manky, pale-brown hatchback slouched at the far end of the lay-by, fading into the fog, just outside the cordon of yellow-and-black 'CRIME SCENE – DO NOT ENTER' tape that boxed off a council wheelie bin and something tipped over on its side. Like a black plastic coffin.

Which was a bit awkward, because that meant half the lay-by was now inaccessible, and Roberta's mini convoy had to all jam together at this end. Bumper to bumper. And not in a sexy way.

The flickering lights they'd been aiming for belonged to a patrol car, parked half on the semicircle of long grass that sat between the potholed tarmac strip and the A96. It should've had a two-person crew, but only a single uniformed PC was visible: arranging a bunch of traffic cones into a defensive wall. She was in the full high-vis get-up, with her sandy hair crammed into a tight bun and a bowler hat.

Because unlike Roberta, she'd clearly bought into all that sexist bollocks about *male* officers wearing peaked caps while women were stuck with stupid bowlers. Like Charlie Sodding Chaplin. Whatever happened to sticking two fingers up to the patriarchy? Then kicking it in the balls?

The unemancipated PC looked up from her task – over her shoulder towards the cordoned-off bin – revealing a faceful of angry acne. Her eyes narrowed.

But she wasn't glowering at Roberta, she was giving a pair of crows the evil eye as they hopped sideways towards that plastic coffin thing.

Then PC Plukes abandoned her cones and charged at the cordon, waving her arms about. 'GET OUT OF IT, YOU THIEVING FEATHERY GITS!'

The crows rattled into the air, cawing in foul-beaked outrage, and the PC lumbered to a stop, shaking her fist until their ink-black tatters disappeared into the woods beyond.

'Hmph!' And she went back to her cones.

No idea where Plukey's partner was, though. Maybe…

Ah, there we go.

A Jack Skellington figure, partially digested by the mist, stood over by the miserable hatchback. Lanky, with a big head, and a high-vis jacket that had 'POLICE' and two reflective strips across the back. He was talking to a dumpy pregnant type in an ugly dress.

Suppose everyone needed a hobby.

That manky smell got stronger as Roberta made her way along the convoy, heading for the cordon. The Scenes Transit was even grubbier up close. As is tradition, someone had scrawled finger graffiti in the grime: 'CAPITALISM KILLS!!!',

'WASH ME!', 'FILTH!', a skull-and-crossbones, and a Dirty Elmo. That was probably best not to dwell on.

Tufty scurried up behind Roberta, phone out, poking and scrolling as he nipped around to block her way. 'Now you is not so catastrophically hungovered, do you want to go through our new list of cases what we did inherit from the Sarge?'

'No.'

'Cool. We has inherited Operations Owlbear and Firedrake.'

Roberta added a two-foot willy to the graffiti collection. 'Feel free to shut up and sod off.' Then shoved Tufty to one side and moved on.

He followed, doing a sort of hoppity-skippity thing so his feet were in time with hers. 'Owlbear am all the camper vans getting nicked, and Firedrake is being The Great Burger-Van Turf War. We can review all the casework when we hand *this*,' pointing at the cordon, 'over to whoever's—' His Airwave gave its incoming-message bleeps. 'Oops. Hold that think.' Pressing the button. 'Safe to talk.' Then the wee squit stuck a finger in his other ear and peeled away to annoy whoever had called him instead. Leaving Roberta on her own.

Thank God for that.

The smell was getting smellier. Growing as she reached the front of the Transit, where a pair of scene examiners were struggling into matching white Tyvek suits. Hopping about as they wrestled their legs in.

Shirley had dressed as a middle-aged golf bore, in a green polo-shirt and knee-length shorts. Clarks sandals and pink socks. Tartan Alice band. Looking every bit as knackered and hungover as Roberta.

Her colleague, Charlie, boasted squint teeth, large arms, stubble, smoky eye shadow, and hot-coral lipstick that was far too warming for his complexion.

Roberta jerked a thumb at the cordon. 'What we looking at?'

Shirley wriggled into her suit's sleeves. 'Give us a chance.' Zipping herself up. 'Technically, shouldn't be going anywhere near *anything* till the Fiscal or Dr Death get here. God forbid we little folk should think for ourselves!'

Typical.

'How come none of you fudgers are any sodding help today?'

Over on the grassy buffer-zone, PC Zitzilla charged at the crows again. 'HOY! BUGGER OFF! RRRRRRAAAAAH!'

Shirley pulled on blue plastic booties. 'Give us a minute and we'll see what we can see.' Turning to her colleague. 'Right, Charlie?'

He gave them a crooked smile, voice deep enough to quarry rocks. 'Do our best, like.'

''Bout time *someone* did.' Roberta got moving again. 'And set that marquee up sharpish, before those crows nick everything!'

Next up: the police van, which had all its interior lights on, showing off the cage at the back for locking people in, the racks of equipment, rows of seats, and PC Owen Harmsworth's hairy bumcrack – poking above the waistband of his uniform trousers as he rummaged about, looking for something he'd probably dropped. Clumsy git.

She banged on the window. 'Cover it up! No one needs to see your furry toast-rack!'

Harmsworth snapped upright. Which exposed a sight not much better than his woolly buttocks: a middle-aged basset hound of a man, who needed to lay off the pies. They'd put a strip of plaster across the bridge of his now squint nose, which kind of drew attention to the nice pair of black eyes he was cultivating. The hair on his head hadn't so much 'gone into retreat' as abandoned its post and fled for the hills.

He stuck that plastered nose in the air and let free an indignant, 'Don't be so rude!'

Roberta gave him a one-fingered gesture, and carried on her way.

By the time she was passing the patrol car, that manky smell had grown into a pong, then a reek, then a stench. She pulled her chin in, blinking. Eyes watering.

Wafting a hand in front of her face made sod-all difference. 'Fruffing skunch… Last time I smelled something *that* bad, the neighbour's dog was rolling in it!'

What she needed was something to mask the honking niff. So she dug her vape from a trouser pocket and had a good long puff of black cherry. Which made it possible to stand at the cordon without retching. Just.

That plukey PC was still fiddling with those stupid traffic cones.

Roberta cupped a hand to the side of her mouth, making a loudhailer. 'HOY! YOU THERE: BUNNET!'

The PC barely looked. 'I'm *busy*.'

Time to turn on the sweetness and light – which should've been a *massive* sodding warning sign, but some people weren't that bright. 'Oh, I *am* sorry. I'll give you a wee mintie to finish up, shall I?'

'Guv?' Tufty appeared, Airwave in one hand, the other covering its microphone. Sounding all bunged-up. 'Pathologist's going to be late – some Trumpwit's jack-knifed a lorry in the fog, just past Thainstone roundabout. Pickled beetroot *everywhere*.'

Yet more bollocks to deal with.

'What about the PF?'

'Unfortunately, they is *miles* away. Had a strangling last

night in Arbroath, and all the other procurators fiscal am in bed with the ague, so we've only got one covering everything from Fort William to—'

'Worry not, dear Constable; not a problem at all.' She raised a hand, before he could say anything else. 'After all, we've got *all* the time in the world.'

His eyes widened, chin pulling in as the gentle, zen-like tone of her voice fully sunk in. 'Oh dear…' Looking as if she'd just pointed a gun at his balls. 'Has I did something that's—'

Roberta plonked a finger against his lips, silencing him. Giving him a big beneficent smile. Then stuck her vape back in her pocket, replacing it with two – different – fingers to fire a shrill whistle at PC Pimples McTraffic-Cone. 'HOY! LOTS'A-SPOTS!'

The PC stiffened. 'I SAID, "I'M BUSY!" Christ's sake, got enough to do without running about after some half-arsed, jumped-up—'

'"Detective Inspector" is the word you're looking for.'

'Oh…'

Tufty lowered his voice to a whisper. 'Don't be mean.'

'So, perhaps you'd like to waddle your plukey wee teuchter arse over here and answer a couple of questions? *If* it's no' too much trouble?'

'Guv. Yes, Guv.' The PC hurried over. 'Sorry, Guv.' A proper beamer making her cheeks glow and her spots throb. 'Only it's a green shift and we've been on since seven yesterday morning, cos everyone's off with the pestilence; and that's *after* getting called in to man the barricades at that riot in Aberdeen, Saturday; and there's only so much Red Bull and petrol-station espresso one person can drink; and—'

'All right, Jeffrey Archer; don't need your life story.' Roberta hooked a thumb at the cordon. 'Give us the headlines.'

'Ma'am.' Snapping to attention. 'Mr Baird and Ms Moncrief

discovered the remains and called 999 at quarter to seven this morning. PC Stratford and I responded to the call, cos we were closest. We secured the locus and called for backup.'

'That *it*?'

'Ma'am?'

'What about this Baird and Moncrief: they see-or-say anything useful?'

'Nah. Moving up to Huntly for a new job, left Dundee at three this morning, she's desperate for a wee, they pull over – bish-bash-bosh – and here we are.'

'You check they're telling the truth?'

'Ah...' Those spots went radioactive. 'I'll get on that, *right* now. Ma'am. Sorry.' Whipping out her Airwave and hurrying off.

Roberta shook her head. 'Unbelievable.' Then ducked under the cordon and snapped on a pair of blue nitrile gloves.

'Er... Guv?' The wee loon clutched at the yellow-and-black tape. 'No. No adventuring!'

See, that was the trouble with today's officers: no initiative.

She stalked across the potholed tarmac, to about six foot from the upright bin. Which was A: keeping a safe-ish distance, for forensic purposes, and B: about as close as she could get without the not-so-dry heaves. Cos the smell was *minging.*

Out came the vape again, puffing away as she clicked her fingers. 'Nerdboy: heel!'

Because why should she be the only one suffering?

'Yeah...' Tufty stayed where he was. 'Maybe best if we leave it for the pathologist, Guv? We're not even wearing SOC suits. Don't want to—'

'Tufty, I swear on Mr Rumpole's fuzzy tummy, if you don't march your bony wee backside over here this *instant*...'

'Eeek... But—'

'The remains are in an advanced state of decomposition. Which means they've been here for a while. Last week it was baking hot. The week before *that*, it was pissing down. There's bugger-all left to contaminate!' She snapped her fingers again. 'Now: *heel*.'

A wee, mumbled, 'Oh noes…' But he did as he was told – treading very carefully in her footsteps, following an imaginary approach path. 'And you does now owe two pounds to the swear jar.'

Oh in the name of … spudge.

That … *flipping* swear jar.

What snidge-for-brains thought a *swear jar* was a good idea?

Anyway.

One extra-large puff of cherry, then Roberta inched closer for a better view. But the stench won, and she had to retreat again. Spluttering. Wafting a hand at the horror-filled reek. 'Frunching heck!'

The wee loon nodded. 'It's the fog.' Pointing at it, as if she couldn't see the sodding stuff. 'When you've got all this water vapour in suspension it acts as an insulator. Imagine there's a smoke alarm going off in your living room, and it's loud everywhere, right? So you wrap the detector in a layer of cotton wool. Only that doesn't make a lot of difference, so you wrap some more around the thing – and you *keep* wrapping and wrapping until you can't hear it anymore. You might *think* it's gone silent, but deep inside the cotton-wool cocoon it's still deafening.' He cupped his hands, then moved them out a little, then a little more, miming concentric circles. 'The fog's like that, only with smells. And sound. And light. Up close: *really* stinky. Not so far away: everything's fine.' Grin. 'That's why I did takes *precautions*.'

Course he sodding did.

'I'll "precaution" you in a minute.'

'See?' He tilted his head back, showing off a pair of yellow blobs – one in each nostril. 'Got a set of those foam earplugs and rolled them into little cones, then,' more miming, '*poink*.'

'You're disgusting.'

'Disgusting like a fox!'

Everywhere she looked: idiots.

Puffing hard on the cherry vape, Roberta picked her way around the outside of that plastic coffin – which turned out to be a second wheelie bin, tipped over onto its side, with the lid lying open on the rutted tarmac – staying far enough back to keep breakfast down: two aspirin, two paracetamol, and half a pack of Rennies.

But it was close enough to get a good look at what had spilled out of the fallen bin.

That was *definitely* a skull, and there were some ribs, and two shoulder blades, a pelvis, lots of vertebrae, and all of the long bones.

Hmm... Didn't seem to be nearly enough phalanges. Ten fingers, ten toes, with three bones each. Should've been heaps of them.

Mind you, they could still be in the bin, couldn't they. Lurking away at the bottom.

The teeth too, because there were none out here. The lower jaw lay separate from the skull, split into three bits, and there wasn't a single tooth in any of them. None in the rest of the head, either – just cracked bone and empty sockets.

Roberta hunched down and frowned at the stinking mess. 'You seeing what I'm seeing?'

Tufty squinted. 'Yes...?'

That pair of crows settled on the upright bin, eyes shiny, beaks sharp and ready. Watching.

'There's no clothes.' She pointed at the remains. 'Even if they were wearing *all* natural fibres, there'd still be zips, buttons.

Body was stripped: no identifying tags or labels. Someone's taken a hammer to the face, so no teeth for forensic dental ID. Can't see any fingers – that means no prints.' A frown, as she pointed at the crows. 'Assuming those beaky bastards haven't nicked them.'

Tufty shrugged. 'Yeah, but the body's a skeleton. There'd be no prints anyway.'

'Killer couldn't know it'd take this long to find the remains.' She stood, brushing the smell from her hands. 'He's covering his tracks.'

'Wow. That's ... not good.' Eyebrows up. 'Professional hit?'

A faint *pwing-twong-pwang* rang through the mist, as if someone was tuning-up a vast, strange, musical instrument.

'Ooh.' Tufty meerkatted onto his tiptoes. 'Did you hear that?'

PC Pimples appeared at the cordon, fixing the Airwave handset back on her stabproof's clip. 'It's the railway lines. Must be the Inverness train. Aberdeen one went south about ... quarter hour ago?'

Oh no...

Roberta stared at her. 'A bloody *train*?'

The twanging grew louder.

Off in the middle distance, Shirley and Charlie – dressed as ghosts in their SOC suits – struggled under the awkward, lumpy, dead-body-in-a-bag weight of their crime-scene marquee. Hauling it across the lay-by, making for the bins.

'Sodding...' Roberta waved both arms. 'GET A BLOODY MOVE ON, THERE'S A TRAIN COMING!'

And just like that, it was on them: thundering out of the fog, all lights blazing, casting spotlights that raked across the lay-by.

The buggers onboard must've seen the flickering police lights approaching through the murk, because a whole bunch of them were standing with their phones pressed against the carriage windows, filming. Probably hoping that something exciting/juicy/horrible was going on so they could record it in HD and share it on their socials.

Rattly-clack, rattly-clack, rattly-clack…

Roberta rushed forward, putting herself between the train and the bones, arms out, blocking as much of the scene as possible. 'DON'T JUST SODDING STAND THERE!'

Rattly-clack, rattly-clack, rattly-clack…

Tufty scurried over to help, keeping his head down as he struck a blocking-starfish pose next to her.

Rattly-clack, rattly-clack, rattly-clack…

And then the train was past, growl-grumbling away into the fog.

'Great.' Roberta slumped, massaging her aching brain again, because God knew how much footage the ghoulish bastards had got. Not to mention the train before *them*. 'That's all we need.'

9

Just after eight, and the not-so-rush hour was in full crawl as a near-solid line of cars crept by in the fog, heading south for Inverurie and Aberdeen beyond. Headlights glowing white, taillights red.

Every so often, a motorcyclist risked this being their last morning on earth by overtaking the funereal procession, but everyone else was sensible enough to tortoise past the lay-by. Especially with a patrol car parked at either end, their blue-and-whites spinning.

Shirley and Charlie had finally managed to wrestle an SOC marquee over the remains – pretty much filling the cordon of yellow-and-black tape – but instead of the traditional parking-their-bums-in-the-Scenes-Transit-to-enjoy-a-sneaky-thermos-of-tea-and-some-crime-scene-custard-creams, they'd been forced to lumber back and forth, humping blue plastic evidence crates.

Muttering and grumbling.

Casting dark glances at the big black Range Rover that had joined the party, parked on the long grass between the main road and the lay-by.

But at least they didn't have to deal with Chief Superintendent Bloody Pine. Because the woman was one of nature's haemorrhoids on the Great Hoop Of Life.

Roberta worked her way along the cordon's edge, putting

one heel in front of the other toe, pacing it out in a wobbly fashion. Vape in one hand, phone in the other. 'Well, what am *I* supposed to do about it? No' my fault these scumbags loaded all that rubbish up to YouTube and the like. Don't remember them asking *my* permission.'

'Really?' Pine had one of those cut-glass I-went-to-a-posh-school accents that *almost* managed to cover up the razor-gang Weegie-Glaswegian beneath. *'You could at least've blocked their view! Honestly.'*

'What do you think I was doing, auditioning for *Strictly*?' A sniff. 'Doesn't matter anyway – it's out there now. No point getting your perky wee bum in a twist.'

Roberta kicked a tangled clump of unmown grass to emphasise the point, only there must've been a wee stone hiding in there, because it flew off the toe of her Doc Marten, soared through the air … and clunked against that black Range Rover's immaculate flank.

Oops…

'I'm still clearing up after the weekend's brouhaha, do you really think I need another dead body to deal with?'

Quick left and right: scanning the fog to make sure no one saw that. 'Oh, I *am* sorry. If you like, I can ask the Ice Queen to stuff all those bones back in the bin and stick it out for collection? We'll forget aaaaall about it.'

'You know exactly *what I meant.'*

Roberta wandered towards the probably completely uninjured vehicle. 'And "brouhaha"? Who says "brouhaha"?'

'Half the force was already off sick, and now another chunk are too injured to work! How am I supposed to run A Division with no officers?'

Oh *poor* Chief Superintendent Pine.

'Let's no' forget all the brave souls, *like me*, who came in *on their rest day* to help out.' In horrible itchy trousers.

With blistering hangovers.

Though it was probably best not to mention that bit.

Or the fact that all the cool kids called it 'NE Division' these days, cos 'A Division' was for oldies and wankers.

Soon as she got to the Range Rover, Roberta had another quick check to make sure no one was watching, before examining the paintwork for damage.

'Yes, well… The important thing is to keep the public safe.' Pine cleared her throat. *'Are we* sure *this is a murder?'*

'Unless you think someone got naked, smashed their own teeth out with a claw-hammer, chopped their fingers off, then clambered into a lay-by bin to die? Yeah, probably.'

Oooh. There it was: a knuckle-sized dent, with a curved scratch leading off from it.

She licked her thumb and rubbed at the tortured paint.

Yeah … that wasn't going anywhere.

'I wouldn't normally assign a case like this to anyone under the rank of DCI.'

Time to vacate the scene of the crime.

'*But…?*' Sneaking away.

'Needs must, when the Devil dances. However, if you don't feel up to the task, I'm sure DI Beattie—'

'Oh no you bloody don't! That glaikit beardy jobbie couldn't investigate his bum for arse-berries; you're *no'* giving him my murder.'

That *pwong-twang* noise grew again, followed by the diesel growl of the 08:02 from Insch station, heading Aberdeenward. The train emerged from the fog – every *single* carriage window was packed with silhouettes, and they all had their phones out, filming.

Kind of hard not to give the buggers a middle finger, but she resisted. Cos let's face it: things were bad enough.

A suspicious tone slithered into Pine's voice. *'What was that noise?'*

'Noise, Boss? I didn't hear anything…' The train dissolved into the gloom again. 'Besides, I've *been* a DCI. Fatty McFart-Face couldn't—'

'Then it's settled. The media's already frottaged itself into a frenzy over the protest; a decomposed, naked body, stuffed in a wheelie bin will have them in orgasmic wanks of outrage.'

Oh aye?

'I love it when you talk dirty.' Roberta headed for the police van. 'If I say yes to this, I get a proper-sized team, right?'

No answer.

'Right?'

'Sorry, got to go: Chief Constable's on the other line. I want updates on my desk every hour on the hour, understand? Good. Bye.' Then silence.

Roberta pursed her lips, squinting at her phone as it glowed the words 'CALL ENDED'.

'Aye, thought as much.' She stuffed it back in her pocket and struck one of those superhero poses – legs akimbo, shoulders back, fists on hips. 'Well, Roberta: looks like solving *this one*'s down to you, the boy, and your trusty Queen Street Irregulars!'

Sniff.

What could possibly go wrong?

Her stomach replied with a gurgling snarl. It'd been a long time since it last saw solid food: two hotdogs; two cheeseburgers; some ribs; chicken wings; and a glollop of tattie salad, because it was important to have your five-a-day. Washed down with a wee sherry or two, in the blistering sunshine of Logan McRae's back garden. Joined by all the other reprobates who'd survived Saturday's 'protest-cum-riot'.

Speaking of reprobates and idiots: Tufty emerged from the milky mist, hands tucked into the armpits of his stabproof, frowning at the Airwave handset clipped to his chest. 'Guv.'

'Where've you been?'

The wee loon shrugged. 'Still nothing from Harmsworth and Gifford.' He turned, looking out over the rosebay willowherb at the woods behind the railway line. 'Sure they're OK?'

'This is officially *my* case now.'

'Maybe we should go after them?'

'They'll be fine.' She lowered her voice to a near whisper, leaning in, all conspiratorial like. 'Besides, I've got a special, top-secret, super-important mission for you...'

Steel slouched in one of the police van's bench seats – sitting sideways, with her feet up, scowling at the bollocks passing for journalism in that morning's *Aberdeen Examiner*.

Headline: 'RIOT CHAOS GRIPS CITY CENTRE', above a photo of the running battle down Union Street, featuring a small group of police officers in full riot gear – hunkered behind their shields as projectiles and fireworks rained down and smoke bombs turned the air blue and red.

She gave the front page a snort, shook the paper, then opened it halfway through, at an article titled, 'MURDOCH IRVINE'S FUNERAL KICKS OFF BY-ELECTION' with a picture of a spud-faced tosser who thought big sideburns compensated for an oversized baldy head that made him look like an infected thumb. 'Political Parties Scramble As Campaign To Replace MP For Gordon And Buchan Hots Up'.

As if anyone cared.

Roberta pulled out a biro and drew a big willy growing out of the dear departed Mr Irvine's forehead. Then blacked out a couple of his teeth. And added a bolt through his neck, for good luck.

Pfff…

She sat up, peering over the seats and out through the van's windows.

The fog was *finally* beginning to thin as the sun baked its way through the outer layers. Making the lay-by glow a brighter shade of horrible grey.

Like being inside a big stinky cloud.

Still no sign of Harmsworth, though. Or anyone else. The lay-by was deserted.

Next article: 'CITY COUNCILLOR "CAUGHT STD OFF RENTBOY" CLAIMS' and another infected-thumb-head. What was it with politicians and their—

The van door clunked open and in clambered Tufty. A little red in the face and shiny of cheek. As if he'd actually been working hard for a change. 'Flipping, blipping thingummy.'

He undid his high-vis waistcoat and flapped the edges – as if that was going to do any good through a stabproof vest. Twit.

Steel gave the dirty councillor a few biro scars and a twirly moustache. Then held her hand out. 'Give.'

'"Top-secret mission", my bunghole.' Tufty sagged into the seat opposite. 'And the Pitstop doesn't *open* on a Monday, thank you very much. It am officially an Food-Free Zone.'

'Oh for God's…' She scrunched her face up and covered it with the paper. 'Could today *get* any worse?'

'There I was, standing outside the Party Bus, all bereft and so forlorn—'

'Aaaaaaaaaaaaaaaaaaaaaaaaaargh!' Roberta slumped back. 'The universe *hates* me.'

'When a mannie does arrived to check something inside, and he tells me,' putting on a deep manlier voice for: '"We don't open Monday–Tuesday."'

'I should've copped a sickie and stayed in bed.'

Weren't a hangover *and* a murder enough to deal with?

'"Oh noes!" cried I, with dejected hopelessness.' Tufty did the voice again: '"You'll have to come back Wednesday," he replied.'

'Wasn't even supposed to be *in* today. Should be at home right now, snoring it up.'

'"Lackaday, woe is me," thinks I, "whatever shall I do? For the Guv will shout at me in a totally unreasonable fashion for this unfortunate happenstance what am *completely* not my fault."'

She crumpled the paper into her lap. 'If those bumlumping *shunts* had turned up when they were *supposed* to, we would've had a working sauna by now, instead of a sodding building site! Could've steamed the hangover right out of me…'

All naked and sweaty.

Tufty grinned. Pervert. 'But *then* I did work my devious charms, and telled him: "We is poor hungry police officers in dire need of sustenance, jolly innkeep!" Well, buskeep, but you get the drift. And…' Whipping out a large-ish paper bag. 'TA-DAAAAAAAAAH! He fired-up the grill, just for us.'

Roberta stuck both hands out this time. 'Gimme, gimme, gimme, gimme!'

Tufty dipped into the big paper bag, producing a collection of smaller paper bags, all of which were promisingly spotted with grease. 'Got bacon; bacon and egg; sausage, egg, and egg; sausage, *bacon*, and egg; and a Neptune's delight.'

She grabbed the bag marked 'SB&E', scrabbling it open to reveal a well-fired and well-filled morning roll. Stomach rumbling in anticipation. 'Sauce?'

He ferreted about in his pocket and presented her with a big handful of multicoloured sachets – slithering them onto the seat between her boots. Then dipped into the bag again for a wax-paper cup of something and handed that over too.

Oooh, *coffee*.

She cricked off the lid and took a soul-restoring sip. Sighed. Let her shoulders sink. 'I take it *all* back.'

Roberta ripped open some sachets of English mustard, tomato ketchup, and brown sauce, liberally dosing the contents of her roll, while Tufty squirted tartare sauce onto his fish-finger-and-fried-egg butty.

The pair of them sat there, slurping and munching.

And maybe the world wasn't a massive fondue-pot full of jobbies after all?

The wee loon nodded towards the lay-by. Munchity crunchity. 'Still no pathologist?'

'In the tent, foostering about with our remains.' Bite. Chewing the words and a chunk of sausage at the same time: 'Apparently I was "not helping" with my probing questions and insightful suggestions. Tell you, that woman could—'

Roberta's phone launched into Scissor Sisters' 'Take Your Mama'. She sooked tomato sauce from the fingers of one hand and answered it: 'What?'

A male voice, knackered, local: *'Steel? It's me, Davey.'*

Eh?

Didn't sound like him, so clearly laying on the 'I'm so sick' routine.

'Barrett! Where the hell are you? Should've been here hours ago.' Munch, munch, munch. Mouth full and mumbly. 'We're no' saving you any butties!'

'Butties? Wait, what?'

'And the auld-mannie voice is fooling *no*body.' Bite, munch. 'Lund said you were faking a cold, but you sound about *ninety*, you skiving wee git. No one goes off with the plague 'less I say so!'

'No, it's Davey. *Davey McLeod? We used to work together, back when it was still Grampian Police? Before the suits and Weegie*

wankers buggered everything up with this "one country one force" bollocks?'

She sat back, eyes wide. 'Detective Sergeant Wee Davey McLeod? Buggering hell; thought you were *dead*!'

Tufty chewed fishfinger butty at her. 'Pound in the swear jar.'

She flipped him the Vs and went back to her phone. 'You're no' dead, are you?'

'Might as well be…' A huffed breath. *'Listen, don't suppose you could do me a* teeny *wee favour?'*

Cos *that* didn't sound dodgy. 'Oh aye?'

'Normally, I wouldn't ask, but everyone I know's off with this bug that's going round. … See, there's a—'

'Well, look what the cat coughed up.' Roberta lowered her phone as Harmsworth staggered into view – beetroot of cheek, shiny with sweat, and breathing as if he'd just run a marathon. When the pie-stuffed snudge could barely run a bath.

He was *clarted* in pine needles, sticky Geordies, rosebay willowherb, and other assorted bits of undergrowth. Both shoulders spattered with what *looked* like splots of yoghurt. But probably weren't.

She slapped her phone against her chest, covering the mic. 'Might've known. You snidgers can smell a bacon butty at six hundred yards!'

Harmsworth collapsed into a spare seat. 'Had to … get across … railway line … before the eight twenty-three … Aberdeen to … to Inverness.' Wiping at his sweaty face. Then a sniff. Chin and eyebrows raised in hopeful expectation. 'Did you say something about butties?'

Tufty tossed him a paper bag.

He caught it, read the wobbly Sharpie letters – 'B&E' – then drooped. 'No sausages?'

Whining git.

Tufty rolled his eyes and reached for the one marked 'SE&E', but Roberta shook her head.

'No sausages for you, Bumcrack Boy. They're spoken for.' Ripping out another meaty eggy mouthful. 'Whnnnnrzz mmmgh vawannnnzeeeg?'

'What?'

Chew, chew, chew. 'Where's my *phalanges*?'

A martyred sigh, then he opened his paper bag. 'We searched and searched and searched…'

'Did you find the crows' nest, or didn't you?'

His face soured as he ripped open a tomato sauce. 'Oh we found the nest all right.' A shudder; squirting blood red all over his bacon and egg. 'Rotten flipping crows.' Biting into the butty and chewing as if it was a bitter chore. 'Pigeons aren't the rats of the air, *crows* are. Rottweilers with wings!'

'Did you find my missing phalanges or no'?'

'I got dive-bombed!' Hunching his pooped-on shoulders. 'Could've put my eye out.'

'Oh for…' What was the point? Useless sods were always going to uselessly sod, because that's what useless sods always did. And Harmsworth had to be the uselessiest and soddiest of them all.

Roberta was chewing at him in a disapproving manner, when a tiny, muffled, tinny voice squeaked into her right boob:

'Hello? Can you hear me? Hello?' Ex-Detective Sergeant Davey 'I Need A Favour' McLeod.

She popped the last chunk of butty in her gob. 'Davey? Yeah, I've got stuff on the boil here, so it's been lovely catching up, but—'

'I'm not asking much! Just run a couple number plates, that's all. I wouldn't ask, but I'm dying *here.'*

'Haven't heard from you in over a decade, Davey, and you call up asking for favours?'

Silence.

She sooked her fingers.

Crumpled the empty butty bag.

Tossed it into the back of the van.

'Jenny's cancer's not responding anymore. We're...' Deep breath. *'I want to do something special, but... It's... I need help, OK?'*

Jenny.

Who the hell was Jenny? Davey's Labrador? Wife? *Child...?*

Yeah.

Roberta sagged. 'Maybe. Text the buggers over and we'll see. I'm no' promising anything, mind.'

'Thanks! Thank you, that's great! That's—'

'Aye, I'm a sodding saint.' Or a soft touch, one of the two.

She hung up.

And there was Harmsworth, polishing off the last corner of his bacon-and-egg butty – already reaching for the sausage-and-double-egg.

'Oh no you don't.' Snatching the paper bag before he could get there. Unwrapping it as she jerked her chin at Tufty. 'You:' then at Harmsworth, 'as Fart Boy here is sod-all use, you're on crow duty.'

'Guv.' The wee loon crammed the last morsel of Neptune's delight into his gob, chewing as Roberta searched through the sauce sachets for more mustard. But while she was distracted by a rogue portion of raspberry jam, the thieving snudge plucked the butty from her fingers.

'Hey!'

Could barely make out a word over the fish-fingery mouthful: 'Need to extract the corvid tax.' Tufty plucked the two sausages from her bun and dropped them, naked, back into the paper bag. Then returned the eviscerated, meatless corpse of her butty. As if that was any sodding consolation.

'Gimme back my sausages!'

'Nope.' And off he scarpered, both hands held high above his head. 'Woo, woo, woo, woo, woo!'

Harmsworth watched Tufty go. 'Told you: we should've had him tested.'

8

The sausage-thieving twunt-wad was waiting for her by the fence that ran along the back of the lay-by. He'd got himself some backup, in the person of that spotty PC from before, who sported the same underbrush accessories as Harmsworth. Only with more bird poop.

She was munching on the last bacon butty, presumably by way of compensation for being shat on.

Roberta marched over there, hauling her trousers up with one hand, disembowelled butty clutched in the other. And yes, it still had two eggs in it, but that wasn't the point. She let go of her trousers and shook a fist at the culprit. 'Sausages, *now*, you skunk-faced … pridge!'

PC Spots curled her top lip. 'Eh?'

Tufty hid behind her. 'We're not allowed to swear, because of reasons, so everyone has to make up their own naughty words.'

Harmsworth lumbered over, picking bits of bracken out of his stabproof. 'Maybe everyone should just calm—'

'HE STOLE MY SAUSAGES!'

'For the *greater good*, Guv.' Tufty eyed the unsausaged roll in her hand. 'You know, we should donate that one to PC Stratford. Only fair, as he hasn't…'

Roberta took a big spiteful bite. Getting yolk all down her chin – a double-booby-trap butty being hard to control.

He pursed his lips. 'Fair enough.' Then checked his watch. 'Any minute now…'

She shook that fist again. 'You're asking for a boot, right up the Farage!'

Silence.

Tufty looked at her, as if she'd just crapped on a kitten. 'Someone's *dead*, Guv.'

She opened her mouth to rip the scrawny wee tit a new bumhole … then frowned and shut it again.

Sodding hell.

He might be a scrawny wee tit, but he was right.

Roberta drooped, hiding the bitten butty behind her back. 'I know.' Turned to frown at the marquee. 'But … when it's a *fresh* body it's still a *person*, you know? When you've got nothing left but sludge and bones… When it happened a long, long time ago…' A big sigh. 'Somehow, doesn't feel as *real*.'

Urgh…

Way to go, Roberta. Way to be an absolute prize prick. An insensitive arsehole. A rancid wank-numptie.

That pre-chewed butty hung heavy in her hand, like it was made of concrete and buttered with shame.

'Sorry.' She held it out to Harmsworth. 'Here. Give it to Constable Whatshisface.'

Harmsworth accepted the proffered butty. Paused. Licked his lips – clearly contemplating just wolfing it himself. Then puffed out his cheeks and wandered off. Hopefully looking for PC Stratford, rather than a safe spot to gorge.

Tufty beamed. 'Thanks, Guv.' He checked his watch again. 'Here we go…'

Those familiar *twing-spwong-twanggggg* noises rang out, getting louder, before a three-carriage train *rattle-clack*ed past – going the other way this time, heading south to Inverurie.

It was standing-room only onboard, and the windows

were full of commuters – staring at the lay-by as they passed. Phones out. Looking disappointed that there was nothing gory on show.

Then the fog swallowed the train again, and the noise faded. Till nothing but the whispering grey blanket remained.

Tufty pointed over the fence, towards the woods. 'Operation Find-Crows'-Nest-And-Not-Get-Pooped-On is go!' He hopped over the chain-link, followed by PC McAcne. Then held a hand out for Roberta.

Yeah, because there was nothing she wanted more than to go wading through the sodding forest underbrush looking for crows that must have diarrhoea – going by the amount of crap on Harmsworth and the spotty PC's shoulders.

But it was a *murder* investigation.

More importantly, it was *her* murder investigation.

Groan…

'Fine.'

The pair of them helped her clamber over the waist-high fence, and off they set across the train tracks…

Fog turned the woods into a horror-film mass of spooky silence and ominous gloom. The trees weren't in regimented Forestry Commission rows, but a mixed jumble, stretching uphill and fading away like ghosts. Filled with a sort of … expectant hush, only broken by the snap and crackle of twigs beneath their feet as Roberta and Tufty followed Police Constable Acne through damp bracken and grumpy blaeberry bushes.

Which *was* kind of mean.

Sure the PC had an actual name.

Had she said what it was?

Must've.

Bet Tufty knew.

The unnamed PC had her phone out – swinging it around as she looked up at the trees, consulting the map on her screen every few paces.

Probably suffered from acne her whole life.

Wasn't fair to make fun of it.

Well, it *was*, but that didn't make it *right*.

PC Lots'A-Spots did a three-sixty, eyes raking the ghostly canopy. 'Not far now.'

Roberta struggled through a waist-high curl of bracken. 'You said you were closest: when the call came in?'

'Yeah. Me and Shaky – I mean, PC Stratford – we were over Oldmeldrum way. Attempted rape.'

'"Attempted"?'

A nod. 'Local tosser snuck in through the garage when the victim's husband headed off to work. Nips upstairs while she's in the shower. Hides. Then jumps her as she's getting ready.' A huge grin ripped across the PC's face. 'Did you know you can circumcise someone with hair straighteners?'

Tufty winced. 'Oooh…'

'Yup, that ironed out his short-and-curlies. Was still screaming when the ambulance took him off.' Shrug. 'So we were only twenty minutes away.' Swinging her phone about again. 'Would've been ten, if it weren't for the fog. … Aha! Here we go.'

They stopped at the base of a big pine tree, that disappeared up into the grey murk. A couple of branches were distinctly lopsided and bent on one side of the trunk, with a broken limb at the bottom – directly above a big flattened oval of bracken.

Looked as if Harmsworth might've got down the fast way.

Everyone peered overhead, into the pine's spiky canopy. Not doing anything.

So Roberta poked Tufty. 'Up you go.'

'Pfff...' A nod. Then he took off his hat and handed it to her. 'That's a *big* tree for a little person.' Pulling on a pair of leather gloves. 'Come on, brave Sir Tufty, you can does it!'

Deep breath and he jumped for the lowest branch – which was a good bit higher than the one Harmsworth presumably broke off on his plummet downward – and failed. Jumping and reaching and jumping and fumbling and jumping and jumping and jumping. Wee arms scrabbling in the air above his head, like a small cat trying to catch a dangled toy.

It wasn't dignified.

'Oh in the name of...' Roberta hooked a finger at the PC, and together they gave the daft wee sod a boost, up to the lowest unbroken branch.

'Hurrah for the intrepid Sir Tufty!' And he was away: clambering up the tree, monkey-style.

Roberta's phone *ding-buzz*ed: incoming text.

Three number plates from an unknown caller.

That would be Wee Davey McLeod, then.

Well, he could sodding well wait.

Roberta put her phone away. 'Your victim: she OK?'

'Pissed off we wouldn't let her take the straighteners to Mr Rapey's balls too. I was all for it, but Shaky took pity, cos of the third-degree burns all over the guy's "bishop's hat".'

A big smile. 'If you get that bit off, you can feed it to your cat.'

The PC raised an eyebrow.

'You kinda had to be there.' Sniff. 'Listen...?' Leaving a wee pregnant pause with a question mark at the end.

'Gifford, ma'am.'

High above, the rustle-crack of a short-arse police officer clambering up a tree died down, then stopped.

PC Gifford stared up into the canopy. 'Generally "Michelle", if I'm not in trouble.'

'OK, *Michelle*. What happened with the check on our two spuds who found the body?'

'Alice Moncrief and Scott Baird. Yeah. ANPR cameras got them on the bypass at ten past four this morning, so—'

'SARGE?' Tufty's voice rattled down from above. *'I MEAN: ACTING GUV? GET UP HERE QUICK!'*

Sodding hell...

7

Roberta leapt for the lowest branch ... and had no more success grabbing it than Tufty had. She jerked a thumb at the thing. 'Would you...?'

But instead of clambering up the tree, Gifford hunched down and stirruped her hands.

Oh for God's—

'GUV! GUV, COME QUICKLY!'

Sod it.

Roberta stuck her foot into the offered hands and was boosted up to within grabbing reach – hauling herself onto the branch. Which was a lot higher than it looked from the ground. Then inched her way along to the trunk and reached for the next limb. Moving with all due care and attention, not wanting to join Harmsworth in the Plummeting-Out-Of-A-Tree-Club.

'GUUUUUUUUUUUUUUUUUUUUU-UV! QUICK!'

'Snudging heck...'

Faster – scrambling through the jaggy branches, boots fighting for purchase, almost losing her footing and crashing to the forest floor below. 'Hold on! I'm coming!'

She struggled and clambered from branch to branch, until Tufty's legs finally appeared through the needles above her.

'GUV!'

One last heave and her head poked above the raggedy

collection of brown-and-green prickles, bringing her eye to eye with the wee loon.

Sweat trickled down between her shoulder blades, gathering like a monsoon beneath her bra. Breath rasping like gravel in a tumble drier. 'What? … What's wrong? … Are you … you OK?'

But the idiot wasn't dying. Instead, he beamed like a proud parent and pointed at the scruffy bowl of sticks and dry grass and twigs and scraps of plastic bag, three crisp packets, and a couple of straws that now sat between them. A nest. Complete with four coal-black puffballs.

Tufty made *ta-daaaaa* hand gestures. 'Look! Like teeny tiny Goth ducklings, with sharp pointy beaks!'

Her mouth pinched. Eyes bugging. 'YOU DRAGGED ME ALL THE WAY UP HERE FOR … *THAT*?' Reaching across the nest to wallop him. 'I THOUGHT YOU WERE DYING!'

'Ow!' Retreating on his branch. 'No, *look*, Guv. How often do you get to see baby crows? Plus, I kinda need someone to lift them out the way, so I can search the nest.' He pulled off his leather gloves and snapped on a pair of blue nitriles instead. 'Ready?'

'I climbed a bloody tree!'

'That's another pound in—'

'Don't you *sodding* dare!' Getting her walloping hand ready for another bash.

'OK! OK. Right. Anyway…?' Gesturing at the chicks.

Really hard not to add another tenner to the swear jar right now. But she swallowed it down, reached out, and plucked a chick from the nest.

The wee thing *chirrrp*ed and *scraik*ed and wriggled, opening its beak to show off a bright-red gob.

Yeah…

Suppose they *were* kind of cute. And extremely fuzzy.

Using her elbows, Roberta braced herself against the branch and scooped up the other three chicks. Holding them in her cupped hands as they complained and swore and demanded food.

Tufty peered into the empty nest. 'Bingorama…' He took a couple of snaps with his phone, then popped it back in his stabproof, before unfurling a clear plastic evidence bag.

High overhead, something gave an angry *cawwwwwwww*!

Steel looked up – a pair of tattered bin-bag shapes whirled above them. Looking *very* unhappy. 'Tufty…?'

He reached into the nest and plucked something small from the feathery bottom. Dropped it in his bag. Then something else.

The circling crows stopped circling and dive-bombed Roberta, shrieking and cawing, wings clattering against her face on the way past. And ducking didn't help.

'Tufty!'

Pluck, pluck, pluck. 'Almost there…'

The second crow joined in, swooping at her head, claws out, beak flashing.

Roberta's peaked cap went flying, tumbling down, bouncing off branches on the way, leaving her floppy, unstyled hair on show.

And yes, *technically* it was a fancy new do: trimmed tight at the sides and back, getting longer and darker as it rose – from grey at the nape of her neck, to a crashing wave of thick hazelnut curls, sweeping forwards. But when you were dragged from your bed at half-six in the morning, with a screaming mariachi hangover, who the hell had the energy to faff about with tongs and mousse and hairspray and all that bollocks?

She pulled her ears in to her hunched shoulders as Crow Number One returned for another go. 'GHAAAAAAAGH!'

Pluck, pluck, pluck. 'Almost there…'

Number Two Crow clattered into the back of her head, pecking and screeching.

'GETOFF-GETOFF-GETOFF-GETOFF-GETOFF!'

PC Gifford's voice belted up from down below. *'ARE YOU TWO OK?'*

'DO WE BLOODY SOUND OK?'

Number One landed on her shoulder, claws raking, beak grabbing at lumps of hair. 'BUGGER OFF YOU WEEE SHITES!'

Tufty had one final rummage. 'And we're done!'

Thank God for that.

Roberta plonked the babies back in their nest and covered her head with both arms as the dive-bombing continued. 'I PUT THEM BACK! I PUT THEM BACK!'

'OK.' Tufty pocketed the evidence bag and produced a grease-spotted paper one instead – pulling out the two sausages he'd nicked. Waving them in the air, like an airport marshal guiding a 747 to its gate.

The crows battered Roberta with their wings, pecking away as Tufty poked both sausages into the nest, so they stuck up like excited willies.

Which the babies immediately attacked.

And that seemed to be enough of a distraction to stop the adults pecking a hole in Roberta's skull. At least temporarily...

Tufty grimaced at her. 'Cheese it!' And he was off, scrambling away down the tree.

Roberta blinked. 'What?'

Crow Number One *craaawwwwwwwwwwwed* at her – ready for another assault.

'Arrgh...'

Sod this.

She hurried after him.

Roberta picked a chunk of pine needles from her itchy black trousers and clambered over the railway fence. Limping along the potholed tarmac towards the SOC tent.

Stupid bloody crows…

The fog had thinned a bit while they were away playing Plank The Sausage, and now not only was the other side of the A96 visible, but the view stretched halfway across the field beyond. A grey-green swathe of barley, waiting for the sun to finally break through.

Someone had been busy with the blue-and-white 'POLICE' tape too, cordoning off the entire lay-by and putting cones on the other side of the road to discourage parking.

Which hadn't stopped a handful of journalists from loitering about on the grass verge opposite – smoking cigarettes and sharing a thermos of tea. Cameras at the ready in case anything juicy occurred.

None of whom seemed to have clocked her crow-pecked, forest-wearing, ankle-twisted scruffitude. Yet.

At least Roberta's recovered hat hid her haystack hairdo and all the bleeding welts left behind by those pointy-beaked bastard birds.

Tufty followed her over the fence, with his bag-o'-things in one hand, and twigs poking out of his stabproof.

The only one of them that didn't look like she'd been dragged through a garden centre backwards was PC Gifford. Blinking and yawning and shuddering as she shuffled along, bringing up the rear.

At the SOC tent, Roberta slumped, then knocked on the door-flap. 'SHOP!'

Gifford showed off all her fillings again, then gave a little post-yawn burp. 'Urgh…'

'You look like poop.'

'Thanks, Guv.' She ran an eye over Roberta, but wisely kept any smart remarks to herself.

Over on the far side of the road, those journos' cameras were watching them. Snapping away.

'Go on.' Roberta hooked a thumb at the nearest police vehicle. 'Sod off out of it. Go home. Get some sleep. No use to anyone if you fall asleep at the wheel of a patrol car doing ninety.'

'But—'

'Detective Inspector's orders. And take your mate, PC Lanky McBig-Head with you.'

Another yawn. Then a nod. 'Thanks, Guv.'

Tufty watched Gifford slouch off, then nudged Roberta in the ribs. 'Look at *you*: doing a nice thing for someone.' A grin. 'Must be going soft in your golden years. Well, golden months. Weeks?' He pulled on an innocent face. 'How long until you do has a retirement again?'

'Shut up.'

She gave the tent another chap, and the marquee's flap flipped open, as if the person inside had been lurking, waiting for the second knock. Ready to pounce.

Sheila Dalrymple: a bony thing, made of broomsticks and twigs, with a wide flat face. Wearing glasses under her safety goggles. She was in the full SOC kit, the fingers of her purple-nitrile gloves constantly in motion. Like twin spiders. Searching for something.

She gave Tufty a creepy smile and Roberta a wee bow. 'Hail and well met, fellow travellers on the journey to knowledge and justice! Of what service may I be today?'

Roberta groaned. 'It's no' gonna be another one of *these* days, is it, Sheila?'

'If it's an update on progress thou seek, then I can confidently predict that my mistress and I shall be about our foul task for *many* an hour yet. The remains of this *poor* individual are numerous and scattered, and ensuring neither bone nor scrap of flesh evade our attentions is a challenging task indeed!'

Why could nobody *normal* work for Police Scotland?

'Aye, OK. Is your mummy in?'

She put her head on one side. 'Professor McAllister is currently consumed by the task in hand and *regrets* that she is unable to attend to thy needs. Hence: my humble presence before thee now.' Another bow.

'Got something for you.' Roberta gave Tufty a gentle thump and he held out the evidence bag.

'We has been a-rummaging!'

'Crows' nest, up in the woods. Might be some of your missing bits.'

Sheila took it, turning the thing over and over in her spidery hands. 'Ah, most interesting *indeed.* Are these metacarpals I see before me? And I do believe that's a hamate, a lunate, scaphoid, and … a rib. Third rib, left-hand side, I'll wager.' It curled across most of the bag, pushing the plastic tight. 'No idea what *that* bit is, though. Or that.'

'You're welcome.'

More peering. 'I shall convey these to my mistress, forthwith.'

Roberta made her sign the chain of evidence form printed on the bag first. Then pocketed the pen. 'PM?'

'Ah, yes: the post mortem.' Shaking her head. 'Sadly, this shall now *not* take place until the morrow, for we already hath upon our slate two suicides, and a man whose unfortunate end was precipitated by the events of Saturday's protest.' She tutted. 'He was set about by pugnacious ruffians on Bridge Street.'

'Shite…' A riot was bad enough without fatalities.

'And so, *wretchedly* does turn the wheel of life. We are but a brief spark of candlelight, flickering in the—'

'Sheila?' A voice, from inside the marquee – with all the warmth of a mortuary slab. *'Playtime's over. Tell whoever it is they'll have my preliminary report by close of business and* not *before.'*

Sheila placed a purple hand over her weird little heart. 'My mistress needs me, and I must be about my allotted tasks.' Then she slipped inside the tent again, closing the flap behind her.

Like a creepy usher in this Cinema Of Horrors.

Roberta stuck two fingers up at the blue plastic marquee. Grimaced. Then turned and limped back towards her MX-5 with Tufty scuffing along behind. 'Swear to God, that woman gets *weirder* every day.' Limp, limp, limp. 'Time is it?'

'About twenty-five to. Give or take.' He evicted some more leaves from his stabproof vest. 'What you wanna do?'

Good question.

Go home. Soak in a hot bath. And plan a monster blowout retirement party *so* debauched that Police Scotland would speak of it forever in awed whispers…

But she had a murder inquiry to run.

Roberta hissed out a long breath and surveyed the crime scene with its police van, and Scenes Transit, and patrol cars – missing one, now that PC Gifford had scarpered… 'Suppose we better get cracking: commandeer an office at the nearest station, draft some bodies in, set up a HOLMES instance, search the misper database, drink some rank coffee, organise … things.' She stuck her hand out. 'Keys.'

Tufty stopped walking. 'Thought you were, and I quote, "hungover like a mother-snudger"?'

'That was *before* my sustaining butty and horrible woodland adventure. Now give me the blipping keys.'

'Nope. Kate and me is hasing an romantic dinner for two tonight, and she'd be upset if I died in a horrible car crash. So Tufty is Mr Does-The-Driving today!' And off he scurried, leaping into the driver's seat and cranking the engine. Grinning and waving at her as he beeped the horn: *ponk-honk*!

Idiot.

She closed her eyes. Pinched the bridge of her nose. Took a deep calming breath. 'Only eight weeks, three days, six hours, and twenty-five minutes to go, Roberta. You can do it.'

Ponk-honk!

'Just try not to kill anyone...'

The MX-5 tootled along, top down, radio off – though Tufty was humming away to himself, nodding along to whatever daft wee tune was playing in his hollow little head – as they approached the ever-expanding outskirts of sinful Inverurie.

Well, maybe 'sinful' was overegging it a bit.

At least the fog had faded to a wispy mist, glowing away as the sun beat down from above. The ground dropped away to the left, across a churned-up field of brown, where bright-yellow diggers and tippers planted yet another crop of cut-and-paste houses.

Roberta went back to her phone, thumbs jabbing away at a motivational text to that useless lazy twunt, Barrett:

> Where the heck are you and Lund? We've got a murder to investigate!!!!!
>
> FINGER OUT, YOU SNIDGING FRUDGER!!!

SEND.

She frowned at the screen. 'I miss swearing. *Proper* swearing.'

Tufty shrugged. 'You're the one who wanted to clean-up the team's language.' He put on a gravelly voice that sounded *nothing* like her. '"Some of us have small children to think of!", "Swearing isn't big *or* clever!", and my personal favourite: "Foul language is indicative of a stunted IQ and limited vocabulary!"' Dropping back into his usual stupid voice for: 'Cos it's not often one hears an Detective Sergeant using big clever words like "indicative".'

So she hit him.

'Ow!'

'I do *not* sound like that.' Roberta scrunched her face and huffed out a breath. 'Besides: got the feeling PC Gifford was mocking us. About the not-swearing.'

'I liked it when we had our Special Mystery Hat of Terms from whence were drawn the day's words of approbation and disapprobation, uniting the discommodious—'

So she hit him again.

'Ow! Stop it!'

'Nobody likes a show-off.'

They drove on in silence for a bit, as palisades of brown fencing reared up on either side of the road, corralling yet more identikit housing.

Tufty drummed his fingers on the steering wheel. 'Gu-uuuv…? Are you really getting a sauna?'

'Wee retirement treat for me.' Well-deserved after all these spudging years. 'Aye, if the sodding builders ever finish. Three weeks, and all they've done is rip everything out back to the stone, and put the electrics in. No wooden panelling; no benches for my pert, sweaty little buttocks; no hot sizzly stones. How am I supposed to—'

Her Airwave chimed out its three bleeps: incoming call.

Then a nasal teuchter accent whined from the speaker: *'Control to Alpha Charlie Nine: safe to talk?'*

Roberta pushed the button. 'Fit like the day, Jimmy?'

'Assistance needed: campaign office, Kingsfield Road, Kintore. Caller reports "violent mob" on scene.'

'Aye, very good. So why don't you call the local bunnets and make them do something about it?'

'From what I see: you sent the last two home. Inverurie are trying to pull officers in off their rest days now. Meantime, would you be a nice *acting detective inspector and go sort it out?'*

'What?' She actually laughed at that. 'No chance: I'm running a major murder Op, here!'

'Oh, I know, but your skeleton in a bin can probably *spare you for a couple of minutes. Unless you're chasing down a hot lead and an arrest is imminent as we speak…?'*

Buggering shiteflaps.

'Aye: thought not. Kintore. Don't make me clype on you to the Big Boss.'

'You wouldn't dare!'

The call ended with a wee snort. Then silence.

Of course he sodding would.

That was the trouble with modern policing – no loyalty. Every sod in uniform was lining up to stab poor, hard-working, beset-by-idiots, honest-as-the-day-is-sharny officers like her in the bum.

Tufty pulled an innocent face. 'Kintore?'

'Oh for … flipping … *scrudge*.'

'Told you: we should go back to the word-of-the-day thing.'

'Urgh…' Roberta slumped in her seat. 'All right, all right: put your foot down, we've got a riot to stop.'

A groan. 'Not *another* one! We just did that *two days* ago! I've still got bruises on my unmentionables.' He wriggled in his seat, face like a spanked buttock. 'Snidgers and snudgers running about, waving placards and attacking each other and chucking fizz-bangs and kicking nice police people in the underparts and smashing shop windows when they should be *celebrating* the nice police people for solving murders and rescuing victims and I don't *want* to…'

Blah, blah, blah.

There was more, but Roberta tuned it out.

OK, new plan:

Go to Kintore.

Stop the riot.

Give everyone a *really* stern talking to.

Then get back to work and catch whoever killed the poor sod in that wheelie bin.

Easy.

Right?

6

The Kintore Fish & Chip Bar crawled by, followed by the Fen Wei carry-out. Because even though the MX-5 should've been ripping along the street, lights blazing and siren roaring – not that Roberta's wee sports car was actually fitted with those – Tufty was sticking to the speed limit. Like a manky, pointy-noised scrunk.

'Will you hurry up?'

He shook his head. 'Nope.'

The town was nice. Genteel, in a sleepy sort of way. Lots of old-fashioned Scottish buildings in various shades of granite. The kind of place where the bus shelters weren't covered in marker-pen genitals and spray-paint profanity.

But it should've been flashing by *much* quicker.

The lights changed at the crossing, outside the local Indian takeaway, and Tufty stopped. Waiting for a harassed-looking mother to drag her horrible screaming children across. Probably not going for an early-morning breakfast bhaji.

He gave Mummy a cheery wave and got a scowl in reply. 'Can you imagine the headlines if we squished some poor member of the public, like her? Or her kids? Not to mention the damage it would do to your car.' A low whistle. '*And* your insurance premiums.'

Urgh… 'Suppose you've got a point.'

The lights turned green and off they pottered at thirty miles per hour, ambling through the town square – which was more of a lopsided triangle – then a hard left at the sign for Hatton of Fintray.

A dour kirk appeared on one side of the road: Kintore Parish Church. It had the welcoming air of somewhere that might end up converting from Christianity to Carpet Warehouse – bless this underlay, for it has sinned – with an attached graveyard and no parking. All enclosed behind a shoulder-high wall.

Campaign headquarters lay on the opposite side of the road. An olde worlde granite bungalow that had two dormer windows and a small portico over the door, which combined to make the place look a little bit like a startled pig. A yellow-and-black sign took up most of one window: 'EMMA DORNOCH: BETTER FOR SCOTLAND!'

And in the middle of the road – halfway between politics and damnation – was a pretty lacklustre riot. If you could call five middle-aged men in chinos and pastel-coloured polo-shirts facing off against nine T-shirted 'young adults' a 'riot'.

They'd only got as far as entry-level pushing and shoving. Some chest-to-chest glaring. A touch of placard-based tussling. No sign of any blows being traded.

But the morning was still young.

A couple of dog walkers looked on, while an auld mannie in the churchyard leaned on the cemetery wall – smoking his pipe and watching the scuffle. Because either he was *freakishly* tall, or the graveyard sat a good bit higher than the road. To accommodate all those dead people…

The youngsters were wearing 'EMMA DORNOCH' campaign T-shirts, in various cheery shades, holding hand-made placards with things like 'SMASH WHITE SUPREMACY!', 'FAR RIGHT: AWA AND SHITE!', and 'NO MORE NAZIS!!!' on them. None of the kids looked a day over twenty-four. Jammy sods.

There were a couple of proper hotties among their ranks too. One had long, wavy rust-red hair and a cartoon tattoo on one arm. Round glasses. Angry freckles. She wasn't just girl-next-door pretty either, she was the kind of pretty that would make you suck in your stomach … if you weren't hungover and full of sausage-bacon-and-egg butty. The other had long brown hair, cute nose, big eyes, and an in-and-out figure that set things tingling in your downstairs.

Something guaranteed to turn your downstairs dry as the Sahara Desert was the gammon-faced bunch of pricks they were shout, sneer, snarl, and scowling at.

Those pastel polo-shirts gave the middle-aged mob an air of soccer casuals who'd gone to seed. Lots of bald heads and double chins. Probably sold used Ford Cortinas and abused whippets when they weren't demonstrating and making tits of themselves.

Their placards were all professionally printed: 'BRITAIN FOR THE BRITISH!', 'THE UK IS NOT OK!', 'NO MORE LIBTARD LEFTIES!', 'NO SHARIA LAW!!!', and the *pièce de résistance*: 'EU FASHISTS! OUT! OUT! OUT!'

Because nothing said 'well thought-out argument' like being too thick to spell the thing you were protesting against.

And each one of their placards had the Anglo-Saxon Defence Group logo in the bottom left corner. Like an advert: if you enjoyed this dose of racism, bigotry, and ignorance, why not try our *other* repugnant views?

The only protester *not* wearing the polo-shirt-and-chinos uniform was a greasy frog-faced fuck in a waxed Barbour jacket, faux-farmer checked shirt, flat cap, and burgundy cords. He was probably in charge, because he stood well back from the argy-bargy, bellowing away into a loudhailer. Which was a bit overkill for a half-arsed tussle on a wee side street. '*...IS TYPICAL OF COWARDLY LEFTIES! OUR COUNTRY IS OVERRUN WITH MIGRANT CRIMINALS, AND YOU'RE ON THEIR SIDE!*'

Tufty parked, and Roberta climbed out into the baking sun. Adjusted her hat. Squared her shoulders.

The wee loon scurried up beside her, fiddling with his Body Worn Video till the little red light came on to show it was recording.

Frog-Face chanted into his loudhailer: 'TRAITORS! TRAITORS! TRAITORS!'

The gammony mob chanted back: 'HOY! HOY! HOY!'

Tufty winced. 'This is going to get horrible, isn't it.'

Not to be outdone, the T-Shirts started up a chant of their own:

'WHAT DO WE WANT?'

'SOCIAL JUSTICE AND INCLUSION!'

'WHEN DO WE WANT IT?'

'NOW!'

Snappy...

'Come on, then.' Roberta hauled her trousers up and marched over there. Stuck her arms in the air. 'All right, you bunch of idiots: I want everyone to take a step back!'

No one did.

But the campaign-office door opened and a snottery sniff of a man emerged. He'd combed all his hair forward, in a desperate attempt to hide the fact that his forehead was already sneaking back past the top of his skull. Trendy glasses and a Super Mario moustache, a rainbow tie, white shirt, and grey suit trousers. 'GO AWAY, YOU ... *THUGS*; I'VE CALLED THE POLICE!'

'We're already here, you numpty!'

'*TRAITORS! TRAITORS! TRAITORS!*'

'HOY! HOY! HOY!'

The man forced his way into the scuffling. 'GET BACK! YOU'RE NOT ALLOWED TO HARASS PEOPLE!'

Was she sodding invisible here?

The shoving got nastier. The chest-to-chest clashes: harder.

Then one of the Polo-Shirts yelped in pain.

This was getting out of hand.

Roberta had another go: 'OK, I want everyone to—'

'TRAITORS! TRAITORS! TRAITORS!'

'HOY! HOY! HOY!'

In the middle of the push-and-shove, that sexy redhead dropped her placard. 'Knife! He's got a—' A scream ripped free, then down she went. Collapsing backwards. *Clunk*: the back of her head bounced off the kerb. And she lay there, still as the graves in the churchyard opposite, with a knife handle sticking out of her stomach. Deep dark red seeped through the cheery yellow fabric of her 'EMMA DORNOCH' T-shirt.

Everyone froze.

The man in the rainbow tie stared. 'NO!' And rushed over to help.

A chubby young man with a pubey beard clutched his placard tight. 'Billie!' Little pink eyes bulging. 'YOU BASTARD!' Swinging 'SMASH SEXISM!!!' like a headsman's axe.

It clattered into one of the Polo-Shirts, catching him right in the face, sending him staggering with a broken-nosed grunt.

And that's when it all kicked off.

Punches flew, teeth flashed, and the boot was put in.

Tufty pulled out his extendible baton. 'Oh dear…' He clacked the thing out to its full length and charged. 'STOP! POLICE!'

Fists whistled through the air, placards clashed, swearing and screaming bellowed out.

Roberta waded into the crowd, making for the injured Billie. 'Get out the way! Move!'

But no one paid the slightest bit of attention.

It was getting dirty now: biting, gouging, kneeing-in-the-knackersing…

'TRAITORS! TRAITORS! TRAITORS!'

'HOY! HOY! HOY!'

And *that* wasn't helping.

She reached the victim, shoved Mr Rainbow-Tie out of the way, and knelt – feeling for a pulse.

Christ that was a lot of blood.

The knife's handle looked like a kitchen job: black, with metal rivets. Probably had a six-to-nine-inch blade, angled upwards from about the middle of her stomach.

Billie's face was pale and slack.

More blood on the pavement and kerb, from where her head cracked into the concrete.

Yeah, this did *not* look good.

And still no sign of a pulse.

'Come on, come on…' No, wait: there it was. Faint, but still beating. 'Bingo.' Roberta grabbed her Airwave handset and pressed the button. 'Alpha Charlie Nine to Control, *not* safe to talk. Need an ambulance and backup at Kingsfield Road, Kintore, ASAP! One stabbing victim. Repeat: stabbing victim. Violence ongoing.'

The same nasal voice as before crackled out. *'Hold on, hold on…'*

All around, the battle raged, while Mr Rainbow-Tie stood in the gutter, hands over his mouth, feet moving as if he needed a wee. 'Ohmygod, ohmygod, ohmygod…'

'Get me some bloody backup!'

'Working on it.'

The man knelt on the other side of the motionless body. 'Maybe we should pull the knife out?' He took hold of the protruding handle. Bit his bottom lip.

Roberta slapped him. 'LET GO: you sodding idiot!'

And he did, snatching his hand away as if the knife was scalding hot.

She glared. 'You want to make it *worse*?'

'I'm sorry, I'm sorry!'

Idiots, everywhere.

'TRAITORS! TRAITORS! TRAITORS!'

'HOY! HOY! HOY!'

She grabbed the moron's hands and placed them either side of the wound. 'Apply pressure *here*. And no touching the knife!'

Tears sparkled in his eyes, welling up as he stared at the blood seeping around his fingers. 'Oh God, Billie... Come on, don't *do* this to me... You'll be fine, you'll be fine... Please, please, please, please, please...'

'OK: ambulance on its way, rerouting all available officers...'

Roberta scrambled to her feet.

Tufty had one of the larger Polo-Shirts pinned to the ground in a lock-and-bar hold, twisting the guy's arm out of its socket – trying to get the cuffs on with his other hand. Which meant the sexy brunette was free to put the boot into Mr Polo-Shirt's ribs and head. Good job those boots were a pair of nice soft trainers, otherwise she could've done some real damage.

But she was bloody well trying.

Tufty fumbled the cuffs again, glaring up at Little Miss Stomps-A-Lot. 'GET OUT OF IT!'

All over the street, blood and teeth and punches flew.

And they already had *one* attempted murder.

Yeah...

No way two police officers were ending this any time soon.

'TRAITORS! TRAITORS! TRAITORS!'

'HOY! HOY! HOY!'

Right.

She struggled free of the riot and marched over to the frog-faced tit. Made a grab for his loudhailer. 'Give me that!'

But he wasn't cooperating. Holding on tight as they wrestled for it, turning round and around and around. Then shoved her away. 'Get off me, you old bag!'

Roberta crashed down on the pavement like a sack of tatties. Breath whooming out of her. Hat flying off to reveal her disaster hairdo.

Frog-Face brought the loudhailer up again. *'TRAITORS! TRAITORS! TRAITORS! HOY! HOY! HOY!'*

That was it. No more Mrs Nice Police-Officer.

Cheeks burning, she scrambled to her feet and ran back to the MX-5. Popped the boot.

Her stabproof, high-vis, and utility belt were right where she'd left them this morning, after clocking in and sodding off.

She hauled the heavy armoured vest over her head and scritched the Velcro sides shut, buckling on the belt as she strode back towards the fight. Teeth gritted. Thunder *growling* through her skull. '"*Old bag*", is it?'

Roberta whipped out her PAVA spray – no bigger than a tube of lube – flicking off the safety catch as she headed for Mr Froggy. 'HEY, *FUCKFACE!*' Holding the thing at arm's length, with the nozzle pointing right at him. 'LOUDHAILER: NOW!'

'Bugger off.' Back to whipping up his gammony thugs. *'TRAITORS! TRAITORS! TRAITORS!'*

Can't say she didn't warn him. One last bit of protocol to go: clearly announce that she was deploying Pelargonic Acid Vanillylamide as a non-lethal incapacitant in an ongoing violent situation to subdue a non-cooperating individual.

'SPRAY!' She pressed the trigger and a somewhat apologetic squirt of clear liquid arced through the air to spatter against the git's face.

He pulled his head back, spluttering and blinking, features all creased like a revolted toad. One hand wiping at his suddenly wet skin. 'What did…' And then a keening yowl broke free: low at first, building in volume and pitch like an air-raid siren as all those lovely chemicals got to work. Turning his ugly mug an angry shade of baboon's arse, screwing his eyes shut. He folded in half, dropping the loudhailer, freeing up both hands to clutch at his burning eyes. 'AAAAAAAAAAAAAAARGH! JESUS, FUCK! AAAAAAAAAAAAAAAAAAAAAAAAARGH!'

Roberta snatched the loudhailer from the ground, and the flat cap from his head – exposing a huge bald spot at the back – using the tweedy fabric to wipe the loudhailer's mouthpiece. Then cranked up the volume and pressed the button. *'THIS IS THE POLICE! EVERYONE STOP FIGHTING* RIGHT *NOW! YOU'RE ALL UNDER ARREST!'*

Which made no difference whatsoever.

Mr Frog collapsed on the pavement, curled up tight as an ammonite, hands covering his beetroot face. 'Oh God, help me! Aaaaargh…!' Deep breath. 'AAAAAAAAAAAAAAARGH!'

Good. Served him right.

'DON'T SAY YOU WEREN'T WARNED!' Roberta tossed the loudhailer and brought up her PAVA canister again, charging into the fight. 'SPRAY!' Squirting everyone in the face who came within range. Didn't matter if it was a T-Shirt or a Polo-Shirt, sometimes both. Leaving a trail of scarlet-cheeked, swollen-eyed, *screeching* destruction in her wake.

Both sides staggered apart, clutching their burning faces. Tears streaming. Kneeling in the road – shrieking and bawling about how much it burned.

She kept going till the PAVA stopped squirting, and pressing the trigger just made farty bubbling noises.

All empty.

Roberta popped it back in its holster and surveyed her handiwork.

It was like something out of a war film – aftermath of the battle – a low-budget Bannockburn, where the cries of the injured mingled with the wails of those who wished they were dead.

Wimps.

Of the assembled riot, only five had escaped her squirty wrath: two polo-shirted gammon tosspots and three T-shirt-wearing bleeding-heart liberals. And Tufty, of course. Who'd got his gorilla cuffed and was now rolling about on the ground struggling to restrain Little Miss Sexy-Brunette, who was resisting arrest in an *extremely* bitey way.

The survivors milled around, still clutching their placards like offensive weapons, everyone bleeding from bashed noses and split lips as they stared at their screaming fallen comrades.

Little Miss Sexy kicked out with her trainers, aiming to emasculate the wee loon. 'GET OFF ME YOU PERVERT!'

'Ow! Ow! Ow!'

Roberta rolled her eyes. 'CONSTABLE QUIRREL! Stop mucking about and spray anyone who doesn't give up *right now*!'

He wrestled his foe into an arm lock, before looking up. 'You sure?' Then he must've seen the expression on Roberta's face because he grimaced and snapped out a crisp, 'Yes, ma'am!' Before letting go of Miss Sexy-Bites and scrambling to his feet. Backing off to a safe distance and whipping out his own PAVA spray. Adopting a Dirty Harry pose. 'Nobody move! Drop your weapons!'

The remaining T-and-Polo-Shirts stared at him.

'OK.' He shrugged and took aim.

At which point they all abandoned their placards and stuck their hands in the air.

Finally: peace.

Roberta produced her Airwave, pressing the button as she hurried back to their stabbing victim. 'Where's my bloody ambulance?'

After a brief visit to the corner store, Tufty had returned with a job-lot of cable-ties, *vwwwwwwwwwwwipp*ing the rioters' wrists together behind their backs.

They all sat on the pavement: Polo-Shirted protesters on one side – slumped against the cemetery wall – and the T-Shirted political volunteers on the other – like little gnomes outside the campaign office. The ones who'd been sprayed had faces like squeezed plukes, eyes clamped shut, whimpering. While the unsprayed moaned about their human rights and how unfair it all was.

Poor babies.

Should've sodding thought of that before they started beating the crap out of each other.

A woman in jeans, a yellow shirt, and her early-thirties was washing one of the T-Shirt's faces with a milky cloth – topping it up from a two-litre container of semi-skimmed. This dairy-based Florence Nightingale boasted a sensible haircut and a strong jaw, broad shoulders and a wide back. The kind of biceps that suggested she could castrate six bullocks, eight pigs, and two Jehovah's Witnesses before breakfast.

A proper farmer's quine.

She'd worked her way around the other blubbering T-Shirts, offering words of comfort as she ministered to their puffy eyes and swollen faces. The kids already looked a lot less tortured and beetrooty, but the Polo-Shirts were all still scarlet-faced and weeping. And Miss Milky didn't seem in any hurry to help them.

Meanwhile, Roberta knelt on the ground, holding the hand of a dying woman.

They'd covered Billie's legs with one of those silvery marathon blankets, which might or might not have been helping on a baking-hot day like this. Difficult to tell. Her skin was pale as the milk being sloshed onto her friends' faces.

Mr Rainbow-Tie kept pressure on the wound, just like Roberta had told him. Snivelling and gurning away to himself, teetering on the edge of a full-fledged bawl.

To be fair: trying to stop someone you know *dying* was probably pretty upsetting.

Especially if it wasn't working…

Tufty appeared at Roberta's shoulder, dangling his leftover cable-ties. 'How is she?'

'How do you *think*?' Stupid sodding question. Roberta glanced at the line of whimpering prisoners. 'If they decide to kick off again, that won't hold them for long.'

'Nope. Some big beefy backup wouldn't hurt.' He peered off down the road. 'But till they get here…?'

Good question.

'Set up a cordon. Should be tape in the boot.'

But instead of hopping to it, the wee loon gazed down at Billie, face as droopy as his voice. 'Be *really* nice if today didn't turn into a double feature.'

'Yeah.'

Because one dead body was *more* than enough.

Tufty huffed out a breath, grimaced, then headed off to fetch the blue-and-white tape.

The farmer's quine finished sponging milk into the last T-Shirt's eyes and wandered over, still holding that dripping cloth and jug of milk. 'Is Billie… Is she going to be OK?'

Roberta bit back the sarcasm this time. 'She's lost a lot of blood. Ambulance should be here any minute.'

Hopefully.

Fingers crossed.

Before it was too late…

The woman frowned down at the horrible tableau for a moment, then put a hand on Mr Rainbow-Tie's shoulder. Gave it a squeeze. 'You OK, Frank?'

His lip quivered, but he bit it and nodded. 'She's going to be fine. She's going to be fine…'

'Good man.' Another squeeze. 'You're doing great.' She scowled across the road at the collection of zip-tied, blubbering political casuals. 'Do you know which one of *them* did it?'

Rainbow Frank shook his head, tears on their way. 'Sorry. I'm so sorry…'

'It's unbelievable. How could anyone have so much … *hate* in them? She's only *twenty-one*!' Squaring up to Roberta, Miss Milky used her carton to gesture at the protesters. 'These bastards've been turning up, every couple of weeks. We keep complaining about it, but no one *does* anything. What's the point of *having* a police force if they don't *do* anything?' Righteous and indignant. Then a sigh, a sag, and a shrug. 'I apologise. That was unfair.'

She stuck a milky hand out for shaking. 'Emma Dornoch: I'm running to take Gordon and Buchan from the Tories, in the by-election … That's the plan, anyway.' She squatted down beside Billie, tears glittering in her eyes as she brushed a strand of hair away from that pale motionless face. 'Billie's been volunteering here off-and-on since Christmas. Doing an MA in Philosophy, Politics and Economics at Aberdeen University; lives with her mum and dad in Ferryhill. I've got her home address somewhere, in case you need to…'

Shuddering. 'Suppose *I* should be the one who tells them what's happened.'

Roberta looked up at the campaign office, with its piggy snout and 'VOTE FOR ME!' signs. Scanning the frontage for a telltale camera. 'You got CCTV?'

There it was – mounted just above and to the left of the front door… Only the wires dangled loose, snipped clean through.

A bitter laugh snorted free. '*Coincidentally* enough, it gets vandalised every night before these knuckle-dragging, middle-aged gristle-wanks turn up with their placards.' Dornoch stuck her nose in the air. 'We complain about *that* too, but nothing happens.'

Of course it sodding didn't.

Why did people think there were an infinite number of police officers, ready to rush round at a moment's notice to pounce on every little annoyance and minor infraction committed against them? Bring the full weight of the law to bear, with fingerprints and DNA and stakeouts and surveillance and round-the-clock foot patrols…?

But if you policed everything *they* did, no matter how small, they'd be screaming about a fascist state and overreach and *'My tax pays your wages!'*

Should be grateful Roberta turned up at all.

This wee street would be knee-deep in bodies if she hadn't taken charge and sprayed the buggers.

Couldn't say any of that though, could you.

Not unless you wanted a lecture from Professional Standards and a two-week training course on Securing Positive Outcomes When Dealing With Awkward Bastard Members Of The Public.

So, instead, Roberta went for a more tactful approach. 'Aye, well: get your arse elected and double our sodding budget. You think policing's—'

A screech of brakes sounded behind her, and Roberta whipped around. About time that bloody ambulance…

But it wasn't an ambulance, it was a fancy dark-grey BMW. One of the electric ones, where you could run old ladies over without the engine noise tipping them off. It slithered to a halt, just outside Tufty's cordon, and the passenger door popped open.

Out stepped a stylish middle-aged woman, dressed for a business casual lunch/affair with her stockbroker and/or tennis coach. Understated jewellery. Thick brown wavy hair that brushed her shoulders. Boot heels clacking against the tarmac as she ducked beneath the blue-and-white tape and marched down the middle of the road, towards them.

Emma Dornoch stood. 'Claire!'

A posh accent: 'Came, soon as I heard.' Completely ignoring Roberta, Posh Claire locked in on Mr Rainbow-Tie. 'Frank, oh my God, is she OK?'

Rainbow Frank blinked back tears and shook his head. Not saying anything.

Why did everyone keep asking the same old *stupid* questions?

'Hoy!' Roberta clambered upright, glowering at Mrs Posh-Bits, then flinging a finger at the tape. 'Cordon. Other side.'

There was a moment of blinking and chin in, as if processing this *bizarre* request. Then the woman's hand came out for shaking. 'Claire Fordyce, MSP.'

'Do I look like I sodding care? Get your arse out my crime scene, *now*.'

The hand was withdrawn.

Emma Dornoch – Better For Scotland – tried a more diplomatic tone. 'Officer…?'

But Roberta maintained a steely silence.

'OK.' She tried again. 'Claire, is my … well, *mentor*. She's been *so* kind, helping us put together a campaign in only a couple of—'

'*Still* don't care.' Roberta stepped closer. 'Either you get your stylish bum on the other side of that sodding cordon, or I arrest it. In five.'

Claire Fordyce pulled on a photogenic smile. 'We appear to have gotten off on the wrong foot,' peering at Roberta's epaulettes, 'Inspector, isn't it?'

'Four.'

The smile slipped a little. 'Surely there's no need for *hostility*, Inspector, I'm only here to support—'

'*Three*.' Putting a bit of darkness in it.

'Look, I recommended Billie for *Emma's team*, it's—'

'Two.'

Took a while, but eventually it must've sunk through that four-inch-thick posh-person skull of hers, because she backed away. 'All right, all right, I'm going, I'm going.' Then, Claire Fordyce, MSP, turned on her heel and clacked off again. Making a big show of ducking under the cordon, followed by a pantomime 'You happy now?' gesture.

Emma Dornoch sighed. 'Was that really necessary?'

'Every bugger watches TV cop shows, but no one understands how forensics work.' Roberta hauled up her trousers. 'Coming in here, prancing about like Lady Muck. It's a *crime scene*!'

'Maybe that's because she actually is? A lady, I mean.' Dornoch pointed at the BMW, where an older gentleman – with fashionably long, swept-back grey hair and a neatly trimmed salt-and-pepper beard – was emerging from the driver's side. Playing up the silver-fox image in a suit that probably cost more than Roberta's car. And a watch worth more than she made in a year. With a fancy-foreign-holiday tan and teeth an unnatural shade of pearly white. 'That's her husband: *Sir* Norman Fordyce.'

Sir Norman strode to his wife's side and gave her a wee

comforting hug. Before pointing at the Polo-Shirts and the T-Shirts. Then whipped out his phone – casting angry glances in Roberta's direction as he talked and paced.

Yeah … that probably wasn't good.

He was exactly the kind of prick who had friends in high places.

And, as if to prove the power of the Mighty Sir Norman Fartface, a siren *whoop-whoop-whoop*ed in the distance. Getting louder, fast. For verily, his mere presence hath summon-ed an ambulance.

About sodding time.

5

The ambulance slowed, mounting the pavement to squeeze between Sir Norman's BMW and the cemetery wall, as Tufty opened the cordon for them.

Rainbow Frank sagged. 'Oh, thank God…'

Right.

Now the paramedics were here, it was time to do something about her collection of prisoners/suspects/idiots.

Roberta stepped into the road, plucking the loudhailer from where she'd dropped it. The plastic housing was a bit scuffed, but other than that? Pressing the button marked 'SIREN' made the thing wail like a slapped child.

Good enough.

Soon as the screech faded, she addressed both sides. *'LISTEN UP! SOMEONE HERE STABBED THIS YOUNG WOMAN! YOU GET* ONE *CHANCE: FESS UP* NOW*, OR I SWEAR TO WHOEVER LIVES IN THAT BIG POINTY HOUSE,'* waving at the church, *'I WILL MAKE IT MY LIFE'S WORK TO CRUSH YOU LIKE A SODDING BUG! ARE WE CLEAR?'*

The ambulance came to a halt beside Billie, the front doors sprung open, and the two-person paramedic team leapt out. The passenger was a toothy yeti of a man with too much beard. The driver: a wee blonde woman, her bare arms and round face a painful shade of sunburnt pork. Both looking knackered and harassed in their kale-green uniforms.

No one said a word as they hurried toward Billie. Peeling off the crinkly tinfoil blanket as if she was some sort of ready meal.

Roberta raised the loudhailer again. *'YOU'VE GOT TILL THEY LEAVE!'* Then hurled the thing to the ground. It bounced, the casing cracking as it blared out a tortured, discordant-electronic-feedback howl.

So she stomped on it – once, twice, three times – shattering the plastic, sending bits of circuit board and casing flying. Putting it out of its misery.

Mr Yeti knelt beside Billie. Purple-nitrile fingers exploring her hairline, searching for damage. 'Hello? Can you hear me, Sweetheart? Hello?'

Sunburnt Blondie tried Frank instead. 'How long has she been unconscious?'

'I don't really ... fifteen minutes? Maybe? It's all been a bit of a blur...'

An emergency vehicle wailed in the distance, approaching at speed. Not the medical *whee-yoo-whee-yoo-whee-yoo* of another ambulance, but the longer *demanding* tones of a patrol car siren on its first setting. More than one car, going by the racket.

Wasn't long before two of them appeared in Kintore's town triangle, followed by a police van caked in dust and grime.

The three vehicles blocked the road behind Sir Norman's BMW, and out piled six officers – two from each – which had to be a good chunk of North East Division's dayshift, given how many of the snudgers were off sick.

And every single one of them was too buggering late to do any good.

Roberta threw her hands in the air. 'Finally!' Taking a deep breath to welcome them properly: 'WHERE THE *HELL* HAVE YOU BEEN?'

Tufty sidled up to her, keeping his voice down so no one else could hear. 'Guv? Are you OK?'

She glared at him, jaw clenched, fists trembling. 'Do I sodding *look* OK?'

'Eeek...' He backed up a pace. Then made himself busy somewhere else.

Because he wasn't as daft as he looked.

'So ...' Logan McRae adopted that slightly patronising tone he used when someone had been unusually stupid, *'you arrested them* all*?'*

'Course I sodding did.' Roberta grumbled her way between the graves, one hand jammed deep in her trouser pocket, the other holding her phone. Kicking at the grass and glancing over the cemetery wall.

The smaller protesters – both Polo-Shirts and T-Shirts – were being loaded into the back of the police van, while the back seats of the two patrol cars were reserved for the biggest and gammoniest lumps.

Mind you, they all seemed to be suffering from the post-riot blues, and not inclined to kick off again. Not *yet*, anyway.

She stepped around a squint headstone. 'Well, what was I *supposed* to do? Can't just let the buggers *go*: serious assault, rioting, attempted murder – which might turn into an *actual* one – resisting arrest, dressing up like a bunch of tits, and one count of being a chinless wank.'

'That's two quid in the swear jar.'

'Shut up.'

Rainbow Frank stood all on his ownsome, by the door to campaign headquarters, arms wrapped around his chest as if trying to keep his innards from escaping. Trembling.

His shirtsleeves were drenched in dark scarlet from cuffs to elbows, the multicoloured tie stained to a gory monotone.

Poor sod looked in desperate need of hot sweet tea and a dark corner to sob in.

Roberta gave the squint headstone a wee nudge with her boot. 'And Sergeant Downie Six-Toes is moaning, cos the cells are still full after the weekend. Says it'll take *days* to get the backlog through court, and "How dare I arrest another big wodge of people, just to spite him?" Pasty-faced, inbred gype.'

'That's violent protests for you.'

Emma Dornoch was on her phone too, marching back and forth with her forehead all furrowed, free hand gesticulating in jabby sweeping arcs. Doing her best to avoid the puddle of blood where Billie had lain. Could be squeamishness, or maybe just not wanting to get all that sticky haemoglobin on her nice boots.

'No' *my* fault, is it. Some buggers just *need* banging-up.'

Sir Norman and Lady Stick-Up-The-Arse Fordyce were loitering by their fancy BMW, both wheeling and dealing on phones of their own. No doubt tag-teaming the Chief Constable to tell her what a rude, insolent, absolute disaster of a disappointment Acting Detective Inspector Roberta Steel was.

'There's dozens of little stations all over the division. Bet they've got plenty of spare cells.'

'Oh aye? And who'll man them, the Not-Off-On-The-Sick Fairies?' This time the squint grave got a wee kick. 'Bloody force is like a ghost town.'

'Could let them go?'

'Nah, attempted murder, remember?' Roberta sagged her bum against a big granite slab with crimped decoration along its curved top, like a carved Cornish pasty. 'Poor wee girl's only twenty-one; lying there with a knife sticking out her guts.'

At least the ambulance was long gone. Billie would be halfway to Aberdeen Royal Infirmary by now. Where she'd be heading straight into surgery. Hopefully. Rather than the mortuary.

'Should be ashamed of yourself, by the way: shirking your duty. Malingering at home, when some of us are out here *working*. Struggling nobly under the weight of monstrous hangovers brought about by your cheap drain-cleaner booze.'

A snort. *'Oh no you don't. You wolfed two bottles of—'*

'Don't interrupt when I'm berating you. It's—'

'Acting Guv?' Tufty's pointy wee head appeared over the cemetery wall. 'That's them ready to go.' Nodding at the patrol cars and police van. 'Any idea where you want them, yet?'

'Hold on.' She took the phone from her ear and covered the mic with her other hand. 'Is Downie still moaning about his sodding cell capacity?'

'Up to his ears and sinking fast. "No room! No room!"' A frown. 'Think she'll be OK?'

'She *better* be, or I'm clambering up someone's backside with crampons and a blowtorch.' Pointing at the wee loon's chest. 'You get the stabbing on your BWV?'

He looked down at the little black rectangle, fixed to the front of his high-vis. 'Won't know till I get it back to the *Palais de Police* and download the footage. What twit designed Body Worn Video units that does not has no screens?' Then peeled off his hat and fanned his sweaty face. 'Pfff... I hates stabbings. Too sudden and easy and random. Not like *guns*. You need to put a bit of work in with a gun.'

Idiot.

'Go away.'

'No, but you do! You have to find a sketchy-criminal type who's selling one, and you've got to buy it for very muchness of money – not to mention the ammunition, which isn't easy to come by – and *then* you've got to go out and shoot your victim, getting all covered in blowback and leaving wads of forensics behind. And even worse: every bullet that comes out the shooty end bears a scratch-etched fingerprint that's unique to the gun what fired it.' Nodding away, as if agreeing with this nugget of daftness. 'Whereas most people's cutlery drawers are *full* of knives. And once you've stabbified someone, you can give the thing a quick squirt with bleach, ditch it in the river, and buy a new one at your nearest supermarket.'

She made a wafting gesture. 'Away. Go. *Now.*' Then back to her phone call. 'So, when you coming back to work, Skiver?'

'Got to keep the leg elevated for a couple of weeks.' Logan made a hmmmmm-ing noise. *'Could wheel me about in a bath chair, I suppose? Might make operational duties a bit difficult, though.'*

'Meh: long as no one commits an "upstairs crime" we'll be fine. Tell you, it's...' She narrowed her eyes, because the wee loon was still hanging about like a wet fart. 'Thought I told you to sod off.'

Tufty shrugged. 'Yeah, but you has not answered The Big Question: where am we taking all these peoples?'

Did she have to do *everything*?

'Find out if there's enough space at Inverurie. If not, distribute the buggers through the...' Oh for goodness' sake: the halfwit had his notebook out, scribbling away. 'Why are you writing that down? It's easy enough to remember!'

'No: is your running total. For the swear jar.'

She jabbed a hand at the vehicles. 'Go! Before I throw a gravestone at you!'

'Eeek...' And away he scurried.

Honestly.

Roberta raised her phone again. 'That boy could numpty for Scotland. Where was—'

'Listen: you've got no CCTV, right? Have you confiscated everyone's phone? Maybe somebody got the stabbing on film.'

She let the sarcasm rip. 'Of *course* I didn't, because I'm a *simpering imbecile* who's *never* run a *murder inquiry* before!' A haughty sniff. 'Now, if you'll *excuse* me, I've got tossers to interrogate.'

Roberta hung up and stuffed her phone in her pocket. Glowered at the pie-topped gravestone for a moment. Then took a deep breath. 'HOY, TUFTY!'

The wee twit stopped, turned. 'Guv?'

'CONFISCATE EVERYONE'S PHONE.'

'Yes, Guv.' Hurrying off to do what he was told.

Leaving her alone in the graveyard – except for the dead – looking at an empty street, with its puddle of dark scarlet glittering on the tarmac.

What a bloody day…

Inverurie police station was a chunky barrel-roofed lump of beige and grey-brown that looked more like a cleaning-services company on the outskirts of a cut-price industrial estate than Scotland Yard. If it weren't for the blue-and-white 'POLICE' sign mounted on the wall, you might never guess it was a vital cog in the criminal-justice machine…

Roberta's MX-5 was the only car parked out front, even though there were loads of spaces – maybe because everyone was off with the lurgy, or maybe because Inverurie was more of a sprawling commuter town than a bustling crime-filled metropolis.

A modest Morrisons sat on the other side of the road, with its supermarket petrol station, and advertising banners promising two-for-one deals on doughnuts, cakes, and biscuits. Which *mattered* as it was officially time for elevenses and ages since Roberta's sausage-bacon-and-egg butty.

Surprised she wasn't wasting away, right now.

A tractor grumbled by on the road, hauling a bogie full of sheep. Off on some sort of sheepy adventure.

She toasted them with her vape, then sagged back against the MX-5 and blew a plume of black-cherry steam at the sky.

Contrails crossed the cloudless blue, following some high-flying intercontinental plane.

Jammy, holidaying bum-rummlers.

Sighing, she slumped even further. Puffed out her cheeks. Scowled at the posted petrol and diesel prices on the big supermarket sign opposite – because nothing *ever* got cheaper these days – then dug out her phone and thumbed a text to Susan:

> Having a sodding lovely day at work.
>
> On the plus side: held baby crows.
>
> Minus: got attacked by their parents, pooped on, found a stinky skeleton, then some poor girl got stabbed.

SEND.

Hmm... Maybe that came off a *bit* whingey.

To soften the blow, she added a second one:

> Can we have something nice for tea? In need of a boost. And booze. And chips.
>
> Or how about Chinese? Or

Her phone *ding-buzz*ed in her hands before she could finish.

Incoming message.

Which earned a smile. Good old Susan – no doubt replying to that first text with words of love, understanding, and support. And maybe a saucy pic of her boobs?

Only it wasn't Susan.

UNKNOWN NUMBER:

> Any luck with those number plates?

Bloody Ex-DS Wee Davey McLeod.

Cheeky bugger. Like she hadn't got more important things to do?

She hissed a few more gouts of fruity steam at the contrails.

Watched some cars go by.

Then an auld wifie with a Dalmatian.

Maybe she should send someone over to Morrisons for some tasty baked treats? A custard slice would go down a—

'Guv?'

Ah well, suppose it was too good to last.

Roberta had one last puff of black cherry. Then turned.

Only it wasn't Tufty this time. Instead, a partially collapsed shed of a man squinted back at her – broad of shoulder and square of head, with an expression that implied he was in a permanent state of constipated puzzlement. A PC's uniform, and a beak big enough to qualify him as an honorary crow. He *almost* came to attention. 'Guv? That's everyone booked in and processed.'

'You get them all in the cells?'

'Nah. The *polo-shirt* tossers are banged up, but half the kids are in the canteen getting glowered at by Shaky.'

The name sounded familiar, but no idea why. That was police nicknames for you, every bugger had one.

'Meh…' She stretched her neck from side to side, making it *crickle-crack*. 'Wanted to do the kids first anyway. Pick one and stick it in an interview room.'

'Yeah. Can't *really* do that till they've seen a solicitor, Guv. You know: procedure and all that.' Throwing in a wee shrug and a pained smile.

'Oh for…' She put her vape away. 'Fine, we'll do it your way.' Then stomped off towards the main doors.

The station canteen looked like every police canteen in the country, with only a couple of framed pictures of Bennachie and some hairy-coo paintings to let you know that *this* little slice of soulless misery lay in Aberdeenshire. Grey terrazzo floor, Formica tables, blue plastic chairs. A machine for crisps and other 'healthy' snacks, and another for cold fizzy drinks – most of which seemed to contain enough caffeine to make a colony of sloths vibrate for a month.

Throw in some uninspiring tea-and-coffee-making facilities, and a full-sized fridge covered in posters – 'Don't Steal Food From Other Officers!' and 'THIEVES Belong In The CELLS ~ *NOT* The CANTEEN!!!' and the picture was complete.

Four of Emma Dornoch's campaign youngsters sat at individual tables, each in a different corner of the room. Presumably to stop them coordinating their stories.

A couple of T-Shirts held ice packs to sore jaws and bruised knuckles, the other pair had piles of canteen napkins on their tables, dabbing away at bloody noses.

They were watched over by a lanky PC with an unfeasibly large head. That would be PC Stratford, from the lay-by earlier. Standing there, arms folded, glaring at everyone. Only ever seen him in the distance, through the fog, but up close he boasted a flattened nub of a nose, and a mean slit of a mouth.

Bet he was fun at parties…

He nodded at the PC who'd fetched Roberta in from the car park. 'Disco.'

Disco nodded back. 'Shaky.'

Roberta marched into the middle of the room and clapped her hands twice. Demanding attention. 'Listen up: you want out of here? You talk to me.' Making eye contact with every last one of the buggers. 'You want to spend the rest of today stuck here, in a manky police canteen, waiting for a spare cell? *Don't* cooperate.'

The T-Shirts glanced at each other. Fidgeted in their seats. Looking shifty. No doubt waiting to see who cracked first.

Then one in the far corner put her hand up – a somewhat dowdy, mid-twenties, teacher's-assistant type. The kind of young woman who was probably 'at home in a cardigan', wink, wink. With a saltire badge on her T-shirt, and a haircut that *had* to be a cry for help.

She didn't say anything, though. Just sat there.

'You volunteering?'

Her chin came up. 'We have the right to talk to a lawyer first.'

Roberta tilted her head on one side. Giving her a good lonnnnnnnnng look. 'You *got* a lawyer?'

'But...' The hand sank. 'I mean, don't you have to provide one?'

Roberta clicked her fingers and Shaky stepped forward:

'Cos of all the illness, and the riots, there's only *one* duty solicitor for the whole northeast. Probably won't be here for hours and hours.' A grim smile. 'Maybe not till tomorrow morning.'

'*Or* you can talk to me.' Roberta turned and marched from the room. 'Take your pick.'

4

Interview One was a wee magnolia room with grey carpet tiles and a half-knackered table – its Formica top covered in scratched graffiti. Most of which was the kind of language that would cost you a fortune in the swear jar. Though whether they'd been carved there by suspects or police officers was anyone's guess. Probably a bit of both.

Cameras were mounted in the upper corners of the room, keeping a beady eye on the four chairs. *Especially* the Naughty Seat, bolted to the floor just in case…

Not that there was anyone here for them to record.

Well, except for Roberta – as she drew the vertical blinds to shut out the scorching day, leaving the fabric slats glowing alien-abduction bright. And the sodding window wouldn't open, so it was already too hot in here.

She sagged into a non-bolted-down seat, with her back to the door; a random file nicked from someone's desk acting as a prop on the table in front of her, as she took her car keys and scratched 'SHITEFLAPS!' into the Formica. Then sent Lund a friendly text:

WHERE THE SNUDGING HELL ARE YOU?!?!

SEND.

Roberta thumped back in her seat with her arms crossed.

What the bugger-wank was taking them so long? Lund and

sodding Barrett should've been here *ages* ago. Lazy pair of twunts. See, that was what's wrong with officers these—

A knock on the door.

Here we go.

She sat up, getting the fake file all lined up and official looking. 'Come!'

The door opened just far enough for Disco to pop his head in. 'Guv.' He slipped through the gap, bringing a mug of coffee with him. Plonked it down on the table for her. 'Two and a coo.'

Yeah…

She gave the mug – 'POLICE OFFICERS DO IT WITH TRUNCHEONS' – a good stare, because some of the junior ranks resented playing Teasmade, and you never knew if your tasty hot beverage came laced with spit and bogies.

Didn't *look* sputumy…

'"Disco", is it?'

He nodded. 'Guv.'

'And do I want to know *why*?'

'Probably best not, Guv.'

Fair enough.

She took a sip. Didn't taste of bogies, either. 'Ever worked a murder before, Disco?'

'Depends on your definition. Do one-punchers at kicking-out time count?'

'No.'

'Oh.' Wrinkles appeared between his eyebrows as he attempted to engage whatever passed for his brain. 'There *was* that farmer out Bennachie way, who skewered a neighbour with the bale spikes on his tractor? Dispute about stirks, a dozen fenceposts, and who was knobbing whose missus. But he was the one who called 999, so not much of an investigation.' Disco hooked a thumb at the door. 'Ready for your first guest?'

'Might as well.'

And off he sodded, shutting the door behind him. Meaning he missed Roberta's phone launching into its jolly ringtone.

The word 'LUND' glowed in the middle of the screen.

Ha: should bloody well think so too.

Roberta jabbed the button. 'Where the sodding *frunch* have you got to? I'm sitting here with a ton of—'

'I'm at the lay-by. You want the good news, the bad news, the worse news, or the really awful news?'

Oh for…

Roberta slumped back. 'Give us the bad news.'

'Barrett, the skiving proink, is now officially *signed off with The Disease. Detective Superintendent Young caught him coughing up a lung in the muster room and sent him home.'*

'Of course he did.' Scrunching her eyes closed and massaging her forehead. 'Worse news?'

'Young also *said he needs a vanful of thugs at Portsoy Harbour: four o'clock this afternoon. Operation Basilisk?'*

'And I care, because…?'

'All the Operational Support Units have the plague, and apparently we "need the practice" after our "monumental cock-up at Charles MacGarioch's place, last week".'

'Well, he can ram it sideways up his hoop. I've already got a murder and an attempted on my dance card the day. I'm no' home to visitors.'

A nasty, ominous wee pause slithered out of the phone. Followed by: *'You want the* awful *news now?'* Deep breath. *'Just caught Sheila Dalrymple creeping out of the SOC tent. They've found a second set of remains in that bin.'*

Nooooooo…

'I hate you, Veronica. Was *one* dead body no' enough?'

'That's not what makes it awful. Second set of bones are tiny and only partially ossified. Which means your victim was pregnant – between ten and thirteen weeks.'

Roberta folded forwards, curling up till her forehead thunked into the stolen file.

Pregnant.

'You still there?'

'No.' It was *really* hard not to add another chunk of cash to the swear jar. But she squeezed it down. 'And the *good* news?'

'There isn't any. I just said that to make you feel better.' A sigh. *'Still, at least now we know* something *about our victim, right?'*

Oh, lucky, *lucky* them.

Roberta thumped her head off the folder a couple of times.

What kind of sick bastard did *that* to a pregnant woman?

'Guv?'

'Grab Harmsworth and a couple of Smurf suits. I want that whole lay-by fingertip searched. And do both sides of the railway line as well.'

'There's only two of us!'

'Better get onto Transport Plod first: all rail services to be cancelled between Inverurie and Insch till you've finished. No point getting the pair of you squashed; staffing problem's bad enough as it is.'

Lund's voice went into a full-on whine. *'But, Guu-uuv…'*

'Sooner you start, sooner you're done.'

Another knock at the door pulled Roberta's forehead from the file. 'Got to go.' She hung up, grimaced. 'Pregnant… Bloody hell.' Then sat upright and gave herself a shake. Pulled on her police face. 'Enter!'

Tufty had ditched his high-vis and stabproof vest, going for a much more casual police-officer-about-town vibe as he shepherded a young man into the room.

Wow.

Talk about *babe* magnet.

The new guy was early-twenties, but had come up with a cunning plan to look older and more mature by growing what could barely be described as a 'moustache'. It was as if he'd brushed his top lip, twice, with mascara and left it at that. His ears pointed in different directions, and his haircut alone was enough to make sure he remained a virgin till his mid-thirties. His general air of unsexiness wasn't helped by the twin wads of bloody toilet paper poking out of his bashed nose. Or the sour yoghurty smell that oozed out of him like baby sick.

Tufty snapped to attention. 'Derek Wickham, ma'am.' All formal and correct.

Derek looked around him, as if he'd never seen a TV crime drama before. Voice all bunged-up and nasal. 'So … if I talk to you, right, I can go?'

Roberta pointed at the Naughty Seat. 'Sit.'

He did. 'Only I've got a paper on Scoddish parliamentary process to hand in for tomorrow.'

She clicked her fingers and pointed at the chair beside her.

Tufty sank into it and fiddled with the AV unit's knobs and buttons, setting it all recording. 'Interview with Derek Albert Wickham, Monday, sixteenth of June.' Checking his watch. 'Eleven twenty-five. Present are Detective Inspector Roberta Steel and DC Stewart Quirrel. Mr Wickham has declined to have a solicitor present. Isn't that right, Mr Wickham?'

Derek nodded.

'You have to say it out loud for the tape.'

'Oh, sorry. Yeah. Suppose. Long as I get to go home afterwards…'

Tufty raised his eyebrows at Roberta, because that wasn't, *strictly speaking*, an unqualified agreement, but close enough.

Roberta glowered across the table at Derek, giving him the full benefit of her police charm. 'You in the habit of rioting, Derek?'

'Rioting?' He shrank back from the table, but his chair was bolted to the floor, so didn't get very far. 'I … thought you wanted to talk about Billie gedding stabbed? I mean, Billie Nesbit. The red-haired girl? Who got stabbed?' Pointing in the vague direction of Kintore.

Roberta jabbed her fake file. '*First* we're going to have a wee chat about your role in the violent affray outside Emma Dornoch's campaign headquarters.' A nasty smile. 'So why don't we start at the beginning...'

The police station's corridors were every bit as inspiring as its canteen. Only without the pictures of local scenery and hairy cattle. Instead, the scuffed walls boasted a crop of not-so-motivational posters, like 'WHAT HAVE YOU DONE TO MAKE SCOTLAND A BETTER PLACE TODAY?', 'DON'T MAKE TIME FOR CRIME!', and 'TERRORISM *ISN'T* COOL!'

Woo-hoo...

Roberta sent a big cloud of black-cherry vape at the picture of some beardy tit in uniform: 'I'M KEEPING THE PEACE WITH A CAREER IN THE POLICE!'

Kinda getting a bit tired of black cherry. And all the other fruity flavours too.

How come no one made nice *savoury* vapes? Like steak-and-kidney, or cheese-and-onion. Bet you'd make a fortune selling smoky-bacon refills. Better yet: chicken-tikka-masala.

The door to Interview One opened and out slipped Tufty, like a sleekit wee jobbie.

There was a flash of Derek Wickham, still sitting at the table, in tears, rocking back and forth as he gurned away. Boo-hoo.

Tufty *clunk*ed the door shut and pulled on a disappointed face. 'Went a bit hard, there, Guv.'

She gave him a dose of fruity steam. 'What kind of person goes to university and studies *politics*?' Pronouncing the word with all the contempt it deserved. 'Wanna know why you go to university?' Counting the reasons off on her fingers: 'Getting laid, drinking too much, sexual experimentation, freedom from your stuffy parents, and banging every hot undergrad you can get your sticky little mittens on.' Another cherry lungful. 'Studying *politics*? See if either of *my* kids does that, I'll disown them.'

'Are we letting Wickham go?'

'Should be studying *art*, or poetry, or Scottish literature. You know: something useful.'

'Not like he saw anything, is it?'

'World would be a better place if just *applying* to study politics was enough to get you carted off. Three years, hard labour, working on a tattie farm in the Outer Hebrides.' Hauling her trousers up. 'That'd teach 'em.'

Tufty shrugged one shoulder. 'And he only fought back cos the ASDG bloke punched him.'

She waved her vape about. 'They want to go from school to university and straight into sodding government, don't pass go, don't get a proper job, don't learn how *real* people live – just hop on the gravy train and lord it over us plebs, with your crappy degree and sharny micro-moustache.'

The wee loon nodded, agreeing with himself. 'I does think we should let him go.'

'This is why we invented the guillotine.' She poked Tufty. 'Where's that BWV?'

'I did downloaded it, but we does not has no stabbing on film.' Shrinking away, hands up. 'Which is *totes* not my faults, before you start biffing people!'

She gave him a glower instead. Seething and vaping. Surrounding herself with clouds of billowing fog, the end of her vape glowing hot red in the mist. Like the eye of Sauron.

'Erm…' Tufty jerked his head back towards the interview room. 'So, Derek Wickham: we're letting him go … right?'

'Our murder victim – Jane Doe, AKA: Body-In-The-Bin – she was pregnant.'

Took a moment for that to sink in, then Tufty sagged. 'Oh … poop.'

Roberta pointed at the interview-room door. 'Turn the boy loose and bring the next bumhole up here. Let's get this over with.'

A bluebottle buzzed its lazy symphony, trapped between the interview room's unopenable window and the vertical blinds, casting a big black shadow as T-Shirt Number Two scowled back at Roberta from the Naughty Seat.

About the same age as the first one, with sideburns on his cheeks and a whole poke of chips on his shoulder. A heavy jaw lent him a belligerent air, an underbite, and a teeny bit of a lisp, while his hair stood up in lopsided clumps on one side – matted with blood, from a couple of *tiny* cuts to his scalp, courtesy of a Polo-Shirt's placard. Or, rather, the chunk of wood it was stapled to. He had the same sour-dairy smell as the last one. Which was either some new foul scent of deodorant, or something to do with getting his face washed in semi-skimmed milk, after the riot.

'Wait…' Roberta blinked at him, cos that couldn't possibly be right. 'No, but seriously … your mum and dad named you "Paddington"? *Paddington* MacInver?'

The scowl darkened. 'I go by "Paddy".'

'Don't blame you. But "*Paddington*"?'

'He proposed to her under the station clock on Platform One, OK? And this was before any of the films came out, so can we *not*, please?' Arms crossed, glaring now.

It was probably meant to be one of those famous Paddington hard stares, but came off more like a dyspeptic Winnie-The-Pooh.

Probably wouldn't help to tell him that, or laugh in his face.

Tempting, though.

Instead, she just sat there, in silence, smiling at him for long enough to make it *really* uncomfortable. Then: 'So … *Paddy*: where were you when Billie Nesbit got stabbed?'

He made a big show of thinking about that. 'Me and Ringpull – that's Declan Tinworth – were over by the bins. I remember, cos there were wasps, and I *hate* wasps. Always following you about.' Curling his lip. 'Nasty, thieving, *stingy* little bastards.'

Probably after his marmalade sandwiches.

'And…?'

'We had this fascist cock-slap sticking his chest out at us, waving his stupid placard.' Frown. 'What was it… Yeah: "Stop immigration, this is our nation". Prick.'

Roberta raised an eyebrow.

'Not *you* – the guy. Looks like a rabid thumb?'

Which could've been any of the Polo-Shirts.

'So then what happened?'

'Pfff… I was staring him down, you know?' Paddington MacInver pulled his shoulders back, making himself look bigger. 'Yeah, I'm putting the fear of a *just* and *fair society* into the wanker, when I hear Billie scream: "He's got a knife!" You know?'

Silence.

Tufty looked up from his pad, pen poised. 'And did you see the knife?'

'… No?'

The wee loon wrote that down.

More silence.

Roberta did her sit-and-stare routine again.

Paddington's shoulders sagged a little, then a lot, as he wriggled in the Naughty Seat, picking at a 'COCKWANK' carved into the tabletop. Until, finally, that big chin of his drooped. 'Sorry.'

She tapped the file – ominous, menacing. 'Tell us about your relationship with Billie Nesbit.'

'Yeah…' He stared at the file. Licked his lips. Wriggled some more. 'Yeah, it was *OK*. I mean, we weren't *in* a relationship, just volunteering on the same campaign. You know, sort of unpaid interns, for the extra credit? We both go to Aberdeen Uni. Other than that… I mean, I never laid *a hand* on her.' His eyes didn't leave the prop file. 'Did someone say something? It's not true!' Fidgeting. Hands leaving sweaty palmprints on the tabletop. A shifty look left and right, then Paddington lowered his voice. 'You should ask Vivian. Vivian and Billie were like…' He made his greasy paws into claws, jabbing them at each other, as if they were fighting. 'You know? *Ask* her. But I was … nope. And yeah, Billie's *really* pretty, but she's only moist for the cause, you know what I mean?'

Tufty curled his lip.

Roberta leaned forwards; voice cold as an icepick to the crotch. 'Oh I know exactly what *you* mean.'

The sexist moron smiled as if that was a good thing. Then it must've sunk in that it *really* wasn't, because he shrank in his seat. No longer quite so keen to be big. He cleared his throat and stared at his sweaty hands. 'Sorry. Erm… Can we start over?'

Nope.

Ethan Rattray had a downy blond beard, round cheeks, and little pink eyes that darted about the place. Curls framed his chubby wee face, making him look a bit like a hamster who did a *lot* of coke. He'd been the one at the protest with the

'SMASH SEXISM' placard – swinging it about, trying to take a Polo-Shirt's head off.

Maybe even the very same Polo-Shirt who'd enrolled Ethan in the Broken-Nose-Boys' club, leaving him dabbing at his crusted nostrils with a succession of napkins that had grown into a grisly little pile on the interview-room table.

He added another one to the collection. 'And then Billie *collapsed*, and I couldn't *believe* it. I mean, she was … *is* always so upbeat, you know? And she's got *all* this experience and knows *all* the lingo, and you can always rely on her to know how things are meant to *work*, cos she was on Lady Fordyce's team at the last Scottish election, which is *so* cool, cos you don't usually get *that* kind of opportunity when you're only *sixteen*, and there we are working – side by side – on a *long* campaign for the next *general* election, years away, when Old Murdoch Irvine pops an aneurism in the *House of Commons* last week and suddenly we're fighting a by-election, and Billie's all, "I know what we need to do!" And *we're*—'

'OK, yes, right, we get it.' Roberta gritted her teeth and tried again. 'Did. You. See. Who. Stabbed. Her?'

A little shrug. 'Well … it all happened so *quick*, and…' Ethan pursed his lips. 'I *think* it might've been the ugly one. Well, they're all *ugly*, aren't they? Hate does that to your soul. But anyway, he had a placard with "No more libtard lefties" on it, if that helps? Cos that's a *tremendously* insulting portmanteau, isn't it? Anyone who's using "retard" as a pejorative in this day and age is, quite frankly, an absolute *fuckspanner*.' Pink flushed Ethan's cheeks. 'Sorry.' He winced at the cameras. 'Can we edit that bit out? I don't want my mum to know I swear.'

In the name of Jesus.

Deep breath.

Do not scream.

Or batter him to death with the fake file.

Roberta hissed the air from her lungs.

And went in for *another* go: 'Did you actually *see* someone stab Billie Nesbit?'

'Erm…' Ethan poked a finger at the tabletop, twisting it from side to side, as if he was trying to screw his digit into the Formica. 'When you say "see", do you mean *see*, see?'

Roberta folded forward and banged her head off the file again. 'Aaaaaaaaaaaargh!'

The interview-room door hung wide open, to let a bit of heat out, as Roberta sipped at a fresh cup of tea. Munching on a biscuit that tasted of dust and disappointment.

Tufty bimbled back into the room. 'Guv?'

Sip, crunch, crunch. 'Well?'

'Went through all the footage again, and…' He held up a printout – grainy and slightly blurred, of an ugly balding middle-aged dick, mouth open in a snarling yell. The placards in his gammony fists: 'NO MORE LIBTARD LEFTIES!' 'MR THE SUSPECT IS ONE TOBY FORBES.'

She sat back and smiled. 'And just like that, renowned policing genius *Roberta Steel* solves the case.'

'Only Toby Forbes is about twenty feets away from Billie Nesbit when she screams "knife!", there's three people between them, and he has his back to her. So, unless he am some sort of knife-throwing-magician-ninja person…?'

'It wasn't him.'

Sod.

That's what she got for listening to bloody students…

3

Roberta poked the fake file, in an I-know-something-that-you-don't kind of way. 'And you didn't see anything *at all*?'

Vivian Staybridge glowered back. Even with a monster scowl on, she was a perky wee treat to sit opposite. About as short as Tufty, but a damn sight prettier. Long dark hair and a small button nose, cheeks still holding on to a glow of puppy fat, and perfect plucked eyebrows. Throw in the slender waist and pneumatic under-shirt bits, and she was the kind of young woman who headed off into the woods with her boyfriend at the start of a horror movie, only to be turned into kebabs mid-bonk by some mask-wearing psycho with a thing for boilersuits.

A scrape marred her forehead, already beginning to scab over, and both sets of knuckles were cracked and swollen. Unlike the three milky pricks they'd interviewed so far, she'd come from the cells not the canteen, and didn't smell of rancid Fruit Corner.

And Tufty eyed her like she was an unexploded velociraptor.

'You want to know what I saw?' Vivian narrowed her lovely dark eyes. 'I saw *fascists* trying to destroy the democratic process. I mean, are you surprised those misogynistic shites knifed a young woman?' Her nostrils flared as she pointed at the wee loon. '*Men!*'

Roberta nodded. 'Aye, they're a constant source of delight. How come—'

'*And* he touched my breasts!'

Eh?

'The guy who stabbed Billie?'

'No: *him*.' Pointing at Tufty again. 'Copping a feel when we were on the ground. Pervert!'

His cheeks went pink as a spanked bum. 'No, no, no, no, no! I didn't touch *anybody's*...' Doing his kicked-puppy look. 'I was fighting for my *life*.' Poking a retaliatory finger in Vivian's direction. 'She bites!'

And, to prove the point, her teeth flashed – snapping at Tufty's finger, making him jerk it out of range with an unmanly 'Eeeeek!'

Yeah... There was no way in hell the wee loon was groping anyone's breasts, backside, or anything else. He'd die of embarrassment before he'd even got the first squeeze in.

Mind you, as boobs go, Vivian's weren't half—

'And don't think I haven't noticed *you* staring at them too.'

Roberta prodded the file again. '*If* we can return to the riot? You assaulted a man while he was being handcuffed; do you no' think—'

'Here: I'll save you the bother.' Vivian grabbed the hem of her 'EMMA DORNOCH ~ BETTER FOR SCOTLAND!' T-shirt and whipped it up – revealing a lacy black bra. Then whipped that up too, revealing its perky contents for them all to see. Glaring over the top of her bunched clothing at Tufty, then Roberta. 'Have a good look, you *perverts*!'

The wee loon covered his eyes. 'Eeeek...'

Idiot.

Roberta, on the other hand, sat there in silence. Taking it in for a good, *lonnnnnnnnnnnng* moment. Because ... well, you know... Then sighed. 'Aye, very good. Now, put them away before the boy here blushes himself to death.' A smile. 'He's no' used to topless women who don't have staples in their bellybuttons.'

Vivian lowered her T-shirt, a frown pulling at her scabbed forehead. Tufty had the same puzzled expression.

Children.

There was a time when the newsagent's top shelf – and funky-smelling bushes in the woods – were the only place to get X-rated material. What was the point of ogling a centrefold when you could download hardcore porn in 4K on your smartphone?

'Never mind.' Time to get back to the case again. 'A wee birdie tells us you and Billie had a falling out.'

A snort from that cute button nose. 'You have to have a falling *in* to have a falling out. She's just jealous, because I've got—'

A knock on the door. Quickly followed by another couple. Urgent. Hurried.

Why could no bugger leave Roberta alone to do her job?

'WHAT?'

Disco poked his head into the room, out of puff, with his face all flushed and sweaty. 'Sorry, ... Guv, ... but there's a ... thing you might ... might want to...' Jerking his head at the corridor outside. 'For a minute? ... Please?' Hopping from foot to foot.

So whatever it was, it was probably horrible.

Don't swear.

Deep breath, growling it out. '*Fine*.' Roberta checked her watch. 'Interview suspended at twelve fifty-three.' She stood and poked Tufty in the chest. 'No funny business.' Then turned to Vivian. 'And *you*: keep them in your shirt.' She marched after Disco. Paused on the threshold. Looked back at Perky Miss Bites-A-Lot. 'Oh, and if you can wheech your bra up over your boobs: it's no' fitted properly. You need to get that seen to, or they'll end up dangling round your knees.'

Vivian froze, both hands up under her T-shirt, returning her breasts to their receptacle. Then a look of horror crawled across her pretty face as she contemplated the sagging to come.

Good.

Because life was nothing without a well-fitting and comfortable bra. Like Roberta's trusty longtime companion: Old Faithful.

Roberta pinged the shoulder strap through her stretchy black Police-issue top, gave an imperious sniff, and stepped out into the corridor. Shut the door with a heavy *thunk*.

Trapping Tufty inside with Vivian.

Then turned...

Only Disco had already scurried halfway down the corridor, looking furtive as he opened one of the office doors and made 'follow me!' gestures.

Which was more than a bit suspicious, given he was breathing like a pervert in a sausage factory.

Well, if he thought he was in for some MeToo action he had another think approaching his knackers at warp factor boot.

She followed the wee prick into an incident room at the front of the building, overlooking the Morrisons opposite. Its car park and petrol station, baking in the noon sun.

Vacant desks lined two sides, separated by elbow-height blue cubicle walls, all of which looked ready for the skip. A rash of Blu Tack acne infested the ceiling tiles in one corner, but other than that it looked virtually abandoned. The fact that every single office chair in here was on the verge of collapse didn't help. Some were missing arms, or their back, others sat lopsided on absent castors – as if this was the place sickly seating came to die. Doubt the carpet tiles would survive another winter.

Whiteboards dominated the wall by the door, but someone had been at them with a permanent marker and hadn't managed to clean it off properly, leaving the ghosts of previous investigations behind.

And all of it coated in a furry layer of dust.

Disco limped into the middle of the room and crumpled, clutching his knee with one hand – arm locked to keep himself upright – while he wiped his sweaty face with the other. Puffing and panting.

Roberta readied her kicking boot. 'This better be good.'

'Oh, it's not ... not good ... *at all.*' He staggered over to the window, scanning the ground outside. Then must've found what he was looking for, because he pointed, backing away from the glass – as if trying not to be seen from below.

OK...

She sidled up next to him, standing on her tiptoes to peer out past the surfeit of dead wasps lined up along the window-sill, and into the station's front car park.

Three new vehicles had joined her MX-5: a crusty rust-bucket that used to be a VW Polo in a former life; a shiny red Porsche Boxter, with the top down; and a fancy, electric, dark-grey BMW.

A hunched, balding bloke wandered about in the far corner of the car park, on his phone, smoking. Wearing a cheap-looking pair of suit trousers, a grey shirt – dark with sweat down the back – and a half-mast tie. Top button undone. He'd dyed his hair shoe-polish black and scraped it from one ear to the other, straight across the top, which didn't stop his bald pate gleaming through the strands.

He wasn't alone out there, though: a sharp-dressed middle-aged man loitered by the Porsche. His linen suit contrasted with the open-necked blue shirt, *big* gold watch, and tousled brown hair. Definitely the kind of man who thought he could charm his way out of any trouble, or into anyone's pants.

Roberta dropped down from her tippytoes. 'And? It's a scruffbag and a slick git.' She belted Disco for being a dick. 'I was interrogating a *suspect*!'

'Ow!' Limping out of whacking range. 'The "slick git" ... arrived just ... just before the Beamer. ... Gave me this.' Disco held out a business card.

Difficult to read without her glasses, but Roberta took the thing and had a good squint:

Elgin Woodburn, LLP	
Private Crime Department Lead	Moir-Farquharson Associates
Partner & Solicitor-Advocate	Mortimer House
	Golden Square
	AB10 1RH

The other side contained a list of phone numbers and email addresses.

‘Shite.’ She peeked up on her tiptoes again. ‘What’s *he* doing here?’

Disco pointed at the BMW. ‘Sir Norman and Lady Fordyce … called him in. … He’s representing the interns. … *All* of them.’

‘Double shite.’

‘I ran up here to tell you.’ Disco grabbed his knees again. ‘We’re to stop interviewing anyone … till he’s spoken to them.’ Wheeze. ‘Flipping heck…’ Rattle. ‘There’s worse…’

Of course there sodding was.

Puff, cough, heech. ‘Sir Norman says … he’s called his old mate, the Chief Constable, and—’

Roberta’s phone launched into ‘Take Your Mama’.

Disco cleared his throat. ‘Are you going to…?’

‘No’ sure that’s a good idea.’ But she pulled the thing out anyway and checked the screen: ‘Sexybum Pine’ glowed in the middle of it. ‘Triple shite, with knobs on.’

Her thumb hovered over the red ‘Decline’ button.

Cos things were bad enough without having to explain everything to the head of North East Division.

Why did senior bloody officers think they could ‘supervise’ things?

Still, might as well get it over with.

Roberta hit the green button, pulling on a shiny, upbeat confident voice. '*Chief Superintendent*, how *lovely* to hear from you. Any word on that team I was promised?'

'Don't you play smart with me, Roberta Steel! I've just had my arse chewed by the Chief Constable, and she wanted to know why we've arrested every single volunteer for a perfectly legitimate political campaign!'

'"Chewed your arse"?' A tut. 'You should've said, Boss – ask nicely and I'll nibble your perky round buttocks for free.'

'Their lawyer's threatening to sue us for wrongful arrest, and assault, because you attacked everyone with PAVA spray!'

Roberta made 'go away' gestures at Disco, but the hollow-headed halfwit just stood there, looking confused.

'We are not some sort of fascistic *force of oppression, here to undermine the democratic process! You can't just go around interviewing people without legal representation!'*

The 'go away' gestures turned into 'bugger off' ones. And still Disco stood there. Gormless twunt.

'They *volunteered*, Boss: all above board.' She pressed the phone to her chest and jabbed a finger at the door. 'Go on, sod off out of it.'

Finally, PC Idiot did what he was told.

Back to the phone. 'I've got a young woman with a knife in her guts. You want me to do a proper investigation, or some sort of half-arsed job? Chewed or otherwise.' Wandering over to the window and its wasp collection. 'Besides, they were rioting. Can't have people thinking they can just get away with that, can we. No' after Saturday.'

Silence.

Roberta pinged a couple of yellow-and-black carcasses off the sill.

Down below, the BMW's doors were hanging open and Sir Norman and Lady Fordyce had joined the swanky lawyer tit:

Elgin Woodburn – which was a stupid frudging name – deep in conversation.

Meanwhile, Scruffy McCombover was sidling closer. Flicking the unsmoked nub of his roll-up out into the street, and straightening his tie. Clearly wigging in on their conversation.

A lonnnng sigh came from Pine's end. *'I'm just asking you to proceed with some* tact, *Acting Detective Inspector.'* As if Roberta weren't the soul of sodding diplomacy and consideration. *'What about the protesters: the Anglo-Saxon Defence Group?'*

'None of the frunkers are talking. They've all got the same bit memorised: "I exercise my right not to answer any questions until I have spoken to my solicitor."'

'And when will that be?'

'Exactly.' Another couple of wasps got pinged. 'You hear about our Body-In-The-Bin? Pregnant. Only ten, twelve weeks, but still…'

A groan. *'Because what this whole thing needed was more complications.'*

'Oh, we're blessed the day, all right.' Roberta looked around at the broken chairs and haunted whiteboards. 'I'm commandeering an incident room at Inverurie station, cos it's closest. Going to need some decent IT and a HOLMES instance, staff to man the phones, and a squad of officers knocking on doors.'

And yes, no idea whose doors they'd be knocking on yet, but every investigation always needed a bunch of poor buggers to schlep from door-to-door, asking stupid people stupid questions.

'Don't want much, do you.'

The well-to-do crowd must've noticed Scruffy McCombover hovering, because they all turned to stare at him.

He pulled on a fake smile and hurried over to shake everyone's hand.

'Better let us have a few hours with the Media Liaison Officer too. We'll need some press releases; appeals for witnesses; regular updates; blah, blah, blah... That kinda thing.'

'I'll see what I can do. Just ... get a result on this one, OK?'

'Do my best, Boss.' Roberta smiled. 'And that offer of a chewy bum still stands, if you...'

But the line was dead.

Pine had hung up.

'Worth a try.'

Out in the car park, McCombover handed each of his new friends a business card. Chatting away like they were old mates.

Roberta narrowed her eyes and leaned forwards, resting her forehead against the warm glass.

Like watching tropical fish in a tank.

No prizes for guessing who'd got the Chief Constable all riled up. Or who'd threatened to sue Police Scotland for spraying a bunch of rioting morons.

Which just left Scruffy McCombover...

'What are you snudges up to?'

Good question.

The station's reception area was a bland little space, with the desk on one side – hidden behind a toughened glass screen – and loads of posters about terrorism and drugs and all manner of fun stuff on the walls. A wilting pot plant. And a row of uncomfortable-looking seats to discourage members of the public.

With no one to man, woman, or person the desk, the room had a sad, dusty air to it. Because clearly it wasn't just the officers and support staff who were off on the sick. *Everyone* had the plague.

Roberta stood by the front door, hands in her pockets, vaping away – ignoring at least three signs telling her not to. Frowning at the wee gathering outside, as Scruffy McCombover shook hands with Lady Fordyce again, then shuffled back towards his rusty rattletrap.

Soon as his back was turned, Her Ladyship wiped her hand on her trouser leg. Brushing off all those common-people germs. Because God forbid these posh—

'Guv?'

'Aaaaargh!' Roberta flinched, spinning around – fist raised – and there was Tufty, blinking at her. 'Don't *do* that!' Thumping him one.

'Ow!'

'Sneaking up on people.'

'I did not do no sneaking!' He backed off, rubbing at his thumped arm. 'Only wanted to know: does you want me to put Mizz Staybridge back in her cell, till she has made talk with her swanky new solicitor? Or is we having another crack?' A wee shudder, then he dropped his voice to a whisper. 'She does gives me the *heebs*.'

Roberta went back to frowning out at the car park. 'The word has come down from on high, Tufters: we can't talk to the poor dears without a sleaze-bag present. No' even Little Miss Perky-Bitey-Bits.' Pointing through the door. 'Because of Sir Tosspot there.'

Outside, the MSP and her knight-of-the-realm husband took their leave of Elgin Woodburn, LLP, heading back to the air-conditioned and leather-upholstered comfort of their swanky electric BMW.

Woodburn waved as it hummmmmmmmed out of the car park, before popping the Porsche's boot and lifting out a brief-case. Ready for the slippery underhand business of 'practising' law.

Tufty pulled his shoulders up to his pointy ears. 'If we're

officially twiddling our thumbs, we could go over Operations Owlbear and Firedrake?'

She held up her whacking hand. 'Do you *like* getting bashed?'

'Eeeek!' Retreating even further.

'Why does every skrunk think they can keep adding extra crudge to my caseload? Camper vans and burger turf wars… I'm frying bigger fish here: murders, stabbings!' Having a bit of a seethe to underline the point.

'OK… Well, we could take another swing at the *protesters* if you like? Unless they're off limits too?'

Pine didn't say anything about not interrogating *them*. Not specifically, anyway.

And like the Chief Superintendent's buttocks: it was worth a try.

Roberta turned on her heel and made for the door through to the police-only parts of the station. 'Get Slick Larry set up with somewhere to work through his new clients, then I want that incident room ready to go: murderboard; printer; phones; support staff; blah, blah, blah, etc. Oh, and I want one of those digital deep dives on our stabbing victim.'

The wee loon's bottom lip poked out. 'And what are *you* doing while I'm getting on with all the work?'

Fair question.

Roberta struck a noble pose. 'I, my dear Watson … am off for a poop.'

2

Roberta sat on her throne, queen of all she surveyed – a barren cubicle of Formica-covered chipboard, with some fairly uninspired graffiti: 'Inspector Menzies Smells Of Cheese!', 'I STINK THEREFORE I AM', and for some reason 'I Wanted To Be An Alligator…'

Because police officers were weird.

Not being weird, and having no desire to be *any* sort of semi-aquatic reptile, Roberta poked away at her phone. Playing Hedgehog Hodgepodge, with her trousers and pants around her ankles. Not doing too badly, either. When the sodding thing rang, vibrating in her hands during a tricky bit. Making her squeal and flinch and drop the phone. Scrabbling to catch the handset before it disappeared to a horrible, unflushed, watery grave.

'Snudging heck…' She took a deep breath before answering. 'Are you *insane*? What kinda time is *this* to call someone?'

A man's voice. *'Hi, it's me again. Davey McLeod? I was just wondering—'*

'Oh for…' Scowling at the cubicle walls. 'I'm in a *very* important meeting, here!'

'Only, I'm on a bit of a deadline and it would really, really *help me if you could just run those plates and I can get out of your hair?'*

She ripped off a streamer of toilet paper, because Davey had officially ruined her special alone time. 'Were you always this big a pain in the hoop?'

A wee whine of desperation entered his voice. *'Look, could we at least* talk *about it? You know, face to face?'*

'We're talking now! And I've—'

'I'm just outside. I'm waving; can you see me?'

Oh no...

Roberta blinked at the graffiti, then leaned sideways, far enough to peer beneath the cubicle door and out into the ladies' loo.

No sign of any legs or shoes. Thank Christ.

She straightened up again. 'Outside *where*?'

'Inverurie station. Look: I bought doughnuts. Custard ones. Your favourite, right?'

Eh?

'How did you know I was—'

'Saw you'd got the body-in-the-bin case. Thought you'd probably set up an incident room at the nearest station: run the Op out of there.' A wee, smug, aren't-I-clever pause. *'Used to be a detective sergeant, remember? Before I retired.'*

Urgh...

So he did. And a right menace when he got his teeth into something too – it was all flooding back.

What to do about it, though? Wasn't as if doing 'little favours' for civilians ever went well. If you got caught, Professional Standards were the *least* of your worries: gross misconduct, dismissal, prosecution, fines, maybe even jail time...

Course the question was: *why* did ex-DS Davey McLeod want to know? The people these number plates belonged to, what had they done? And what would she find if she did the search then went poking about?

Hmmm...

Knowledge was power, after all. And if she *did* find

something, there was no reason to share it with Davey. Take the credit, do a victory lap, then head off into the retirement-flavoured sunset.

She kept the evil smile from her voice. 'If I help you, will you sod off and leave me alone?'

'Cross my heart and hope to die,
Stick a truncheon in my eye.'

'OK.'

'That's great*! Thanks, Robbie! I appreciate it, it's really—'*

She hung up.

Grinned.

Then finished her meeting.

The incident room had improved *slightly* since she'd been away. A few of the more disreputable office chairs had gone – swapped out for ones that didn't look like drunken toadstools – and a scarred duplex laser printer now sat in the corner. A proper monster. About the size of a photocopier.

Tufty was foostering about with it, lying on the floor, plugging yellow cables into floor ports.

He'd also managed to scare up a cardboard box full of old desk phones, in various shades of smoker's-teeth beige.

But no support staff, no extra officers.

Just him.

'Hoy!' Roberta kicked his foot. 'Where's the sodding team I was promised?'

Which is when the door opened.

But it wasn't a phalanx of constables who marched in, ready to obey her every whim, it was Disco. And he didn't march, he ambled – carrying a small box, about the size of a hardback book. 'Hi, Guv.' He held it up for Tufty to see. 'Sorry, these are all I could get.' Then tipped the contents out onto the nearest desk.

A handful of manky whiteboard markers and a dry eraser clattered onto the dusty desktop.

Be still her beating heart.

Roberta curled her top lip. 'Is this *it*?'

Disco shrugged. 'Blame the plague. We're skeleton-staffed, same as everyone else.' Perching his bum on the bepenned desk. 'Good job all the scroats and stots and fiddlers are laid up with it too, or we'd be buggered.' Looking around the incident room. 'So…?'

Tufty emerged from his labours, dusting off his hands as he wandered over to the Big Desk in the corner – a double-sized cubicle with a fancy executive chair that had *definitely* been stolen from a DCI or superintendent's office. A couple of manilla folders sat on the desk, next to an antique laptop.

The wee loon pointed at the left file. 'Operation Troglodyte. PNC searches on everyone we arrested in Kintore, plus all the major players.' Then the right one. 'Operation Demogorgon. Got you every missing person reported in the last six months. And I went a-hunting while you were … indisposed.' Pulling out his phone and poking at the screen, before holding it up so she could see.

Aye, but he wasn't running the show. *She* was.

Roberta snatched one of Disco's pens, produced her own mobile, and squinted at Davey's text. Printed those three number plates on the whiteboard by the door in squeaky red letters. Then snapped her fingers at Disco. 'PNC check. And see what you can dig up on any registered drivers too.'

'Wow…' He gazed at the three lines. 'We've got leads

already? Cool.' Then he scurried off to a vacant, dusty desk to do what he was told.

About time someone did.

Tufty shuffled closer. 'Did you find a witness? Did someone come forward with info? Ooh ... or was it *dashcam footage* of suspicious vehicles at the scene of the crime?'

'None of your business.'

'Oh.' Drooping a little, before remembering the phone in his hand. 'Anyway, *speaking* of footage: we does has *stuff*.'

He set a video playing and held his mobile out again.

A lumpy young woman appeared, who'd applied so many 'beauty' filters when she'd filmed it that she looked shrink-wrapped. It was a head-and-shoulders shot, eyes wide and mouth open in a shocked 'O'. Like a bullet hole. *'Ohmygod, ohmygod, ohmygod; you won't* believe *what happened on my way into work this morning!'*

Her image shrank down into one corner of the screen, still cropped so the top of her head was missing and most of her shoulders too. There was clearly some sort of half-arsed in-camera green-screen wank going on, because the background was a streaky fuzz of out-of-focus grey that kept cutting in and out around her hair.

Then the fuzzy grey swayed as a faint blue-and-white glow rippled on the right-hand side.

A clunk and what might've been the bevelled edge of a train window appeared in the bottom left, then darker streaks wheeched past like a huge barcode, and those blue-and-whites turned into the flickering glare of a patrol car's lights – filtered through heavy fog.

And then the lay-by swept into view.

Must've been before Roberta and her convoy turned up, because there was no sign of the Scenes Transit, or the police van, or her MX-5, but the video zoomed right in on the wheelie bin. Tipped over. Its contents sprawled across the tarmac: long bones and ribs and that toothless skull…

And then the train was past, and grey descended once more.

The picture swung around, showing more of the carriage and the back of a dozen people's heads as they strained to get more footage of the crime scene.

Then the background froze and Little Miss Lumpy raised a pair of eyebrows that she must've drawn on with a toilet brush. *'I know, right? That was* completely *a dead guy! Just lying right there, where anyone could see it! It's totally disgusting!'*

Behind her, the footage looped back to the start.

'Swear to God, it's like something off a horror movie. Utterly *traumatising! I mean, so, how could the police just* leave *it like that, utterly uncovered and bones and that? Are they* trying *to damage us? On, you know, purpose?'*

This time, when the video got to the lay-by, it froze. Then the picture went in for an extreme close-up on the remains. Pixelly and blurred, but clearly a human skull – lying there in the sludge of its decomposed owner.

Miss Lumpy shuddered. *'It's just* horrible. *I might need therapy to get over the shock; for my mental health? No one should* ever *have to see stuff like that…'*

As the remains loomed behind her.

Tufty peered over the top of the screen and swiped up.

There was no Little Miss Lumpy this time. The fogginess outside was the same, but a quick pan around the carriage showed a load of commuters on their feet with their phones out filming. Eager little faces waiting for the horror show. Which meant this had to be a later train.

Just to make things extra annoying, the footage came with a pounding drum-and-bass beat.

The patrol car's lights shimmered in the fog, the trees

strobed past – going left-to-right this time, so a northbound train – and then Roberta and Tufty appeared. The wee loon had his head down, hiding his face, but she was on full view: arms and legs spread wide, trying to hide as much of the remains as possible.

And as if all that wasn't bad enough, a man's voice broke through the terrible music, rapping, machine-gun fast:

> *'Sittin' on a* train, *feeling ma* pain,
> *Can't* explain *all the ways that this life is* insane,
> *And then Death's standin'* there, *in the fog and his* stare,
> *Says that life doesn't* care, *for the—'*

Thankfully, Tufty swiped again and the awful racket stopped. 'You get the drift.'

Another grey screen with a ripple of trees through the fog—

Roberta snatched the phone out of his daft wee hands. 'All right, Steven Spielberg, that's enough for one day.'

A pout. 'But it's—'

'We *know*: fog, remains, police, the train. No' like it's helping, is it.' She tossed the mobile back to him. 'And where's my murderboard?'

'Well, we didn't have no pens, and then Disco went and got pens and now we has pens, but does not has much to put *on* a murderboard with our new pens, cos we has just started the investigation and does not know much about the case or the victim or *anything*.'

'No excuses.' She picked up the Firedrake folder. Pointed it at Disco. 'You: get those number plates searched. And I expect a *proper* murderboard done by the time I get back!' Then grabbed Tufty by the ear. 'You: with me.' Marching for the door, dragging him along.

'Ow, ow, ow! Let go! Let go!'

And yes, it wasn't dignified, but sometimes you had to make your own entertainment.

Grace, the Police Custody and Security Officer, led the way across Inverurie station's custody suite. Which consisted of a wide magnolia hallway with rooms leading off. The offices and cupboards were hidden behind faux-beech panelled doors, but others were heavy blue metal things with wee porthole windows, while two were proper bars-and-big-steel-locks affairs – leading through to the twin cellblocks. One for the ladies, one for the gentlemen.

Steel slapped the Operation Firedrake folder against Tufty's chest, leaving him to carry it while she wandered over to one of the portholed blue doors. Standing on her tiptoes to peer inside, because whoever designed this place did so with freaky tall-arsed weirdos in mind.

Inside, the wee room featured painted breeze blocks, with a barred and frosted window. It did contain a plain table and matching uncomfortable chairs, but they were all bolted to the floor.

In the custody suite, *every* chair was a Naughty Seat.

That slick dick, Elgin Woodburn, LLP, was in there, sitting opposite the perky wee ball of simmering rage known as Vivian Staybridge. No doubt being schooled in the art of 'No comment.'

Wonder if she'd shown him her boobs yet…

Out here though, a *rattle* and *clank* preceded a *clang*.

Roberta abandoned her peeping and there was Grace, holding one of the barred doors open. She was one of those middle-aged ex-cop types. The kind who couldn't really hack retirement, so went to work as a PCSO, cos it was *like* being a police officer only with a lot less running about.

Which was tempting.

What with retirement looming and all that.

But you still had to spend your days dealing with drunken scroats, perverts, and scumbags. So maybe not.

Grace had a marked limp to the left, with a severe haircut and rectangular glasses. Chunky, in a I-can-lift-heavy-things-and-throw-people-through-plate-glass-windows kind of way. She wafted a hand at Tufty. 'After you.'

He gave her a wee bow. 'No, please: after *you*.'

'I have to lock it behind us, you numptie.'

Took a moment for that to sink in. 'Oh! Right. Right.' And through he scurried.

Roberta sauntered over. 'Lost none of your charm, I see, Grace.'

'*You* can talk.'

Soon as they were all inside, Grace locked the gate with a *clanggggg* that echoed away into silence.

Which was weird.

Normally, any cellblock would contain at least one blootered idiot, singing or swearing or screaming about snakes, but here? Nothing. Even though nearly every cell was occupied.

Ten heavy blue doors lined a double-wide corridor, each one with a little whiteboard built into the sliding hatch – for notes and warnings. Five of them had 'POLO-SHIRT' scrawled on them, three had 'T-SHIRT', and one down the end was marked 'RED TROUSERS'.

That's the cell Grace stopped outside, jingling her keys. 'And you're categorically *not* questioning the suspect?'

'Heaven *forfend*.' Roberta fluttered her eyelashes. 'We're just here to check he's no' desperate to talk to *us*. On account of being all lonely.'

Tufty grinned. 'Etcetera.'

'No.' Grace poked him with an iron finger. 'There will be no *"etcetera"*, no "and so on", *or* "and so forth", or I will clatter down on you from a great sodding height.' Another poke. 'Are we *clear*, Constable?' Because once a sergeant, always a sergeant.

'Eeek...' Nodding.

'Good.' She pressed the grey button on the hatch – *click* – then lowered it, moving the transparent section downwards until it lined up with the gap in the door, showing off the cell's interior. Exposing a printed notice saying '↑ HATCH UNSAFE, CLOSE FULLY ↑' and 'WARNING'. As if the chinless tit inside was Hannibal Lecter.

Instead, the loudhailer's owner sat on the thin, blue, plastic-covered mattress, like a sulky teenager. Grace had confiscated his Barbour jacket, tie, belt, and shoes. She'd also wheeched his flat cap, revealing that big shiny bald patch. It *gleamed* in the overhead light.

He glared at the open hatch, then levered himself to his feet. Adopting a parade-rest stance, even though – according to Tufty's file – he'd never served a day in his life.

Roberta gave the nod, and Grace unlocked the cell door. Pushed it open.

'Ta.' Roberta stepped forwards, leaning on the doorframe. 'Well, well, well; if it's no' Lewis Kelman.'

He snapped to attention, heels clicking together – as much as they could in just socks – shoulders back, chin up.

'Aye, Louie, if you're about to crack off one of them "Roman salutes" gotta warn you:' jerking her head at Tufty, 'my sidekick here is militant Antifa, and I *might* no' be able to restrain him from rushing in there and booting your knackers into orbit.'

Took a while, because clearly Tufty hadn't plugged his brain in this morning, but the wee loon finally twigged. 'Oh. Yeah: *down with fascism!*' Striking a gangsta pose which, let's be honest, wasn't exactly all that threatening, but Kelman clasped both hands in front of his groin and shuffled backwards anyway – out of knacker-booting range.

'You can't assault me in custody – I have witnesses!'

Roberta tutted. 'You've got the sharny end of the stick there, Louie. No one's *assaulting* you, because I stepped in with a friendly warning on your behalf. Mind?'

He let go of his bits and stood up straight again. 'I am a political prisoner.'

'And I'm Keira Knightley's arse double.' Pointing at the frog-faced prick. '*You* assaulted a police officer in the lawful execution of her duties, Louie. No' to mention all the incitement to commit violence against your political rival.' Roberta shook her head. 'A wee girl got *stabbed*. See if she dies: you're up on "joint enterprise" charges, cos you don't have to be holding the knife to still go down for eight to life.' Wink. 'Wee bit of poetry there to lighten your day.'

That saggy not-quite chin raised a little more. 'I exercise my right not to answer any questions until I have spoken to my solicitor.'

'This is no' an *interrogation*, Louie, it's a friendly chat. Mind how I saved your bollocks, just now?' All innocent and disarming. 'Wanted to give you a chance to put your side of the story.' She snapped her fingers. '*File*.'

'Eh?' Tufty blinked at her, then the manilla folder in his hands. 'Oh, yes. File. Erm…' Rummaging through the paperwork. 'Here we go: "Lewis Jeffery Kelman, fifty-three, two-years-suspended for racially aggravated assault, ninety hours community service for embezzling funds."'

Kelman sniffed. '*Youthful* indiscretions.'

'It was four years ago.' Tufty went back to the file. 'Three points on your licence for speeding, another three for running a red light, and three for careless and inconsiderate driving.'

'Oh dear, Louie.' Roberta gave him a sad look. 'One more motoring offence and you win a *prize*.'

'Currently living in Flat Seven, Mochie House, George Street, Aberdeen. First Warden of the Anglo-Saxon Defence Group, Aberdeenshire branch. Favourite book: *Wind in the Willows*.'

'Eh?' Kelman frowned. 'Isn't that for kids?'

Tufty took a moment to look him up and down, no doubt taking in the Toad-Of-Toad-Hall outfit. 'My mistake.'

'We were merely exercising our legally protected right to protest a political campaign that plans to ruin our country by *flooding* it with illegal immigrants.'

'Aye, and a wee girl got stabbed.'

Kelman scowled at her. 'You want Scotland to become an Island of Strangers? Cos that's where we're headed. Bit by bit they're *replacing* us, taking our jobs, taking our benefits, molesting our kids, raping, stealing, abusing the system! That what you want?'

'A. Wee. Girl. Got. *Stabbed*.'

He waved it away. 'There are casualties in every war. I'm fighting for the survival of our sodding *species* here.'

'Actually,' Tufty raised a hand, 'Anglo-Saxons aren't a species, they're just an inhomogeneous and arbitrary grouping based on a shared geographical—'

'Our *race*, then.'

'Yes, but "race" is a social construct that has no scientific meaning, because—'

'Thank you, Constable.' Roberta gave him a light thump. 'Can we get back to the stabbing? Mr Kelman here knows which one of his little friends did it, don't you, Louie. Could make things *so* much easier on yourself if you told us who.'

The scowl deepened.

And so did the stony silence.

She had another go: 'We'll find out soon as we run fingerprints and DNA anyway. Might as well do yourself a favour…?'

For a moment, it looked as if he was actually considering it, then he pulled his shoulders back and clicked his stockinged heels again. 'I exercise my right not to answer any questions until I have spoken to my solicitor.'

Grace shifted in her comfortable shoes.

Tufty stood there, pointy features arranged into a vacant expression that went with his hollow wee head.

Kelman glared.

OK.

Roberta faked a worried face. 'And when might one of these mysterious solicitors turn up, Louie? Would've thought your sugar daddy, Graeme Anderson, would be back from his US jolly by now. All *greasy* from pressing the tangerine flesh.' A grin, as she hunched down, arms out, knees bent. 'Or do you far-right grifters prefer to strip off and *wrassle*?'

'I *exercise* my right *not to answer* any questions until I have spoken to my *sol-i-ci-tor*.'

She dropped the wrestling pose and stood. Hands in her pockets. Giving Toad-Of-Turd-Hall one last look. Curled her lip. Then turned on her heel and slouched off. 'Lock him up.'

1

No sooner had Grace thumped the cell door shut again, than Kelman's voice launched into a wobbly baritone, getting louder with every line:

'Our nation pure, our nation fair,
Our nation—'

Tufty joined in, loud as a foghorn: 'In its underwear!'

Which wasn't professional in the least bit.

Couldn't help but smile, though. What with Kelman being a racist twat.

Roberta stopped and gave the wee loon a token thump. 'Naughty. Bad Tufty. Back in your box.'

He grinned at her, throwing in two thumbs up.

Having been knocked off his stride, it took Kelman a couple of breaths to try again:

'Our nation pure, our nation fair,
Our nation brave and bold and true,
Our people joined in holy prayer,
Our proud flag flies: red, white, and blue!'

Urgh…

Preferred Tufty's version, to be honest.

Roberta took hold of the barred gate back through to the custody suite, giving it a rattle as one of the other Polo-Shits sang along:

'Our hearts beat for this hallowed isle,
Our Celtic blood flows staunch and true,'

A T-Shirt banged on their cell door. *'SHUT UP, YOU FASCIST WANKS!'*

Roberta gave the gate another rattle. 'Shop!'

'All right, all right.' Grace unlocked the thing and swung it open.

'Our sacred land none shall defile,
Our proud flag flies: red, white, and blue!'

The police contingent exited the cellblock as a second T-Shirt made their contribution: *'SHOVE YOUR FLAG UP YOUR ARSEHOLE!'*

Which seemed to be the cue for *all* the Polo-Shirts to join in on the chorus, belting it out:

'We'll drench the beaches in their blood,
With sword and shield, beat back the flood,'

'THE ONLY THING YOU BEAT IS YOUR MEAT!'

'Till Scotland's glens and hills are free,'

'WANKERRRRRS! WAAAAAAANKERRRRRRRS!'

'Pick up your blade and FIGHT WITH ME!*'*

Then all the T-Shirts took up the cry, football-chant style: '*WAAAAAAA-NKERRRRS! WAAAAAAA-NKERRRRS!*'

Grace slammed the bars shut again and locked them, staring icy needles at Roberta. 'Did you have to get everyone all riled up? They'll be at it for *hours* now.

'*WAAAAAA-NKERRRRRS! WAAAAAA-NKERRRRRS!*'

Roberta gave her a wink. 'I do what I can.' And escaped, out through the custody suite and into the station stairwell, leaving chaos in her wake. Which was the best place for it.

The stairs were those metal anti-slip ones, with painted breeze-block walls and a stale-sock smell.

'Gu-uv?' Tufty scampered along behind her. 'If I is to be an "militant Antifa" does that mean I gets a special hat? You know, for fighting fascism with. Look upon mine hat, ye shitey and *despair*!' Pausing on the stairs to perform some half-arsed ninja moves. 'Pow! Zap! Kerblooie!'

She blinked at him. Gave herself a shake. Then set off climbing again. 'I am *no'* going to miss working with freaks and sodding weirdos.'

Tufty followed. 'What is we doing now? Does we has An Cunning Plan?'

She stopped again.

The wee loon had a point.

A plan would probably help...

Trouble was: 'We're screwed on the interview front. Can't interrogate any more interns without their sodding solicitor, and there's only *one* sodding solicitor, so that's going to take all sodding day. And our wee racist friends don't even *have* one yet, so furch knows when we'll get round to them.' Chewing on the inside of her cheek and frowning, because none of that actually helped. 'Basically: the whole thing grinds to a halt, till—'

Ding-buzz.

'Hold that thought.' She checked her phone.

UNKNOWN NUMBER:

Much though I hate to nag?!?

Bloody Davey, *again*.

'Oh for … *scrunks'* sake.' Did the man have nothing better to do than haemorrhoid her bumhole?

She rammed her phone back in its pocket and stomped up the stairs, setting them ringing beneath her Doc Martens.

Should've stayed in bed this morning and to hell with the lot of them.

Roberta clattered into the incident room, jaw set, ready to tear someone a new Boris.

And as PC Disco Whatever-The-Hell-His-Real-Name-Was had his arse parked in an office chair, swivelling back and forth like a teenaged girl, while on the phone and doodling in a notebook, this was his chance to get ventilated.

He didn't even look up as she thundered into the room. Still swivelling: 'OK, right. … Uh-huh. … Uh-huh.'

She slammed a hand down on his desk, making him flinch. 'Where's my *twunting* murderboard? And those PNC checks?'

He pointed at the handset held to his ear, mouthing the words 'I'M ON THE PHONE!' in silent pantomime mode.

As if she couldn't scrunking tell.

Then he swung himself around and pointed at the Big Desk instead. Where a brand-new blue folder had joined the laptop and Operation Demogorgon file.

Then Disco whirled back to face front, wiggling his finger at the wall beside the door she'd just stormed in through. 'Yup. … I understand. … Uh-huh.'

Roberta turned to see what the lazy wee shite was pointing at. Whatever it was, it was hidden behind the open door, so she thundered back over there and slammed the thing shut.

Her murderboard seemed to consist of two diagrams of the lay-by, some printed-out photos of the crows' nest where she and Tufty had found the stolen body parts – which must've come from the wee loon's phone – along with a train timetable for the Inverurie-to-Insch stretch of line that had an extra column in the middle for 'ESTIMATED TIME AT DEPOSITION SCENE' for both north-and-southbound trains.

And yes, it was all very *neat and tidy*, but not a massive amount of use.

Pff…

But until they made some progress, it was all they had.

She slouched over to the window, sneaking a peek into the car park below, where that manky old VW Polo still sat, rusting away. Bet that was Davey's car. Couldn't make his face out from up here, but that was definitely an arm, resting on the driver's windowsill as he smoked a fag and munched on a custard doughnut.

The incident-room door swung open and Tufty loitered on the threshold, face all spanked puppy dog as he rubbed at his stupid pointy noise. 'What was *that* for?'

She snapped her fingers at him. 'You, Bumnuggets: PNC check.' Reading out the VW Polo's number plate nice and loud. Making sure that Disco had to poke a finger in his free ear and curl away from her to still hear his phone call.

Tufty copied it down into his notebook. Muttering away to himself. Scowling and pouting. 'Slamming doors in people's faces when they've not done nothing wrong…'

She left him to it, cracked the window open an inch and had a wee vape. Puffing out black cherry as she pinged dead wasps off the sill, into the baking afternoon. Watching Davey lurk outside.

Waiting for her…

Disco took his finger out of his lug again. 'Uh-huh. … I see. … Yeah, OK.' Writing whatever that was down.

Meanwhile, Tufty finished poking at the room's ancient laptop and that massive printer whirred and clicked for a bit, then wheezed out a sheet of A4.

'No, no: I understand. … Uh-huh.' More notes.

Tufty wandered over to the machine, skimming the printout on his way back. 'OK: registered owner is one David McLeod. No priors. *Does* has an weeny collection of parking tickets. Home address: 32 Kingswood Place, Kingswells. Former detective sergeant of this parish. Well, Grampian Police, but that am being *way* before my time, when dinosaurs roamed the Earth and— Ow!'

'*I* was Grampian Police.' Flexing her whacking hand. 'Get into whatever system it is and pull up his record.'

Tufty rubbed at his arm. 'That was a really *stingy* one!'

'You want another?'

'And I can't just "get into" other officers' records. Wouldn't be right. Need to go through proper channels, and Professional Standards, and the like.'

'Sod that.'

Last thing they needed was the Rubber Heelers poking their beaks in.

'Yeah, OK. … Thanks. … Bye.' Disco hung up and scribbled some more in his notebook. Then waved at them. 'That was the hospital, Guv. Our stabbing victim's been in surgery for two and a half hours.' Frowning at what he'd written. 'Knife went in and up, so the blade's gone through her small *and* large intestine, then into the liver.' A wince. 'Apparently, it's all a bit of a mess in there. Every time they gave her a blood transfusion it just came squirting out again. Think they've got the worst of it now, but there's still a heap to do.' Waving a hand at his notes. 'Not to mention all these potential medical complications I can't even *pronounce*.'

Bugger.

Poor Billie Nesbit.

'She going to live?'

Disco just scrunched up his face and shrugged.

'I *hate* today.' Roberta went back to scowling down on Davey and his crappy car.

Bugger must've been psychic, because her phone went *ding-buzz* and there he was, sneaking into her messages again.

UNKNOWN NUMBER:

Hello? Is everything OK? I'm still outside if it helps?

No, it sodding didn't.

OK. Time for that cunning plan.

She pointed at Tufty. 'You, Nerdarama: grab a patrol car: we're going out.'

'Don't we have to be here for when the solicitor—'

'Don't be a prune.' Grabbing the blue folder Disco had left on her desk. 'Slick Larry has to consult with his client; then he has to sit in on the interview, so he can stop her saying anything useful; then he has to debrief her afterwards, before moving on to the next one. Rinse and repeat.' Opening the folder revealed a trio of printouts: PNC checks on those number plates. 'And while Sleazy McLawyer-Pants is consulting and debriefing, *we're* bobbing around like spare jobbies in the hot tub. Instead, we head out and get some actual police work done while he's faffing about with his interns.'

The wee loon's mouth made an uncomfortable sine wave. '*Suppose* so…'

'Patrol car. Now!'

He backed off a pace, probably worried the Whacking Hand would make a return visit to Stingy Town. 'Yeah, but why a patrol car? Don't you want to take the wee …' miming driving her MX-5, '…vroom-vroom, beep-beep?'

Because it was still sitting out there, parked not far from Davey's rustmobile.

Sigh.

But sometimes you had to make sacrifices for a distraction to work.

The benefits of commandeering a patrol car were twofold – one: members of the public didn't like to look too closely at them, cos *looking* at them might make you appear suspicious, which might make the police officers *driving* said patrol car interested in arresting you. And two: unlike pool cars, they weren't mobile skips, full of empty crisp packets, coffee cups, sandwich wrappers, crumpled pie-shop bags, and that funky bin-bag smell.

Roberta and Tufty had the windows rolled down, to release the sticky heat, as the wee loon drove them through the reinforced gates that separated the private rear car park from the public one out front. Humming away to himself.

Teeny beads of sweat were already glistening on his forehead, because the idiot was wearing his stabproof and high-vis again. Should've ditched them on the back seat, along with his utility belt, like Roberta. But maybe he *enjoyed* having a pair of handcuffs digging into his kidneys?

Being much wiser, Roberta scootched down in the passenger seat, hiding her face with her peaked cap – peering through a wee gap between it and the car door.

There he was: Davey, loitering beside his rustbucket again, phone in one hand, frowning up at the station.

Good.

You keep looking that way.

Stay nice and distracted while they made their escape.

Tufty nodded at the folder in her lap. 'So … is we going to visit the peoples what owns the vehicles what Disco did make PNC checks on?' Stopping where the station entrance met the main road to let a minibus and a couple of mud-spattered four-by-fours rattle past.

'Nope.' Not yet, anyway.

'But we is—'

'They're not *for* us, they're for Davey.'

Maybe. Possibly. Depending on what turned up.

'Eh?' His forehead wrinkled up in a parody of thought. '*Davey?*' Taking a left, following a filthy Ford Ranger. 'Why can't Barrett do his *own* PNCs?' More wrinkles. 'Anyway: thought he was off sick.'

She wriggled down a little further. 'Not *that* Davey, you pustulating twit, the other one.' Pointing ahead. 'Up to the roundabout and left, back into town.'

Captain Slow-On-The-Uptake finally twigged. 'The *ex*-cop?' His eyes widened. 'But… No… That's…'

They drifted past the front car park, so close you could almost reach out and slap Davey on the back of the head as he poked away at his phone, then held it to his ear.

Well, if you had really, *really* long arms.

Might be able to spit on him from here, though.

Tufty stamped on the brakes. 'You can't interrogate the Police National Computer for funzies! What does he need PNC checks for? Is he a stalker? A murderer? Is he doing something illegal with the info?'

'Well, that's what we're trying to—'

Her phone launched into its jaunty disco-pop tune, belting it out. And as all the patrol car's windows were down, the car's interior must've acted as a sort of loudspeaker, because Davey spun around.

And locked eyes with Roberta.

'Bugger.' She scooted down even further, till the seatbelt threatened to choke her. 'Drive. Drive!'

'I'm not being party to anything illegal! I has a bidie-in; I is a pillar of the community; we're talking about getting a goldfish!'

Roberta thumped his leg.

'Ow!'

'Then *drive*, you idiot!' Declining the call.

But Davey was already yanking open the door to his VW Polo McRusty.

Tufty accelerated again. 'Just because *you're* retiring in a couple of weeks, doesn't mean the rest of us don't have careers to—'

'Stop driving like a drunken granny and put your foot down!' Roberta poked the button for lights and music. The siren wailed, the lights flickered.

Tufty switched them off again. 'You can't just— Ow!'

'And there's loads more where *that* came from!'

He put his foot down.

0

Tufty navigated the big roundabout at the bottom of Westhill Drive, slipping into the Kingshill Commercial Park like a high-vis suppository.

A trio of uninspiring office buildings lumped-up on the left side of the road, but it was the big Tesco opposite which seemed to pull a gurgling growl from the wee loon's guts.

He gave Roberta the side-eye as those angry noises faded. 'Where are we going?'

'Straight through the next roundabout. I'll tell you when to stop.'

Clearly not wanting another stingy one, he did what he was told.

More bland offices went by, and some even blander warehouses too. Lots of flat-fronted rectangles. Lots of car parks. Lots and lots of *bleh*. All arranged around a winding labyrinth of dull, dull streets.

Until, finally, a sign appeared up ahead: 'SILVERMOSS BUSINESS CENTRE →'.

If anything, this bit of the industrial estate was the blandest of them all, surrounded by warehouse-style commercial units with big roller doors, lots of chain-link fencing and a twenty speed limit.

Only one business had abandoned the grey-on-grey colour

scheme – a bright-pink food van with 'HUNGRY HELEN'S NOODLE DOODLE!' down the side.

Which set Tufty's stomach howling louder than any patrol car's siren. He slowed to a crawl, pining out through the driver's window at it. 'Can't we just—'

'*No.*' She gave the wee loon a gentle thump. 'Right here.'

He let loose a starving-dog whine, then took the turning into Silvermoss Business Centre. Whimpering away to himself. 'Poor Tufty. Poor, *poor* Tufty…'

It was a new-build cul-de-sac of eight smaller units, one half facing off against the other across a wide area of tarmac – divided up into parking spaces and areas for dumping dirty-big bits of equipment. Like the huge wiggly-pipe things, sitting on pallets outside 'DEMETER VALVE MANAGEMENT SERVICES LTD'.

It also seemed to double as a space for right-wing-nut-bag press conferences, because a podium had been set up outside the unit next door, beneath a sign saying 'UK.EPF ~ UK ECONOMIC POLICY FOUNDATION' in big red, white, and blue letters. It looked more like an office than a workshop, devoid of the roller doors and loading bays of the other units.

They'd even put a couple of banners on either side of the podium, featuring smiling families – all of whom were Tipp-Ex white – and Dover's famous cliffs, and union flags, Spitfires, all that malarkey.

A quartet of big bald men, in the classic bouncer's outfit of black bomber jacket, black jeans, and black boots, lurked in the background, scowling at the rows of seating set out for the audience.

Had to be thirty or forty folding chairs, which was kind of overkill for the half-dozen journalists who'd actually turned up. Smoking tabs and kicking their heels. Waiting for something interesting to happen.

The parking area was half-empty too – couple of hatchbacks, a DEMETER-liveried van, two Jags, and a pair of minibuses with blacked-out windows from a local hire company. What it *didn't* feature was a single Outside Broadcast Unit. Probably because this was a wee press conference, on an industrial estate, in northeast Scotland, at ten past two on a Monday afternoon.

Tufty reversed into a space across-and-along-a-bit from the UK.EPF offices – between an engineering firm titled 'ALL THE WELD'S A STAGE' and a mechanic's called 'BANNANER-SPANNER'. Parking the patrol car under the company logo. Which they'd clearly made themselves out of metal sheeting, bolts, and girders: a gorilla's hand, holding a banana that had the stalky bit at one end and a spanner's head at the other.

At least it brought a bit of colour to the place.

The wee loon killed the engine, gave a big theatrical sigh, then hauled his droopy arse out of the car.

Roberta stayed where she was, scowling through the windshield at whatever bollocks was about to begin.

Tufty poked his head back in. '*What?* Thought this was what you wanted!'

She waved a hand at the podium and seating and teeny clump of journos. 'It's all a bit … Four Seasons Total Landscaping, isn't it?'

He sagged even further. 'I don't even know why we're *here*! And I'm hungry. And I'm tired. And I'm hot. And I'm *hungry*.'

'One: have you got *worms* or something? And two: we are here, because while you were snidging about, back at the station, *I* was multitasking on the toilet. Doing a bit of research.' Cracking out her vape for a black-cherry-nicotine hit. 'Our Anglo-Saxon Defence Group friends from this morning: they have a boss. Graeme Anderson, Grand Master of the ASDG Aberdeen branch. And he got back from the grand olde US-of-A today. And he's giving a press conference right here.'

'Yeah, but why are *we*—'

'Because I want to know why he sent his thicko thugs after Billie Nesbit. Does he know her? Is there a connection? Or was she just a victim of opportunity, and Emma Dornoch's *campaign* was the target? Apparently, they've been protesting outside her office for weeks. That no' seem suspicious to you?'

'Can't tell: I'm too hungry to think straight. Wasting away. Fading fast. Tell my wife and children I love them…'

She rolled her eyes. 'Fine.' Digging out her wallet. 'Go: get us something nice from the van.' Holding up a twenty-pound note. 'After all, it's no' like Anderson'll talk to us till this nonsense is over.'

'Woot!' Tufty wheeched the note from her hand and scampered off in the direction of Hungry Helen's.

'And I want a cold drink too! Lots of ice!' Cos it was sodding boiling.

Roberta took her hat off and plonked it on the dashboard, letting her disaster hairdo slump free. Grimacing at it in the sun-visor's mirror.

Yes, it looked terrible, but it was too hot to wear a stupid hat.

She flipped the sun-visor up again.

Puffed out her cheeks.

Settled back to wait.

And wait.

And wait.

Pfff…

Roberta blew another whoomph of fruity steam at the windscreen. Watching it roil and billow down the glass, fading away like the dying embers of her career.

Just over eight weeks.

Going to be weird after all this time…

One of the bouncers muscled up to the podium microphone and tapped on it – the sound *whump-whump-whump*ing out of a set of PA speakers. *'Testing, testing.'*

The mini press corps sat up as the UK.EPF office door opened and out stepped the man of the hour: Graeme Anderson. Sort of a cut-price Sir Norman Fordyce. Slightly rougher around the edges, but in a *manufactured* way. As if he'd hired a stylist to make him look more like a man of the people. His suit was a *little* less flashy, his watch a bit smaller, but he had the same well-heeled tan and easy smile. Even if his teeth don't look as if they'd come out of a packet. But his hair was a Hugh-Grant flop of dark russet brown, with a hint of grey at the temples – just enough to imply wisdom without appearing too old and decrepit.

A red-white-and-blue rosette bloomed in his suit jacket's buttonhole.

Anderson paused for a moment, leaning in for a private word with a woman who looked as if she'd either already done time for murder, or was about to. A stocky stumpy *lump* of a quine, with broad shoulders to go with her gravestone face.

Ding-buzz.

Better not be bloody Davey McLeod again.

It wasn't.

SUPT. YOUNG:

> Why haven't I heard back from you about Operation Basilisk?
>
> Portsoy Harbour: 1600

> Six bodies
>
> Full MOE gear
>
> Liaise with dog unit

Cheeky snudger.

Her thumbs jabbed out a suitable reply:

> Don't know if you heard, but I'm a bit BUSY today. So take your "request" and shove it up your hoop!

Her finger hovered over 'SEND'.

Frowning at the screen while she chewed at the inside of her cheek.

Maybe not the *best* of ideas, even if Young was acting like a massive toss-wank. Sometimes you just had to pick your battles.

DELETE.

On the far side of the car park, the minibuses' doors slid back and out poured about two dozen men and women, all dressed smart-casual. They formed an orderly queue, and the drivers distributed a bunch of placards – one for each of them – then the instacrowd took up position between the podium and the press. So any photos would have to be taken *through* the mini-throng, making it look as if there were loads of people here.

They'd even made the placards double-sided, because God forbid the coverage didn't feature what they were protesting for or against. Which looked like a toned-down version of what Lewis Kelman's thugs had been wanging on about outside Emma Dornoch's campaign office. Something a bit more 'palatable' for the national news...

Conversation over, Mrs Lumpy patted Graeme Anderson on the back, and he marched over to the podium. Tapped the microphone. Then put on his I-might've-gone-to-a-hooringly-expensive-public-school-but-that-doesn't-mean-I'm-posh voice – amplified through the PA system, echoing off the industrial units. *'Ladies and gentlemen, thank you for your time today.'*

Rent-A-Crowd cheered, and the press filmed them cheering.

Anderson waited for the adoration to die down before loosening his tie, throwing in a wee dramatic pause, before: *'We're here, because our very nation is in jeopardy…'*

Roberta scowled. 'Aye, from narrow-minded, bigoted wee pricks like you.'

According to the dashboard clock, it was ten minutes since Anderson had got up on his hind legs to wang on about how awful Scotland was, how it was all the lefties' fault, and how unfettered immigration was ruining this green and pleasant land – blah, blah, bollocks, and *wank* – and the bugger was still going.

The crowd were lapping it up though, whooping and clapping and waving their crappy placards in all the rehearsed places.

Roberta wound up the patrol car's windows, which cut down the volume a bit, but not enough to shut him out entirely.

'…unsustainable! One point two million *immigrants in 2024 alone! That's one immigrant for every man, woman, and child living in Aberdeen – Shire* and *City – Moray, Angus, Perth and Kinross, the Highlands, Orkney, Shetland, the Western Isles,* and *most of Clackmannanshire…* combined*!'*

Tosser.

She flipped him the Vs – not that he was looking – and finished her text to Lund:

Have you lazy bumholes found ANYTHING yet?

SEND.

Still nothing back from Susan.

'The sad truth is that we cannot afford to absorb these endless waves of people. We are a proud nation, and we've always *shouldered our fair share, but there comes a time when we have to say, "enough is enough!"'*

A muffled cheer from the crowd.

A big pantomime sigh from Roberta.

Where the hell was the wee loon?

Both hungry *and* bored, here.

She thumbed out a text to Logan, filling in a bit of time:

You're a lazy sod, you know that don't you?

Leaving me with all this work.

And all these idiots.

'We can't take any *more immigrants!'* Anderson waited for the cheer to end. *'How are we supposed to afford foreign aid when we can't even pay our doctors and nurses properly?'*

Speaking of idiots: the wee loon's getting on my nipples!!!!

Good job I'm retiring.

Couldn't cope with you useless poops for another 30 years!

SEND.

As that wafted off into the aether, Roberta glowered out at Graeme Tit-Face Anderson. Wonder if you could hate someone hard enough to make their head explode?

Worth a go.

She narrowed her eyes and gritted her teeth.

Die. Die. Die. Die.

'We have to put Scotland first. Put Britain *first. Put our hard-working families, struggling to get by,* first*!'*

Maybe cranial detonation was a bit ambitious for a first go?

Poking two fingers against her temple she screwed her whole face up, sending out the mental rays:

Rectal prolapse. Rectal prolapse. Rectal prolapse.

Still nothing.

Starting to think this telekinesis thing was a load of old bollocks.

So she slumped in her seat again. Checked her phone again. Sighed again.

Still no reply from *anyone*.

Urgh...

'We've got a cost-of-living crisis; a spiralling debt crisis; a GDP crisis; and a high-tax, low IQ, authoritarian *government bleeding us dry!'*

With the windows wound up, it was getting claggy in here. Cramped too. Muggy. Suffocating.

Not as bad as a wheelie bin, though.

Imagine being crammed into one of those: all your teeth battered out with a hammer, fingers hacked off with a knife, or an axe. Flesh melting away as the flies feasted...

Roberta's shoulders dipped.

Only upside was the poor woman must've been *long* dead by the time she ended up in the bin, because there was no way anyone could do all that to a living human being, in a lay-by, on the side of the main road north to Inverness.

Talk about small mercies.

Just had to hope she hadn't been alive for *any* of it, otherwise...

Yeah, that was a cheery thought.

Roberta's head lolled back to stare at the ceiling.

Who the hell could *do* that to a pregnant woman?

With any luck, the bastard would resist arrest when they eventually caught him – at least long enough for her to get the boot in a few times. Turn his cock-and-balls into eunuch mince.

This probably wasn't helping.

Of course, what she really *should* do is get back to Detective Superintendent Young. Tell him, politely, where to cram his request.

Could just kid-on she never got the text?

'It's not enough for political parties to just pretend they're listening to the people. It's time to roll up our sleeves and do *something about it!'*

Yeah, but then there would be repercussions and shouting and all that rubbish. And she'd have to act all chastened and humble and 'Oh, I *promise* I'll never do it again!'

When everyone knew she definitely would.

Pfff...

Better get it over with:

> Unable to provide OSU support.
>
> Working on a murder: pregnant woman in a bin.
>
> You'll need to find alternative dogs and thugs.
>
> Sorry.

SEND.

Young couldn't complain about *that*, surely. She hadn't even told him to Foxtrot Oscar.

Bet he'd still whinge to Pine, though.

Oh, boo-hoo, naughty old Roberta won't do what I tell her, she's so *mean* to me!

As if she wasn't up to her ears as it was.

Roberta tossed her phone onto the dashboard and reclined her seat a little further.

Anderson was *still* wanging on. And on. And on.

And where was that idiot with her cold drink? And her lunch. And her change, thieving scumbag.

Still, at least Wee Davey 'Pain-In-The-Hoop' McLeod was nowhere to be seen. But then Tufty's driving was probably enough to put anyone off.

'Our nation is crumbling all around us! Potholes, poverty, cost-of-living crisis. We're the sixth biggest economy in the world, and we've got teachers using foodbanks*! That. Is. A. Disgrace!'*

Speaking of Davey: she wriggled a hand across the back seat, searching for that folder... Bingo.

Roberta opened it and pulled out the three PNC checks.

First up: a nearly new, red, Jaguar F-Pace – whatever the hell that was – belonging to a Rory Hatton, registered address, Tremuda Knap Steading, Stonehaven. One warning for drunk and disorderly; lots of parking tickets; and six months, suspended, for Class A possession.

Next: an eight-year-old, lime-green, Toyota Yaris, registered to one Charlotte MacNeal; 16 Creel Terrace, Cove Bay. No record.

And last: a brown Daihatsu Fourtrak that had been on the road since the first of January, 1997. Jeremy Yarrow; 8K Fairview Court, Danestone. Four months for soliciting under a Section Forty-Six, which meant Jeremy was *selling* sex, rather than buying it.

Hmmmm...

'And now the government are talking about reopening the EU money-pit – handing billions of pounds and our hard-won sovereignty *back to the unelected bureaucrats in Brussels – when our brave veterans are sleeping rough!'*

Huge round of applause and cheering.

Not really any obvious connection between Hatton, Yarrow, and MacNeal. They didn't live in the same area; didn't share an offender profile; and going by the cars they drove, they came from *very* different income brackets.

So why was Davey so interested in them?

The idiots were still at it, cheering Anderson, clapping away and honking like seals.

But finally, some good news: here came Tufty, scampering back to the patrol car, carrying a clump of four cardboard containers and a couple of wax-paper cups.

About frunking time.

Roberta folded her trio of PNC printouts and stuck them in her pocket. Something to peruse later, when the wee squit wasn't watching.

The wee squit opened the driver's door and Anderson's voice got a lot louder:

'Well, I think it's about time we took care of our own!'

And the crowd really went for it, waving their placards and yelling and jumping up and down. Like the pricks they were.

Tufty thumped into his seat, bringing with him the rich sticky scents of honey and five-spice and soy sauce and deep-fried loveliness. He handed her one of his boxes – a proper cardboard rectangle, slightly tapered towards the bottom, like they had on American TV shows. Hot in her hands.

'Flipping heck!' He took off his hat and popped it on the dashboard, next to hers. 'It's *boiling* in here!'

Then he placed the pair of smaller containers beside it, before digging into the armpit of his stabproof for two sets of cheapo bamboo chopsticks in crumpled paper wrappers. Tossed one set to Roberta and ripped open the other with his teeth. Whittling his chopsticks against each other, as if sharpening a carving knife. 'Noodles, noodles, noodles, noodles.'

At long last the cheering died down.

'It's time we stood up and showed the Great British public what responsible government looks like!'

She whacked him with her chopsticks. 'Close the bloody door! You're letting all the fascism in.'

Ding-buzz.

Incoming message.

But whoever it was, they could wait. *Especially* if they were Detective Superintendent Young. No point spoiling lunch, after all.

And in the *spirit* of lunch: she grabbed Tufty's box too. Because the wee snidge was *bound* to be hiding something.

'Hoy!'

'*I* paid for them, *I* get first choice. Door: close.'

'All right, all right.' *Clunk.* 'If I knew you were going to be a complete frunt about it, I would've parked out on the street. In the shade.' He let free a whingy groan. 'Car's like a *microwave.*'

It was his own fault for not ditching his stabproof in the back, like she had. Idiot.

With the door shut, Graeme Anderson wasn't as loud, but sadly still audible. *'No more money for foreign wars! No more money for foreign courts! No more money for foreign nationals who don't respect our way of life! No more money for* anything *until we've taken care of our own!'*

Tufty licked his greedy lips. 'Speaking of being all *sweaty*… See when your sauna's up and running, can me and Kate—'

'*No.* I'm no' having you besmirching my lovely new wooden-bench thing with your drippy wee bum.'

'But I'd totally wear a towel!'

Christ, there was an image…

'Doesn't matter: your arse-sweat would seep into the grain – and no amount of Dettol is shifting *that.* Have to burn the whole place down.' She opened one of the smaller, dashboard cartons. 'Ooh, spring rolls.' All golden and crispy.

'We need to say, "No more" means, "no more"!'

The crowd joined in, chanting it out: 'NO MORE! NO MORE! NO MORE!'

Roberta helped herself, crunching through the flaky carapace and into the savoury delight of Far-Eastern hotness – doing that monkey *ook-ook-ook* thing, breathing cool air over each scalding mouthful. Then mumbling through the chewing. 'Defective Superinfectant Young wants us to drop everything and go play dress-up for him.' Crunch-crunch, *ook-ook-ook*, mouthful-mumble. 'What's "Operation Basilisk" when it's at home?'

'And that's why, today, I'm announcing the launch of a fresh political vision for Britain: the UK New Horizons party! And I'm running to represent the proud people of Gordon and Buchan in the upcoming by-election!'

Wild cheers.

The wee loon watched her eating, clutching his unused chopsticks to his stabproof vest. 'But I'm *famished…*'

She gave him The Look.

'OK, OK: Operation Basilisk is all those Lithuanian teddy bears coming into the country, stuffed full of drugs.' Wriggling in his seat, whimpering like a Jack Russell terrier on the verge of starvation. '*Pleeeeeeeease*, Guv, can't I just…?'

Gah…

She rolled her eyes, then held out the open carton, so he could steal a spring roll. Because never let it be said she wasn't kind to small animals.

His chopsticks flashed, grabbing a crispy tube of delight. All whingeing forgotten. 'Thanks! That's—'

A flash of searing light tore through the small business park, slashing at Roberta's eyes – then the *BOOOOOOOM!* arrived, riding the shockwave.

The patrol car's windscreen shattered, hurling a blizzard

of safety-glass shrapnel into her face and chest, as the blast rocked the car back on its springs.

She raised her arms to protect herself, even though it was *far* too late for that.

Then the car's back end jerked upwards as a dishwasher-sized chunk of offshore-valve-equipment slammed into the bonnet, tearing through the metal with a shrieking *CLANG!* and burying itself in the engine block.

Her airbag went off – the white fabric zooming into focus as it shoved Roberta back in her seat, blocking out the tattered windscreen and adding the fizzy-pepper spice of gunpowder to the air. Competing with the choking fug of whipped-up dust.

And in the aftermath, the only sound was the deafening howl of tinnitus, like a thousand rape-whistles screeching in her ears.

She battered the airbag out of her face, deflating the thing, shoving it away. 'JESUS CHRIST, WHAT WAS THAT?'

Tufty's bag had inflated too, so she battered *it* down as well.

The wee loon was all squint in the driver's seat, caught side-on as he went for a spring roll. Glassy-eyed and shaking his head, blood dribbling down his cheeks and forehead. Mouth hanging slack. The same expression he usually had after six pints.

'TUFTY! ARE YOU OK?'

No answer.

Outside, a blanket of glowing white smothered the world, as if this morning's fog had returned for revenge. Only instead of water vapour, it was dust – so thick that the car's crumpled bonnet faded away about halfway down.

'CONSTABLE!' She grabbed Tufty's arm. 'CONSTABLE QUIRREL, CAN YOU HEAR ME? ARE YOU HURT?'

He blinked at his hands, and then at her. His eyes widening. 'GUV? ARE YOU ALL RIGHT? GUV?' Reaching across the car, his trembling fingers touched her cheeks.

She slapped his hands away. 'GET OFF ME, YOU IDIOT!'

Opening the car door, Roberta staggered out onto the tarmac.

The wail of car alarms filtered through the tinnitus, accompanied by people screaming.

Sodding hell…

She grabbed her peaked cap off the dashboard, shook the safety glass out of it, then crammed the thing on her head. 'YOU:' pointing at Tufty, 'CALL FOR BACKUP!'

'WHAT?' He struggled out of the car, but his legs didn't seem to be working properly and down he went. 'EEEEK!'

'OH FOR GOD'S…' Roberta punched the button on her Airwave. 'DI STEEL TO CONTROL, WE NEED BACKUP AT SILVERMOSS BUSINESS CENTRE, WESTHILL.'

…

No reply.

Unless…?

'CONTROL?' She turned the volume up full. 'HELLO?'

A barely audible voice whispered out of the handset: *'No need to shout. Any reason you want—'*

'I NEED BACKUP NOW! FIRE AND AMBULANCE TOO.' She lurched out into the dust, making for where the press conference *should* be. If it were visible. Following the shrieks of pain.

Coughing and spluttering.

Every breath burning.

Ghostly bodies came into focus through the gloom. Some sat on the tarmac, moaning. Others were sprawled across the ground, not moving.

Oh God…

She knelt and felt for a pulse on a middle-aged bloke in a torn shirt and bloodstained trousers. Gash across his forehead.

Come on, you little—

Yes. Unconscious, *not* dead.

Roberta slumped. Took a deep breath. Coughed. Coughed some more. Then arranged Mr Still-Alive into the recovery position, and moved onto the next prone figure: another middle-aged man, a placard's handle lying across his slack palm. 'It's Time For A Better Britain!'

She was still struggling to find a pulse when he groaned, so *probably* still alive. Recovery position.

A woman ran past, clutching one arm to her chest, blood streaming down her face from a tattered hairline.

Yeah... This whole situation needed more than just one sexy Acting Detective Inspector and a halfwit PC with concussion.

She pressed the Airwave button again. 'EXPLOSION AT BUSINESS PARK! MULTIPLE CASUALTIES. POSSIBLE FIRES, DON'T KNOW.'

'Backup on its way. Secure the scene.'

'WHAT?'

Why did everyone have to mumble?

Roberta fiddled with the volume again, but it was already as loud as it would go. 'HELLO?' She gave the handset a shake. 'WHAT'S WRONG WITH THIS BLOODY THING?'

There were no more unconscious bodies here, so she lurched on into the dust, waving one hand in front of her to clear some of it away – which made sod-all difference – the other clasping a hanky over her nose and mouth as a makeshift breathing mask.

Scattered chairs.

A digital camera.

A vague grey shape resolved itself into a small knot of journalists and, going by the cluster of fallen placards, rent-a-mob supporters. About six of them in total, and half were motionless, lying beneath a chunk of corrugated-metal sheeting.

Right, that needed shifting.

But before she got there, Graeme Anderson strode out of the dust cloud. A cut snaked its way across one cheek, scarlet dribbling down to soak into his shirt. He took one look at the fallen, got both hands under the metal sheet and wrenched it up and away. Letting it fall to the side with a reverberating *clang* that cut straight through the high-pitched screech in Roberta's ears.

Then Anderson slipped his suit jacket off and draped it over one of the injured journalists.

A couple of reporters already had their cameras up, filming and snapping away, even though the dusty bastards should've been helping the injured.

Hope all their pictures turned out crap. Wasn't as if they'd get much, anyway: with the sun blazing down on all this dust, it was like wading through milk. But milk that tasted of stale bread, mouldy jam, and raw mince…

Roberta had another go at wafting it away. 'ANYONE SEE WHAT HAPPENED?'

Anderson helped one of his rent-a-crowd sit up – a large gammony man in tears, both hands curled into bloody claws.

And still the sodding press were more interested in getting this on film than sodding *helping*.

She tried her dodgy Airwave again. 'WHERE'S MY BASTARDING BACKUP, YOU USELESS BUNCH OF—'

CLUNK.

It was almost as loud as the initial blast.

Then a galaxy of stars exploded straight through Roberta's

skull and out through her eyeballs. Sharp and callous. So bright that they turned the dust-cloud grey, then the colour of clay, then black…

The tarmac rushed up to meet her knees as they buckled.

She blinked.

But nothing was in focus anymore.

And everything went—

In Which Tufty Has A Close Call With A Banana And DI Steel Has A Lie Down

Flipping wingwang…

Tufty lay flat on his back, beside the ruined patrol car, blinking up at all the fog. Letting the world whoooooosh round and round and round. It had stopped going up and down, which was an improvement. But wasn't getting any quieter.

A screechy *wheeeeeeeeeeeeeeeeeeeeeeee* bagpiped through his poor fizzing brain, bringing with it a weird creaky-*squeak-groan* kind of noise. Getting louder. Like a huge robot mouse was approaching, or some *very* heavy metal thing coming loose from its moorings.

Oh noes…

He did some industrial-strength blinking.

A very heavy metal thing.

Coming loose.

'Eeek.'

Scrambling to his feet – not easy in a great-big stabproof vest – he stumbled away from the patrol car. Which was probably going to need more than a quick once-through-the-car-wash on their way back to the station, what with the Godzilla-sized chunk of pipe-and-valve-work sticking out of its bonnet. Smashed windscreen. Scratched paintwork.

One of the front tyres was flat too.

Hope they weren't going to take that out of his wages...

A dull *burny* sensation faded up in the middle of his chest. Like indigestion after a far too spicy curry.

Looking down revealed a thing poking out of his tattered high-vis waistcoat. Sort of dark, and plug-like. A fizzy-wine cork, only made of threaded metal.

He pinched the twisty end between his fingertips and pulled, tugged, and finally yanked, till it popped free of his stabproof vest.

Snidging *snudge*.

It was a bolt.

A seventy-millimetre solid-metal bolt.

Tufty stuck a finger in the hole it left behind, wiggling through the layers of torn Kevlar and whatever else his stab-proof was fashioned from, till the questing digit made his chest sting like a great-big wasp had been at it. Not quite all the way through, but it was Womble-*funt*ingly close. And right over his heart, too.

Talk about a near-death experience.

This was—

The robot mouse went *twang...*

Tufty hunched, like a *ninja*, spinning through a quick three-sixty, Kung Fu hands at the ready as he checked his surroundings for immediate threats. Only when he stopped turning, the universe didn't – whooshing by at warp factor eight, making him stagger sideways a bit. Holding onto the murky air for balance till it all slowed down again.

Wow.

That was *much* cheaper than buying booze. But the hang-over wasn't a lot of fun.

The robot mouse's squeaky-*creak-groan* turned into a tortured *squeeeeeeeeeeeeal*, then a *CLANG*.

He stared as that massive Bannaner-Spanner logo peeled away from the industrial unit's wall and *smashed* to the ground – crushing the patrol car's whole driver's side and burying spiky metal struts deep into the tarmac *exactly* where he'd been lying only moments before.

Nearly deaded *three times* in ten minutes.

An explosion.

A deadly heart-seeking seventy-millimetre bolt.

And a huge metal bannaner-spanner.

'Double eek.' And a Klingon called Derek.

Wait, that wasn't right…

Tufty wiggled a finger in his ear.

'Tripple eek?'

Nope, could barely hear himself over the *wheeeeeeeeeeeeeee.*

Should probably find Steel. Everyone knew she was lost without him, because he was the bestest sidekick in the whole wide thingummy. And *who knew* what kind of trouble she'd get into if he wasn't there to help.

'GUV?' A deep breath made him cough and hack for a bit. 'DETECTIVE INSPECTOR STEEL!'

Of course she *might* be calling for help at this very minute, but he just couldn't hear her over the tinnitus? And the car alarms.

Right. Well. Nothing for it, then.

He unclipped his Airwave. 'ALPHA CHARLIE TEN TO CONTROL. ASSISTANCE NEEDED AT SILVERMOSS BUSINESS CENTRE!'

A really, *really* quiet voice whispered back at him. *'We know! No need to shout. And it's on its way. ETA: five minutes.'*

Fair enough.

Tufty straightened his ragged high-vis, brushing weenie cubes of safety glass away – to *ping* and *clitter-clack* against the tarmac. Pulled his shoulders back.

Time to do the Big Brave Police Officer thing, and—

Oooh!

No: hat.

No hat.

Wasn't wearing his hat.

Mustn't forget the hat.

It added a touch of gravitas to the uniform. Let people know you were trustworthy and dependable. Could always trust a man in a hat. Like Indiana Jones, or Santa.

And *his* was still in the car, on the dashboard.

But when Tufty turned to fetch it, the patrol car hadn't magically unflattened or unexplodified itself, and his hat remained crushed beneath a huge steel banana/spanner.

Poop.

Just have to do this hatless…

He strode out into the glowing white blur of dust.

The first couple of people he discovered had somehow managed to arrange themselves into the recovery position. Which was helpful.

Then, up ahead, a silhouette faded into view. Turning into a photographer's back-end. Her front-end was snapping away, the flash kicking-in every now and then, making the dust-fog shine even brighter.

What on earth were they photographising? It wasn't as if you could *see* anything through all this…

Graeme Anderson emerged from the haze, back straight, blood smeared on his crisp white shirt. Tie missing. And he had DI Steel's limp body in his arms.

She was on her back, one arm dangling over the side, face crimson with blood. Mouth hanging open.

Oh *fuck*.

Tufty rushed forward. 'GUV?'

And the photographer snapped on.

bedpans and broomsticks

2.01

'Gnaaaaaaaaaaaaahhh...!' Roberta jerked out of the empty swaying darkness and into a weird stuffy wee room that smelled of disinfectant and carbolic soap.

Unable to sit up, because an invisible bear was sitting on her chest, pinning her to ... a bed?

Why was she in bed?

This wasn't her bed.

Eyes darting about.

Stuffed animals stared at her from the windowsill and bedside cabinet. Most were brand new, but some looked as if they'd crawled out of a skip – balding, with buckled limbs and tentacles. Loads of supermarket flowers in makeshift vases. A trio of mylar balloons in various stages of droop: 'GET WELL SOON!', 'THINKING OF YOU!', and 'SEXY MUFFIN TIME!' A wall of lurid cards, and even a dangle of streamers.

Hospital.

She was in hospital.

There should've been a heap of equipment, pinging and buzzing and bleeping away, but all she had were a drip stand and a heart monitor – the wires disappearing into her open-arsed gown.

The blinds were open, letting in the grey.

A blocky, black-and-white wing of Aberdeen Royal Infirmary dominated half the view, the other half looking out over Westburn park. But instead of an uninterrupted vista of Powis, the Links, and off to the North Sea, the whole thing faded away at Mounthooly Roundabout, because it was absolutely *pishing* down. Rain crackling against her hospital window.

There was someone else in here: could hear them moving about in the toilet. Then a flush sounded.

'Susan?' Roberta's voice was almost inaudible. Not because of post-explosion tinnitus this time, but because the words barely made it out of her dusty throat and Sahara mouth. A parchment-paper whisper of gravel and sand.

Some clunking and rattling.

Then a weird *squeak-squeak-squeak…*

And the toilet door opened.

'Susan?'

But it wasn't Susan who emerged from the bog, it was Logan McRae, notorious wastrel and layabout, who should've been at sodding work this morning. Because then maybe *he'd* have got blown-up instead of her.

He was hamming it up – milking the broken leg for all it was worth, in a hospital wheelchair that needed a damn good drenching with WD40. It even had one of those bolt-on bits to keep his left leg elevated while sitting – a grubby grey cast from the knee down, clarted in signatures and graffiti.

No idea how he'd managed to grow his hair so quickly. Normally, it was scalped almost to the bone, now it was almost an inch long. Bloody hippy.

Did nothing to hide his sticky-out ears though, or the daft smile on his face when he saw her. 'The Kraken awakes!'

Roberta's eyes widened.

Holy crap on a Cornish pasty…

Logan wasn't the only visitor.

Three figures in long white doctors' coats stood at the foot of her bed. One in blue scrubs, one in green, and one in pink. All with stethoscopes and clipboards.

'What the ffff…?'

Dr Blue was perfectly normal, *except* for the fact that he'd swapped everything above his shoulders for the fully-feathered head of a barn owl. Big dark eyes staring at her. Dr Green had a magpie's sharp head and beady stare. While Dr Pink sported the black leathery head and long curved beak of an ibis.

'Why—'

Dr Green cocked her head to one side and let out a high, corvid, rattling cackle.

'Eeek…' Roberta shrank back into her pillows as Logan wheeled himself around the three doctors, squeaking his way to the side of her bed.

'You're in hospital, remember? You were awake a couple of hours ago and we explained what happened?'

OK, Logan seemed far more accepting of horrible human-bird hybrids than she was.

He put on the wheelchair's brake. 'I sent Susan home, because lovely and devoted though she is – she was getting a bit stinky.' Patting Roberta's leg through the blankets. 'How you feeling now?'

Roberta stared back at the three bird-headed monstrosities. 'Fine?'

'Just make sure you *behave* yourself this time. They tried to take you off the sedatives, Monday morning, and apparently you were a nightmare – which I can well believe – making off-colour remarks and trying to chat up the nurses.'

Dr Green checked her notes. *'I say we operate. No one really needs a* whole *liver after all, and it* is *nearly dinner time.'*

Logan grimaced. 'Even the *male* ones.'

'I see…' Roberta flattened herself against the mattress. But her medical team just inched closer.

Dr Pink turned her reaper's-scythe beak to Dr Green. *'You surgeons are all the same: always diagnosing with your stomachs. Let the poor woman be.'*

'You were like a randy octopus.' Logan patted her leg again. 'Thought that whack on the skull had really rattled something loose.'

Dr Blue's voice was deep and woody, like a bass recorder. *'Perhaps it wooould be kinder just to put her dowwwn?'*

'No!' Roberta pulled the itchy blanket up around her chin. Eyes flicking from the Birdheads to Logan. Who frowned at her as if she needed a padded room and a buckle-up cardigan.

She raised a wobbly hand, waving it at them. 'Can you not...?'

He turned his head towards the doctors for a moment, then frowned at her some more. 'Can I not *what*?'

'Erm...' Roberta forced a smile. 'Not see ... I need ... a drink? Thirsty. ... Drink.'

'Oh, God. Yes. *Sorry*.' He half-filled a small plastic tumbler from the jug on her bedside table and held it out. 'You gave us quite a scare.'

Bloody tumbler was too slippery to hold properly, but Logan helped her take a sip. Then another one. And it just rolled down her throat, lukewarm, barely touching the parched surface of her insides.

Roberta coughed, spluttered, groaned. Kept her eyes on the horror-show medical team. 'What happened?'

'You got blown-up. Tufty too. And most of Silvermoss Business Centre. They say it was probably a faulty acetylene tank in the valve-management place next door. Welding spark hits the wrong place and ...' he mimed a slow-motion explosion, '...*boom*. Next thing you know: every gas tank in the place goes up, and scruffy detective inspectors end up in hospital. Where you have spent the last two-and-a-bit weeks under the watchful eye of NHS Grampian in general, and Dr Barbara "Big Babs" Turner in particular.' A smile. 'Even though you made some *extremely* raunchy comments about her arse, Monday morning.'

Two-and-a-bit *weeks*?

She tried another sip of water, holding it on her hedgehog tongue until it softened the spines a little. Swallowed. Tried to move. Failed. 'Getting blown-up sucks arse.'

'Yeah,' nodding, 'it's not as much fun as people think…' Sigh. Shrug. Point. 'Plus you look like crap with your head all bandaged, and face clarted with plasters and those little sticky microporous-tape stitches.'

'Stitches?' She reached up with quivery fingers, feeling the mass of things glued to her cheeks and chin and forehead. And the vast turban of bandages.

'At least the bruising's gone down. You were like a human aubergine.' He fiddled about, below the level of the bed. 'And then there's this:' pulling out a copy of the *Aberdeen Examiner*. 'From the day after the explosion.' Tossing the paper onto her blankets.

Took a bit of doing, with the cannula jabbed through the back of one hand, but she got it unfolded. No idea what the headline was, because they'd printed it in some sort of special *wobbly* ink that wouldn't sit still, but the photo splashed across the front page was clear enough: Graeme Anderson, emerging from a cloud of glowing dust, like some sort of messiah, carrying a limp body in his arms. All bloodied and dripping and dangly. And holy shite, it was *her*.

She was the body.

Logan tapped the front page. 'That photo's been on the front of every newspaper up and down the country. *And* the telly. There wasn't a single news programme that didn't lead with it for *days*.'

The article text wormed and writhed, refusing to settle down into proper words. She blinked. Shook her head. Blinked again. But nothing made it or the headline decipherable.

Dr Pink clacked her beak. *'We should open her head up too. Might be something broken in there.'*

Dr Green stalked closer… *'Something tasty.'*

Roberta flinched back. 'There's nothing tasty for you!'

'What?'

Dr Blue hugged his clipboard. *'I still think the kiiiiindest thing to doooo is put her to sleeeeeep. So she doesn't suffer.'*

'Hello?' Logan gave Roberta's hand a squeeze. 'Are you OK?'

She dragged her eyes from the Birdheads. 'Yes?' Then held out the paper. 'You read it to me. Haven't got my glasses.'

'*Sure* you're OK? Want me to call the nurse?'

Doctors Blue, Green, and Pink *stared.*

'I just … haven't got my glasses.'

He watched her for a couple of breaths, frowning. 'Fair enough.' Then picked up the paper and read. '"Anderson saves stricken cop in bomb horror!" Blah, blah, "explosion at business park", blah, blah, blah, "fifteen million pounds' worth of damage" – which is *way* more than it probably should be. Bet you someone's fiddling their insurance claim for every penny they can get. Blah, blah, blah. Here we go: "Even though he'd been directly in the path of the blast, reformed 'hardman', self-made millionaire, and head of the newly founded 'UK New Horizons' party waded into danger to rescue Acting Detective Inspector Roberta Steel," brackets, "fifty-seven, who had—"'

'Fifty-*seven*?' Roberta shoved herself upright. 'Cheeky bastards!'

The Birdheads swooped in, crowding around her bed, so close that their beaks pressed into her cheeks. Breath hot and buzzing against her skin.

She scrunched her eyes tight as the room spun faster and faster – a warm yellow glow blooming inside her skull, lifting her teeth out of their sockets, making her sinuses throb-throb-throb with each surge of blood.

Then Roberta crashed back into her pillows. Blinking at the retreating ceiling as it darkened and whirled.

Logan grabbed the call button…

Rain rattled the window as Roberta blinked herself awake to a far prettier sight than Logan Sodding McRae: Susan.

She couldn't have noticed that Roberta was conscious yet, because she was click-clacking away with a pair of knitting needles and dark-blue wool, fashioning what looked like a little fluffy Dalek.

Bags darkened her eyes, and there were fresh lines around them too. Probably been tough on her, all this… Still a decade younger than Roberta, though. Like a middle-aged Doris Day, in a Breton top, no doubt still beating herself up for not shifting those extra lockdown pounds. But it just meant there was more of her to grab – a satisfying handful for rampant sexytimes, and something extra to snuggle into afterwards.

Warm and soft and lovelier than she'd ever know.

Susan must've felt Roberta's eyes on her, because she looked up and blushed. Hiding her knitting away, as if caught doing something naughty. 'Hey, sleepybum.' She kissed Roberta's cheek. 'How's the head?'

Nothing came out but a croak.

So Susan poured a little water and helped her sip it. 'You don't have to say anything, if it hurts.'

'Just a bit … dry is all.'

Susan helped her finish the tumbler, then topped it up again.

The door clunked, but Susan didn't seem to notice as Dr Blue and Dr Pink slid into the room. Smooth and silent, as if on castors. No sign of Dr Green and her magpie surgeon's beak.

Doctors Pink and Blue loomed at the side of Roberta's bed, opposite Susan. Who paid them no attention whatsoever as they *whispered* to each other and made notes.

'Your wee loon, Tufty, came past. He got you these…' Susan dipped into the bedside cabinet, coming out with a paperback novel and a weird rubbery thing, about the size of an orange. Pink, with floppy blond hair on top, and a sleazy grin on its round face. Familiar, but not immediately placeable.

Susan popped both on the bed.

The novel was some sort of Science Fiction bollocks, with a planet-and-starships cover: *The Eternal Fall Of Gravity's Children* by some J.M. Brewster dick – which could sod right off – but what the hell was the wee-rubbery-head thing?

'Tufty's been here every day. It's sweet. You should be nicer to him.' Pointing at the wall opposite her bed. 'And look what he made you.'

It was some sort of noticeboard, with the day of the week and the date in big easy-to-read letters, who the prime minister was, and a flip-over-numbers-bit marked 'THIS IS DAY:' It was set to '16'. As if she was a dementia patient.

Well thank you *very* sodding much.

'We weren't entirely sure if it should be "Day *One*", starting today, as you've only just woken up, or how long you've been here in total.'

Roberta glowered at it, then picked up the severed head, turning its glaikit face over in her hand. 'Want to go *home*.'

'I know you do, Robbie, but the doctors need to make sure your skull's all in one piece first. Don't want your brain falling out like a bucket of strawberry Angel Delight.' Straightening the itchy blankets and fussing at the pillows. Taking charge.

'Anyway, you've only been conscious a few hours. There's still physio and scans and tests and tubes up your doodah to go before that happens.'

'Urgh...' And the stupid head thing just grinned at her. So she crushed it in her fist.

Both of its eyes popped out on stalks with a weird plasticky *pkongk* noise. She let go and they went back in again: *glonk*.

Which meant it was either one of those executive stress-relief things, or a *really* weird sex toy.

She made its eyes pop a few more times: *pkongk-glonk, pkongk-glonk, pkongk-glonk...*

The door clattered open and Dr Green glided in, legs still as fenceposts as she cackled over to Roberta's bedside, joining her colleagues. *'Sorry I'm late. Had to see if the mortuary had any nice internal organs going spare.'*

Roberta retreated into her pillows, pulling away from the three of them.

'Robbie? Are you...' The wrinkles around Susan's eyes deepened as she squinted around the room. 'Are the animal people here again? The lions and the tigers?'

The Birdheads edged closer. Beaks clacking.

'No?'

'Because they've got you dosed-up on a *lot* of morphine, and it takes some people funny.'

Oh, that was bloody typical.

'Thought morphine was supposed to be groovy?'

Susan plucked the squeezy head from Roberta's grasp and plonked it on the bedside table. Then took Roberta's hand. Winding their fingers together. Holding on tight. The lights turned sparkly in Susan's eyes as she welled up just a little. 'Oh, Robbie, I thought we'd *lost* you.'

'How come everyone else takes drugs, they get a big-whooshy-fun-time trip, and I get a total arse-munch?'

'No more getting blown-up, understand?' She wiped at her eyes. 'As the only breadwinner in the house, I hereby put my foot down: *c'est verboten*!'

'It's not like I *wanted* to…' Hold on. 'Wait. No, no, no, no. *I* win bread too. What about *my* breadwinning?'

Susan re-straightened the already straight blanket, not looking her in the eye. 'Well, now that … *this* has happened, and you're only six weeks away from retiring, and it's not as if they're going to *discharge you* any time soon, then there's a period of convalescing at home, so you'll be on medical leave for ages anyway…'

Oh God.

'But—'

'I'm *sorry*.' Susan raised a hand to silence any argument. 'You can go back in to pick up your gold watch, if you like, but basically, that's *it* for you.' Then a serene smile dimpled her cheeks. '"Lay down your truncheon, brave officer, for now your shift is done."'

Roberta tried to sit up. 'But I've got *cases*! *Murders!*'

The silencing hand eased her back down again.

'Don't be *silly*, Robbie. They've given your investigations to someone else. It's not as if they could just put everything on hold for a fortnight while you were at death's door, is it?' She nodded. Squeezed Roberta's hand again, much tighter this time. Going into bulldozer mode – sweeping away all before her: 'No. This is the best option all round. You're basically a kept woman now.' And the smile was back. 'It'll be *lovely* to *always* have someone to come home to: a lady of leisure, my very own *domestic* goddess!'

Roberta did her best to fake a smile, as if the prospect wasn't terrifying.

And all the doctors cackled…

2.02

Thursday wasn't much better.

Roberta lay flat on her back, blankets draped over her like a funeral shroud, grimacing up at the ceiling. *Not* looking at the hyena-headed nurse making notes on the chart at the end of her bed.

The rain had devolved into a miserable drizzle that robbed the outside world of its colour, leaving it gloomy and depressed and feeling very, very sorry for itself – because it couldn't go home and sleep in its own bed, where it wasn't surrounded by monsters with human bodies and animal heads. And didn't feel like *crying* all the time…

At least she was out of that arse-split hospital gown. Swapped for a pair of pink pyjamas with little piggies on them. Yup: nothing said long-term hospital stay like festive PJs.

A knock on the door, and Tufty poked his head in. 'You decent?'

Little squit didn't wait for an answer, just slipped inside and closed the door behind him. He was wearing the full on-patrol kit: high-vis and stabproof, cluttered utility belt, and peaked cap. All a bit shiny from the drizzle. Carrying a pair of hessian tote bags. He flipped the number '6' over, so now the dementia noticeboard said 'THIS IS DAY: 17', then pulled the visitor's chair right up beside her bed. 'Can't stop long, but it's lunchtime, so I does come bearing muchness of treats!'

Dipping into one of the totes, he produced a quartet of white paper bags, spotted with grease. 'Ta-daaaaaaaa!' Popping them onto her cantilevered-table thing. 'Seems a bit transgressive to be eating butties at lunchtime, but I is a wild and crazy dude. How you feeling?' Going back in for a clump of napkins and a slithery handful of assorted sauce packets.

She scowled. 'A lot worse now *you're* here.'

'That's the spirit.' Opening one of the paper bags and peering inside. 'Sausage, double egg – on account of the crows and Shaky getting the other one. Does you wants: brown, red, tartare, mustard, or a mystery mélange thereof?'

'Urgh…'

'I'll surprise you.' He shuffled the sauce packets like dominos, then got to work. 'Don't suppose you'll be keeping up with current events, but it's by-election day. Dan-ta-ta-taaaaa!'

Idiot.

Roberta folded her arms. 'Why do *I* care about some stupid by-election?'

'Cos you did single-handedly manage to swing the result. Potentially.' Making a tortured-frog face. 'Unfortunately.'

He unhooked the bed's control pad and fiddled with the buttons, till she was half sitting up with her knees raised a little. Plumping her pillows and shifting the table closer. 'It was that photo, you see? You've *seen* the photo, right? Of Graeme Anderson being all Gort, "*Klaatu barada nikto*"?' Miming carrying a body. 'And it did has a *being everywhere*. Turns out saving a police officer's life is a real vote winner.'

'Didn't save anything.' Folding her arms tighter.

Tufty held out the overstuffed butty, little dribbles of sauce-fusion beige oozing from its multiple layers. 'Mmmmm… Munchable.'

Yeah…

Normally, she'd have his arm off at the elbow for one of those, but that healthy *rapacious* appetite for fried delight in a floury bun wasn't really doing it today.

Still, be rude not to even try.

She accepted the thing and gave it a nibble.

Why did everything taste of dust and gunpowder these days?

Tufty hummed away to himself, saucing up a sausage, egg, and bacon butty, with tomato and English mustard – leaving it looking like a crime scene in a pluke factory, all red and—

A woman ran past, clutching one arm to her chest, blood streaming down her face from a tattered hairline.

Roberta shuddered.

The wee loon munched away, talking with his disgusting mouth full. 'Nearly forgot: has a present for you.'

She struggled forward on her elbows. 'Is it my phone? They said I'm no' allowed screens, but what they don't know, etcetera…' Sticking one hand out. 'Gimme, gimme, gimme!'

He reached into the other hessian tote and pulled out an evidence bag. A chunk of pipe sat inside the clear plastic – about twice the size of the squeezy-head thing. Bent in the middle, with sheared metal at one end and a flange at the other. Covered in dried blood.

She dropped her gimme hand. 'That's *no'* my phone.'

'Nope: this am what beaned you.' Clunking it down on her table. 'Far as they can tell, it either went whoosh upwards, got caught on the sign in front of the building, then fell off – goes *clunk*. Or it did just go boom: allllllllllll the way up,' he tilted his head back, ogling at the ceiling, 'then allllllllllll the way back down again.'

Tufty followed the imaginary trajectory with his eyes,

slamming his hand against the table at the appropriate point – making everything there rattle and jiggle.

Nurse Hyena flinched.

So did Roberta.

'Sorry.' He poked the metal lump. 'Apparently you was like *completely* lucky, cos if it'd been even *one* inch further forward, it would've gone straight through the top of your skull like an sledgehammer through a watermelon. *Spwooooosh…*' Munching away, like the happy little monster that he was, with tomato-sauce on his lips. 'And now, Graeme Anderson's "UK New Horizons" party's up twenty-eight points in the polls.'

'Urgh…' Pushing her butty away.

'And if it makes you feel any better, look: I does has one too…' He went rummaging in his pockets, then held up a three-inch metal bolt. 'Mr The Explosion tried to blast it *right through* my poor little heart, but I did has my trusty stabproof vest on, so it did not manage in its evil—'

'Are you telling me I've helped elect a right-wing, racist, misogynistic, *fuck*nugget?'

A shrug, and he put his bolt away. 'Won't find out till polls close this evening. But yeah, looks like it.' Munch, munch, munch. 'If it's any consolation, that naughty *pre-nugget* word won't count towards the swear jar, on account of you being all traumatised in hospital.'

Oh for the name of *sod…*

As if the world wasn't bad enough without helping pricks like Graeme Anderson make it worse.

Tufty polished off his butty, licked his fingers clean, then opened the remaining two paper bags. 'For dessert, you can has an custard slice, or a apple turnover?'

She covered her face with her hands and groaned. Sagged. 'At least tell me we caught whoever stabbed that wee girl.'

'Ah…' There was some rustling of greasy paper. 'So: slab O'custard, or apples overboard?'

'Gaaaaaaahhh!' Deep breath. Trembling sigh. Because it was pretty obvious where this was going. 'And the poor cow in the bin?'

Silence.

More silence.

Great.

Why did everything fall apart the minute she took some time off?

Roberta let her arms flop on the blankets. Jaw set. Staring.

Tufty shifted in his seat. Cleared his throat. Licked his lips. 'So, we've started talking about your *retirement* bash, and it's—'

'Have you at least found out who she is?'

He bit his top lip.

Fiddled with the paper bags.

Pulled both shoulders up…

'Tufty, I swear on my puckered bumhole, I will climb out of this bed and beat you to death with a bedpan!'

'Well … you see … *Acting* DCI Beattie—'

'WHAT?'

The wee loon shrank back in his seat. 'OK, so he's maybe a *little* unorthodox and—'

'They *promoted* him? He couldn't detect flies on shite!' Blood whumped behind her eyes, innards fizzing. 'How could they give *my* cases to that halfwit, incompetent, fart-faced tosser?' *Whump-whump-whump-whump*…

Beside her bed, the heart monitor let out a bleep as it crossed some pre-programmed threshold, getting louder and faster.

Nurse Hyena's ears pricked-up and she padded forwards, sniffing the air. Mouth widening in a bone-crushing grin.

Tufty stood. 'Guv, maybe you should… *Deeeeeep* breaths.' Putting on a calm, smooth, end-of-the-pier hypnotist voice: 'Picture a cool, calm lake.' Stroking her arm like it was a wee dog at risk of peeing on the carpet. 'See the swans, swimming gently on the rippled surface as— Ow!'

'Get off me, you idiot!'

Something on the monitor must've triggered an alarm, because the door thumped open and in marched a nurse with a *human* head for a change. A middle-aged powerhouse of a woman, who had shining Ghanaian skin, exuberant hair, and competition-level bingo wings that quivered with matronly outrage as she stormed over to the bed. 'What's all this ruckus?' Fiddling with the heart monitor as she glared at Tufty. 'I told you not to get her excited.'

Excited?

Roberta threw back the blankets and hauled one leg over the mattress edge. 'Get me out of this bed, I've got work to do!'

'Hmmph!' The nurse shoved the leg straight back in again. '*You* are going *nowhere*, young lady. They had to weld the back of your skull together with a three-inch metal plate. You're staying put till Dr Turner says otherwise.'

'I'm no'—'

'Do you *want* to die? Is that what you want?'

Roberta glared at her.

'Because if it *is*, I can arrange for the hospital psychologist to visit every *single* day for the next *three* weeks to make you talk about your suicidal ideation.' Nurse Bingo-Wings stuck her nose in the air. 'Is that what you want? Or maybe you'd rather be sedated again?' She stood over the bed, arms crossed – and hoicking up her parcel-shelf bosom.

Heat flushed through Roberta's neck, blossomed across her cheeks. 'They gave my murder inquiry to a moron!'

'Then you'd better concentrate on getting better, so you can get back to work and *solve* it, *hadn't you*.'

Gahhh...

Hate it when other people were right.

She sagged back against her mattress.

The heart monitor slowed its angry bleeps, until her pulse slipped beneath whatever level was considered normal enough not to need warning noises anymore.

Nurse Bingo-Wings nodded. 'Better.' A regal finger came up to point at Tufty, 'You:' then the door, 'out. And take that filthy thing with you.'

'Sorry.' He gathered up the evidence bag and stowed it away again. 'Shall I leave the...?' Nodding at the untouched apple turnover, custard slice, and barely-nibbled butty. 'Or...?'

'*Roberta* is having lovely, nutritionally balanced, cauliflower cheese and strawberry jelly for her lunch. Not some deep-fried atrocity in a bun.'

'OK...' He repacked dessert, then grabbed her sausage-double-egg and took a huge bite, getting yolk all down his high-vis. Chewing through an eggy smile. 'You want me to pop back when we know the by-election scores, Guv?'

Which set her heart monitor bleeping again.

That regal finger jabbed. 'Out!'

And away scurried Tufty, still chewing.

Greedy wee shite that he was.

Friday could go wank itself to death. With a sandpaper glove on. In a bath full of sodding lemon juice.

Roberta slammed that morning's *Aberdeen Examiner* down on her cantilevered table and scowled at the hospital ceiling for a bit.

Bastards.

The rain had buggered off, which was a shame, because it would've been a lot more sodding appropriate than the sun streaming in through her window.

She grabbed the paper again.

HOW COULD THEY VOTE FOR THAT RACIST TIT?

There he was: Graeme *Pissing* Anderson beaming out of the front-page, arms up, Vs out, while behind him, a line of miserable-faced tossers drooped in their losing-this-election suits and defeated rosettes. Saying ta-ta to their political ambitions, on a makeshift stage in a decrepit community centre.

Emma Dornoch stood off to one side, looking thunderous as Anderson did his Richard Nixon impersonation. Turned out she wasn't BETTER FOR SCOTLAND! after all.

The headline declared 'WIN FOR UK NEW HORIZONS', subheading: 'FIRST MP FOR BRITAIN'S NEWEST PARTY IN NARROW VICTORY'.

And if *that* wasn't bad enough, there was a second story on the front page, reduced to a sidebar. 'BODY IN BIN: COPS CLUELESS' with a still from one of the YouTube videos, zoomed in on the victim's skull.

She slammed the paper down again.

Then did it three, four, five more times, till the edges got all ragged and torn.

Crumpled the bloody thing up and hurled it into the corner of her room.

Snarling as the heart-rate monitor launched into its *stupid* bleeping song again.

'AAAAAAAAAAAAAAAAARGH!'

Saturday brought visitors. Not that no one had visited her before – though nowhere near often enough, the heartless, uncaring sods – but these were *new* people. Suspicious people.

In both senses of the word.

The hook-nosed man, whose forehead took up about half of his head, had glasses, grey hair that was on the long side, a dark suit and green tartan tie. He'd introduced himself as Detective Superintendent Rifkind in a posh Scottish voice. Something Lothian-and-Borders-ish.

His sidekick, DI Kensington, was half-bulldog half-silverback, with a bald head stippled by moles and freckles. Wide nostrils. Matching suit, but a paisley-patterned tie, and an unapologetic aye-tae-a-pie Dundee accent. Taking notes as if stood at the foot of a scaffold and it was Roberta's turn to swing.

Rifkind lounged in the visitor's chair, one leg hanging over the arm rest, shiny black shoe swaying. Like a slightly louche headmaster. 'And you're *positive* you didn't see anything suspicious? Really?'

'I was eating noodles.' Because to hell with cooperating with these sketchy bumwanks. 'What did you expect me to see? Some bugger streaking across the car park with a big black ball in his hands marked "Bomb!"? Willy flapping in the breeze?'

A smile. 'Quite.'

Kensington's heavy brows knitted together into a cardigan of disapproval. 'No need to be *crude*.'

Roberta frowned back at him. 'And why are two spuds from Police Scotland's Mob Squad sniffing around? Last I heard it was a leaky acetylene tank. … Or *was* it?'

Rifkind made lazy loops with one hand. 'The Organised Crime and Counter Terrorism team like to lend a hand from time to time, when things go "boom".' The smile took on a distinctly carrion edge. 'Keeps us in a job.' Tilting his head to one side, like the Birdheads did. 'Just out of interest, what *would* you think if the explosion was …' another twirly gesture, '…intentional rather than accidental?'

'Oh aye?'

'Ah, I see you have a Boris Johnson.' Rifkind plucked the squeezy-head thing from her bedside cabinet.

So *that's* what it was meant to be.

The likeness was crap, but now someone had pointed it out…

Rifkind turned Johnson over in his long, tapered, surgeon's fingers. 'Didn't take you for a closet Tory, Roberta.' Crushing the head in his hand, making the eyes pop. *Pkongk.* 'That *is* rather satisfying, though.' *Glonk.* 'Your friend, Mr Anderson, seems to think it was a terrorist attack.'

'I'm no' a Tory! And Anderson's no sodding friend of mine.'

'Really?' *Pkongk-glonk.* 'But he saved your *life*, Roberta. Carried you from the scene of the blast. Never fails to mention you in all those interviews.' Looking around the room. 'I'm surprised he hasn't dropped by to pay his regards. Politicians, eh? And after you gave such a *boost* to his campaign.'

She just glowered.

'Anyway, *hypothetically* speaking: what if he's right and someone *has* decided this new political venture is likely to succeed and spread, upsetting the balance of power…?'

'Hmmmph…' The real question then, was who saw Anderson as a threat? 'It's no' like he's going to pose a serious challenge to Labour or the SNP up here – no' with only the one MP. Conservatives are too busy stabbing each other in the back to care. … But the more *hard-right* parties might get their beaks out of joint if someone's muscling in on their wannabe-fascist patch.'

A shrug. 'I couldn't *possibly* comment.'

'Bit … *showy* though, isn't it? You want to bump Anderson off – loads of ways to do it that don't involve dynamite and a press conference. Why no' make it look like an accident?' Which would be a fun game. 'He could drown in the bath, have a car crash, fall off a cliff, or better yet: strangle-wank.' Grinning. 'That kills the bugger off and makes him look like a proper twat for all eternity.'

Kensington stiffened, no doubt shocked by such a *crude* onanistic practice.

Rifkind's leg stopped swinging. 'Interesting, isn't it. *Hypothetically* speaking.' *Pkongk-glonk.*

'But you'll have forensics that say one way or the other…?'

That twirly gesture was back again. 'Our inquiries are ongoing.'

Bet they bloody were.

He abandoned the slouch. 'I've promised to show Matthew here a slice of Aberdonian nightlife. Maybe visit a local hostelry for a wee nippy sweetie or two.' Sitting forward. 'What's *your* favourite tipple, Inspector?'

Yeah, that wasn't what he was really asking, was it. He was fishing for something. Could see it in the bugger's eyes. Hungry and searching. Magpie-like.

Roberta pulled her chin in. 'Whisky. Malt. Neat. Water on the side.'

'Good girl!' Beaming. 'So many people seem to favour *vodka* these days, but I don't see the appeal myself. Bit too … *Kremliny*, don't you think? One has to be so *careful* not to support Russian businesses, these days. What with the war and everything.'

Patronising bastard.

She sat up. 'Who the *hell* are you calling "good girl"?'

A wink, because clearly all this patriarchal bollocks wasn't insulting enough. 'I do so like a woman with *spirit*.' He stood, towering over the bed as he buttoned his jacket. 'Shall we, Matthew? I'm sure the detective inspector needs her rest.' Then Rifkind stalked to the door. Stopped. Turned. Graced her with a corvid smile. 'Get well soon, Roberta.' He gave Boris Johnson's head one final crush – *pkongk-glonk* – and tossed it to her. 'We'll be in touch.'

Yeah…

Why did that sound like a threat?

2.03

Day 20 – Sunday (18:15)

Susan sat at the side of the bed, knitting away and babbling on, while Roberta lay there like a flattened Smurf, in her fuzzy pyjamas – sky blue today, and covered in penguins.

'So I said to her, I said, "the legal precedent is quite clear: Krys versus KBC Partners LP – brackets, 2015, close brackets, UKPC Forty-Six – shows that distribution of a partnership's assets on dissolution of the commercial entity..."' On and on and on and on.

Love her to bits, but by *Christ* commercial law was *boring*.

'And the judgment *clearly* states that once you take out the interim payments allowed under clauses Eight-point-Two-point-Three and Eight-point-Two-point-Four, clauses Seven-point-Two-point-Two and Seven-point-Two-point-*Three* are the *only* things granting any allocation of income to the Special Limited Partners...'

Roberta removed the crunkly pillow from behind her own head and tried to smother herself with it.

Day 23 – Wednesday (17:40)

'Throwing his weight about like a *total* snudgeweasel!' Naomi stomped a squeaky foot. She'd come dressed as her big sister today, even though Jasmine was a whole eight years older than her. The pair of them, standing beside Roberta's hospital bed with their matching long brown hair, jeans, and oversized trainers. The only points of divergence were their heights and their T-shirts – both black, but where Jasmine's featured a Mozart-as-an-Andy-Warhol-style-punk print, Naomi's had more of a pink pirate-octopus vibe.

Neither of them seemed to have got the memo that the sophisticated woman-about-Aberdeen-Royal-Infirmary was wearing lime-green PJs, with lions and tigers on them this season.

Naomi dug into her pocket and produced a pound coin. 'For the swear jar.' Clicking it down on the table. 'So I called him a *cunt*, and he went running to teacher, cos he's just a cunty little cunt, and he shouldn't push people over in the playground!'

Jasmine looked up from her phone. 'Damn straight. Should've kicked him in the knackers too.'

'Might've done.' A grin. 'But I played the my-mummy's-nearly-dying-in-hospital card, so I didn't even get detention!'

Nice to know all this having-your-head-caved-in-with-a-lump-of-metal had been good for something. But Roberta tapped the tabletop with a finger anyway. 'That's *three* quid you owe. Make with the extra two.'

'Ghhhaaaaaa…' Naomi slumped, arms dangling, head hanging back like a boneless teenager, even though she was only nine. 'But Muuuuuu-um!'

'Hey, I don't make the rules.'

Which was a complete lie, but hey-ho.

Day 28 – Monday (03:56)

Every. Bloody. Thing. Hurt.

One hand on the bed frame, the other clutching her drip stand, Roberta limp-shuffled around the foot of the bed, in the dim nighttime glow of her room's emergency-exit sign.

Each step was on broken glass.

Each movement driving rusty nails into her hip.

Each breath grating against her barbed-wire ribs.

And all of it topped off with the clattering, *burning*, throb of blood swirling around her battered brain.

The bathroom was only a couple of feet away, but it might as well have been miles. Through a minefield. That was on fire.

Finally, she made it to the toilet, pulled down her pink-piggy-PJ bottoms and thumped onto the seat.

Then sat there and cried.

Day 29 – Tuesday (10:05)

The nurse placed a cup of tea down on Roberta's table, with a digestive biscuit tucked into the saucer. 'You're popular today: got a delivery.' He was one of those hairy-little-terrier types, who looked as if he chased parked cars and combed his beard with a fork. Would probably hump your leg and pee on the rug, if you took your eyes off him for thirty seconds.

Nurse Terrier went for the big reveal – whipping out a brown-paper parcel from behind his back. He held it out.

About the size of an expensive box of chocolates.

Which was the best news she'd had in ages.

Ho, ho, ho...

Roberta accepted the thing, ripping through the paper.

'Yeah, they couriered it over and everything.' He sniffed. 'Surprised it got here, to be honest, and they didn't just leave it in the neighbour's hedge.'

It wasn't chocolates.

It was some sort of wooden frame.

'We ordered a case of wine three weeks ago and it turned up in next-door's shed. Bugger had drunk most of it before we found out.'

She turned the thing over.

And stared.

Oh in the name of...

It was an oil painting.

A wee oil painting.

Of Graeme Wanking Anderson, carrying her out from the post-explosion dust cloud.

It didn't look like either of them, but she'd seen that rotten, *sodding* photo often enough to recognise what the 'artist' had been aiming for.

'I'm tempted to order a mixed case of dog-shite and turpentine. Let the bugger get his laughing gear around *that*.'

There was a note tucked in with it, typed on official House of Commons stationery:

> Dear Mrs Roberta Steel,
>
> I am sorry that I can not be there in person to visit you, but here is a little token of my esteem to let you know that I am thinking of you in this troubling time.
>
> I hope you are feeling better, and that you get home soon.
>
> Best wishes,
>
> Graeme Anderson MP

About as warm and comforting as a bucket of day-old sick.

Wasn't even signed.

The nurse sighed. 'Anyway, better get back to it. You know what Matron's like. I blame the hot flushes, myself.' Wink. 'I'll try to get you a *decent* biscuit next time.' And off he bustled.

Leaving her alone with this ... *monstrosity*.

Because getting blown-up wasn't bad enough.

Day 30 – Wednesday (14:15)

'That's great, you're doing great.' The physiotherapist's hands were cold against her feet, pushing back gently as she gritted her teeth and shoved as hard as possible.

Which made sod-all difference.

Doing great, her sharny arse.

But then how could you trust *any* man who thought it was a good idea to shave off most of his hair and bleach the remaining tuft blond. Then head down to the tattoo parlour for a Thora Hird on one arm and a Joyce Grenfell on the other. He had too many teeth as well. And smelled of rubbing liniment.

'OK, great. Now, knees together …'

She did, and he put his hands on either side, pressing lightly.

'…and try to push them apart.'

Could barely move the sodding things.

Buggering hell.

This was *not* what passed for a sex life.

Day 31 – Thursday (10:45)

Tufty lounged in the visitor's chair, crunching his way through another pinch of crisps. '…cos let's face it, Beattie couldn't detect *stink* if you trapped him in a lift with Biohazard Bob, after Biohazard's binged on brussels-sprout vindaloo and extra-fizzy Guinness.'

The wee loon wasn't in uniform this time, but a pair of cargo shorts, knock-off Converse trainers, and a vintage T-shirt for some stupid kids' show – with 'Timmy & The Timeonaughts' on it, three cheap-looking puppets, and 'Ducking About In Space & Time!'

He stretched out his hairy little legs. *Crunch, crunch, crunch.* 'And don't get me started on McPherson! Two days back from the sick and he gets his hand slammed in a filing-cabinet drawer; and *he* was the one slamming it!' Holding the bag's open end out to Roberta. 'I just need him to fall down the stairs now, and I win a tenner on the office sweepie.'

Urgh…

Idiots. They gave her cases to *idiots*.

She dipped a hand into the bag and dug out a wodge of salt-and-vinegar crispiness. Munching on them, even though they were cheap and nasty. Getting crumbs down the front of her PJs, like greasy little snowflakes falling on the penguins. 'Where's my sodding phone?'

'Number the First: you is not allowed no phone, on account of your massive cranial trauma and stuff. Number the Second: it was taken into evidence after we did get blowed-up. Number the Third: I had a look and it's borked. Must've got squashed in the boom.' A shrug. 'Look on the bright side: better it than us, right?'

'Yeah, but you could *get* me one, couldn't you.' Not even bothering to keep the wheedle out of her voice. 'Must have a spare handset knocking about you could stick a SIM in?'

'I does refer you back to Number the First.' *Crunch, crunch, crunch.* 'No phones is no phones. Besides, Susan would kill me.'

'Gaaahhh….' Sag. Droop. Groan. 'But I'm *bored*!'

'You know, when you has retired, you should *totes* come join our Wednesday game. We currently does has a *Quest For The Dreaded Golden Dragon Of Glairmoch's Acurrrrrrr-sed Treasure*!' Hamming it up, like the dick he was, before dropping back to normal. 'We could use a new wizard.'

She snatched another wodge of crisps. 'I'd rather be blown-up again.' Stuffing them in.

Crunch, crunch, crunch…

Day 32 – Friday (14:15)

The physio kept one hand in the small of Roberta's back, easing her forward as she limped and shuffled across the room, leaning heavily on a Zimmer frame, in her lion-and-tiger jammies.

Performing a tortoise-slow clunk-shuffle to the door and back.

'That's great, you're doing great.' Smiling at her. 'Better to be slow and get there, than rush and end up on your arse...'

Day 33 – Saturday (11:35)

Bored. Bored...

Roberta sagged in bed, like a peely-wally starfish, hands and feet hanging over the mattress edge.

Only one thing for it.

Desperate times called for desperate measures.

She huffed out a long breath.

Then reached over to the bedside cabinet and picked up the paperback novel lying there, next to Boris Johnson's squeezy head: *The Eternal Fall Of Gravity's Children.*

That she'd been reduced to *this*...

Pfff...

Might as well see if this J.M. Brewster could actually write, or if it was all woo-woo spaceships and aliens and whatnots.

She got halfway through the introduction, before slamming it shut again. 'Buggering wank's sake... I'm no' a teenage boy!'

Then frisbeed it into the far corner.

Where it bounced off the cornice and onto the windowsill. Sliding to a halt against the glass.

Ten points, and the crowd goes wild.

Another big sigh.

Still bored.

Why couldn't Tufty have got her a nice *dirty* book? Like a Sarah Waters, Sylvia Day, Miranda July, Salwa Al Neimi, Anaïs Nin… Or one of the Marian Keyes with lots of riding in it? Even a Jilly Cooper would do in a pinch.

Roberta starfished across the bed again, grimacing up at the ceiling.

Bored. Bored. Bored. Bored. Bored….

Day 34 – Sunday (12:10)

The problem with hospital food was that people were expected to eat it. Don't think you were supposed to *enjoy* it, just cram it down, get better, then sod off out of there and vacate the bed for somebody else. Or die. Either was good as long as it freed up space.

Whatever happened to Jamie Oliver, kicking the hospital-kitchen doors down and whipping up fresh pasta and pesto and pizza and porchetta and perfectly presented porcini polenta…

Instead of which, what did Roberta have for lunch today?

Skin-graft salad.

And yes it was probably *meant* to be ham, but it looked far more like a surgical offcut.

Could kill for a curry.

She adjusted her glasses and scowled at this morning's *Scottish Daily Post* – the bumper Sunday edition with all the crappy magazine bits and supplements that no one ever read. 'DID SICKO JIHADI THUGS BOMB BRAVE ANDERSON?' above yet another photo of the bastard carrying her through the dust. 'HERO MP SAYS BLAST WAS "TERRORIST ATTACK": EXCLUSIVE'.

That Specialist Crime Division spook, Rifkind, had mentioned Anderson's bomb theory two *weeks* ago. How come the *Sharny Dick Plop* was only just publishing it now?

The front page was light on detail, big on conjecture and sensationalism. 'CONTINUED ON PAGE 6→'

She turned to a double-page spread, crammed full of hyperbole, speculation, and downright lies. They'd married it with a photo of Silvermoss Business Centre after the blast – the units peeled open like the foil on a Chocolate Orange, chunks of machinery scattered all around. There was a pic of Anderson too: some sort of official MP portrait, where he was obviously trying to look like a statesman, rather than a wife-beating, racist thug. Wanging on about how important it was to stand up to Islamic extremists invading the UK in small boats, raping our sheep and stealing our jobs and wank, wank, wank...

Roberta snatched Boris Johnson's squeezy head from the bedside cabinet and crushed it in her fist. *Pkongk* – out popped his eyes.

Then in again: *glonk*.

Bloody Graeme *Bastarding* Anderson.

Pkongk-glonk.

And she'd helped get him elected...

Pkongk-glonk. Pkongk-glonk. Pkongk-glonk. Pkongk-glonk-pkongk-glonk-pkongk-glonk-pkongk-glonk.

Day 35 – Monday (16:50)

Was there anything more depressing than an off-brand Rich Tea Biscuit? Pale and disappointing at the side of her cup. Sucking all the joy from the room as the young man wheeled his trolley away, off to spread depression and despair, one biscuit at a time.

Pfff...

Roberta dunked it anyway.

Munching on the hot soggy mush. The culinary equivalent of sackcloth and ashes.

The door swung open and in rolled Babs, with her cheery middle-aged smile, unruly mop of hair, and a thick Alice band that made her look as if she'd lost a bet and this was the forfeit.

She wheeched the chart from the foot of Roberta's bed, running a podgy finger across the data. 'And how are we today?'

'*We* are contemplating horrible NHS biscuits.'

'Good, good.' Babs produced a wee pen-torch and shone it in Roberta's eyes. Humming something bland and repetitive as she moved it from side to side.

'I'm bored. I want my phone back.'

'You should've thought of that before you got blown-up. No screens till your noggin settles down a bit.' Playing follow the finger. 'How are the headaches?'

'If I say they've all gone away, can I go home?'

'Nope.' Running her fingers along the back of Roberta's skull – light as cotton wool. Tracing the scar tissue.

'Then they're a massive pain. Like some big hairy tosser is drilling away with a jack hammer.'

'Hmmm…' Her eyes narrowed. 'Sharp and stinging, or hot and throbbing?'

'Steady on, Babs, you randy sexpot: I'm a married woman.'

'It's *Doctor Turner* to you, if you're going to be cheeky. How's physio going?'

A grimace. 'Shouldn't *need* physio. Head got bashed, no' my legs.'

She tapped Roberta's forehead with a knuckle. 'See the contents of this rock-hard skull of yours? Sixty percent fat, forty percent neurons and glial cells and nerves and blood vessels and all that mushy stuff. It's a finely balanced network of chemical signals and electrical charge. And *you* scrambled all the wiring by getting your head caved in. That's why you need physio.' She made a note on the chart and stuck it back where it came from. 'We'll try upping your pain meds again. Everybody loves opioids!'

And off she sodded, with a cheery wave and a wobbly bum.

Leaving Roberta to her horrible biscuit.

Day 36 – Tuesday (01:24)

Doctors Pink and Green and Blue clustered around Roberta's bed in the darkness. Looming. Beaks clacking away as she lay there, one hand covering her face, stifling the sobs.

Day 37 – Wednesday (10:35)

Sunlight streamed in through the glazed corridor, making the hospital air sticky as golden syrup. Roberta clunk-shuffled her Zimmer along. Leaving Aberdeen Royal Infirmary's Pink Zone behind and heading into the hospital proper.

Wearing her brand-new pyjamas: orange, festooned with hedgehogs, badgers, and squirrels. Tartan slippers on her feet. Like a proper auld wifie.

Through here, in the Yellow Zone, the hustle and bustle of the hospital's main entrance and reception area throbbed against the old familiar hospital noises – squeaks and beeps and rattles and that ever-present *hummmmmmmmmmmmmmmmmmm…*

Kind of tempting to just keep going.

Make a break for it.

Call a taxi and head *home*.

Babs would love that.

But Roberta was on a mission – an expedition to explore uncharted territory.

Searching out that mythical far-off land: the Green Zone.

(11:20)

Sodding hell…

Pfff…

For anyone with working legs – who wasn't lugging around a three-inch titanium plate in their skull – it probably would've taken five, maybe six minutes *if* they dawdled to look at the paintings and whatnot hanging in the hospital corridors. But she'd been on this slow-motion clunk-and-shuffle slog for *hours*. Days. Weeks. Sodding *years*.

Roberta staggered into the Medical High Dependency Unit, found room six, and sagged against the observation window. Forehead making greasy marks on the cool glass.

Inside, it was far bigger than her one, back in Neurology and Neurosurgery, large enough for four beds and a ton of monitoring equipment. Flashing lights and bleeping things. Graphs and charts and wavy lines on monitors...

Its occupants: all flat out and motionless.

Billie Nesbit was in the bed nearest the window, pale as a whittled bone. Freckles grey and faded. Even her hair had turned a dusty shade of rust.

They'd taped her eyelids shut. Which didn't inspire confidence. Doubt Billie would be waking up any time soon...

Day 38 – Thursday (16:06)

Roberta drew a hairy willy on the Prime Minister's forehead and turned to page nine of that morning's *Aberdeen Examiner*. Safe in the knowledge that no one would want to read it after her. Not by the time she'd finished defacing all the photos with willies, defamatory speech balloons, tattoos, scars, fangs, blacked-out teeth, horns, and glasses, anyway.

Well, everyone needed a hobby, right?

So, who was next for a biro makeover?

The pen drooped in her hands.

A whole quarter page had been devoted to '"INEPT" COPS STILL KNOW NOTHING ABOUT BODY IN BIN'. They'd accompanied it with another grainy photo of the wheelie bins, sitting in the foggy lay-by. Taken by some TikTok ghoul on the train to work. Skull and bones spilled across the potholed tarmac.

The article that went with it wasn't exactly *flattering* about Police Scotland's efforts to identify the victim or killer.

And just to rub it in, they'd included a second pic, near the end of the story: Roberta and Tufty, trying to block the remains from view as the 07:42 from Inverurie headed north to Insch. At least the wee loon had the brains to keep his head down, face hidden by his peaked cap. Sodding Roberta was on full display, all stretched out like Leonardo da Vinci's *Vitruvian Man*.

Only not naked.

Thankfully.

That would've given the commuters something to wank about.

But it meant the dick who wrote the article could crowbar in some guff about Graeme Arseing Anderson 'rescuing' her from the explosion.

She grabbed Boris Johnson and dug her fingers into the bugger's rubbery head.

Pkongk-glonk. Pkongk-glonk. Pkonnnnnnnnnnnnnnnnnngk-glonk.

Day 39 – Friday 25 July (14:15)

Tintin the Tattooed Twat was back, doing his can-you-push-against-my-hands routine again. Only this time her feet were *not* to be defeated.

He gave her a toothy grin. 'That's great, you're doing great.' Increasing the pressure a little. 'Keep this up and we'll have you whizzing about with a walking stick before you know it!'

(16:50)

Dr Babs flicked her pen-torch to the side and back again, making stars race across the world. Leaving blood-red streaks behind as Roberta slumped there in her woodland animals.

One more flick. 'Good. That's a real improvement on last time.'

Thank God for that.

'So, I can go home?'

'Nope.' The pen was replaced by Mrs Finger, moving from side to side. 'But I think we can let you watch a *little* TV, if you like? Won't hurt at this stage.'

Roberta sat up. 'Phone?'

'Also nope.' Making notes on the chart. 'And don't make me explain why: it takes ages, is really complicated, and I need a wee.' Slipping the chart back into its holder. 'But there's bound to be *something* good on this weekend – as long as you don't watch more than an hour a day, knock yourself out.' Frown. 'Only not *literally*. That titanium plate in your head is expensive and we don't want it damaged.'

'Urgh…' Flopping back against the pillows again. Groaning like a stroppy teenager. 'And I repeat: urgh!'

'With a positive attitude like that, you'll be out of here in *no* time.'

She should be so sodding lucky…

2.04

Day 42 – Monday 28 July (18:14)

Roberta glowered at the TV screen as the *Six O'Clock News* chuntered away and a beige sklodge of cauliflower cheese congealed on her plate. Ignored in favour of the pink-square-and-custard. Like being back in school again, only with fewer sweaty gymslips and lunchtimes spent fantasising about Lisa Armstrong in the year above.

Wonder what happened to her…

Bet she ended up marrying some prick like Graeme Anderson – currently slithering his way through a pre-recorded interview, while a heavy-set-and-pretty journalist tried to make him answer the sodding question instead of immediately pivoting to his nasty little talking points.

They were in the House of Commons lobby, with the occasionally recognisable political stinker slinking about in the background.

Miss Curves-And-Bumps gave up on the hard questions, lobbing the bastard a softball instead: '*…and is that why you've introduced this private members' bill?*'

A slippery smile. *'That's right, Olivia, we must* rise *to this challenge and give our police officers the powers they need to take these people off the streets.'* He frowned: serious and resolute, hamming it up. Tit that he was. *'We know extremists tried to silence me with a cowardly bomb, but it's just made me more determined to stand up and say, "Enough is enough!"'*

The news cut to a shaky video of white and grey, and then Graeme Anderson emerged from the dust cloud, carrying Roberta's unconscious, bleeding body. Him looking all noble and manly, while she damsel-in-distressed in his arms, like a half-deflated sex doll.

It was from a different angle to the photo in every paper, so must've been one of the other journos who took it. When the bastards *should've* been helping the injured.

Back to Westminster, where Anderson stuck his rugged chin in the air. *'It was my honour and* privilege *to save that brave officer's life. After all: the police do the same for us, seven days a week, three hundred and sixty-five days a year. And we* must *stand behind them, every step of the way.'*

Roberta grabbed Boris Johnson and crushed his stupid grinning head: *pkongk-glonk.*

'I know that Detective Inspector Roberta Steel would support this bill to make her, and every *police officer's job safer. Especially as it'll help them be more* effective *in keeping* hate *off our streets.'* Churchill pose. *'That's why I'm calling it "Roberta's Law".'*

She bared her teeth, growling.

How *dare* he.

How sodding bastarding *dare* he stick *her name* on his racist shitefest legislation.

Pkongk-glonk-pkongk-glonk-pkongk-glonk-pkongk-glonk-pkongk-glonk-pkongk-glonk-pkongk-glonk-pkongk-glonk-pkongk-glonk-pkongk-glonk-pkongk-glonk-pkongk-glonk-pkongk-glonk...

Day 43 – Tuesday 29 July (13:45)

'Well, I don't know, do I.' Logan hobbled along beside her, leaning heavily on one of those NHS crutches with the elbow brace built in. Fibreglass cast thunking against the polished floor in its fat leather Frankenstein boot. 'Maybe it'll be cool having a law named after you?'

'Grrrrrrrrrrr…!' She'd abandoned the Zimmer frame, taking a heavy wooden walking stick out for a spin instead. Lumbering along the corridor in her pink piggies.

The view wasn't half bad from up here: all the way out to the beach and the North Sea beyond. Supply ships and offshore wind turbines sparkling in the sunlight. Seagulls wheeling in the sapphire sky.

Logan smiled at her. 'Moan, whinge, complain.'

The corridor art was that experimental abstract embroidery-and-collage stuff. What happened to good old-fashioned *traditional* paintings of naked women? Nice roundy ones, getting their Titians out.

'Is it no' bad enough, every time I open the paper, there's Buggering Beardy Beattie making a cat's-arse of my cases?' She gave Logan a wee scowl. 'Thank you *very* sodding much.'

'Don't look at me, I didn't pick him – that was all the Chief Super. *I* was laid up with Stinky The Itch Monster here, remember?' Pointing at his manky cast.

She harrumphed. 'Beattie couldn't investigate—'

'His nose for bogies, his pants for skidmarks, poop for sweetcorn, the … American president for stupid. Yeah, we get it.' Shrug. 'Nothing we can do about that now.'

'But you could take my investigations *off* him.'

'And how do I do that? I'm up to my ears in crap as it is. Don't need *his* disasters as well.'

They'd reached the end of the corridor, which was the perfect place to give Logan a proper glowering at. Useless sod that he was.

Not that it seemed to bother him. 'Look on the bright side: I get my cast off on Friday.'

'And how does *that* help?'

'It's really itchy.' He leaned against the windowsill, gazing out at the sun-glittered city. 'Besides, you know what *Beattie's* like: by the time you're out of here, he still won't've solved the murder or the stabbing. You can ask for both cases back – bet he'll be glad to get shot, after cocking everything up.'

'Ghaaaah…' She slumped against the windowsill, directing her glower at the wheeling gulls instead. And the glowing trees. And the shiny traffic. Took a deep breath. 'Susan says I should malinger about on the sick till I retire. Wants me to be a stay-at-home mum – waiting for her every evening, in my pinny and gingham dress, with a cocktail in one hand and a tray of freshly baked scones in the other.'

'Yeah … don't do that. I've had your scones: volcanoes spit out rocks that are more edible. *And* less burnt.'

'Hoy!' Cheeky sod.

'Besides, they stuck a metal plate in your head, remember? That's going to take a while to get over. Even for you.' He nudged her with his elbow. 'See how *supportive* and *compassionate* I am? You should remember that when you make your retirement speech. About how I've always been an inspiration. Someone to admire and look up to.'

Roberta boinked her forehead off the window. Drooping beneath the weight of it all. 'She was *pregnant*, Laz. Someone cut off her fingers, bashed all her teeth out with a hammer, and ditched her naked body in a lay-by wheelie bin. How do I let *that* go?'

Logan reached out and put an arm around Roberta's shoulders. Pulling her in for a sideways hug. 'You've just got to do your best.' As they both frowned out at the horrible, unfair world.

Far below, a patrol car raced up Westburn Road, lights flashing.

Young families played in the park.

A pair of herring gulls squabbled over a dead pigeon.

Roberta sighed. Smiled. Then shrugged Logan's arm off. 'All right, that's enough mushy stuff. Don't want the nurses to think we're shagging.'

2.05

'And here we is.'

The pool car drifted to a halt.

Home.

Actual, proper, genuine *home.*

In all its lovely granite splendour. A big grey two-and-a-bit-storey lump with bay windows and pointy bits, a nice front garden, and scarlet rose bushes in full bloom – like blood spray. Cast-iron railings. Surrounded by like-minded properties: big and granity, on a big-and-granity street. In a swanky and exclusive part of a big-and-granity city.

Home.

The only thing bringing the neighbourhood down was Roberta's MX-5. Someone must've retrieved it from the Inverurie police station car park, abandoning the poor thing beneath a big sycamore tree outside her house. Leaving it all covered in leaves and lumps and sticky tree drips. Not to mention a bird poop or twelve.

Talk about a metaphor for her career: this thing that she loved, just rotting away…

Tufty parked in front of it, then hopped out – wearing his on-patrol kit, utility belt clanking as he jogged around to the passenger side and opened the door for her.

He stepped back, performing a deep butler bow. 'M'lady.'

Took a bit of effort, but she wriggled around, making sure

the walking stick was all set and her not-so-reliable legs firmly placed, before hauling herself upright to take a couple of limping steps towards the gate.

Weird to not be in pyjamas anymore. As if normal clothes were a foreign skin. And boots were *nowhere near* as comfy as slippers.

Tufty was still stuck in his bow, all bent over with his bum in the air.

Well, be a shame not to…

She hauled back a hand and let it fly with an almighty *SPANK.*

He yowled, leaping into the air, both hands clutching his tormented buttocks. 'OW!' Dancing away from her, face all scrunched up, holding onto his arse as if it were about to fall off. 'OW, OW, OW, OW, OW, OW!'

Roberta shook her stingy hand. 'Fifteen points.'

'Owwwwwwwwwwwwwwww!'

She hurpled around to the back of the car and popped the boot. Reaching in to drag out the holdall – packed with brightly coloured jammies and all her hospital odds-and-sods – and the knotted black bin-bag they'd handed over with her discharge letter. Everything she'd been wearing before the explosion.

Roberta had barely made it through the gate before both the holdall and the bin-bag slipped from her grasp. Because it wasn't easy when you needed your other hand for your walking stick, and staying upright was a bit of a challenge. 'Sod…'

The wee loon was still doing that high-stepping dance of his, like a hillbilly at a barn raisin'. Clutching his down-below. 'Ooooooh, that was *sore*!'

'Serves you right for leaving them on display.'

'Ow, ow, ow, ow, ow…'

'Grab the bags, eh?' She tottered along the path, unencumbered. 'Don't see why Susan couldn't take the day off and come get me. Your Sex-Goddess wife gets home from the hospital? That should be a *celebration*!' Digging out the house keys. 'Six weeks of lukewarm sponge baths and beige cauliflower cheese – I deserve a flipping parade. And a *massive* Chinese carry-out.'

Tufty rubbed at his bumcheeks. 'You better not've broken my poor pert buttocks!'

Blah, blah, blah.

She squinted at her keys, blinking to get the stupid things in focus. As if they were written in too small a font. Flipping lock was all blurry too.

'Kate says my bottoms are like unto an Greek Adonis's. She'll be *really* upset if you've made them all wonky.'

Finally, the key slid home. The lock clicked. And Roberta pushed open the old familiar door. Closed her eyes and took a deep breath – inhaling home. Which *didn't* smell of disinfectant, cabbage, and despair.

Then turned. 'You getting those bags or not?'

One hand clutching his ruined derrière, Tufty retrieved the fallen holdall and bin-bag, then limp-limp-grimace-limped his way up the garden path after her. Scowling. 'That's sexual harassment in the workplace: I should sue!' Doing a lopsided bum wince. 'Owwwwwwww…'

It was nice to spread a little joy in this heartless world.

She hobbled inside.

Home.

Framed photos festooned the walls: her and Susan on holiday in sunny places, and rainy places, and snowy places; her and Susan and Jasmine in *slightly* less exotic places; her and Susan and Jasmine and Naomi in a caravan park on Skye. Photos of Mr Rumpole in his grey fuzzy coat; and old Joseph Vissarionovich Stalin, tottering happily along the Beach

Promenade; and Genghis Khat fetching sticks in Hazlehead Park…

The rack by the door was thick with jackets and overcoats, a jumble of boots and jimmies and shoes on the tiled floor. A sideboard with a special drawer for your keys – because bowls were a bit wife-swapping-parties-esque, according to Susan. A wooden staircase reached up, its handrail dark and shiny from three generations of Steels and one of Wallace-Steels too.

Home.

Roberta threw her arms wide, keys in one hand, cane dangling from the other. 'Hello?'

Nothing.

A bit louder: 'Girls? Hello?'

More nothing.

Louder still. 'Mr Rummmmmm-pole? Gennnn-ghis?' She lumbered over to the foot of the stairs. 'ANYONE?'

No padding of little paws, or oversized trainers thumping down the wooden steps.

So much for a triumphant welcome home.

'Pish.' Roberta drooped. Then dumped her house keys in the drawer, with all the other assorted keys and key fobs.

Tufty limp-waddled into the hallway, clunking the door shut behind him. 'Bet that's going to leave a big vicious bruise.' Dropping her bags to rub at it. 'Don't understand how *anyone* could be into BDSM. Too ouchy…' Then he picked the holdall and bin-bag up again, heading for the living room. 'You want I should dump these in here?'

Little sod didn't wait for an answer, just opened the door and stepped inside. *'Any chance of a cuppa?'*

Cheeky bugger.

She pulled her shoulders back. Time to hobble in there and teach the demanding wee shite a lesson he wasn't going to forget in a…

Hold on a minute.

Aha.

Of *course*.

It was all a set-up.

The *reason* Susan hadn't come to pick her up – the *reason* the kids were nowhere to be seen, the *reason* there was no sign of Mr Rumpole or Genghis Khat – was obvious when you thought about it: they were throwing a sneaky wee party to celebrate Roberta getting out of hospital.

They were all hiding in the living room, waiting for her to walk in, so they could jump out and shout 'SURPRISE!'

Pfff…

Took her long enough to work it out. Clearly, being in hospital all that time had dulled her normally razor-honed investigative instincts.

But she got there in the end.

Roberta tried out a quick oh-my-gosh-this-is-so-unexpected! face in the hall mirror. Perfect. Meryl Streep couldn't do a better job. Then swapped the look for something more beneficent and motherly as she followed Tufty through the living-room door.

And stopped.

It should've been draped with bunting and balloons and a banner: 'WELCOME HOME LOVELY ROBERTA!' Maybe some streamers too…

Instead of which, it was the same nicely decorated, slightly old-fashioned room: two leather-buttoned sofas and matching armchairs, standard lamps, an upright piano, more framed photos, and a mantelpiece liberally sprinkled with trophies: golf, swimming, music, football, etcetera, and a taxidermied mouse, wearing little trousers and a scabby grey bra. Holding a chamber pot.

It also had an idiot in a police uniform, standing in the middle of the rug, gently massaging his own buttocks.

'What's the point of a stabproof vest if it doesn't protect your bottoms? We should be issued with … spankproof vests too! Well, spankproof *pants*.' A frown. 'I should patent that, before someone steals my idea.'

An ornate carved screen hid one corner of the room, over by Susan's collection of antique golf clubs. That was new.

Aha…

Time to get into character. 'Why *of course* I'll make you a cup of tea, young Tufty. After all, you were *kind enough* to drive me home.' Laying it on nice and thick.

Ready to be surprised in five, four, three, two, one…

But no one jumped out from behind the screen.

She shuffled over there and peered around it.

Nope.

Just the telly and its collection of audiovisual gubbins.

Maybe they were hiding behind the sofas?

Roberta tried both. No one there, either.

Tufty pulled his chin in. 'You OK, Guv?'

Hobbling back out into the hall, she made for the dining room. Which wasn't as nice as the lounge, because the large oak table was covered in one of those padded wipe-clean-vinyl things – its chairs stacked sixty-nine-style in one corner, freeing up space for piles and piles of big plastic boxes packed with craft stuff and Lego and boardgames and Airfix kits and all the kind of tat that kids and un-grown-up grown-ups liked.

But no sign of a surprise party.

Back in the hallway, Tufty was still nursing his skelped arse – forehead all wrinkled as he watched her hurple towards the kitchen. 'Should I call the hospital?' Hurrying after her. 'Are you having an "event"?'

OK: the kitchen was certainly *large* enough for a surprise party – could put sausage rolls and fancy finger sandwiches on the breakfast bar; cake, jelly and ice cream on the granite worksurfaces; streamers on the oak units; messages of love and adoration on the huge fridge-freezer…

But nobody had.

The patio doors and all the windows looked out over the long garden with its high walls; climbing frame; verdant honeysuckle, ivy, trees, and bushes; the narrow outbuildings along one side, that doubled as sheds and coal cellars and their brand-new sauna…

Where was the sizzling barbecue? The bouncy castle? The crowds of happy party guests?

No one.

Not one *single* bugger had turned up to celebrate her homecoming.

Surprise…

Roberta wilted into a seat at the breakfast bar.

'Erm… OK.' Tufty looked around, as if he hadn't been here a million times before. 'Why don't *I* make us a nice cuppa, and you can get your breath back?'

A pile of post sat on the breakfast bar, along with copies of that morning's *Press and Journal* and *Aberdeen Examiner*. The *P&J* had gone with 'THIRD BODY DISCOVERED IN DUNDEE PARK' but the *A&E* screamed 'GRISLY HORROR AS "TAYSIDE RIPPER" STRIKES AGAIN'. They both had near-identical photos, though: a blue SOC marquee, erected outside what looked like an old-fashioned observatory in a leafy park somewhere.

So everyone had just moved on from the poor pregnant cow, butchered and dumped in a wheelie bin. Distracted by something new and shiny and bloody.

The kettle rumbled to a boil.

Roberta tossed the papers in the recycling. 'There never *was* a surprise party, was there?'

Tufty made his thinky face. 'If there *was*, they didn't invite me. Poopheads.'

Urgh...

She slumped even further. 'The world is a crapshow, and all the jobbies in it fight to make life worse for each other.'

'I can nip out and gets you a cake, if it does make you feel better? *Or* ... you could bakes one!' Making head twitchy gestures at a brand-new book, lying on the countertop, with a red ribbon tied around it and a note tucked into the bow:

To Robbie, my very own Domestic Goddess!!!
With squidgles of Love,
♥♥♥ Susan ♥♥♥

Urgh...

Nigella Lawson had a lot to answer for.

Tufty bustled about, hunting down teabags and spoons and mugs, while Roberta pushed her present away and poked through the mail instead.

Bills, bills, junk, bills, junk, junk, junk... Because nothing exciting or nice ever came by post anymore.

She'd tossed all the unsolicited and 'TO THE OWNER/OCCUPIER' crap by the time the wee loon returned to the breakfast bar, carrying a pair of mugs.

'Here you goes.' Handing her the one marked 'WORLD'S #1 LESBIAN!'

Roberta frowned. 'I don't need a cake, but do you know what I *do* want?'

'Yup: ta-daaaaa!' Tufty reached into his stabproof and came out with a packet of Wagon Wheels. 'Found them when I was a-rummaging.' Grinning. 'That's what makes me a grade-A sidekick – an uncanny ability to ferret out hidden biscuity—'

'No: post-mortem report on our victim.'

He waggled the packet. 'Wouldn't you rather have *biscuits*? Biscuits are good too. Much tastier. Mmmmm... Nom-nom-nom?'

'And get me everything on that stabbing outside the campaign office too.'

The Wagon Wheels went on the worktop and Tufty watched them for a bit. As if he expected the packet would do something exciting. Which it didn't, as the silence grew.

And grew.

And—

Tufty's head snapped up, eyes wide, that daft smile back on his daft face. 'Ooh, ooh! I does has a *special thing* for you! Nearly forgotified...'

'If it's that bloody bit of pipe again—'

'No: look, look.' He delved into one of his combat trousers' many pockets then held out a small cardboard box, cupped in both hands. Like a proud father presenting a newborn. 'I has *fixed* it!'

Should've had *him* fixed.

He opened the box and there was Roberta's phone.

The screen was cracked in an almost perfect X, but when he poked the power button the thing lit up.

'I did thought it was completely borked, but then I does has *second thinks* and after much research into dark-telecommunications magics on the interwebs, applied all my technomancy skills to raise the patient from the dead! *Including* soldering.' Looking desperately pleased with himself as he struck his half-arsed gangsta pose again, addressing her phone directly: 'Oh, yeah, I did *totally* void your warranty, Baby.'

She picked the thing up.

Case was scratched, and the dangly bit Naomi had made for her was torn and half missing, and she *should've* been really grateful that he'd got her phone working at all … but somehow it was impossible to summon up the enthusiasm. For anything.

Still, better show willing: 'Thanks.' She plonked it down beside her tea.

'They wasn't going to let me have it, till I promised you wouldn't use Mr Phone to be a monster pain-in-the-hoop to anyone on the team.' A wee scowl scrunched his face. 'Not that you deserve it, after maiming my poor bottoms!'

'Speaking of which:' she gave him a steely glower, 'don't think I didn't notice you changing the subject.' Poking his stabproof vest. 'I want that post-mortem report and those stabbing updates, or it's spanking time again.'

'Ah… There's a *teeny* bit of a problem there.' Busying himself unwrapping a Wagon Wheel, not looking her in the eye. 'See: the Sarge, and Susan, and the Boss *all* thought you might ask for stuff like that and they has made it *quite* clear that poor Tufty's bottom will get more than a spanking if he aids and abets you not-resting-up-and-getting-better-at-home.' Pushing the unwrapped chocolate biscuit across the breakfast bar to her. 'Sorry.' Then unwrapping one of his own. 'But you can gets all that stuff yourself, soon as you is back at work, right?'

Not if Susan had anything to do with it.

A calendar hung on the kitchen wall, beside the fridge/freezer/monolith: 'HAIRY PUSSY OF THE MONTH!' July featured a Maine Coon Cat disporting its tummy for all to see, and beneath it, almost the whole month was crossed out – one day at a time – except for today. Scoring through the kids' extracurricular activities and Susan's meetings.

Roberta flipped the month up to see August underneath, where a fuzzy black kitten was pouncing on a pink toy mouse.

Susan had marked up a handful of things, but the month was dominated by the fifteenth. Ringed and highlighted, with loads of arrows pointing towards the two words written there. 'ROBBIE RETIRES!!!' A couple of hearts thrown in for good measure.

Two weeks, tomorrow.

Crap.

...

2.06

Lazy bees bumbled through the honeyed air, house martins swooped and twirled, while high overhead, a seagull circled like a huge fishy vulture.

Probably looking for something to poop on.

Well he could sod right off.

Roberta stretched out in her garden recliner, absorbing some sun for the first time in a month and a half. Back in her woodland-creatures jammies, because they were *far* more comfortable than the outfit Susan had provided for the journey home. Bare feet poking out. Toes wiggling in the warm, early-evening glow – skin the colour of frozen milk.

Fresh mug of tea on the patio table, glasses perched on the end of her nose, newly reunited phone in her sticky little fingers. Thumbs ticking away at the cracked screen as she texted Logan 'Missing-In-Action' McRae:

> How come you sent the wee loon to get me?
>
> You too busy being important, oh Great Emperor Laz McLimpalong?

SEND.

All the time they'd worked together, you'd think he would've made the effort.

She sipped her tea. Sighed. Stared up into the pale-blue sky.

That seagull had sodded off, but the house martins' ballet swirled on.

Chitter-cheeping erupted in the cherry tree, and a bunch of weenie birds *phrrrrrrrrr*ed out from the leafy branches as Mr Rumpole appeared on top of the wall at the far end of the garden. Resplendent in his furry tabby coat of grey and black, tail like a thick plume of smoke. He padded along the side wall on delicate white paws. Maybe a little rattier than he used to be, but then Roberta wasn't exactly a fresh-faced young thing herself.

'So *there* you are!'

He hopped into the apple tree, clambering down it with all the grace of a breeze block. Then sat in the grass, a good six foot away, staring at her with narrowed yellow eyes.

'I'm the one who should be sodding sulking. I was in that hospital for *ages*, and you never came to visit once!'

Mr Rumpole did a bit more staring, then had a wash – schlurping away at his furry tummy.

Typical man.

Ding-buzz.

LOGAN:

> Been seconded to D Division, helping out on this Tayside Ripper thing.
>
> Bit far to nip back from Dundee.
>
> Happy to be home?

Hmph…

She poked out a reply:

> Didn't discharge me till after 4!
>
> And there's nobody here!
>
> Welcome bloody back Roberta!!!

She frowned at the screen, with its furry X of misfiring pixels beneath the fractured glass. It wasn't fair that she was stuck here, all on her own, signed-off on the sick *like some sort of invalid*, while Logan gallivanted around Dundee hunting serial killers.

What's your Tayside Ripper like?

SEND.

A *clunk*-and-*rumble* sounded behind her, and there was Susan: hauling open the patio doors.

Soon as the gap was wide enough, a tootie-wee Jack Russell terrier bounded out into the back garden, barking his daft wee head off as he scampered across the patio. Making straight for Roberta. Squirrelling around her naked feet, yipping and squeaking, tail going like an over-clocked metronome. Doing his happy dance.

So at least *someone* was pleased to see her.

'Hello, Genghis Khat. Who's Mummy's little one-dog barbarian horde?' Rummling his ears and setting his back leg twitching. '*You* are, yes you are.'

Susan bustled over. 'What are you doing out here?' Leaning in, to kiss Roberta on the head. 'Sorry I'm late. Flipping partners' meeting went on and on and on and on… You know what Mortimer's like when he gets a bee in his kilt.' She clapped her hands. 'Genghis, leave that woman *alone*, you don't know where she's been.' Heading back inside, voice raised over the distance. *'I've got a bottle of Veuve Clicquot in the fridge to celebrate, or there's very nice chardonnay if you're not feeling fizzy?'*

Ding-buzz.

LOGAN:

Not good.

> He's butchered 3 male prostitutes: slit them from mouth to anus & hacked out their insides.
>
> Got search teams finding chunks of lung & liver all over the park.

Which sounded absolutely horrible. And interesting.

Lucky sod.

Susan emerged from the kitchen again, carrying two champagne flutes and a chilled dark-green bottle with a bright-yellow label. 'The kids are *both* staying over with friends, so it's just you and me tonight.' Saucy wink. 'Thought we'd order in a nice big Chinese banquet, and sit around getting all noodly in our pants.' Waggling the bottle in a suggestive manner. Then wrinkles pinched between her eyebrows. 'Are you allowed to drink, what with the ... you know ... *plate*,' silently mouthing the words: 'IN YOUR SKULL?'

Because Susan was sweet, and lovely, and sexy, but a bit daft at times.

Roberta reached for her, grinning. 'Let's find out.'

2.07

Monday: 11 days to go...

The kitchen clock ticked over to quarter past eight as Susan did her best to wrangle Naomi and Jasmine through breakfast and out the door.

Naomi was in sports shorts and a rugby top, shovelling in Chocolate Frosted Sugar Bombs and slurping from a glass of milk. Jasmine sported black jeans and a black polo-shirt, crunching away at the more sophisticated toast-and-marmalade-with-a-mug-of-tea combo. While Susan fussed and fiddled, throwing sandwiches and bananas and little packs of nuts into lunchboxes. Wearing a smart navy business suit that flattered her curves and hid the bulgy bits.

Leaving Roberta marooned at the breakfast bar, surrounded by turmoil, mayhem, and uproar – underdressed in her green lions-and-tigers jammies.

You'd think, what with it being the school holidays, Monday morning would be a bit more sedate and orderly, but no. Mayhem and anarchy reigned in the Steel-Wallace household.

Roberta screwed one eye shut to stop the text from doubling up and had another go at that morning's *Aberdeen Examiner*. 'PSYCHIC SUE SAYS "BODY-IN-BIN DEMANDS JUSTICE"' above the photo of a middle-aged woman wearing too much eye make-up and feathers in her hair. Subheading: 'MESSAGES FROM BEYOND THE GRAVE SLAM "HOPELESS" POLICE'.

Which, to be fair, was going easy on *Acting* DCI Beardy Beattie. Useless bugger could only *dream* of being hopeless. He'd have to give up being useless, incompetent, bungling, incapable, and inept to achieve the giddy heights of *hopelessness*.

Susan clapped her hands, grimacing up at the clock. 'Come on, come on, come on! Move it or lose it, mothersnudgers! Time is *money*.'

Jasmine crammed about a quarter slice of toast into her gob in one go. 'Mmmmmgh nnngh, mmmnnnnnffgh snnnrrfff?'

No idea.

Roberta put the paper down. 'I can take them.'

'Both of them? In a two-seater sports car? Is Naomi going in the boot?'

'Cool!' Naomi gave them a chocolaty grin. 'Like a mob stoolie, on their way to get whacked!'

'Besides, you're not even dressed. And I'm pretty sure the doctor said no driving for *at least* three months.' Glancing at the calendar.

The HAIRY PUSSY OF THE MONTH had moved on to August, with its fuzzy black kitten and pink toy mouse. The first three days were already crossed off. The fifteenth: *looming...*

Susan tried clapping again. 'Jasmine, Naomi: more hustle-bustle, less chatty-munch-crunch!' Kissing Roberta on the top of the head. 'Anyway, thought you were having a lie-in?'

'I did. It's quarter past eight; should've been at work over an hour ago.'

'Come on, Mum.' Jasmine pulled on her Waterstones lanyard and ID. 'I'm going to be late!'

'Then get your bum *in the car*!'

'Urgh…' Grabbing her little sister. 'Move it, Squirt, we're leaving.'

'Gennnnnn-ghis! Come on, Mummy's going.'

The cat flap flicked open and in charged Genghis Khat, claws making tap-dancing noises on the tiled floor. Barking and grinning away, like the idiot wee dog that he was.

And then it was all bags and elbows and last mouthfuls and a lead being clipped onto Genghis's collar and they were off – sweeping from the kitchen, leaving Roberta behind.

Susan's voice boomed down the hall. *'Everyone in the car, now!'*

Genghis barked and yipped.

Jasmine: *'Shotgun!'*

Naomi: *'No fair! You always—'*

Then the front door clunked shut and silence descended on the house once more.

Roberta sat at the breakfast bar, with her lukewarm coffee and half-eaten rowie. Blinking.

Jesus…

It was like starting the day in a *war* zone.

The kitchen was littered with dirty mugs, plates, and glasses; cutlery strewn everywhere, including enough buttery knives for a family of twelve, most of which made greasy splots on the worktops. They hadn't even put the bread and milk and boxes of cereal away.

There were even clumps of butter in the marmalade.

She lived with absolute sodding *minks*.

And then, into the kitchen padded Mr Rumpole. The only other sensible person in this whole asylum.

He paused in the middle of the room to stretch out his arms and back, then did one leg at a time, before looking around at the debris left behind by his noisy people.

Roberta toasted him with her mug. 'Well, Mr Rumpole, looks like it's just you and me, the day.'

Mr Rumpole examined her for a moment, then sauntered out through the cat flap and away across the garden. Disappearing over the wall.

'Thanks a flipping heap.'

Living Room (11:25)

Roberta lay on the comfiest of the two couches, knees up on the leather-buttoned arm, feet dangling, drifting through the channels on the TV. Spinning the never-ending carousel of cooking shows and daytime dramas and talking heads.

'*…the importance of setting boundaries at the very beginning of a new relationship is—*'

Click:

'*…damn it, Lieutenant, I can't be responsible for every mob—*'

Click:

'*…always loved the taste, but if you don't like coriander you can—*'

Click:

'*…day of wildfires sweeping through Oxfordshire, leaving devastated communities in its—*'

Click:

'*…because people don't really appreciate the cultural* significance *of Bananarama. They—*'

Click:

'*…bought the property at auction, but renovating it to sell has turned out to be an absolute—*'

Click:

'*…no good, Marjorie! I love you, but I simply* can't *allow you to put yourself in this intolerable—*'

Click…

Kitchen (12:05)

Roberta stood at the open fridge, leaning on her stick, staring in at the vast array of thingummies, whatnots, and takeaway containers. None of which looked even vaguely appetising.

She grimaced.

Sighed.

Then closed the fridge again.

Top Floor Hallway (12:30)

She haunted the corridor like a lumbering, three-legged ghost, looking in on the two girls' rooms. Both of which were a disastrous mess of clothes and toys and books and assorted crap.

And yes, she *could* tidy it up for them. But sod that.

She was their mum, not their maid.

Kitchen (12:50)

Roberta opened the fridge again.

For some weird reason, its contents hadn't mysteriously rearranged themselves into something deliciously exciting and interesting.

Pfff…

Back Garden (12:55)

Standing on the patio, Roberta puffed out a steamy lungful of pineapple-raspberry vape – aiming for a smoke ring, getting a lopsided bagel instead.

Chilly out here, in jammies and slippers.

Puffing away with her nips like rivets, all because Susan banned smoking and vaping indoors.

Roberta had another go: sending two amoebas, a smudge, and a blob drifting away into the grey afternoon.

God, the days were just packed…

Mistress Bedroom (13:05)

She lay on the bed, with her bare feet on the floor, toes digging into the carpet as she sighed up at the ceiling *for a change*.

Throwing in a groan for good measure.

At least back in the hospital she had nurses, and support staff, and porters, and cleaners for company.

Kitchen (13:30)

Fridge time again. Same old show.

Utility Room (13:50)

Laundry overflowed the basket. It looked as if the girls had half their wardrobes strewn across their bedroom floors and the other half down here, waiting to be washed.

Yeah… Didn't matter how bored Roberta was, she wasn't bored enough to do it. Not *yet*, anyway.

Instead, she hefted her going-home holdall onto the work-surface and unzipped it – pulling out pair after pair of cheery jammies and cramming them into the already stuffed basket. Followed by a worm's nest of socks and a pile of pants.

Next out of the bag was Boris Johnson. His eyes had gone a bit wonky from all the head-squeezing – as if he'd been on a legendary bender with Yeltsin and Berlusconi.

Then her washing kit.

And finally: that sci-fi novel the wee loon bought for her. The one that got hurled. *The Eternal Wank Of Wankity Wank-Wank*, by J.M. Wankster.

She opened it and flicked through a couple of pages.

Nope.

Dumped it on the worktop.

Stuck two fingers up to the thing.

Sagged.

There had to be *something* in the fridge.

Kitchen (14:10)

Roberta stood hunched over the breakfast bar as the microwave *burrrrr*ed away – nuking leftover beef chow mein, discovered at the back of the devious refrigerator, where it'd been hiding behind a cauliflower.

The *Aberdeen Examiner* lay open at the centre-page spread: 'UKNH CANDIDATE "RACIST RAPIST" CLAIMS EX-COP' stretched over a photo of some gammon-faced spud in a blue suit and red tie, posing with a sharp-featured woman. Both wearing red-white-and-blue election rosettes.

Graeme Anderson's political party was barely seven weeks old, and *already* mired in scandals.

Ding!

Here we go.

She removed her lunch from the microwave. 'Aaargh… Stingy, burny, hot-hot-hot…' hurrying it to a waiting plate with scalded fingers. Then creaked the top off, letting loose a huge whoosh of steam and the scents of five-spice and garlic and ginger and—

Roberta held the cardboard container of spring rolls out to Tufty – sitting there, eager as a Labrador, with his chopsticks at the ready.

'Thanks, that's—'

Searing light slashed through the car, followed by an ear-ringing BOOOOM! as the windscreen shattered into a million little pieces.

—she trembled the lid back onto her takeaway container. Grabbed her stick. And lurched from the room. Free hand clamped over her mouth to stop breakfast escaping.

A flush thundered around the toilet bowl, sweeping away the chunks and lumps.

Urgh…

Roberta levered herself to her feet, leaning all her weight on the sink. Washing her hands and face, before rinsing her mouth out with toothpaste and water.

So now everything tasted of bitter-parmesan and mint.

No idea what brought *that* on.

Didn't have any problem on Thursday night – ate enough for four people: noodles, spring rolls, prawn toast, the lot. Not a flashback in sight.

But now that old familiar jackhammer was clattering away inside her skull again.

Back in the kitchen, she broke into the tub of pills they'd sent her home with. Knocking back two co-codamol with some cold tea.

Why did nothing *nice* ever happen?

Why couldn't she just…

Hang on a minute: been forgetting something.

'The sauna! I can have a wee sweaty sit in the sauna!'

And just like that, all was right with the world again.

Ten minutes later, she was hobbling across the back garden, making for the outbuildings lined up along one wall.

Ho, ho, ho.

She'd slipped out of her PJs and into a furry dressing gown and bunny slippers, towel under one arm, bottle of chilled water clutched in her free hand.

Should've thought of this sooner.

Nice long roast in some lovely hot heat. Get a bit of steam going. Sweat the yuck right out of her.

A little wooden sign was screwed to the sauna door: 'The Police Scotland Memorial Retirement Sauna' with an extra message dangling beneath it, inscribed in Naomi's unmistakable scrawl: 'No Boyz Allowed!!!' with a skull-and-crossbones.

Quite right too.

Roberta opened the door … onto an abandoned building site. They'd bricked up the window – presumably so no pervert could cop an ogle at Susan and Roberta in the nip – making the space gloomy and grim. The walls were stripped back to the dusty stone, with a bare concrete floor, and a naked lightbulb dangling from the rafters.

Oh for *God's* sake.

She flicked the switch and a cold light picked out the thick grey snakes of electrical cabling that poked up through the concrete – one of which had a socket wobbling about on the end of it – a drain hole that was clearly going to need tiles and things to make it workable, and a blue plastic pipe with a tap attached.

It looked more like a serial killer's torture pit than a sauna: no beautiful lining of Scandinavian pine, no wooden benches, no duckboards, and nothing to make it baking sweaty hot in here. Just a big … nothing.

Wasn't easy pulling your trousers on, single-handed, when your balance wasn't up to much and you had to sit on the edge of the bed. Two hands would've been better, but Roberta needed the other one for the phone.

'Why didn't you *tell* me? I looked a right wazzock standing there in my dressing gown.'

Susan sighed. *'I didn't want to upset you.'*

'Useless lazy *bastarding* builders!' Working up a head of steam. 'I'm gonna call a taxi, head round there, and rip a strip off their arses a *mile wide*! They'll finish that sodding sauna if it's the last thing they—'

'It was me.'

Hang on.

'What?'

'I cancelled the sauna.' This time the sigh had that *resigned* tone to it. *'You've got a metal plate holding your skull together, Robbie. Do you think it's a good idea to get that sizzling hot?'*

'But...' She stopped struggling with her trousers. 'I was looking forward to—'

'So was I. But it's not worth roasting your brain for.'

Roberta opened her mouth.

Then closed it again.

Frowned at the rumpled reflection in the mirrored wardrobe doors: so much older and pastier and droopier than she'd been seven weeks ago.

Buggering hell.

Susan was right, wasn't she.

Nothing was *ever* going to be the same.

Stupid bloody explosion...

OK, so it was only five to three on a Monday afternoon, but sod it: today was officially a cocking disaster that could only be ameliorated by the application of a restorative whisky. Balvenie, Caribbean Cask, fourteen-year-old. Glass of water on the side. Wearing jammies in the garden again. Scowling at the flowering honeysuckle as if it had just crapped in her slippers. Replying to Logan's text:

Of course I'm fine.

Why wouldn't I be fine?

I'm a lady of leisure now.

No more rat race for me.

SEND.

She took a sip, rolling the sweet spicy burn around her mouth, holding it there till her gums went numb.

Butterflies chased each other between the spiky purple flowers – no idea what they were called, gardening was Susan's domain; weenie birds fought over peanuts in the feeder; somewhere, off in the distance, someone sang a sad sweet song.

And Roberta slumped in her recliner. Sipping whisky and glowering at the glowing blue sky.

Supposed to rain later in the week.

Maybe she *should* put a wash on?

...

Was *this* what the rest of her life would be: weather and washing?

How sodding depressing was—

Ding-buzz.

She scrabbled for her phone, unlocking it like a druggie, desperate for a fix.

LOGAN:

Didn't they give you a therapist to talk to?

Getting blown-up isn't your everyday experience.

You should TALK to someone!

Another sip.

Couldn't reply right away: it'd look needy. Desperate.

So, she counted to ten first.

Then thumbed out:

> You caught your killer yet?

SEND.

Roberta turned her gums numb again. Waiting.

Waiting, waiting, waiting, waiting...

Still no reply.

Gah...

Being a lady of leisure *sucked.*

She poked at the screen, coming out of her texts with Logan, and clicked on Tufty's name instead. But her last message was still at the bottom of the chain, so he hadn't replied either.

His last one sat at the top.

TUFTY:

> Just a reminder ~ we still need a wizard!
>
> You could get a character rolled up and start adventuring next Wednesday!

Then her reply:

> Roll your wizard sideways and jam him up your crumph-hole.

And her follow-up:

> Where's my post-mortem report, you wee snudge?
>
> I might be off on the sick, but I'm still your DI!
>
> DO NOT INVOKE THE SPANKING HAND'S TERRIBLE WRATH!

Yeah...

That might've been a *little* harsh.

But once you'd invoked the Terrible Wrath of The Spanking Hand you couldn't really take it back…

And he genuinely could ram his wizarding idea.

Detective Inspector Roberta Alexander Steel, playing Dungeons and Dragons? Like some spotty teenaged boy? No sodding chance in hell.

Didn't matter *how* bored she got, she wasn't doing that.

She drained the last of her dram.

Puffed out her cheeks.

Looked around the garden again…

Maybe it was time for another whisky?

2.08

Tuesday: 10 days to go...

A harsh, insistent *rinnnnnnnnnnnnnnng* cut through the darkness, bringing with it the *throb-throb-throb* of whatever the hell was trying to make Roberta's skull explode.

Ngahh...

Sunlight slashed across the room, barging in through the open curtains to attack her pale-yoghurty body. Lying buck-naked on top of the duvet, spreadeagled, taking up the whole bed. Throat dry as a mummified pharaoh's arsehole.

And then the taste hit.

Sour as bile, scorched as burnt toast, rancid, foetid, stinking...

Like a turd had died in her mouth.

The doorbell rang again.

Roberta rolled over, and the bed disappeared, sending her thumping down onto the carpet. 'Sod!'

Then she was up. Fumbling for her walking stick. Lurching like a faulty clockwork toy to the door; pulling her dressing gown on as she pushed through into the hallway.

Rinnnnnnnnnnnnnnng!

'All right, all right!' She hobbled down the stairs – the top of her head threatening to fly off with every step. 'Jesus...'

The hall tiles were cool beneath her bare feet.

Kinda nice.

Be even *nicer* if she could just lie down and rest her forehead against them. Might stop what was left of her brain from pounding its way out through her skull.

Which was *entirely* due to her traumatic head injury, and nothing to do with the half bottle of Balvenie she'd put away yesterday afternoon, before Susan and the kids got back.

Though everything after that third large dram was a bit hazy.

Did she even put herself to bed?

Roberta hurpled to the welcome mat, stepped over a small-ish rectangle of paper, undid the deadbolt, and threw the front door wide.

No one there.

A white van pulled away from the kerb outside her house, sodding off down the street with ceilidh music skirling out through its open windows.

As if her headache wasn't bad enough.

She scowled after it – because sod giving chase with a walking stick and a gammy leg – mouth smacking on that God-awful taste. The turd must've had friends over…

Shutting the door again, she bent to retrieve the bit of paper – sending the world fizzing round and around like a catherine wheel – closed her eyes and stood up again. Which only made everything spin faster. Holding on to the doorknob till her house stopped whirling.

It took a while…

Roberta peeled one eye open. 'WE TRIED TO DELIVER, BUT YOU WERE OUT'. The card came with a complicated set of instructions for how to rearrange delivery or pick-up from the depot.

'Gah…'

She tossed the thing over her shoulder, turned, and wobbled her way to the kitchen.

Today was going to require a *lot* of coffee.

The train growled into the station, but every stick of clothing from her suitcase was scattered under her seat. And although there were about a hundred pairs of shoes down there, none of them were *hers*. Scrabbling, naked, to get everything repacked – when a voice came over the carriage intercom:

'Oh, Robbie, not again!'

'Mmmmmph...?' She jerked awake.

Garden.

Lying in the back garden.

On her recliner.

A copy of today's *Aberdeen Examiner* was draped across her chest. 'BRAVE BILLIE BATTLES FOR BREATH' above a photo of Billie Nesbit, still and pale in her hospital bed. They'd included a wee picture of her from before the stabbing – all smiling and pretty, with her long red hair, cute little nose, and freckles. 'STABBING VICTIM PUT ON VENTILATOR AS DOCTORS FIGHT TO CURE HOSPITAL SUPERBUG'.

Roberta scrubbed a hand across her own, much saggier face, working a bit of life back into the skin. Stifling a yawn. 'Time is it?'

Susan towered over her, fists on hips. 'Hmph. Well, at least you're *sober* tonight.' Pulling her chin in, doubling it up. 'You *are* sober, aren't you?'

Bit harsh.

Roberta sat up. 'That's no—'

'You can't just lounge about drinking whisky all day!'

'I know, I know.' Waving at the cold mug of half-drunk tea. 'See? No whisky. I'm just...' What? What *was* she? A frown. 'I don't know. A wee boat, rudderless on a stormy sea of shark-infested shite?'

Susan raised an eyebrow. 'You? A "wee boat"?'

'I got blown-up! Stuck in that hospital bed for ages—'

'Six weeks, one day, sixteen hours, and twenty-seven minutes. Not counting the time you were in surgery.' The hands slipped from her hips, an indulgent smile on her lips. 'And how are sharks supposed to live in a sea of shite? They're fish: they'd suffocate.' Clearly trying to lighten the mood.

But... Roberta sat there, frowning out at the garden.

Silence.

The bees buzzed.

Down at the far end, Mr Rumpole descended from the back wall and slunk his way towards them, through the long grass.

Roberta's shoulders curled forwards, knees together. Shrinking. 'Being a police officer's a pain in the arse, but I've been doing it for *thirty years*: it's all I know. And now...? Who even *am* I?' Because there was only so much not-thinking-about-it one person could do. And the whole thing was so much *worse* than it should've been. Maybe it was the hangover, or maybe it was the three-inch titanium plate in her head, but it was *something*. A knot tightened in Roberta's throat, making her voice squeak as the garden slipped out of focus. 'I'm lost, Susan. I'm *lost*.' Wiping away a burning tear. 'And I'm terrified.'

'Oh, Robbie.' Susan wrapped her up in a soft warm hug. 'Shhh...'

Mr Rumpole wound his ratty-old-self around their ankles. Purring.

Roberta hugged her back, squeezing tight. Sniffing. 'What am I going to *do*?'

'Want to know who you are?' Susan let go. Taking Roberta's face in her hands instead. '*You*, are Roberta Alexander Steel: wife, mother, and all-round pain in *my* arse. And you promised to love, honour, and obey me, so—'

'I did *not*!' Forcing a brave wee smile. '"Love, honour, and cherish," I said.'

'*So*, as your responsible adult-slash-carer, I'm telling you we'll work it out. Together. You just … need something to keep this busy.' Tapping Roberta's forehead. 'Till this,' the fingers moved down to tap Roberta's chest instead, 'figures out what it wants to do.'

'My left boob?'

'Your *heart*, you idiot.'

Roberta squeegeed a palm across her damp cheeks. 'Can it involve Keira Knightley and a jar of Nutella?'

'Not according to the restraining order, no.' Susan pulled her close again. Lips warm and soft against Roberta's ear. 'Now, how about we find you a nice hobby instead?'

Thursday: 8 days to go…

Stupid bloody golf.

'Did you no' hear what I said? She's got me playing *golf*! Spudging golf!' Roberta hobbled about in the knee-high grass at the side of the thirteenth fairway, phone in one hand, swinging her walking stick like a scythe every couple of limping steps. Still looking for her *sodding* ball. Which should've been pretty easy to spot, given it was the same shade of embarrassed-pink as the shirt Susan had laid out *specially* for her to wear this morning.

It really set off the ugly, green, diamond-pattern tank-top, pink knee-high socks, and tan plus fours. All of it at least one size too big for her, because they were Susan's clothes. Which meant Roberta couldn't even complain about how much of a tit it made her look.

Even though it did.

A complete and utter buggering *tit*.

At least there weren't many people out here to see her, whacking away like a … tit.

The fairway was a long stretch of manicured stripy grass, gone slightly green-and-yellow after the unseasonal heat wave. Her golf bag sat on its wheely stand, parked about a third of the way down – also borrowed from Susan.

Pines bordered both sides of the thirteenth hole, with the fourteenth clearly visible through a thin strip of trees. Because there were still another five flipping holes to go after this one.

Assuming Roberta ever found her wanking ball.

Logan's voice was flat, distracted. *'Uh-huh.'*

She whacked the crap out of a clump of bracken. 'And don't get me started on the clothes! I look like a comedy sex offender from the nineteen seventies.'

'Hmmmm…'

Whack, whack, whack.

'Stupid way to spend a morning.'

'Uh-huh.'

She stopped swinging. 'Are you even listening to me?'

'Whinge, moan, complain: golf, clothes, and whatever?' A grunt. *'You remember I'm trying to catch a serial killer, right?'*

She glowered out at the idiots on the fourteenth hole. '*I* should be catching serial killers. Not spaffing about on a scrunking golf course dressed like a clown's testicle!'

'And yet, here we are.' His voice went all muffled, as if he'd put the phone against his chest. *'OK. Bill: let's try cutting the numbers a bit. Can you bring up everyone with previous for kerb crawling? Male* and *female; don't care if they were trying to pick up same or opposite sex. … Thanks.'*

Yeah, here they were. With him lording it up on a juicy case, while she was stuck on the buggering *golf* course.

If the man had *one ounce* of decency – or common sense – he'd be falling over himself to ask her for help. What with all of her experience and expertise and knowing how to catch dodgy bastards.

Time to try laying on a bit of the old guilt…

'One week tomorrow, Laz. That's all I've got till it's "Goodbye, Roberta, nice knowing ya!" And *then* what've I got to look forward to – twenty years of whacking a stupid golf ball around?' Sniff. 'You think that's a proper use of my talents?'

Hint, hint, hint.

Logan was back to full volume. *'Well why don't you try Tufty's Wednesday game, then?'*

'No' you as well!' Whack! Whack-whack-whack!

'Look at it from his *point of view: you're old enough to be his nan, and he's* still *asking you to come play make-believe with him and his little friends. Wee loon's doing you a favour.'*

Cheeky sod.

'I'm nowhere *near* old enough to be his grandmother!'

'You keep telling yourself that.' Logan went all muffled again: 'Now *we're getting somewhere. … Do the records say who our kerb-crawlers tried to pick up? … Uh-huh. … OK.'*

Whack. Whack. Whack!

'And do I look like the kind of person who goes about pretending to be a wizard, or a … flipping troll, elf, whatever?' Throwing her free arm wide, walking stick poking straight up like an oddly shaped sword. Standing there, looking down at herself.

Yeah. That was *exactly* the kind of person she looked like. Only worse.

'No, I'm guessing he's maybe tried to pick up a male prostitute in the past. Or tried to pick up a female one and got an unwelcome surprise. … Or maybe that's what he tells himself?'

She sagged back against a tree. 'And this afternoon, after golf and "lunch with the girls" do you know what we're doing? Bloody pottery class!'

'*Got to be some reason he's targeting gay sex workers.'*

Someone must've replied to that, their voice reduced to a muted rumble in the background.

Then it was Logan again. *'Course I'm not sure. But it's worth a punt, isn't it? … Exactly.'*

'Yesterday it was basket weaving, followed by a spa trip.' She thwacked a pinecone out onto the fairway. Which was the best shot she'd made since embarking on these eighteen holes of horror. Which sounded like a very dodgy porn film that she'd *definitely* watch. 'Susan's taken three days off to "entertain" me, like I'm a sodding six-year-old on half term. I'm in my prime here, sharpest officer NE Division has ever seen, a sodding detecting *machine*!' Kicking at the long grass…

A hot-pink golf ball winked up at her from the depths.

'Oh. There it is.'

'OK, get a car and we'll work our way through them.'

Clearly, Logan McRae was too thick to pick up on her subtle cues. 'Are you going to beg me to help you catch this Ripper, or no'?'

And just like that, he was back at full volume. *'Look, I've got to go; might have a lead on our killer.'*

Bloody *men*.

'You haven't heard a word I've said!'

'Nope. But that's what friends are for. Tell Susan I said "Hi."'

Then the line went dead. He'd hung up.

Typical.

She slumped, staring up through the needled branches at the pale-grey sky. Still, at least she'd found her stupid ball.

Roberta carried the thing back to the fairway. Holding it up as she waved her walking stick at the green. 'GOT IT!'

Susan waved back. Because unlike Roberta, she'd got all the way down there with two shots on a par four. As opposed to Roberta's nine to just get *this* far.

And the humiliation wasn't over yet.

She dropped her recovered ball, then pulled a random golf club from the bag. Sighed. 'Come on, Roberta: only twenty years or so till you can drop dead and never play this idiotic game ever again…'

OK.

Deep breath.

She set up her shot, just like Susan taught her: feet shoulder width apart, knees slightly bent, lean forward, weight on the balls of the feet, tap the club on the ground, just behind the ball, line everything up, twist into the backswing, then *strike* – smooth and fast – like a cobra. Follow through, hips facing the green, weight on the front foot…

And her ball was still right where she'd dropped it.

Missed.

Oh for God's sake.

Roberta tried again.

Missed again.

Once, twice, three times.

Stupid *bloody* golf.

2.09

Tuesday: 3 days to go...

Chaos ruled the kitchen once more, as Susan attempted to sheepdog the monsters out the door. 'All right, that's time: all aboard who's coming aboard!' Taking one last swig of coffee, before clunking the mug down and giving Roberta a sweet, decaffeinated kiss.

Susan was in her linen power suit this morning. Jasmine: back in bookseller black. Naomi: wearing denim dungarees and a red-and-white stripy top. Sort of *Deliverance* meets *Where's Wally?* While Roberta sagged there, keeping out of pandemonium's way, in her woodland-creature jammies.

Grey light drooped through the windows and patio doors – the miserly glow of a dark day, threatening rain.

Susan stroked Roberta's back. 'You going to be all right today? I'm sorry I can't—'

'Never better.' Holding a hand up to forestall any fuss. 'And don't worry: the wee loon's taking me for my check-up. They'll just have a prod about, declare me a "magnificent sexy beast of a woman", and send me on my way.'

'I *am* sorry.' Frowning at the *Aberdeen Examiner*, laid out on the breakfast bar. 'And you shouldn't be reading that stuff. It'll only upset you.'

The front page was dominated by '"GAS LEAK" WAS "COVER-UP" SAYS TOP COP' with yet another photo of Roberta being carried out of the dust. Subheading: 'WESTHILL BLAST WAS "A TERRORIST PLOT" CLAIMS EX-SUPERINTENDENT'.

A hug, a quick smooch on the forehead, and Susan gathered up the pre-packed lunches. '*Move* it, you two! Genghis!'

In he skittered on clicker-clack nails that still needed trimming. Almost wagging his back end off as Susan clipped on his lead.

Roberta buttered a second slice of toast. 'You know, you could leave the wee man with—'

'It's no trouble, honestly, and I got used to having him around the office when you were away. Stops Adriana from stealing all the fancy client biscuits. Three months pregnant and she's the size of a caravan. Swear that woman can unhinge her jaw and swallow a whole packet of Tunnock's Caramel Wafers in one go.'

'But—'

'KIDS! I'm leaving, *right* now. If your bum's not in—'

'All right, all right.' Jasmine pulled on her lanyard. 'Jeesh, what a total Vogon.' Pausing only to give Roberta's cheek a peck as she stole her buttered toast. 'Thanks. Catch ya' later, investigator.' Chomping as she strode off.

Naomi slurped the last gunky-brown-milky residue from her cereal bowl, gave Roberta a chocolaty kiss, then scarpered after her sister. 'Shotgun, shotgun, shotgun!'

'They'll be the death of me, I swear it.' Susan straightened her jacket. 'If you can put a load of socks and pants on, and empty the dishwasher, that would be great.' Clapping her hands. 'HAS EVERYONE GOT EVERYTHING?' Marching out of the kitchen. *'Move it, people: clock is ticking!'*

Naomi: *'I called shotgun, I called shotgun!'*

Jasmine: *'God, you're such a—'*

The front door clunked shut.

Silence.

This must've been what it was like at the Battle of the Somme, when the artillery finally stopped. Only with fewer dirty dishes and abandoned buttery knives.

Roberta puffed out her cheeks and surveyed the devastation.

Life was so much easier when she was up and out of the house while they were all still asleep.

The utility-room door hung open – letting in the *hummmmm* and *whoosh-whoosh-whoosh* of an expertly loaded dishwasher – while Roberta sorted socks and pants into two piles. Colours on one side, whites on the other. Because she wasn't making *that* mistake again.

The first load got stuffed into the machine with a cap of squirty liquid. *Beep, beep, click*. And it was off.

Right.

She stuck the lid on the laundry basket and pushed it into the under-counter alcove it came from. Only the stupid thing wouldn't go.

Haul it back out. And shove it in again.

As the actress said to the bishop.

Still no.

Had to be something blocking the hole…

Ooh, *Matron*.

So Roberta pulled it all the way out – fnarrrr… – and checked the alcove.

A black bin-bag lay crumpled in the space, half-filled and tied at the top. Which was weird, because the rubbish went straight from the kitchen bin to the black wheelie outside. Even if it was raining. Because otherwise, what was the point of having kids?

Suspicious.

Police radar pinging, she fished the thing out with her stick, plonked it on top of the worksurface and untied it – releasing a funky, sweaty-sweet, cloying fug. Somewhere between fusty meat and manky mildew.

It was her clothes. The ones she'd been wearing when the explosion went off at Silvermoss Business Centre. Bagged up on admission to Aberdeen Royal Infirmary and returned when she was discharged.

Urgh…

Given that everything in there was covered in dried blood and dust and hairy mould, it probably wasn't wise to touch anything with her bare hands. So she dug through the cupboard under the sink for a pair of yellow rubber gloves. Snapping them on, as if about to perform an *extremely* intrusive full-body-cavity search.

Time to make the bag bend over and grab its ankles.

There was no sign of her stabproof, high-vis, or utility belt. But they'd been in the back of the patrol car, crushed beneath a big metal logo. Instead, she pulled out what remained of her clingy black T-shirt and itchy black trousers – both slit open when the trauma team cut them off her. Her pants were severed on both sides too, though thankfully skidmark free. Which was a worry when you'd just been blown-up. That kind of thing could startle even the most stoic of bumholes.

Her socks were hard as boomerangs, but the Doc Martens looked salvageable. Just need to clean off the mould and air them out a bit; they'd be good as…

Oh God.

Roberta let go, and a fusty boot tumbled down to bounce against the tiled floor.

Please no, please no, please no…

Trembling yellow-gloved fingers reached into the bin-bag,

easing out Old Faithful, her long-serving, long-suffering, Playtex 'Magic Feeling' bra.

Normally, it was a sort of ancient-grey colour, all the white washed-out by years and years of use and abuse, but now Old Faithful was stained dried-blood brown and speckled with mildew.

She cradled the poor thing in her hands, like an injured kitten, biting her bottom lip as she took in the sheer *horror.*

Barbed wire coiled in her throat.

They'd cut both bra straps and one of the wings.

Old Faithful ... was dead.

Mr Rumpole lurked beneath the rhododendron bush – staying out of the drizzle, because he wasn't an idiot – watching Roberta dig a wee grave in the flower bed.

One shovel wide and two shovels deep, not far from a small granite headstone engraved: 'JOSEPH VISSARIONOVICH STALIN ~ A BRAW, STINKY, LITTLE OLD DOG, MUCH LOVED & MISSED ~ 2002–2021'. Even though they'd only had him for his twilight years.

The rain misted her face, giving her jammies a velvety fuzz of tiny droplets to go with the muddy cuffs.

She put her spade to one side and gently lowered Old Faithful into the hole. Then stood there, with her head bowed and her right hand over her heart. Swallowed. 'You were a good and faithful bra, and we had some bloody wonderful—'

'Take Your Mama' blared out from her jammie-jacket's top pocket, ruining the solemnity of the occasion.

'Sonofafarting...' She checked the screen: 'TUFTY', then answered. 'What do *you* want?'

'We still on for this afternoon, Guv?' Sounding cheery. Because

he was an idiot. *'You know, for the hospital visit-slash-check-up thing?'*

She pinched her face closed, locking the shouting-and-swearing in a grave, two shovels deep. Because the wee loon might be an idiot, but he was doing her a favour. 'Yes.'

'Coolio. See you at one, and we can talk about your wizard character!'

'I'm no' having *any* bloody…'

But he'd already gone.

Roberta blinked out into the rain, put her phone away, closed her eyes, shook her head, then grabbed her shovel and filled in the grave.

Her soggy pyjama bottoms *schlapp*ed into the utility-room sink, followed by the soggy top. Both stained brown-and-black with grave dirt. Leaving Roberta standing there in the nip, with only a pair of bunny-eared slippers to cover her modesty. AKA: feet.

Cool air crept across her damp skin, goosepimpling it as she frowned at the mound of cut-off pre-explosion clothes sitting on the draining board.

Kind of forgotten all about them, what with the impromptu funeral and everything…

Might as well stuff it all in the bin, then head off for a nice warm soak in the tub.

She pulled on the yellow rubber gloves again.

Then paused.

Bet someone out there would find the butt-naked-with-Marigolds look *unspeakably* kinky.

Might try it on Susan, later.

But first: bin the mouldy crap.

It would be a shame to throw out her last ever set of official inspector's epaulettes, though. So she unbuttoned them from the T-shirt before tossing the remaining rag back in the bin-bag. Then went through the hacked-open trousers' pockets, making a little pile of bits and bobs: one hanky, cardboard-stiff and brown with dried blood; wallet, featuring credit, debit, and library cards; twenty-six quid, thirty-tuppence in notes and smush; a lottery ticket, now completely unreadable; her vape, all dented, cracked, and spidered with musty growth; and last of all – three folded sheets of A4 paper.

They were stained around the edges, but the inside bits were still perfectly readable: printouts from the Police National Computer. This would be the number plates Wee Davey McLeod begged her to run for him. Rory Hatton's red Jaguar F-Pace, Charlotte MacNeal's lime-green Toyota Yaris, and Jeremy Yarrow's ancient, brown Daihatsu Fourtrak.

Whoever the hell *they* were.

Hmmm...

Never did find out what the old bugger wanted with these.

Maybe Tufty had been right and Davey *was* up to something sketchy?

Drugs?

Could be.

Extortion scam?

Or some sort of people-smuggling thing?

The northeast of Scotland had a whole *smörgåsbord* of criminal activities, and Davey could be tucking in to any of them.

Roberta crammed her ruined trousers, pants, socks, vape, and that crusty hankie, back into the bin-bag and retied the top. Leaving her Doc Martens and epaulettes on the draining board for cleaning later. Then headed through the house, dressed only in bunny slippers and Marigold gloves.

She stuffed the black plastic bag in the kitchen bin. Then

snapped off her rubber gloves, perched her naked bum at the breakfast bar, and called up her texts.

Clicked on the thread titled 'UNKNOWN NUMBER' and scrolled through Davey's messages.

UNKNOWN NUMBER:

> Much though I hate to nag?!?

UNKNOWN NUMBER:

> Hello? Is everything OK? I'm still outside if it helps?

Hadn't seen the most recent one before, but going by the timestamp he'd sent it eight weeks ago, just before the explosion:

> You didn't have to run away like a weird little kid! We worked together for years! Thought we were friends!?!
>
> I covered your arse heaps of times!
>
> The least you could do is talk to me!!!

She wriggled her uncovered arse in her seat, frowning at that last message.

He was definitely up to *something*, but what?

Only one way to find out.

She thumbed out a reply on the cracked screen:

> I survived the blast, thanks for asking.
>
> What did you want those number plates for?

Should really get dressed; this wasn't Ibiza. Couldn't just paint your exciting bits happy colours and go dancing on Aberdeen beach. Get frostbite, apart from anything else…

Besides, the Idiot Child would be here to pick her up soon. And she was *far* too much woman for a wee squit like him to see in the nip. He'd die from excitement, and—

Her phone launched into 'Take Your Mama' again.

And there it was, glowing in the middle of the screen: 'UNKNOWN NUMBER'.

Of course, it *could* be anyone.

But kind of guessing it wasn't.

Roberta let the call ring through to voicemail, then went upstairs to change.

The patrol car took a left, between the blood transfusion centre and what looked like a clandestine incinerator. Taking the long way around, because going straight up Foresterhill Road was verboten for anything other than buses and bicycles. Which just gave Tufty extra time to bore Roberta to death before she reached the hospital.

'…and *then* you roll a D-twenty to determine your *Wisdom* – which is different from your Intelligence, of course – and that gets a modifier too, based on the base roll and the corresponding value in the table in the player handbook…'

He was wearing the full Police Scotland outfit again, which was nowhere near as stylish as Roberta's purple-'LESBIAN MAFFIA'-T-shirt-and-blue-hoodie combo.

Didn't matter how many times she yawned at him, he just kept droning on. And on. And on.

The drizzle had thickened to a light rain, pattering down from an ashen sky as they crawled around the staff car park at the mandatory twenty-miles-per-hour.

Roberta checked her phone.

The 'UNKNOWN NUMBER' call she hadn't answered came from 0770 090 0382. The same mobile as Davey's texts. Which meant he must've rung *seconds* after getting her message.

Talk about keen.

And *suspicious*.

His voicemail sat there un-listened-to, because Tufty had turned up – honking his horn and waving like a moron.

'...so: you've rolled for Strength, Dexterity, Constitution, Intelligence, Wisdom, and Charisma, and now we get to feed those scores into the rest of your character...'

On and on and on and on.

She saved the 'unknown' number in her phone, creating a new contact called 'SKETCHY DAVEY', because at least this way she'd be forewarned when he called.

A big, brutalist, metallic fishing creel loomed up ahead. The multistorey car park.

Tufty slowed even further, indicating right, to take the turning. '...cos your Saving Throws are determined by adding your Ability and Proficiency modifiers together, so— OW!'

'No. No multistorey. Drop me off: front of the hospital.'

He stared at her, mouth hanging open. 'But ... is ambulances and buses *only*!'

'You're a patrol car, for snudge's sake. It's *raining*. And I'm practically disabled. Got a traumatic head wound, here!' Jiggling her walking stick at him. 'Might no' be able to walk far, but I can still batter wee farts unconscious with this!'

'Eeek...' His eyes darted from hers, to the stick, to the multistorey, and back again. Then he switched off the indicator and drove past the car park in silence. Slightly shrunken into his stabproof vest like the cowed little turtle that he was.

Good.

She put her phone away. 'Where did you get with ID'ing our bin body?'

'I *told* you: I'm not allowed to—'

'Hey!' Mr Stick raised his vengeful head again. 'You want a traumatic head wound of your very own?'

'*Encore la* eeek!' He slowed for the junction, turning right, down the hill towards ARI proper. 'We've got no idea who she is. Was.'

'Oh for... How can Beattie *still* no' have—'

'She'd been in that bin for maybe a month and a half, which is bad enough, but it'd been baking-hot for *weeks*, and the bin's *black* so it just sooked up the heat. Like a big ... wheelie ... slow cooker.' Tufty shrugged. 'Everything inside, basically, *casseroled*. Right down to the bone marrow. TLDR? The DNA's borked. If we'd found some teeth, then *maybe* it would be different, but we didn't so it's the same.'

He winced as the patrol car violated the box junction outside the hospital's main entrance. Grimaced at the no-left-turn 'EXCEPT BUSES' sign. *Cringed* as he defied it and did indeed turn left, crawling between twin no-entry signs. Squirming on the short drive to the entrance proper, cheeks going nuclear-scarlet, little wisps of metaphorical steam fizzing out the top of his beetroot ears. 'So we've got spudge-all DNA, no dental, no fingerprints, nothing obvious on the bones – no old breaks that've healed we can match against doctors' records – *or* implanted medical devices with nice traceable serial numbers, and all the hot sludge stewed her hair to a grey fibrous moosh.' He parked outside the double doors. 'Even *Sherlock Holmes* couldn't identify her, never mind Beardy Beattie.'

Maybe the wee loon had a point?

Didn't stop Beattie being an idiot, though.

Tufty fidgeted in his seat. 'No offence, Guv, but any chance you could get out of the car? I has the *major* squeams sitting here, and I'd like to go park somewhere that does not has an "Against the Rules!"'

Hmph...

Roberta struggled her way out of the passenger seat and

into the rain. Turned to glare at him through the open door. 'You better be waiting here when I get out.'

Then *clunk*ed it shut, and hobbled towards the entrance.

The patrol car was off before she'd taken more than a couple of steps. Coward.

She limped past a knot of soggy smokers and into an entrance that should've been impressive, given how massive Aberdeen Royal Infirmary was, but somehow managed to look more like the side exit from a failing shopping centre in some Teuchter hick backwater town.

Past the wee Markies, a café, and a couple of shops.

The reception area was a bustling open space, with visitors in their rain-dripping jackets; patients in their gowns, jammies and scuffing slippers; porters, doctors, nurses, and support staff in their scrubs and uniforms…

Roberta kept going, ignoring the information kiosk and making for the glazed walkway through to the Pink Zone.

Which was going to take a while at this speed.

Might as well entertain herself on the way.

So she dug out her phone, scrolling as she lumbered across the scuffed Terrazzo floor, bringing up her voicemail and poking Davey's message. Setting it playing:

'Hello? Hi.' He cleared his throat. *'I was… I saw what happened on the TV. Wow. Quite something, eh?'*

Bit of a sodding understatement.

She stepped into the glass-walled corridor, leaving the Yellow Zone behind. It was toasty-hot last time, in the blazing sunshine, but now it was drab and cold, rain streaking down the glass, rippling the grey world beyond.

'Here: do you mind Martin Lynch? PC, hairy, had that thing on his bum? Two of Wee Hamish Mowat's goons ran him over in a hearse. Mind him?' Sounding all nostalgic. *'What were their names … Kenny Something. And Big Steve McHugh?'*

Did Davey really think she'd fall for this?

Oh, yeah, it was dressed up as a harmless wee shamble down memory lane, but he was just trying to establish a rapport. Look at this anecdote from our shared past: aren't we the best of friends! You want to help your *friends*, don't you?

Manipulative tosspot.

'You'd think, if you were nicking a vehicle to go ram-raiding, you'd want something sportier than a hearse, but Kenny aye had something loose up-top.' A laugh. *'Back of the hearse is full of stolen VHS recorders, and there's Mikey, trying to flag the buggers down – and* bang*! Goes flying.'*

Roberta limped off the walkway and into a gloomy corridor with magnolia walls and a padded grey bumper strip. No windows. No natural light. Only doors.

They'd painted a hot-pink bar along the top of the wall, and put all the signage in fuchsia, but it didn't help. The corridor still looked like a well, and everyone who stepped into it was falling…

'Broke both his legs and three ribs, cracked two vertebrae, then the buggers reversed over him, trying to finish the job. Twice. Was in traction for months.'

She turned the corner to where the lifts lurked. Each one boasting hot-pink doors with a big white '2' on them. Even though she'd just come straight through from the ground floor.

Roberta picked the nearest and pressed the call button.

'Rumour has it, Wee Hamish had Marty picked up from the hospital, day before he was discharged, and whisked him off to a farm out Loch of Skene way.'

Ding.

An unconvincing voice scratched out of the lift's speakers: *'DOORS OPENING.'*

She stepped inside.

No need to consult the magenta-backed list of wards and offices, she'd been here long enough. The only other splashes of colour were the strips of blue duct tape, holding the peeling grey floor together.

'Plonked him down in an armchair, gave him a beer, and let him watch as Reuben battered the living shite out of Kenny and Steve. Then treated him to a fish supper on the way back to the hospital.'

Roberta poked the button for the third floor, then did it again, poke-poke-poke-poke. Because a harassed-looking mother, with two snottery kids in tow, was rapidly approaching.

Come on, come on…

Davey sighed. *'Wonder what happened to him…'*

Poke-poke-poke-poke!

'Doors Closing.'

And they did, *just* in time to make sure Mummy Dearest and her disgusting mucus-dripping children would have to spread their germs all over the next one.

There was silence from the phone as the lift juddered upwards.

Then: *'Yeah. Sorry. The good old days, eh? Anyway: I'm glad you didn't die.'* This time the pause had a sleekit edge to it. Here came the big sell. *'Erm…'* Another throat clearance, every phlegm must go. *'Look, I don't suppose you've – I mean, if you're back at work, after the explosion – cos … those number plates would still be a* huge *help.'* Followed by a hopeful, *'If you've got them?'*

Ding.

'Doors Opening.'

Roberta stepped out into the old, familiar, claustrophobic half-light of Neurology & Neurosurgery. With that unrelenting background hum, and the paintings she'd limped past hundreds and hundreds of times before.

'Doors Closing.'

Making her way along the well-trodden corridors.

'Right, well, you've got my number.' Deep breath. *'I'm sorry you got hurt. … Anyway, bye.'*

Followed by a harsh electronic voice: *'End Of Messages. To Replay This Message, Press—'*

Roberta hung up.

Then flattened herself against the corridor wall to let a porter trundle someone past in one of those chairs that looked like a cross between an instrument of torture and a mobile toilet.

The porter gave her a cheery wave on his way past, but the teenaged girl in his chair just sagged there, all the hair missing on one side of her head, a puckered scar making an 'S' shape across the pale-grey skin. Stitches poking out of it, as if a score of spiders were trying to escape from her skull.

Roberta stood there, watching her disappear down the corridor. Sighed.

Poor wee thing…

Still, no point moping about it.

Got an appointment to keep.

2.10

Roberta sat in her creaky plastic seat, in the corner of the waiting area, as far away from the other three patients as possible. Frowning down at her phone as she poked out a reply to Davey.

> I'm not giving you sod-all until you tell me WHY you want those number plates.

SEND.

The room wasn't exactly inspiring. Wasn't really a room either, more a doglegged corridor with a dozen cheapo plastic chairs, some posters about getting vaccinated and not doing drugs and looking out for diabetes and how to spot someone having a stroke... And the obligatory coffee table, covered in ancient magazines and local newspapers.

Most of which seemed to be *Aberdeen Examiners* from last week. Their front pages were split between pointing out how crap NE Division was for not solving the Body-In-The-Bin murder, and how crap D Division was for not catching the Tayside Ripper, and how crap N Division was for not arresting whoever it was that kept leaving jobbies under the windscreen wipers of all the councillors in Inverness.

The most recent edition had broken the mould with 'BRAVE BILLIE BEATS SUPERBUG', featuring a blurry photo of Billie Nesbit sitting up in her hospital bed, looking pale as snow, with heavy purple bags under her eyes – no doubt covertly snapped by some nosy arsehole on their mobile. An insert pic, taken at the mini-riot, which showed Billie lying on the road with a knife in her guts. 'STABBING VICTIM "IN GOOD SPIRITS" SAY GRATEFUL PARENTS'.

Which was a relief, after everything the poor—

'Take Your Mama' blared out from Roberta's phone, and there it was, glowing in the middle of the cracked screen: 'SKETCHY DAVEY'.

The waiting patients all turned to stare at her.

Tempted to answer it, just to spite them.

Still, that would mean *talking* to the bugger.

She hit 'DECLINE', then *tic-tic-tic-tic-tick*ed out a message instead:

> Not taking any calls till you lay it out for me.
>
> IN WRITING!

A nurse bustled into the waiting area, clutching a clipboard to his pigeon chest. Long hair pulled back in a pigtail, which made his already sharp features even pointier. Like he'd heard about Roberta's Birdheads and fancied the look. He checked his clipboard. 'Victoria Bervie?'

A large woman wearing a damp tweed jacket and sex-free cardigan levered herself out of her chair and was led away into the bowels of the ward.

Ding-buzz.

SKETCHY DAVEY:

> You think I'm murdering people or something?

Tick, tick, tic-tic-tic-tic-tick:

> OK.
>
> Bye Davey.

SEND.

Should've brought a magazine or something – glancing at the coffee table, with its prehistoric copies of *Good Housekeeping* and *Boring Wank Monthly*. Or a book. Even that stupid Sci-Fi thing would be better than nothing.

And there was only so much Hedgehog Hodgepodge one woman could play, before—

Ding-buzz.

SKETCHY DAVEY:

> It's a divorce case.
>
> Mrs X thinks Mr X is screwing around behind her back and hiding cash/shares/bank accounts.
>
> These are 3 cars from staking out his business premises. Regular visitors.

Roberta sat back in her seat, lips pursed, chewing on that little revelation.

Tasted kind of fishy.

> So, you're Sam Spade now?

SEND.

A second nurse appeared: short and pencil-thin, with dark hair in a manky-mushroom bob. Another clipboard. 'Peter Waring? Peter Waring?'

Peter scrambled upright in his baggy skater-dude clothes. Like the girl in the porter's chair, his long hair was shaved on one side, only his was growing-in around a twisted curl of pink scar tissue. His hoodie declared 'SMASH THE SYSTEM!', but he trotted after Nurse Mushroom like an obedient puppy.

Ding-buzz.

Only if Sam Spade did nothing but nasty divorces and missing person cases.

No mysterious dames or maltese falcons in ABZ.

Well, well, well... Who'd have thought it: Wee Davey McLeod, private eye. Aberdeen's answer to Humphrey Bogart... Only not so much 'Bogie' as 'Snotters'.

Her thumbs got to work:

I'll do you a deal. We

'Roberta Thteel?'

She looked up and there was a nurse with dozens of holes in his ears and a couple in his nose too. Add in the pointy black fringe, ink-black hair, and missing eyebrows, and it was a safe bet he was a full-bore Goth, playing it vanilla during work hours.

Roberta put her phone away, wobbled to her feet, and raised her free hand – flashing the horns of the devil.

That got her a big smile, revealing a tongue piercing the size of a midget gem. Which explained the lisp.

'Dr Turner will thee you now.'

Babs was hunched over a laptop, un-pierced tongue poking out the side of her mouth as she pecked with two fingers at the keyboard.

Her office was a cluttered little room, stacked with files, journals, and reports, plastic models of various brain bits, a map of the nervous system, and a life-sized skeleton-on-a-stand called Gary – currently sporting a Santa hat, even though it was only August. Every shelf was stuffed, the overspill forming towers and piles on the floor. Leaving *just* enough space for an examination bed, a small desk, a saddle seat, and yet another cheap-arsed squeaky plastic chair for her patients.

Some of whom featured in polaroid photos mounted on the back of the door. Each one sporting a shaved-patch-and-scar-tissue, a big grin, and two thumbs up.

Roberta knocked on the desk with her stick. 'Hey, Babs, how's that eminently chewable arse of yours?'

'Free of tooth marks, thankfully.' She shut the laptop. 'Got a haemorrhoid the size of your fist. Thinking of naming it "Elon" and charging the bugger rent…' Babs winkled a pen-torch from her top pocket. 'Park yours, and let's see those eyeballs. You know the drill.'

'When do I get to drive again?' Thumping down in the groaning chair.

'Depends.' She flicked the light across Roberta's eyes a few times, making humming noises. 'Headaches, nausea, dizziness?'

'Only when I pay attention to the news. So, about driving: three months seems a bit—'

'Uh-huh. Let's play follow the finger.' Moving a digit from side to side. 'What about the animal-people-hybrid things?'

'Should never've told you about those.' Eyes left, eyes right, eyes left again. 'No. No' since coming off the morphine.'

'Good.' The torch went back in her pocket. 'Right: kit off and get on the exam table. Let's see if you need your oil changed…'

Roberta leaned on her walking stick, propping herself up as she gazed in through the observation window.

Billie Nesbit had graduated from the High Dependency Unit to a private room in the Green Zone's General Medicine ward. Unlike the other patients, who maybe had a bottle of Lucozade and a get-well-soon card, Billie's room was bedecked in fancy floral bouquets, teddy bears, and floaty mylar balloons, with a blizzard of cards pinned up behind the bed. All very bright and cheery.

Which didn't really go with the pale, thin, semi-corpse sagging back on top of the itchy hospital blankets. Watching some cheesy daytime show. Even her *Adventure Time* tattoo was washed out.

But at least she was alive.

Hard to know whether to pop in and say hello, or leave her alone and sod off home.

Only really came down here out of curiosity anyway. Being in the neighbourhood and all that.

Maybe it would be better to just—

Billie must've felt Roberta's gaze, because she turned to look.

Frowned.

Then her eyebrows raised, which somehow managed to make her circled eyes look even more sunken. Billie killed the telly, then pulled on a knackered wee smile, and made a droopy 'come in' gesture.

Meh, why not.

After all, the wee loon could wait. Serve him right for boring the arse off Roberta with all that Dungeons & Dragons bollocks.

She limped through the open door and over to the bed. 'Hi.'

Billie wasn't hooked up to anything that pinged or bleeped or dripped, but she still had a cannula plumbed into the back of one hand. And instead of stylish woodland-creature jammies, she'd gone for an XXXL 'DEMOCRACY ROCKS!' T-shirt which swamped her emaciated body. Nowhere near the hottie she used to be, but still pretty enough to make Roberta stand a little straighter and pull in her gut.

A pained look twisted those porcelain features. 'You're *her*, aren't you?'

'Depends. She owe you money?'

'From the papers. You got blown-up.' Sigh. 'And helped elect that racist, fascist, sexist prick.'

Now wait a sodding minute.

'Bugger right off. I was investigating *your* stabbing when it happened!' Roberta poked the bed. 'So if *you* hadn't got stabbed, I wouldn't've been there, I wouldn't've suffered a *traumatic* head injury, and that greasy shiteflap wouldn't've got elected.' Nose in the air, triumphant. 'So *technically* it's *your* fault.'

'Urgh...' Billie sagged further into her pillows. 'Suppose that's fair enough.' She waved a hand at a bag of sweeties sitting on the cantilevered table. 'You want a jelly baby? I can't: they've got boiled-up cow bones in them.'

Yummy.

Roberta helped herself to a green one – which everyone knew were the *king* of jelly babies – and collapsed into the visitor's seat. Stretching out her left leg with a groan. Because it was still a major trek from the Pink Zone to here.

Got to admit the flowers were pretty impressive. And she'd got a lot more of the things than Roberta had too. Jammy cow.

'How you getting on?'

Billie shrugged. 'Hoping I don't have to poop in a bag for the rest of my life.'

Well, at least Roberta was winning on *that* front. She plucked the printed card from a *very* fancy bouquet. 'FROM THE OFFICE OF CLAIRE FORDYCE MSP ~ GET BETTER SOON, BILLIE, WE'RE ALL ROOTING FOR YOU! ~ WITH LOVE FROM CLAIRE, SIR NORMAN, AND ALL THE TEAM.' The arrangement next to it had a handwritten note from Emma Dornoch.

Billie watched her tuck the card back in among the roses.

'They've been very good about visiting. Think that's probably why I got a private room.'

Because there was nothing like rich folk throwing their weight about. Nice to see the bastards using their privilege for a good cause, though. Bet *that* didn't happen often.

Roberta ripped the head off her jelly baby. 'You remember anything about that morning? Getting...' Miming stabbing someone.

'I went over all this with ... DCI Whatshisname.' Frown. 'Large, with a beard and—'

'Beattie.'

She nodded. 'Beattie. Right.' A pause. 'Is he *OK*? Because he seems a bit ... challenged? Not that there's anything *wrong* with being *neurodivergent*, I just didn't expect someone like that would get promoted to Detective Chief Inspector. Suppose Police Scotland are more progressive than I thought.'

Roberta helped herself to a red baby. 'Oh aye. Sometimes they even let *lesbians* be DCIs.' Chewing away. 'So, given that Beattie is "nae the full shilling" as my old mum used to say, how about you tell *me* what you remember?'

Billie opened her mouth, frowned, then closed it again. 'I was ... I was leading the counter-protest against those ASDG thugs, and they were chanting ... and Frank called the police.' She bared her teeth. 'These *bastards* turn up every few weeks, shouting and being dicks. Because why try to make the world a better place when you can cheer the oligarchs' capitalist boot on our throats?' Levering herself upright with her elbows. 'Do you know their boss is a multimillionaire? People are starving, can't afford to heat their homes, and he's sitting on more money than you or I could spend in three lifetimes!'

'Aye, I'd give it one hell of a go, though.' Roberta went for a yellow baby, keeping it casual. 'Your man, Frank...?'

'Oh he's not *my* man. No. Frank isn't into women, literally *or* figuratively. He works for Emma, though. Emma Dornoch?'

Roberta raised a fist. '"Better for Scotland"!'

'He's her campaign manager. We were going to put her in parliament...'

Not this time.

'So, Frank calls the cops?'

'Then it's all ... you know? Shoving and pushing and there was a knife.'

Roberta sat forward. 'Who had the knife, Billie?'

The lines between her eyebrows deepened. 'It... Maybe... It was one of the Neanderthals, I know that.'

'And you can describe him?'

She bit her lip again, squinting into the middle distance, her whole face twisting with the effort. 'All I can see is the knife...' Her eyes glittered in the overhead light, then her head dipped as tears spilled out. Shoulders trembling. Breath coming in jagged little gasps.

Yeah.

Roberta stood, putting a hand on Billie's shoulder. Voice soft and kind. 'It's OK.'

'I'm sorry.'

'Hey: when someone pulls a blade on you, that chunk of sharpened metal becomes the most important thing in the world. Why *wouldn't* you stare at it? It's not your fault everything else falls away.' Giving her shoulder a squeeze. 'Seriously: it's OK.'

Billie wiped a hand across her face, but the tears just flooded back. 'I'm supposed to be the *strong* one.'

Yeah...

Roberta let loose a long, long sigh. 'Me too.'

The various multicoloured zones of ARI were stitched together by a long corridor that was sometimes underground, sometimes overground – Wombling free – lined with art and murals designed to fool people into thinking they were somewhere far nicer than a hospital.

Roberta limped along it, leaving the Purple Zone – bolted sideways onto the Green one – and into the Yellow Zone. One hobble closer to escaping. Not going as fast as possible, because it wasn't easy to text one-handed and limp-along-with-a-cane at the same time.

As predicted:

Doc says I'm a MAGNIFICENT SEXY BEAST OF A WOMAN, but my recovery would be aided by more rampant steamy sessions with a randy blonde.

A porter speedwalked past her, pushing some poor bugger who was almost completely wrapped in bandages. No doubt on their way to wreak revenge on some olde-timey archaeologists for disturbing the wrong tomb.

How do you feel about Marigold gloves?

SEND.

The corridor ended with a wide set of stairs, leading up one flight to Level Two. Urgh… Why did everything have to involve *stairs*?

She lumbered up them, one step at a time. Pausing for breath every ten or twelve, because this was getting to be a bit of a sodding struggle as her legs ached and her back grumbled and every breath *whoomph*ed in her throat.

Should've got one of those porter's chairs. Would be home by now…

Finally, she staggered off the top step and back into the

hospital's reception area again, with its collection of saggy visitors and stressed staff.

Just take a quick breather.

Flipping heck.

Pfff…

Right.

Swift pitstop at the wee Marks & Spencer, then she'd go give Tufty a hard time for not offering to wheel her about, instead of abandoning a poor injured police hero to limp through this labyrinth of sick people and experimental art.

Urgh…

Roberta hobbled out through the sliding doors, clutching a packet of Reversy Percies and a wee hospital bouquet of cheery yellow flowers. The rain had stopped while she'd been inside prowling the corridors, but it looked as if there'd been a proper downpour in-between. Every concrete surface was stained a darker grey and the tarmac shone, a wee lochan spreading around the nearest drain. And going by the heavy clay-coloured clouds another downpour wasn't far away.

A bus rumbled past on Foresterhill Road, hissing up a miasma of dirty spray.

'Oh, for *buggering…*' Scowling out at the afternoon. Because although there were a couple of smokers loitering about, there was no sign of Tufty *or* his patrol car.

And yes, *maybe* she'd been a little longer than promised, but the wee shite could've waited!

Roberta pulled out her phone and jabbed his contact. Listening to it ring, and ring, and ring. Until:

'Please don't shout at me. It's been a—'

'Where the hell are you? "Out front," I said!'

'Yeah... About that: got a call – domestic in Mastrick. I was closest so...' He made a little hissing noise. As if inhaling through his teeth. *'Not a nice one, either.'*

Rustling and scrunking sounds filled the pause. Hard to be entirely sure what was going on, but he was moving through somewhere.

'Not that they're ever *nice, but ... Christ. You can do a lot of damage to a human being with a steam iron. Especially if it's hot.'*

The scowl fell from Roberta's face. 'You get there in time?'

'Don't know, Guv. Ambulance just left.' A big sigh rattled from the earpiece. *'Why do people have to be so* horrible *to each other?'*

It must've been *really* bad to make Tufty sound like a normal person for a change – no tortured grammar or weird speech tics.

She leaned against a bollard. 'Are *you* OK?'

Silence.

Then another sigh. *'No. But this is what we do, isn't it: pick up the terrible pieces when all the screaming stops.'* Voice flat as an ironing board. *'Anyway, gotta get going. Suspect to process, paperwork to do...'*

'Don't worry about me, I'll get a taxi.'

Another long pause.

But this time, when Tufty came back, his words were laced with a hint of evil glee: *'Or you could give* Rennie *a call. He's on a day off; sure he'd* love *to give you a lift!'*

Good idea.

After all, there was nothing like spreading the misery...

2.11

Roberta puffed out another lungful of maple-pecan, leaning back against the 'WELCOME TO ABERDEEN ROYAL INFIRMARY' sign. Showing solidarity with the half-dozen other smokers gathered beneath the front portico in violation of all the notices about it being forbidden within fifteen metres of hospital buildings. Because it was pishing down, and sod that.

She had her flowers tucked under one arm, walking stick propped beside her, freeing up the other hand for phone-holding duties as rain *battered* out of a gunmetal sky. Gurgling in the gutters, hissing through the trees, bouncing off the tarmac.

'What?' Lund's voice had a flat echo to it, as if she'd answered from a toilet cubicle. Dirty bugger. *'Nah, I'm pretty sure I'm not allowed to just do PNC checks for poops and giggles.'*

'It's an official order from your superior officer!'

'Oh aye, till Friday. *And you're off on the sick!* And *you didn't say please.'*

A furious hiss of nutty smoke billowed down Roberta's nose. 'See when I retire? I'll have all this free time on my hands, and nothing better to do than come up with ways to make people's lives miserable.'

An ambulance *neee-nawwed* away into the distance.

A drenched family hurried in from the downpour.

An elderly smoker folded over, one hand covering his face, the other holding a drip stand as he sobbed.

And on the rain fell.

'Fine.' Lund let loose a long-suffering groan. *'Who do you need me to look up?'*

Roberta grinned, because they always cracked in the end. 'One David McLeod, ex-detective-sergeant, Grampian Police.'

This time, the pause dripped with suspicion. *'Why?'*

'Cos I want to know if he's legit, or a greasy wee shunt.'

'Pfff… Hold on.'

Keyboard noises clacked away in the background. So, Lund can't have been on the bog after all.

'How you getting on with *my* cases?'

'Oh no you don't. We've got strict *instructions not to tell you anything: doctor's orders. … Well, Chief Superintendent's, but you know what I mean…'* One last clack, then: *'OK: here we go. … Uh-huh. Right. David McLeod, Thirty-Two Kingswood Place, Kingswells. Couple of parking violations, … shotgun licence is up for renewal in September, … registered with the Security Industry Authority as a private investigator. No outstanding warrants, complaints, or warnings that I can see.'* She hummed and hawed a little. *'You should ask the wee loon: get him to do an internet search and burrow down into all the guy's socials, like a weevil.'*

Probably.

Might take his mind off that horrible Domestic Violence case…

A scuffed-yellow people-carrier emerged from the downpour, swinging through the NO ENTRY 'EXCEPT BUSES' sign with gay abandon. Not exactly the most stylish of vehicles – a Ford Galaxy. As if a Transit van shagged a hatchback.

It stopped right in front of Roberta, and the driver's window buzzed down.

Simon Rennie grinned out at her. Swear he'd got even porkier since she'd been in hospital. At this rate, he'd be self-basting in time for Christmas. His bleached-blond mop was thinning at the front, but still teased up into short spikes, like a porcupine's testicle. Wearing a 'Top 10 Dad*' T-shirt and sunglasses, even though it was bucketing. Like a tit.

He ponked his horn. 'Taaaaaaaxi!'

Roberta hunched her shoulders and hurpled around to the passenger side.

Lund must've heard that. *'We done now? Only I've got* actual *police work to be getting on with.'*

'Aye: when did Davey leave the job, and was it under a cloud?' Roberta yanked the door open and scrambled in, out of the rain.

Then sat there, looking around at the absolute craphole that was the Rennie family car. The footwell carpet was basically invisible beneath a layer of sweetie wrappers and toys, while dust and mud and splots of grease and what you had to *hope* was chocolate covered nearly every other surface. All of it clarted in a furry blanket of dog hair.

Smelled more than a little funky in here too, even though a trio of lemon air-fresheners dangled from the rear-view mirror.

Bunch of minks.

She plonked her flowers on the dashboard, pinning the phone between her ear and shoulder to do battle with the seatbelt. 'And while we're at it, what the hell's going on with Billie Nesbit's stabbing? Poor cow's stuck in ARI and we're twiddling our thumbs like … flipping snudges.'

Click.

Rennie put the Mankmobile in gear. 'Home, James?'

'God's sake…' Lund gave a wee grunt. *'I'll do what I* can, *but I'm promising squit-all. Like North Korea round here, now – we do not question the Great Leader.'* Then hung up.

'Well?'

Roberta put her phone away and turned. 'Kingswells?' A nod. 'Aye: Kingswells. Got to see a man about a thing.'

'Hmmmm… Thought this was supposed to be a *quick* favour?'

'The longer you moan about it, the longer it'll take. Besides, you got something better to do on a sharny Tuesday?'

Rennie's lips pursed as he peered out at the downpour. 'Well … I *suppose* Emma's got the kids all day. But I was planning on spending it playing Minecraft and arguing with strangers on the internet…' He huffed out a lonnnnng breath, then pulled away from the kerb. 'Meh, why not. But we're stopping for coffee on the way, and *you're* paying.'

The Rennie Family Yuckmobile stopped outside the smallest house on Kingswood Place.

Number thirty-two was about half the size of its boring neighbours, but every bit as dull. For some strange reason, there was no pavement, and instead of a tarmac road and lock-block driveways it was the other way around. As if the developer had got the plans upside down. To add a frisson of excitement, the pantile roofs alternated between russet-brown and grey, but the buildings were the same colour as the lowering sky.

Each one had a teeny garage, set weirdly far back from the road, behind the houses, at the arse-end of the garden. Much too small to fit anything bigger than a child's pedal car. A line of trees lurking behind them.

Even though the front gardens were minute, most were well maintained – the grass short, the bushes trimmed with the precision of a super-model's bikini line – but number thirty-two boasted a shaggy clambering rose, losing pale-pink petals in the hammering rain. Dandelions peppering the tiny unmown lawn. House martins nesting in the eaves, spattering the weed-choked flowerbeds below with bird shite. Letting the rest of the street down.

And while all the other homes had at least one hatchback or Smart Car parked on its inside-out driveway, Wee Davey McLeod's place had the crusty brown rustbucket VW Polo last seen outside Inverurie police station.

Rennie turned the blowers down to a gentle howl, peering out through the windscreen as it began to fog over. 'Want me to wait?'

'No, I want you to sod off and leave me stranded out here, in the rain, with my walking stick.' Giving him a good dose of the evil eye. 'Cretin.'

'You've got a *funny* way of asking for favours.' Taking a sip of white chocolate mocha frappuccino. 'Lucky I've got the patience of a saint.' Reaching into his door pocket for a greasy paper bag with the coffee shop logo on it. 'And a double-toffee-chocolate-crunch muffin.'

Roberta tutted at the idiot, hoicked up her collar, and climbed out into the monsoon. Leaving her flowers in the car, but not the Reversy Percies, because you couldn't trust Rennie with confectionery. Biscuits. Or cheese.

She hurried up the driveway, her walking stick making little sploshes in the puddled tarmac, ducking in beneath the climbing rose where it prolapsed out above the door. Getting a bit of shelter while she rang the bell.

The neighbours had two steps up to their front door, and a wee built-in handrail, but Davey's house featured a concrete ramp instead. Which didn't excuse not answering the sodding door.

Come on, come on, come on…

She thumbed the button again.

Sodding *drowning* out here.

This time, she left her finger on the bell, letting it *rinnnnnnnnnnnnnng*. 'DAVEY!'

A *clunk*, then the door swung open, and there he was – playing dress-up in a blue pinny and pink rubber gloves. Instead of the sexy yellow ones.

He goldfished at her for a bit, like he was having a stroke or something. 'It… But… What are you…?'

She barged past, into a tiny vestibule/porch thing, with a set of hooks for hanging your keys and a place to put your dirty outside shoes.

Roberta gave herself a shake, spraying second-hand rain. 'Flipping took you long enough. It's *pishing* down.'

'Watch it! You're getting water everywhere!' Voice low as he squeezed by, to stand between her and the internal door. 'God's sake, what are you *doing* here?'

'I think you mean, "Oh, lovely Roberta, it's such a *delight* to see you again! *Do* come in for a cuppa and a chocolate biscuit."'

He wriggled his rubber gloves at her. 'Will you keep your voice down? Jenny's sleeping.'

'At half two in the afternoon?' Wink. 'Have a post-lunch knee trembler, did you?' That explained the gloves.

'Just…' He scrunched his face, took a deep breath. 'Why are you here?'

'Can't one *old friend* visit another old friend who asked the first old friend to do dodgy PNC searches on the sly? After all, it's…' Looking over his shoulder, eyes widening. 'Is that…?'

'Jenny.' He turned to look, even though it was the oldest trick known to man, and soon as he did, Roberta slinked past, through the door.

The hallway on the other side was … really, really, *weirdly* clean. As if no one actually lived here.

A bunch of landscape prints adorned the walls, and a cheap bookcase sat in one corner, but other than that, the only thing in here was a threadbare pale-green carpet, hoovered to within a millimetre of its life.

Five doors led off, but one of them lay open, revealing a hospital-style bed with siderails, and a pump-controlled drip stand beside it. A wheelchair and sling-hoist for getting the patient out of bed.

Not that she looked as if she did much of that.

An emaciated woman lay slumped beneath the duvet, looking about a decade older than Davey with her white hair, sunken eyes, and hollow cheeks. There was a yellow tone to her papery skin, like parchment. Sickly.

That would be 'Jenny'.

Davey tiptoed over there and closed the door. Careful and quiet. Then bustled Roberta through into a compact and antiseptic living room. Not a speck of dust, discarded book, or abandoned coffee mug in sight.

To be honest, this whole place made Roberta and Susan's home look like the inside of Rennie's car.

An ancient fabric suite was arranged before an old-fashioned, bulky TV, while a glass coffee table contained nothing more exciting than a little wooden stand with coasters in it. Patio doors took up most of the end wall, showing off a ratty garden not much wider than the house. And it was *not* a wide house.

Weeds grew up between the paving slabs of a deserted patio, and the lawn was about knee-deep. Which seemed a bit out of character, given how fastidious Davey was in here.

There wasn't room for a shed, but that weeny garage sat off to the right, against the back fence. Another drooping rose rambling up the side wall.

Davey closed the door to the hall, cheeks all pink and flustered. 'It's not that I'm *ungrateful* or anything, it's… We have a routine.' Pulling off his embarrassed rubber gloves. 'No one comes to visit. … Not friends, anyway.'

Maybe she'd been a *wee* bit hard on him. What with the ill wife and everything.

Yeah.

Give the poor sod a break.

Roberta held up her bloodstained printouts. 'Got your PNC checks.'

He licked his lips. Nodded. Looked back at the closed door, as if peering through it, across the hall, through the door opposite, and into his wife's sickroom. 'Do you mind if we do this in my office? I don't like mixing home and business…'

A crazy-paving path twisted its way through the long grass, past a row of quivering bushes, to a little door in the garage wall. Surrounded by the weeping rose.

Davey led the way, with Roberta limping along *right* behind him – staying close, because he only had the one golf brolly, and it was still dinging down out here.

The garage side door was peppered with about six different Yale locks, and Davey worked his way through a bundle of keys, undoing each one. Then shuffled sideways on the narrow path. 'After you.'

She gave the bundle of keys a pointed look. 'This better no' be one of them "Suburban Sex Dungeons" we hear so much about…'

But instead of leather straps and shackles and paddles, whips, ball-gags, and dildos-of-all-nations, the weenie garage had been turned into a home office, complete with lined walls, a proper ceiling, and carpet on the floor.

Not a sex swing in sight.

A collection of corkboards ran along one wall, covered in photos and diagrams and missing-persons posters. Four of which were for cats.

The room was rounded out with a small desk, a micro-kitchen area, and a pair of matching filing cabinets.

Davey kicked off his little ankle wellies and slipped on a pair of tartan baffies. Frowned at Roberta's soggy boots. Then wisely didn't ask her to do the same. Forced a smile instead. 'Jenny got tired of me slouching about the house after I retired, so this was all her idea.'

Bet it was.

Roberta had a good squint at one of Davey's cases: a stakeout on a bungalow in Mintlaw. Floor plan, photos of the participants, notes, a telephone bill that looked as if it'd been scrounged from a bin. 'You should get yourself some red string, Davey: tie the bits and bobs together. Go for a proper conspiracy-theorist-slash-serial-killer vibe.'

He furled his brolly, then filled the kettle. Set it boiling. 'So … you've got those PNC checks for me?' All casual, like.

'I'm a classy broad, Davey. Need a bit of foreplay before the full-on shagging starts.'

He shrugged, then produced two mugs. 'What do you want?'

'Tea.' She watched him get the bags out. 'Tell me about Mr and Mrs X.'

'I can't.'

'Aye, you *do* know I catch *murderers* for a living, right, Davey? All this…?' Pointing at the little groups of photos. 'Beneath my pay grade. Doing you a favour, here.'

'I still can't.' And a withering look didn't shift him. 'Client confidentiality. Like being a doctor, only with less money.'

Not as if she really gave a toss anyway.

Only being nosy for the sake of it.

Mind you: given that she wasn't allowed anywhere near a *proper* case, thanks to Chief Superintendent Pine being a toss-weasel, might as well meddle with Davey's caseload.

And Susan said she needed a hobby…

'OK.' Roberta raised a finger. 'But say I'm here as a *consulting detective*, what with all my expertise, experience, and PNC checks. That means it's all OK again, doesn't it. *Ethically* speaking.'

'Suppose…'

She plonked down into his office chair, swivelling from side to side as the kettle *hiss-click-grumble*d. 'So, you staked-out Mr X's place of business…?'

Davey stared at the ceiling. Pulled one shoulder up. 'OK.' Let it drop again. 'Four months ago, Judith Sherman wakes up in the middle of the night to find her husband downstairs, on the phone. Muttered conversation, clearly hiding something. She confronts him over breakfast, he denies everything. Accuses her of being paranoid.' Kettle boiled, Davey filled their mugs. 'Two days later, husband Noel's wearing a nice new pair of jeans, a nice new shirt, and a nice new leather jacket. Very swish. Two weeks after *that*: gets himself a nice new BMW convertible.'

'Sports car and an affair.' Roberta pulled on her best Jane Austen voice: 'How *frightfully* midlife-crisisey!'

'This goes on for a couple of weeks, and she's sure he's at it. So, she calls me. Wants to make sure she's got all her financial ducks in a drawer, because her husband's a sneaky wee shite who's probably hiding a whole heap of assets from her, which she intends to plunder in the divorce.' Mashing the teabags with a spoon. 'I follow him for a couple of days – nothing special – then stake out his business.'

'Which is?'

The teabags *splatch*ed into the bin. 'Coillewood Development and Resolution Specialists Limited. Joinery, mostly. Runs a few guys out of his workshop just outside Stonehaven, putting up timber frames for kit houses. Does a bit of "debt management" on the side.'

Now *that* was a bit more interesting.

Roberta pushed off one side of the desk, setting the chair rotating all the way around, in a slow-motion twirl. 'Loan shark?'

'Nah: strictly legit. You've got an outstanding bill needs paid, or a County Court judgement, he'll enforce it for a fifteen-percent cut.' Milk in the teas. 'You still take sugar?'

'One. And a biscuit. None of your stingy knock-off-rich-tea shite, though. Something with chocolate.'

He plonked a mug down in front of her, along with a depressing disc of brown.

'What the hell's this?'

'Ginger snap. All I've got. I'm not exactly making KitKat money, here.' He wandered over to one of the corkboards, crunching. 'I stake out Noel Sherman's office-cum-workshop, record all the comings and goings. Thought maybe the woman in the electric-bogey-coloured Toyota Yaris might be his fancy piece. She's a regular.'

'And the other two: Red-Jag Man and Rusty-Jeep Boy?'

'Gay people can have affairs too. Just cos Noel's hetero at home doesn't mean he's not factory-floor fabulous.'

Roberta did another three-sixty.

Hmmm…

'Gimme a bit of paper and a pen.'

He raised an eyebrow.

'Well I'm no' giving you an official Police Scotland printout, am I. Be incriminating.'

'Thanks.' Davey dug out a pack of Post-its and a chewed biro. 'This is—'

A hard *buzzzzzzzzzzzzzzzzz* cut across the room – joined by a red light, flashing above the filing cabinets.

He dumped his tea and hurried to the door, swapping slippers for mini-wellies again. Grabbed his brolly. Then bustled out into the rain. 'Jenny needs me. Don't touch anything!'

And he was gone, shutting the door behind him.

Leaving Roberta alone with her mug of tea and disappointing biscuit.

Right.

She stood.

Time to have a rummage…

2.12

Roberta finished digging through Davey's desk drawers – nothing interesting – and had a good nosy at his corkboards instead. Sipping her tea and crunching her biscuit. Because ginger snaps were actually quite nice, once you got used to the idea that they weren't slathered in chocolate.

Already seen the Great Mintlaw Bungalow Inquiry. Next in line was the Huntly Crown Green Bowling Club Investigation – thrilling stuff – and the Strange Case of the Lusty Lumphanan Librarian and her Loch Street Lothario… All of which were at the duller end of surveillance photography: cars in car parks; people sitting together in restaurants; snaps of one couple hand-in-hand on the beach…

The last pics in the 'Soon To Be Divorced' section were of what looked like an agricultural shed, with a 'CD&RS Ltd' sign on its corrugated-metal walls. One snap each of the red Jaguar SUV, snot-green Yaris, and a rusty Fourtrak so *decrepit* that the rear bumper was held on with hairy string. What had Davey said the business was? Coillewood Developy Something Somethings?

Close enough.

Then it was on to the missing-persons posters, starting with a ginger tabby: Mr Wibbles, a tortoiseshell: Captain Floofypants, a longhair: Rincannaroth, and a Burmese called Bob.

Which left the people.

Davey had far more of them than cats. Most were late-teens, early-twenties, but a few middle-agers and OAPs had gone walkabout too. Like Evan MacGath, a balding pensioner, photographed in his droopy wattles, shirt and tie. Missing for six months. Last seen heading out from his home in Portsoy, carrying a bag-for-life, bundled up in a parka jacket and woolly hat against the February sleet.

Tina Hannay hung next to him: a *squashed*-looking woman, in her forties, a cardigan, and flustered-mumsy haircut. Long nose, dark eyes, pinched mouth, overbite. As if a rat had been granted its wish to become human, then instantly regretted it. Last seen on CCTV walking away from the Elgin bus station, ten months ago.

Don't think the bus station even existed anymore.

Ding-buzz.

Lund:

> DS David McLeod > retired Feb 2013
>
> No big cockups or Prof.Stand investigations
>
> B.Nesbit stabbing > Beattie at standstill

Of course he sodding was – the man was an idiot, wrapped in a moron, and stuffed up an imbecile. How did it take someone eight-and-a-bit weeks to solve a stabbing with two dozen witnesses?

Scowling, Roberta went back to the wall of mispers.

Next up was a Ruby Burrows: thirty-seven, longish straight brown hair, prominent ears, wide mouth. Really wide. Like, *pedal-bin* wide. OK, in a girl-next-doorsy kind of way, wearing a grey shirt under a navy jumper and a dark-grey sports coat that did nothing for her. According to the text beneath Ruby's photo, she went missing on the first of June – nearly eleven weeks ago. Last seen driving out of the staff car park at Kirkenwell Academy, where she worked as a music teacher.

Fortunately, someone much more to Roberta's taste was pinned-up by the filing cabinet: Megan Lockheart. Twenty-one with long black hair in a centre parting, dark eyebrows and darker eyes. Pouty lips, small nose, little dimple in her chin. She was pictured in a blue-and-yellow T-shirt with a Ukrainian tryzub on it. Looking serious and determined as she gazed into the camera. Which somehow made her even prettier.

There was something weirdly … *familiar* about her.

As if they'd met before, but long enough ago that the memory was blurred out of focus. Though that might've been something to do with the ballistic chunk of pipe that tried to tear its way through Roberta's skull.

The accompanying write-up pegged Megan at five-foot-two – so a proper pocket rocket – last seen on Saturday, third of May, at the big B&Q in Garthdee. Though her wee Fiat 500 was found six miles away in Portlethen, near Nicol Park, a week later.

Wonder if they looked at the boyfriend for it? Because a fiver said Megan had terrible taste in men. The seriously pretty ones often did. Too used to everyone being nice to them to develop a fully functioning dangerous-dickhead Radar.

Whoever Megan was shagging, bet he'd be the kind of guy who—

'*Sorry about that.*' Davey bustled in from the rain, thumping the door shut behind him. 'Sometimes Jenny has difficulty settling after a … visit.'

Roberta tapped the missing person poster. 'This one: Megan Lockheart. Where do I know her from?'

He shuffled out of his mini-wellies and joined her at the corkboard. 'You've seen her? What, *recently*?' Bouncing slightly in his tartan baffies. 'Are you sure it was her? Cos her mum and dad are frantic. And probably going to fire me if I don't make some progress soon.' Grabbing a battered notebook and another half-eaten pen. 'Where was this?'

'Anyone grill the boyfriend?'

'Didn't … *doesn't* have one. According to her friends, the only thing she's in love with is helping people. Volunteering, that kind of stuff.'

Hmmmm…

Roberta had a good long squint at the photo, but it wasn't coming. 'Nah. No idea.' She pointed at the three Post-its she'd stuck to Davey's desk. 'Copied out your PNC checks. You didn't get them from me, or anyone like me, or anyone who's even *heard* of me.'

His shoulders dipped as the chance of not-getting-sacked slipped away. Then scuffed over there to check what she'd written. 'You given any thought to what you're going to do? Cos you're retiring soon, right?'

'End of the week.' As if she needed reminding.

'Could ride along with me if you fancied it? Now I've got these,' holding up the Post-its, 'might *actually* make some progress before Mrs Sherman fires me too.'

Roberta folded her arms, leaning back against the filing cabinet. 'I solve sodding *murders*, remember?' Sniff. 'Besides, why do I get the feeling *everyone's* on the verge of canning you?'

'It's not my fault! I can only do Mondays, Wednesdays, and Fridays, cos someone has to be here for Jenny. You got any idea how hard it is to get a care package these days? Health visitors, someone to help turn her, or take her … for a visit? She *hates* strangers doing that.' Getting smaller and wetter with every word, till there was nothing left of him but a teeny puddle of self-pity.

Roberta groaned, rolled her eyes, then turned to scowl at the corkboards – with their crappy divorce cases and missing people.

'Well...' He huffed out a breath. Tried again: 'How about we give it a trial run? You and me see if we can nail Noel Sherman's cheating arse?' Neediness oozing out. 'We could go noise-up this ... Hatton, MacNeal, and Yarrow tomorrow? Rattle their cages: see if anything bites?'

Leaving a pause that *ached* with desperation.

Pfff...

Not as if she had anything better to do, was it.

And at least this would be better than stupid *golf*.

Roberta set her jaw and turned. 'If I *do* help you – and I'm no' saying I will – remember *I* was a Detective Chief Inspector, *you* were a DS, so there'll be no sexist bollocks: no throwing your weight around, thinking you're in charge. You're no' in charge, *I* am.'

'Deal! Cubs' honour.'

'OK then.' She stuck out her hand. 'File.'

He almost skipped to the nearest filing cabinet, ferreting about in its bottom drawer, and returning with a folder. Then paused. Biting his lip as he clutched it. 'But ... doctor-patient confidentiality.'

'Consulting detective *immunity*.' Ah, what the hell – why not? 'But fair enough.'

Davey handed the file over and she tucked it under her arm.

Roberta gave him a wee nod. 'Pleasure doing business with you. Maybe.' Then headed for the door. 'And get some decent biscuits in next time!'

She hurried down the driveway, coat pulled up over her head, like Quasimodo in stylish boots.

The Rennie Family Tip was parked where she'd left it, rain

bouncing off the roof, bonnet, and windscreen like a snare drum at an execution.

The boy himself was still behind the wheel, rocking in his seat, flailing his hands about, as if attending a one-idiot rave.

Roberta yanked open the passenger door and hurled herself inside. Thumping the door closed on the downpour. 'Buggering shiteflaps!'

Up close, it was clear that Rennie had earbuds in, still 'dancing', and making high-pitched sort-of-joining-in-with-whatever-the-song-was noises. 'Yeah, yeah. … Ooh, ooh…'

She gave herself a good shake, sending water pattering into the footwell.

'Doobie, doobie, doobie-doobie. … Waaah, waah…'

'What the hell are you listening to?'

His voice was far too loud: 'GIVE US A MINUTE, THIS IS THE BEST BIT.' Throwing in a shoulder wiggle. 'Yeah, yeah, yeah, yeah, *yeahhhhhh*!'

Idiots.

Just … *surrounded* by idiots.

While he seat-shimmied, she opened Davie's manilla folder and slid the contents into her damp lap.

Top of the pile were a couple of photos of the not-so-happy couple, with their names written on them, in case you couldn't tell which was which.

Judith Sherman had a vaguely Slavic look, with dark blonde hair long enough to put in a plait. Bow-shaped mouth, very red lipstick, long face, long nose, heavy eyebrows. Early-forties, doing her best to look mid-twenties.

'Uh-huh, uh-huh, doo, doo…'

Her cheating husband, Noel, was one of those short-back-and-sides-with-an-order-of-stubble kind of guys. As if he were desperate to star in a Guy Ritchie film. Larger ears than his head was designed to accommodate. Strong jaw, turning a bit saggy, with a hint of the double chin about it. Still a big lad, though. Someone who went to the gym every now and then, and didn't mind throwing his weight about.

Mr and Mrs looked happy enough in the first pic, taken at some sort of party when they were both much younger, but in the second one, it wasn't just Noel's jawline that was heading south. Stony-faced, they sat at opposite ends of the couch with their three kids in the middle, like sticky little human shields. Two boys, one girl – soon to be from a broken home.

'Bam, bam, bim-bam, oooooh-oooooh!'

Other shots showed the big metal shed/workshop. And the last three were the now familiar pictures of Davey's suspicious vehicles.

And then it was on to handwritten notes from four stake-outs: times, number plates, comments. Blah, blah, blah.

Nothing even vaguely interesting.

Rennie grinned across the car at her. 'BIG FINISH…' Then into an air-guitar solo, because apparently, he had no shame at all. 'Yeah, yeah… Gonna,' his voice jumped an octave into a falsetto shriek, '*Yeaaaaaaaaaaaaaaah*!'

The only things left were a couple of zip-lock freezer bags, containing credit-card receipts and phone bills – smeared and splotted with grease-and-food stains, crumpled, creased, then straightened out again. Because clearly Davey was big into his bin diving.

Which, to be honest, showed more initiative than he had when he was a detective sergeant.

Good for him.

Rennie performed his big finish on the invisible drums, then slumped back, breathing hard and beaming. Before popping out the earbuds. 'Get everything you needed?'

'Not yet.' She returned the photos, notes, and bills to their folder. 'Back to town. Think we'll pop in past the big Asda in Garthdee. I've always wanted to run amok in one of those mobility scooter things…'

2.13

Wednesday: 2 days to go…

This morning's tea-and-toast chaos came with a hefty buttering of Jasmine moaning about the weather – cramming down breakfast with her hair like an electrocuted bird's-nest.

No idea why, but Naomi was dressed as a pirate today, wolfing cereal while Susan did her best to get everyone out the house:

'Come on, people: move it or lose it! Car. Car. Car. Car!' Shepherding both kids towards the door. 'GENGHIS! Mummy's leaving!'

The wee lad scurried in on his tap-dancing nails, tail wagging so fast he could barely keep his little hind legs on the floor.

Susan clipped on his lead then bent to give Roberta a lingering smooch. 'You look very smart … *and* pleased with yourself.'

Roberta beamed at her. 'Marigold gloves: who knew?'

'Robbie!' Pink bloomed across Susan's cheeks. 'Why *are* you all dressed-up, though?'

As if there was anything suspicious about ditching the jammies for once, and going with a nice new pair of jeans and a nice new purple silk shirt – not to mention the extra perky boobs, thanks to a nice new swanky bra. Courtesy of her shopping spree yesterday. 'Can't slob about *all* week in my PJs.'

Which was technically true, and therefore not a lie. So didn't count. And what Susan didn't know wouldn't hurt her. Or cause a blazing row about how Roberta was just a wounded wickle birdie who had to stay in the nest and not go galivanting about town playing freelance detective.

A wail echoed through from the hall. Jasmine: *'Muuuuuu-um, I'm going to be late!'*

Susan rolled her eyes. 'I love them to death, but some days…' Deep breath. 'THEN GET YOUR BUMS IN THE CAR!'

'Thought I might have a wee hobble around the neighbourhood if the rain lets up. You know: what the physio said – keeping active.'

'That's the spirit!'

'Muuuuuuuuuummmmmmmm!'

She slumped. 'Now I know why gerbils eat their young.' Marching for the door. 'ANYONE NOT IN THE CAR GETS LEFT BEHIND!'

Naomi: *'Arrrrr, me hearties, I calls "shotgun", so I does!'*

Jasmine: *'You had shotgun yesterday!'*

'Move it, move it, move it, move it! Honestly, you're such a pair of—'

The front door clunked shut.

Peace at last.

Roberta closed the paper: 'TAYSIDE RIPPER: NEW VICTIM EXCLUSIVE', above a photo of a narrow, cobbled alley cordoned-off with blue-and-white 'POLICE' tape. Bars on the windows, graffiti on the walls. A patrol car blocked most of the shot, but Logan was visible in the middle distance, between its swirling lights – on his phone and scowling at something out of sight. A blue SOC tent filled the alley behind him. 'FAMILY'S HORROR AS "BELOVED" SON'S BODY PARTS DISCOVERED IN CITY CENTRE'.

Told Logan he should've hired her as a consulting detective. Would've solved it by now.

She gulped down the last mouthful of coffee.

Then an evil wee smile bloomed.

Instead of filling the dishwasher and tidying up, Roberta snuck down the hall and peered through the glazed panels either side of the front door.

Outside, Susan helped Genghis hop into the back of her grey-blue Volvo XC40, then jumped in behind the wheel. A *vwwwwmmmmmmmmmmm* of electric engine as the Big Car pulled away. And they were gone.

Roberta was *all* alone.

Which was cue for a sinister chuckle, rubbing her hands together. Because if you couldn't ham it up at the start of a devious plan, when could you?

And now: keys.

She went for a rummage in the sideboard drawer.

Keys, keys, keys, keys, keys…

First up would be a trip through the car wash. Maybe two, given how sticky her MX-5 was. And then…

Where they hell were they?

Roberta pulled the whole drawer out and peered into the hole left behind. No keys.

'Oh for God's…'

Right.

Carrying the drawer through to the war-zone-cum-kitchen, she tipped the contents out on top of that morning's *Aberdeen Examiner*. It made a massive mound of assorted keys and fobs, many of which didn't fit anything anymore, because in the sixteen years they'd been married they'd never thrown a single key out. There were even keys in here that she'd inherited from her parents – big and rusty, like her dad. Keys for every car she'd ever owned. Keys for about a dozen wee stations that no longer existed, because Police Scotland sold them. Keys upon keys upon keys. Keys for everything *except* her MX-5.

'Bugger-wank.'

Back in the hall, she shoved the drawer into its slot again, then searched through every single coat hanging by the door. Even the kids' ones.

No keys.

Up in the mistress bedroom, she rifled through both big wardrobes, patting down anything with pockets.

Still no keys.

Down in the living room – stuffing her arm in down between the sofa's leather back and its leather cushions. Then doing the same with the other one. And the armchairs. Producing nothing more useful than a couple of Mr Rumpole's toy mice, a half-chewed rawhide thing, three Lego men and a small handful of spare change.

Which she pocketed.

Roberta stood in the middle of the room, turning round and around. Hauling in a deep, deeeeeep breath then bellowing it out again. 'AAAAAAAAAAAAAAAAAAARGH!'

Pacing the living-room rug, like a lopsided tripod.

Come on, they had to be *somewhere.*

Where did she have them last?

...

Inverurie.

They were in her pocket when she and Tufty sneaked out in that patrol car. Which meant she'd had them on her when everything went BANG!

OK.

This was progress.

Through in the utility room, her mouldy Doc Martens and epaulettes still sat on the draining board, awaiting a good clean. Along with her wallet and the other bits and bobs.

But no keys.

'Oh for *Christ's...*'

The bin-bag?

Maybe she'd missed a whole set of car keys when going through her cut-off clothes?

Worth a try...

Roberta rummaged through the bin, wearing last night's yellow Marigolds for a *far* less noble purpose.

Why was there so much sticky slimy yuck in here?

Why did—

Got you: one fusty hospital bin-bag, hidden beneath a layer of malignant cat-food pouches.

She dumped the foul-smelling thing in the sink, untied the knot, and pulled everything out, going through all the pockets again.

Still no buggering keys.

Just to be sure, she searched them a third time. Slow and steady. Jaw clenching tighter and tighter with every sodding pass.

WHERE THE WANKING *FUCK* WERE HER KEYS?

Ramming her cut-off fusties back into the bag, Roberta slammed it into the bin, then shoved that back into its cubby-hole.

Glared at it.

She snapped off her rubber gloves and hurled them into the sink.

2.14

Roberta grabbed Boris Johnson's head and collapsed into the sofa. Crushing his squishy skull in one hand as she opened her phone and selected her number-one contact. *Pkongk-glonk. Pkongk-glonk. Pkongk-glonk.* Forcing her face into a smile as the number rang. *Pkonnnnnnnnnnnnnnnnnnnnnnnnnnnngk…*

Oh for the piffering *snidge.*

A splot of something stained the front of her new silk shirt. Clean on this morning, never been worn. She curled her lip and gave it a sniff.

Rancid, cat-food-gravy, bastarding—

'Robbie?' Susan's voice. *'You OK?'*

Glonk.

'I've got *yuck* on my top!'

Silence.

'Right… And you thought I could do *something about that?'*

'What? No. Sorry.' She tossed Boris Johnson's severed head onto the other sofa, and unbuttoned her shirt. 'Listen, I think I left that book I was reading in the Wee Car's boot. You know, before I got blown to smithereens?'

'Did you?'

'And, funny thing: I can't find the keys…?'

'That's right.'

Roberta wiggled one arm out of its sleeve then froze. 'When you say—'

'Dr Turner thinks you're not safe to drive right now, so you won't find your keys anywhere. *Not even the spare set. And there's no point whingeing at me, because I am every bit as stubborn and bloody-minded as you are.'*

'But ... my book!'

'I'm not falling for it, Roberta Alexander Steel.' And there was that flinty lawyer edge. *'Now, is there anything else, or can I get back to work?* Some *of us don't get to retire for over a decade yet.'*

Urgh...

She peeled off the other sleeve and sagged back on the couch. Not bothering to hide the sulky droop to her voice. 'No.'

'Good. Love you.' And Susan was gone.

Roberta gave in to a full-body slump, head lolled back to glare at the ceiling. 'The woman's a *monster*.' Quite a few cobwebs up there. Wonder if Wee Davey McLeod fancied popping around with his feather duster and pinny?

Speaking of whom.

She thumbed out a text to 'SKETCHY DAVEY':

Change of plan.

Can't drive: car trouble.

You need to pick me up.

SEND.

OK, so Davey's crapbucket VW Polo was a rusty heap, but inside it was spotless. Like his house.

Sounded as if the engine needed tuning, though. Or taking out and shooting as they puttered down the A92, a couple of minutes south of Stonehaven.

Outside, the sky was dark as a smoker's lungs, a misty drizzle mixing with the filthy road-spray, smeared by the windscreen wipers into grubby beige arcs. Trees bordered the fields to the right, but on the left they gave way to the looming slate-grey slab of the North Sea. Full of foreboding. And fish. While the radio was full of bland sub-par rock, one step above elevator music.

Roberta slouched in the passenger seat, wearing a blue shirt rescued from the laundry basket, while Davey had opted for a pair of wicker-furniture-style driving gloves that made him look like an OAP pervert.

A junction appeared up ahead '← DUNNOTTAR CASTLE ¼'.

He indicated left, slowing for the turn. 'All I'm saying is we should've started with Jeremy Yarrow, then did Charlotte MacNeal, and *finished* with Rory Hatton.'

'Uh-huh.' Poking away at her mobile, texting Logan:

> See you got yourself a new Ripper victim.
>
> Spill the beans, Limpalong.

SEND.

Davey took the turning. 'It just makes more sense to start with the nearest and work our way out.' Leaving the old main road behind.

'And how is that different from starting furthest out and working our way back? Got to get home anyway.' She stuck her phone away. 'Or were you planning on abandoning the car and starting a new life, down here? Cos I'm flattered, but you're no' my type.'

He opened his mouth, then clicked it shut again.

Which is why *she* was in charge.

Roberta grabbed the case file and pulled out the map she'd printed off last night – with each of the three suspected-husband-shaggers' addresses ringed in yellow highlighter. 'Next right.'

A track headed off towards the brooding sea, guarded by a pair of squint wheelie bins and an even squinter wooden sign: 'TREMUDA KNAP STEADING'.

The car lumped-and-bumped along the rutted stretch of mud and gravel, like a ship on stormy waves.

She held onto the grab handle above her door. 'How much are we getting paid for this job anyway?'

'"We" aren't getting paid anything; *I'm* getting paid. And not enough.' Baring his teeth as something scraped along the bottom of the car. 'You got any idea how hard it is to keep the wolf fed these days? In your big fancy house, with your big fancy lawyer wife?'

'No' my fault I married well. Anyway, you got your pension, didn't you?'

His face soured even more. 'Sore point.'

A steading appeared at the end of the track. A long low rectangle of misshapen granite blocks, topped with grey slate. Behind it, a bunch of fishing nets were hung on poles for mending. Like a kinky big top.

Roberta stared at him. 'Oh, *Davey*, you didn't…?'

That insipid song blanded to a halt, and a tit DJ faded himself up. *'I bet you were rocking out on your air guitars to that one, weren't you?'* Adopting a teasing tone as if he wasn't tittish enough. *'Aye, you were. We seen you. Ha, ha.'*

She rolled her eyes. 'You bloody did, didn't you.'

'Well, there were all those adverts about cashing your pension in, and how much better off you could be with the money as a lump sum.'

No sign of that flashy red Jaguar from the surveillance photos. Instead, a knackered-looking old Landy sat outside the steading.

'You took out *all* of it?'

'You're listening to Fit Like the Day *wi me, Murray MacDuff, on a sharny Wednesday morning.'*

He squirmed in his seat.

'Oh for God's… Davey!'

'So let's kick it up a bit and wheel out oor very own The Electric Ceilidh Company and their hot new release: "Skirl And Jiggle".'

'Don't, OK?' Parking next to the Land Rover. 'I know. *Believe me*: I know.'

Bagpipes howled out of the speakers, followed by a coked-up accordion. But before they could get anywhere, Davey killed the engine and clambered out. Probably thought that would save him from a proper bollocking.

Wrong.

She wriggled free of the car – not easy with a walking stick and an umbrella. A fancy blue-green-and-yellow one, from one of Susan's corporate clients. 'How could you cash-in your pension just cos some slick prick in an ad said so?'

He stuck his hands deep in his pockets, shoulders up to protect his ears. 'Bet this is bleak in the winter. Wind howling straight off the North Sea…'

It had probably started life as a cow byre, way back in the century before last, but someone had clearly lavished a bit of love and money on its conversion to a family home. Even had planters out front, with flowers in them – hard up against the walls to shelter from Davey's change-the-subject gales – but they were sad and wilting in the drizzle.

She gave him a disappointed tut. '*Never* trust people off the telly, Davey, they're all wanks.'

Away to the left, Dunnottar Castle was just visible through the drizzle, like a broken row of rotten teeth.

He pocketed his driving gloves and sparked up a cigarette that smelled like burning dog shite. 'What's the plan for talking to this Rory Hatton?'

'Same as any suspect: we start off sarcastic; move onto downright horrible; and if that doesn't work, chuck him down a couple flights of stairs.' Grin. 'You can be "Good Cop", if you like?'

He rang the bell. 'Not allowed to be *any* kind of cop. Police Act 1996, Section Ninety, brackets, One, close brackets.' Deep breath. '"Any person who, with intent to deceive, impersonates a member of a police force or special constable, or makes any statement or does any act calculated falsely to suggest that—"'

The door opened and a wee girl peered out at them through thick round glasses. Not *wee*, wee. Maybe thirteen? With a trendy haircut and a 'NUCLEAR KILL SYNDROME' T-shirt from their recent world tour. So, she had better taste in music than Davey. 'Can I help you?'

'Aye, is Rory Hatton kicking about?' Roberta hooked a thumb at the Landy. 'Don't see his Jag.'

The kid backed away an inch, frowning. '*Why?*'

'Need to talk to him about a bloke he knows. Sort of get his advice on stuff.'

Nothing.

Then the frown faded, and she gave Roberta a one-shouldered shrug. 'Dad's out. Gone fishing. On his boat?'

Davey mimed casting with a rod, putting on a sing-song voice. 'Is your daddy going to catch a lovely fish for your tea?' Fag poking out the corner of his mouth.

She blinked at him. 'We're having *sausages*.' Then shook her head and went back to Roberta. 'Dad sells lobster and crab. He's got creels.'

Davey had another go, scootching down, eye-to-eye. 'What about your mummy?'

'Bitch fucked off when we were little.'

Sounded as if Daddy Dearest had done a great job of poisoning the well, if that's how his daughter talked about her mum.

'But...' Davey's eyes widened. 'But if your daddy's away, who's looking after you, Sweetie?'

Roberta hit him. 'She's a young woman, no' a bloody puppy!'

The wee girl stuck her chin up.

Davey shuffled his feet.

Roberta hit him again. 'You have to excuse my colleague, he's an idiot. Any idea when your dad'll be back?'

'Not till ages.' Pointing in the vague direction of Stonehaven. 'Only just missed him, though. Might get him at the harbour, before he sails: *The Nippy Partan*. Red with a white stripe.'

'Cool. Ta.' Hobbling back towards the car. 'Do us a favour: make sure you lock the door, eh? Lots of weird freaks out there.' Hoicking a thumb at Davey. 'Like *this* numpty.'

'Yes. ... Well...' The numpty cleared his throat. 'Stay safe.' Then hurried around to the driver's side and climbed in. Starting the engine to perform a laborious six-point turn, the wheel bearings squeaking and squealing with every laborious twist, until they were facing the right way again.

And throughout this display of motoring ineptitude, the wee girl stood there, in the doorway, watching with her arms crossed, face scrunched. As if trying to figure out how anyone could make such a mess of driving.

Roberta gave her a wave, and for a moment the hard-girl act slipped, and Little Miss Sausages smiled and waved back. Before retreating inside and clunking the door shut.

Soon as she was gone, Roberta thumped Davey again. 'What the hell was *that*?'

'Will you *stop* hitting me!' Rubbing his arm. 'And I don't—'

'You sound like a sex offender.' Putting on a high-pitched mocking voice: '"Oh, wickle girlie, is your *daddy* catching tasty fishie-wishies for your yummy *din-dins*?"'

'I was just—'

'And how come we didn't know he was a fisherman?'

'Well, how was I supposed to—'

'Check his social media! No bugger does anything these days without posting three million sodding photos about it. Look him up!'

Idiot.

'And no smoking in the car!' She yanked the cigarette from his mouth. 'You no' got enough cancer in your life?'

Davey's ears went bright pink, cheeks too.

Cracking her window, Roberta pinged the smouldering remains out into the drizzle. 'Bloody things smell like creosote and singed pubes.'

There was silence as they lump-and-rolled their way back up the track. Then Davey cleared his throat. 'How do you think Rory Hatton manages this road in his fancy Jag?' Trying to change the subject *again*.

'I gave you those names *yesterday*, did you do *no* research?'

'Well … it was … and the house needed tidying before the carers came this morning, because Jenny's—'

'Honestly: I have to do *everything*.' She dug out her phone and called Tufty, letting it ring and ring and ring. 'And that's the last time you get to interrogate witnesses *or* suspects. You've forgotten how to—'

'Ghaaaargh…' Puffing and panting and *lurchy* noises whoomped out of the earpiece. *'Is this … important … only … only I'm sort of … in the middle … of chasing … someone.'*

'I need you to do your techno-geek thing on a few people.'

'Can it … can it wait? … As mentioned: … chasing someone!'

'You're such a—'

'HOY! STOP, POLICE! COME BACK HERE!' Peching and heeching. *'Flipping blip-blop. … Why do they … Never… Pfff…'*

'Fine, I'll *text* you. But I want it done today, understand?' Hanging up before he could whine some more.

Lazy wee snudge.

That was the problem with these young DCs nowadays: no work ethic.

The windscreen wipers *thunk-squeeeeeeal*ed back and forth as the drizzle turned into something far wetter.

Stonehaven's High Street was a lot less grand than it sounded, walled-in by sandstone terraces, darkened by the slithery rain. Made gloomier by the heavy sky and general lack of trees and bushes or any living thing.

Thankfully, the car radio was off and Davey was keeping his yap shut. Probably fearing the Terrible Wrath of The Spanking Hand. Leaving Roberta free to sit there, texting the names and addresses of their three suspected adulterers to Tufty. And the cheating husband's too. For luck.

The road narrowed, curving left as they puttered past a dumpy clock tower. Then a smear of grey appeared in the middle distance, between the buildings, and the narrow vista opened up as the soggy buildings on the right came to an abrupt end with a rumble of granite setts beneath the Polo's wheels.

Even in the drizzly yuck it was kind of picturesque – the headland rising up to the right; a line of quaint olde worlde shortbread-box buildings on the left, bordering the Old Pier.

Just a shame the water was even greyer than the sky.

Davey leaned forward, wickerwork hands at ten-to-two on the steering wheel, as he peered through the windscreen. 'Any idea what bit of the harbour he's parked?'

'*Moored*, you twit.' She pointed across the car at the marina area. 'And it won't be that bit, will it. Nothing but noddy boats and poncy yachts. Keep going.'

The setts disappeared and they were back on damp tarmac again, drifting past the old bit of the harbour, where thick stone arms encircled a wide sandy beach. A handful of boats were stranded there, the low tide leaving them nothing to float on. Then, past the old harbour wall to the newer bit, driving by the public loos, harbour office, and a bulky lump of white steelwork – where a single orange lifeboat hung, so people could practise *not* dying in a catastrophic offshore disaster.

This outer bit of the harbour must've been deeper, because there was no sand on display here, just a slick green line of algae and seaweed growing on the harbour wall to mark the usual tidemark.

The first human being they'd seen since turning onto the High Street was an auld mannie in yellow wellies, blue ovies, and a fluorescent-orange waterproof. Loading blue plastic barrels into the back of a rusty pickup.

All the berths here were empty, the only vessel: a solitary fishing boat, puttering away from the quayside. A tiny thing, no more than twenty feet long, with a small wooden wheelhouse at the front and a stack of empty creels in the back. Red, with a white stripe, and '*The Nippy Partan*' painted across its stern.

Buggering heck.

'Stop the car!'

Davey did and Roberta struggled free.

No time to sod about with umbrellas. She limped as fast as her legs and stick would carry her, to the harbour's edge. Waving both arms at the departing boat. 'HOY! COME BACK HERE!'

But either *The Nippy Partan*'s captain couldn't see/hear her, or he didn't care. Either way, he kept on going.

She whipped out her phone, firing off some snaps as the boat puttered around the breakwater and out to sea.

Davey shuffled up beside her, sheltering beneath his stupid golf brolly. 'Told you we should've called first.'

'Oh aye, because what we *really* want is to give the buggers plenty of notice, so they can come up with lies and excuses.'

Hmmm...

There was nearly sod-all water in the *old* harbour bit, and you could see the green line where the sea should've been, and the only vessel still here was that survival-training lifeboat. And it wasn't going anywhere.

She hobbled over to the auld fisher mannie.

Up close, his face was craggy as an elephant's scrotum, with a grey-and-white Captain Birdseye beard. He'd accessorised his wellies-overalls-and-waterproof ensemble with a crumpled fisherman's cap and a rollie cigarette that smouldered evil-smelling smoke out into the rain – even worse than Davey's.

His blue plastic barrels were peppered with holes not-quite big enough to post a tin of Irn-Bru through. As if he'd cobbled together DIY creels from old cooking-oil drums.

He tied the last one into place, thunked the pickup's tailgate shut, then turned to find Roberta standing right behind him. Flinched. 'Gaaaaaagh...!'

'Aye, see the boy in the boat?' She pointed at the empty harbour. 'Is it no' a bit low-tide to be heading out? That usual?'

'Hrrrmph...' The auld mannie's voice was gravel deep, but stuffed with posh-boy plumminess. 'Man's free to sail whenever he wants, no matter *how* stupid it is.'

'You know him? Rory Hatton?'

A drip formed on the end of that wrinkly nose. 'They say time and tide wait for no man – some men think they're better than the sea.' Sniff. 'They tend to end up on the bottom. Feeding the crabs.' Frowning off into the rain. 'I suppose that's the circle of life for you. You'll excuse me if I don't burst into an Elton John number, though.' A final draw on his burnt-down rollie, then he ground the stub out on the bed of his truck. Ferreted a wee tin out of his overalls and lit another. Not offering her one.

Probably just as well.

He looked her up and down. 'You police?'

'That a problem?'

A shrug. 'Not for me.' Puffing away as he stared out at the briny deep. Motionless as a carved figurehead. 'That's the thing about the sea, you never know what you're going to catch…'

And with that unhelpful bit of fortune-cookie wank, he climbed into his truck and buggered off.

Davey wandered over. 'What did he say?'

'Sod-all, useful. You stick an auld mannie in a fisherman's cap and he thinks he's Captain Flipping Ahab.' She gave herself a wee shake.

Getting soaked here, standing in the rain like a halfwit.

'Gah… Back to the car. Let's go see the next numpty on your list.'

2.15

Davey pulled up outside number sixteen, face like a skelped arse. 'I take it *you* want to do all the talking.'

'When you've got fillet steak, why eat dog food?' Roberta climbed out into the drenching drizzle of a dreich Scottish August – sloughing down from a pewter sky.

Cove had oozed outwards over the decades into a sprawling suburban maze of housing developments and cul-de-sacs. Like Creel Terrace: semidetached two-storey boxes with linked garages. Semidetached two-storey boxes *without* garages. Little terraces of four-or-five two-storey boxes, all smooshed together... They'd been clad in red brick from the ground up to just below the first-floor windows, with cream harling above. As if there'd been a terrible flood and that was the high-water mark.

Number sixteen formed the left-hand side of a garage-free semi, with that fluorescent-snot-coloured Toyota Yaris parked out front. A grey Transit van sat on the driveway at the side of the house, hooked up to a fast-food trailer that had a lime-green sign bolted on top: 'BURGER THIS FOR A GAME OF SOLDIERS!'

Davey stayed in the car, squeezing its steering wheel, face all pinched. As if he *reeeeeally* wanted to say something, but knew he needed her more than the other way around.

Roberta gave him a big smile. 'You've been in the private

sector too long, Davey. Gone soft.' Opening her arms wide, like the messiah-adjacent figure that she was. 'But look on the bright side: with my *kindly* mentoring – a wee prod here-and-there – we'll soon get you toughened-up again. Can take the man out of Grampian Police, but…?'

He gave her a grudging shrug.

'There's my boy.' She hobbled up the path and in under the wee cantilevered portico. Getting a little shelter as she rang the bell.

Davey joined her, Uncle Festering beneath his golf brolly, as if a bit of drizzle was going to kill him. 'Remember: we're looking for evidence of an affair, and-slash-or proof Sherman's been hiding money.'

'Oh aye. I'm betting that comes up in casual conversation *all* the time. It's—'

The door swung open, revealing a young-ish man in nothing but Y-fronts and a collection of tattoos. Some of which looked a bit … white supremacy-ish. A little pot belly swelled between his skinny legs and broad shoulders. Well-muscled arms. So either he spent a *lot* of time just lifting weights, or wanking himself ragged. His hair looked as if it'd only just woken up.

He gave them a cave-sized yawn and had a scratch at his arse. 'Yeah, what?' A belch rattled free. ''Scuse me.'

Roberta pulled on her official voice. 'Is this *your* vehicle, sir?' Pointing at the Yaris.

Something magical happened when you called scroats like this 'sir'. A Pavlovian reaction, born from years of being pulled over and searched, made him stand a little straighter. Made him cover the front of his pants with his hands. Made him worry if she knew what he'd been up to.

Bet Adolf McSkinny-Legs here had a criminal record thick as his skull.

His forehead wrinkled as he battled with the three brain

cells in there. Should he lie and antagonise her? Or tell the truth and maybe get off with a slap on the wrists? In the end, he went for the sensible option. 'No?'

'Course it isn't. It belongs to one Charlotte MacNeal, does it no'?'

He pulled his chin in, chewing on his bottom lip. 'Mebbe...?' Backing off a couple of paces and shouting over his shoulder, into the house. 'CHARLIE! CHARLIE, IT'S THE *POLICE*!'

At which point Davey opened his gob – probably wanting to clear up any misunderstanding and explain that they weren't *actually* police officers, what with that being illegal under Section 90(1) and everything – but Roberta elbowed him to shut it again.

'May we come in, sir? It's a tad on the soggy side out here.' She stepped inside anyway. 'My what a lovely home you have.'

Not really.

It was a long narrow hall, barely shoulder width, with a tiny loo on the left and stairs going up. A whole heap of coats bulged from a rack, meaning Adolf had to turn sideways to get past, making for a glazed door at the end of the hallway.

The laminate floor needed a sweep, and a mop, and pulling up and burning; and it was a safe bet that the stair carpet had never seen a hoover in its life. Scuffed walls. Furry cobwebs dangling from the ceiling...

Bet Davey's clean-freak little heart was shuddering at the sight.

Roberta advanced on the retreating idiot. 'Down here, is it, sir?' Past the jacket barricade. 'You won't mind if my colleague stays behind, will you? He's what we call "claustrophobic"; likes to stand by an open door.'

And with any luck, Davey was bright enough to stop anyone from doing a runner out the front.

'It... Er...' Adolf's skinny legs failed him, and he stumbled in his retreat. 'CHARLIE! THE POLICE ARE HERE TO SEE YOU!' Disappearing through the door at the end of the corridor.

Roberta followed him into a small living room, connected to a dining/kitchen by a little archway. In *here*, the manky laminate boasted a couple of pot plants long past their compost-by date, two saggy leather couches, and a rug that was more stains than pattern.

It was a motif that featured in the dining area too, where who knew what colour the floor tiles originally were?

A small round dining table boasted a trio of chairs and the remnants of last night's meal. Along with a bottle of Chardonnay, still one-third full of wine – with about two dozen little black flies bobbing about in it.

No sign of any 'Charlotte', though.

Roberta shadowed Mr Tattoo McY-Fronts into the kitchen bit, blocking him in.

A miserable little back garden lurked outside the French doors, where a border collie sheltered from the drizzle beneath a rickety picnic table.

She gave the dog a wee wave. 'You didn't give us your name, sir.'

'Ah…' Backing up against the sink. 'Brown. Campbell? Campbell Brown.'

'I see.' Roberta tipped her head on one side. 'And did you…'

A woman plummeted past the French doors, landing on the soggy grass outside with a plus-sized *thud.*

She was late-forties, large, and dressed in a red, lacy, babydoll negligee – the matching thong on full display as she lay there in a crumpled heap. She'd paired it with a brown furry bathrobe, which had the unfortunate effect of making her look like a disembowelled turd. Long bleached-blonde hair, and a cigarette dangling from the side of her mouth – which any sensible person would've extinguished *before* clambering out of an upstairs window. Health-and-Safety, and all that…

This would be Charlotte MacNeal, then.

Roberta opened the squeaky French doors and the sound of defenestrated moaning filtered into the dining area.

The dog whined, but stayed where it was.

Brown Campbell, on the other hand, squeezed past Roberta, into the drizzle. Falling to his knees and cradling Charlotte's head. 'Jesus, are you all right? What did…? It's…?'

Roberta leaned on the door frame. 'A little *underdressed* to play Santa Claus, aren't we, madam?'

'Ow…' She coughed and the cigarette fell into her hair.

He scooped it out, but she slapped him away.

'Get off me. Off!' Covering herself with the dressing gown. 'Don't just stand there – help me up!'

Campbell put on his best little-boy-lost look, then pulled her to her feet.

She stood there, all lopsided and bleary, with skinned knees and grass stains, one hand pressed into the small of her back. Teeth gritted. 'Buggering…'

Roberta gave her a cheery grin. 'Shall we talk inside, or are you comfier out here in the rain?'

Mr Y-Fronts helped Charlotte limp inside, where she collapsed into the nearest chair with a groan.

Fussing at her. 'Are you *sure* you're all right?'

She grabbed one of last night's empty wine glasses and poured herself a hefty measure of Chardonnay. Scowled at all the floating flies. Then fished them out with a scarlet-painted fingernail. Because Charlotte was clearly a classy kind of girl. Taking a big swig. Grimacing as it went down.

'Mmmmm… Dead insecty.' Roberta sat opposite. 'You know, when most people think the police want to talk to them, they don't immediately leap out an upstairs window.' Giving her a nice bland smile. 'Is there something you'd like to *tell* us, Miss MacNeal?'

Charlotte coughed, winced, then smacked her smeared lips. 'Go get Mummy's special medicine, Baby.'

And away trotted Brown Campbell, like a good little doggie.

Soon as she heard the living-room door close, Charlotte rolled her eyes. 'Thick as mince, but he goes like a steam train, so what you gonna do?' Patting the pockets of her dressing gown and coming out with a packet of twenty Bensons. Sparking one up and blowing the smoke at Roberta. 'Am I under arrest?'

'What is it with you people and skipping the foreplay? We're just having a lovely chat, you and me.'

'Oh, I'm fucking *loving* it so far.' One eye screwed up as she rubbed at her back again.

'So why the leap of faith?'

Overhead, the gurgling *whoosh* of a flushing toilet raged. Because Sugar Mummy's Good Little Boy had stopped for a wee before finishing his mission.

Charlotte took a sudden, close interest in the ash disc forming at the end of her cigarette. Working on whatever lie she was about to tell. 'It was … a *late night* last night. Up till well past three, shagging the boy's brains out. … Though I may have been a *bit too* thorough with poor Campbell. … I must've been disorientated. And dehydrated. After all the sex. That we had. All night.'

'Oh, I *see*. OK. That makes sense.' A big generous shrug. 'And, of course, you'd be happy to repeat that, in an interview room, *under oath*?'

Another flush from above.

Maybe it wasn't a wee? Maybe Brown Campbell had produced a floater?

Charlotte puffed away. 'What do you *want*?'

'Let's start with Noel Sherman.'

'Ah...' She downed the rest of her glass in one, then topped it up, emptying the bottle. Threw back a *hefty* mouthful. Not bothering to fish the flies out this time. 'Never heard of him.'

'Really? Cos we've had his place under surveillance for *months*, and guess who we see: coming and going on a regular basis.'

That flush sounded again. Must've been one *stubborn* jobbie.

Charlotte swirled her glass, sending the dead flies on a merry-go-round. 'I don't have to say anything without my solicitor present.'

'True. But you'd be cutting your boobs off to spite your bra, wouldn't you.'

She licked her lips. Cleared her throat. Sooked on her fag so hard the thing *hisssssss*ed. Swilled down the last of her fly-infused Chardonnay.

Upstairs the world's floatiest jobbie got yet another flush.

Followed by a little wailing voice: *'CHARLOTTE? CHARLOTTE, I'VE GOT A PROBLEM!'*

Roberta curled her lip. 'Your wee loon needs to eat more fibre. It's...'

Something went *pitter-pat* at the kitchen-end of the room. Like tiny feet on the filthy tiles. Only it wasn't tap-dancing mice, it was a trickle of water – coming from one of the ceiling spotlights. The trickle built into a stream, then a mini-waterfall. Spreading out across the floor.

A panicky *'CHARLOTTE!'* rang out. And then another sodding flush, because clearly Campbell wasn't the brightest of toyboys. *Spwoosh*ing down from the light fittings.

'In the name of fuck...' Charlotte folded forwards, burying her head in her hands as Roberta scrambled out of her seat and through to the living room. Into the hall. Round the bottom of the stairs – hobbling up them, walking stick thunking into the grubby carpet.

Breathing hard before she was even halfway there.

Using her spare hand to pull herself up the banister.

The landing at the top was tiny, with six doors off, but only one of them lay open – exposing a messy bedroom with rumpled sheets, the duvet lying on the floor, and the window wide open.

The landing carpet had probably started life as 'oatmeal' but had ended up 'burnt toast', getting even darker as a wet patch spread out from beneath the door at the top of the stairs.

Squelching under Roberta's boots.

But that didn't stop Campbell from flushing again.

She banged on the door. 'You better no' have your pants round your ankles!' Then shoved the thing open.

The bathroom inside wasn't massive – just enough room for a bath, a sink, a toilet, and another dead pot plant.

It also contained a tattooed young man in his Y-fronts, standing there with one foot on the floor, crying as he tried to jam something down the overflowing toilet bowl by stamping on it. Like a toddler in a puddle, splashing bog-water everywhere.

'Flipping heck…' Roberta froze, because it was already like a paddling pool in there. 'That must be one *hell* of a jobbie!'

Campbell froze, then looked up at her, with his eyes all pink, face wet with tears and *eau de toilette*.

Could *see* those three brain cells rattling around his hollow little head: fight or flight, fight or flight, fight or flight?

She raised a hand. 'Don't even think about—'

He leapt from the bog, barging past, knocking Roberta off her feet.

She crashed down on the soggy carpet, walking stick flying off to *bang-crash-rattle* down the stairs after Campbell as he legged it.

Her head hit the floor, and a bright-brown *whoooooooooooomph*ing noise detonated through her skull, making the walls shake and the ceiling ripple.

Downstairs, Davey got as far as, *'Hoy: you! Stop right—'* A clattering sound echoed up the stairs, followed by: *'Aya, bastard!'*

Which was probably Campbell being an unstoppable force to Davey's very moveable object.

God's sake...

Roberta rolled onto her side, grabbed at the balusters, and dragged herself upright. Stood there with her other arm out for balance. Doing a really good job of not being sick as Sixteen Creel Terrace waltzed around her.

Deep breath.

She staggered along the landing to the only door that faced the front of the house. Dragged it open.

A weeny bedroom, containing a part-collapsed crib full of catering supplies: pots, pans, trays, scrapers, spatulas... All of it heavy and industrial. So probably for the fast-food trailer outside.

There were boxes and boxes of napkins too, condiments, wee paper packets of salt and pepper, cases of fizzy juice, and boxes of burger buns – filling the room, chest high.

Roberta hurpled forward, one hand on the wall, shoving her way through, clambering onto boxes that really weren't robust enough to take her weight. Her boot went straight through one of them and into something soft and squashable. Because what could be nicer on a burger than an artisanal foot-flattened bun.

She battled to the window and peered out at the road below.

Identikit houses lined the street opposite – in all their bland, tidemarked glory – but Campbell Brown was determined to add a bit of excitement: sprinting away from number sixteen, heading for the town centre, wearing nothing but his soggy, almost-transparent Y-fronts.

Still no sign of Davey, though. Lazy bugger should've been giving chase by—

'STOP! NO! YOU ARE UNDER—' Another thumping collision. *'AAAAAAAAAaaaaaaaargh…'*

And then Charlotte MacNeal appeared out front, wobbling off at a fair clip. Bare feet slapping on the pavement, brown dressing gown flapping out behind her. Babydoll nightie on full show.

And *still* no Davey.

Useless tit.

Roberta struggled back through the boxes and onto the landing again. Leaning hard on the banister as she squelched across the soggy carpet and into the drowned bathroom.

Splish, splosh, splish.

Then risked a quick peek at the toilet bowl.

And there, surrounded by the blast-residue of a thousand skidmarks, was a brick of something white – about the size of a paperback book – wrapped in clear plastic and secured with heaps of duct tape. Looked *properly* wedged in there. You'd have to be an absolute moron to think it would ever flush.

That would be 'Mummy's special medicine'.

Well, it could stay there till backup arrived, because there was no way Roberta was putting her hand anywhere near that filthy crapper.

Instead, she lumbered down the squishy stairs, phone to her ear as it rang.

A nasal voice picked up: *'Aye, aye. I heard you weren't allowed to—'*

'Need all units to Cove. Suspects are an IC-One male, wearing sod-all but his skiddies, and an IC-One female in a turd-brown dressing gown and scarlet underwear. Both to be considered unarmed and *extremely* stupid.'

'Thought you were retired?'

'No' till Friday. Now am I getting them cars or no'?'

Mr Nostrils treated her to a long humm-and-haw... Then: *'I can't just send out vehicles willy-nilly. I mean, it's not as if—'*

'They're both suspected of possession with intent. A lot of intent. At least a kilo.'

'Oooh... In that case, I'll see what I can do.'

She hurpled off the bottom step, squeezed past the jacket barricade, and there was Davey – standing in the front doorway, propping himself up against the frame with one hand, while the other cupped his undercarriage. Knees bent, face screwed shut, forehead pressed against the painted wood.

Roberta hunkered down to retrieve her walking stick, taking it slow and careful, because sod having another go on the whirling-*whoooooooooooomph*-and-waltz machine.

By the time she'd straightened up that old familiar headache was clawing at the base of her skull anyway.

And Davey hadn't moved an inch, still clutching his knackers.

She hoicked up her damp trousers. 'Good job you're too old to be a dad, eh?' Peering off down the street. 'But next time, maybe *try* stopping the bad guys?'

Davey just groaned...

2.16

The drizzle had given up – for now – but the sky was heavy and bruised, ready to have another go. Looming over the soggy world.

Down here, patrol-car lights flickered off the rain-slicked tarmac. One sat empty, but Charlotte MacNeal glowered out from the back seat of the other. Hunched there like a babydoll scarecrow, shagged-out, with her hair scruffed into a sideways haystack, a muddy scrape covering one side of her face.

And the glower got darker and more murderous every time Roberta gave her a cheery wave.

So Roberta threw in a thumbs-up for good measure, before finishing up a text to Tufty:

> Hoy: Snidger!
>
> Have you done that digital deep dive yet?

Which sounded like a *very* dodgy euphemism…

Davey limped up the driveway to number sixteen – apparently still feeling the after-effects of Charlotte's knee. Which must've been remarkably bony for a well-padded lass.

He arrived bearing a large tartan thermos. Gave it a wee jiggle. 'First rule of any stakeout: stay hydrated.' Popping the lid off, then filling it with steaming pre-milked tea. 'Second is: make sure you've got a bottle to pee in too. Third is: *never* get the two mixed up…' He winced, adjusted his tormented testicles, then poured himself a plastic-mugful. 'Anything from our barely dressed friend?' Lighting one of those foul cigarettes of his and making a big show of blowing the smoke *away* from Roberta.

'Aye: a torrent of inventive swearwords even *I'd* never heard before, and sod-all else. Tell you, she's… Hold on.' Pointing away down Creel Terrace.

A uniformed PC marched into view, driving Campbell Brown before him. They were both sweaty and flushed – appropriately enough – but Campbell was still four-fifths naked, with both hands cuffed behind his back. Going by the mud and scrapes, he'd put up a bit of a fight…

'*See*, Davey? It *is* possible to apprehend a suspect.' Roberta gave Campbell the big-grin-and-cheery-wave treatment too. 'Nice to have you back with us!'

The thick sod clearly didn't know whether to smile or scowl. So he just looked … *uncomfortable* as the PC folded him into the back of the other patrol car.

She toasted him with her plastic-lid-mug. Then had a sip. 'No' bad. But full-fat milk next time, eh? Can't expect to do proper police work on this semi-skimmed bollocks.'

And as if her plastic-lid-mug didn't runneth over enough, a sleek black Mercedes turned onto the street. Heading their way. Which could only mean one thing:

'Better stand up straight, Davey, here comes the Big Boss. Time for pats on the head and, "Oh, Roberta – you clever, *sexy*, sapphic goddess you!"' Throwing in a wee smug head wobble. 'Wouldn't be surprised if there's a King's Medal coming my way.'

The Merc parked opposite the patrol cars, and the driver's door popped open, releasing Sergeant Brookminster. He'd skipped the stabproof vest, high-vis, and utility belt, opting for an official black Police Scotland fleece instead, with his epaulettes on it. Rocking a WWII wing-commander's haircut and moustache, with an upward tilt to the corners of his eyes. Like an RAF elf.

He pulled his peaked cap on, gave Roberta a curt nod as he hurried around the car, then opened the rear passenger door.

Davey really did stand a little straighter. Then had a wee panic and pinged his horrible cigarette away into the next-door neighbour's garden. Waving a hand about to clear away the charred-pube stink, like a teenager caught with a joint…

Charlotte scowled.

Campbell looked glaikit.

Roberta had a puff on her vape, releasing a steamy cloud of blackcurrant-mint. Because she wasn't a crawly wee sook.

And then, *finally*, Chief Superintendent Pine emerged from the Merc. Because it was always fun to make an entrance.

Cut quite the elegant figure in her clingy black T-shirt and crown-and-pip epaulettes, pert bum shown off to nibbling perfection in a pair of non-itchy black trousers. Got to love a woman confident enough to go grey disgracefully.

Like Roberta, Perky Pine smashed the patriarchy by donning a peaked cap instead of a bowler. Only hers came with oak-leaves and piping. Just in case any sexist moron wanted to complain.

She took a quick look up and down Creel Terrace, then tugged her T-shirt down – making it go all tight across her excellent boobs – and marched across the road. Not stopping until she was right in front of Roberta.

Being a crawly wee sook, Davey snapped to attention, hiding the thermos behind his back. 'Ma'am!'

Roberta had another sip of tea. 'Aye, aye: if it's no' Roslyn Pine and her delicious perky bum. Come to tell me how great I am?'

Pine's eyes narrowed. 'Would you care to explain what the buggering *fuck* you thought you were playing at?'

Oh, it was going to be one of *those* days, was it?

Well, two could play that game. Laying on the sarcasm: 'I was *playing* Catch-A-Drug-Dealer. Pretty big one, too, going by the size of that toilet blockage. It's—'

'Your suspect told PC Shand the pair of you came in, impersonating police officers and conducted an illegal search!'

Roberta pulled her chin in. 'Now wait a sodding—'

'And before you peddle your pathetic half-truths about—'

'*Impersonated*? I never impersonated nothing!'

Davey shuffled his feet. Not making eye contact. 'Well ... actually ... you sort of did.' Standing even more rigid as he weaselled at Pine. 'I did *try* to warn her, ma'am, about contravening Section Ninety, brackets, One, of the Police Act 1996, but—'

'Who are you throwing under the bus, you traitorous wee shite?'

Pine curled her lip. 'Even giving people the *impression* that you're a police officer is an *offence*! You don't have to flash a fake warrant card for it to be illegal.'

'I told her, ma'am, I said: "Any person, who with intent to deceive, impersonates a member of a police force or special constable, or makes any statement, or does any act calculated falsely to suggest that he, or *she*, is such a member or constable, shall be"—'

Roberta thumped him. 'Oh, shove it, Judas!'

Pine stepped closer. '"Shall be guilty of an offence and liable on *summary conviction* to imprisonment for a term not exceeding *six months* or to a fine not exceeding level 5 on the standard scale, *or both*!"' Nose in the air, like Cruella de Vil. 'Now: what have you got to say for yourself?'

Oh no...

'Wow.' Roberta sagged. 'Even… Even if I don't flash a fake warrant card?'

'I just *said* that!' Getting louder.

'Even for just calling them "sir" and "madam"? It's illegal to be polite now?'

'IT IS IF YOU DO IT SO THEY THINK YOU'RE A COP!'

'Ah…' She hung her head. Nodded. Let loose a long wobbly sigh. All droopy and contrite… Then gave Pine her best vulpine smile. The one that struck fear into scroats and Detective Inspectors alike. 'Then it's a good job I *am* a cop, isn't it?' Producing her very real warrant card and showing it off. 'I'm not impersonating *anything*. I'm still a police officer till end of shift, Friday, and *last* time I checked today's *Wednesday*.'

Pine goldfished for a moment or two, the wind leaking out of her imperial sails. 'But you're not even on duty: you've been signed off on the sick!'

'*Normally*, when off-duty police officers solve massive crimes, they get commendations and medals. Not bollockings!'

'It…' Pine tried again. 'I'd hardly call a little Class A possession a "massive crime". You still can't—'

'Boss!'

They all turned, and there was Detective Superintendent Young, emerging from the front door. Broad-shouldered, with a scalped haircut of grey-and-white. The knuckles on his grizzly paws criss-crossed with scar tissue. His wee dark eyes sparkling as he beamed at them. 'You're just in time.' Holding up a slightly squashed teddy bear with an inside-out nose/muzzle.

Pine frowned at it. 'Why are…?'

Young flipped the bear over, showing off its bum. The

washing instructions sewn into the crack of its arse waved in the breeze like a wee flag. 'Made in Lithuania.' He hooked a massive thumb at Charlotte's house. 'There's a whole box of them upstairs, in the nursery, with the lid caved in.'

Ah, so *that's* what Roberta stepped on. Not burger buns at all.

Young clapped a hand down on Roberta's shoulder and gave it a squeeze. 'This is the biggest break we've had on Operation Basilisk in *months*. Drugs, plus teddy bears, equals…' He turned the bear around again, jamming both thumbs into the seam running down its back. Cracking it open in those massive paws of his, splitting the stitching.

About two dozen teeny zip-lock baggies were nestled in among the kapok, each about the size of a second-class stamp.

Pine stared.

Young plucked one of the bags from the bear's back. Holding it aloft, as if it were the most beautiful thing he'd ever seen. 'Now, we take Madame MILF back to the station and we sweat her till she gives us the entire operation.' Giving Roberta's shoulder another squeeze. 'Good work. *Damn* good work.'

Then he was off, the eviscerated bear clutched in one paw as he waved the other at a loose PC. 'SHANDY: GET SCENES UP HERE! AND I WANT A DOG UNIT TOO! QUICK AS YOU LIKE!'

Davey cleared his throat, did some more foot rearranging, cheeks ablaze. 'Yes, well, I suppose I'd better…' Licking his top lip. 'Yes.' And away he slunk, like the two-faced chicken-spined prick that he was.

Then crept back again with a wheedle in his voice: 'Don't suppose there would be any sort of *financial reward* for…'

He made the mistake of catching Roberta's eye, and his

cheeks glowed even brighter. 'Right. I…' Taking a sudden interest in his shoes. 'We can talk about it later.' Slinking away once more.

And then there were two.

Roberta chucked the dregs of Davey's traitorous tea. 'You were saying, Boss?'

Pine scrunched her eyes shut, pinching the bridge of her nose. 'Friday, you retire. *Please* try to stay out of trouble till then.'

Roberta just grinned.

Davey's crappy old Polo growled along Rubislaw Den, blending in with the collection of fancy granite houses, villas, and mansions like a hairy wart on a pornstar's knob.

His car radio filled the brittle silence with some cheery, cheesy, poptastic nonsense, that was *still* better than listening to the git-faced tosser apologise for the umpteenth time.

'Sarah knows to feed the crows,
With chocolate and pistachios,
Every time the north wind blows…'

Roberta thumped back in her seat, arms folded tight, glaring out the passenger window. Radiating Chernobyl levels of radioactive sulkiness.

Davey turned onto her street, those stupid rattan gloves at ten-to-two.

'And sweet Francesca, In her Ford Fiesta,
She hotwired a desire,
To own an orchestra…'

He took a deep breath and pulled his shoulders up to his ears, as if the motion was physically painful. Probably working himself up to say something stupid.

'Cos Jane's insane in the pouring rain,
She ain't been the same,
Since she swam in champagne…'

He pulled up outside Roberta's house. 'Look…'

The radio idiots launched into their big chorus:

'Sing it loud, and let them hear,
All the—'

Davey killed the engine. 'I'm *sorry*, OK? I… It's not easy, we—'

'Don't.' She opened her door. 'You're a crawly bum-licking bastard, Davey McLeod. Feel free to go fuck yourself.'

'It's just…'

She struggled her way out into the gloomy afternoon.

Didn't stop him whining, though. 'I lost it *all*, OK? All of it. Took my pension lump-sum and invested the lot in high-momentum small-cap growth stocks on the US market.' A grunt. 'Was making a decent return … then *Trump* happened.'

Roberta turned and scowled back into the car as Davey wriggled in the driver's seat.

'Stock market crashes. We sell; get the hell out of there. Then it's *up* again, so we buy, you know? Trying to recoup some of our losses… And it crashes again. And again. And *again*. Up, down, up, down…' Davey buried his head in his stupid driving-gloved hands. 'He's standing in the sodding Oval Office boasting about his mates making billions, and we're left with *nothing*. Nothing!' Davey's shoulders curled inwards, back hunching. 'AAAAAAAAAAAAAAAAAAAAAAAAAAAAAAAAAAAAAAAAAAAAAAAAAARGH!'

Tough.

She straightened up and slammed the car door.

Turned on her heel and hobbled away.

Leaving him to stew in his own misery.

Roberta sat at the breakfast bar, with a proper *decent* mug of tea and a chocolate biscuit, giving *The Eternal Fall Of Gravity's Children* another go. Because, according to Jasmine's mate who worked the Sci-Fi section at Waterstones, there was a *lot* of shagging in it.

Maybe that's why Tufty gave it to her?

Dirty wee monkey that he was.

And speak of the pervert…

Ding-buzz.

TUFTY:

> Have done your Digital Deep Dive [fnarrrrr...]
>
> Results available for collection this evening.
>
> 19:00
>
> My Place.
>
> Bring crisps and disps or chips and dips.
>
> Either is good!

Pfff…

Not like it mattered anymore.

Davey could take his pish-flavoured divorce case, slather it in Ralgex, and cram it up his hoop. Investigating that kind of thing was beneath her anyway.

Mind you: knowledge *was* power.

And sometimes power meant *revenge.*

She plonked the novel down, and replied to the wee loon:

> Just text it to me.

Lazy wee shite that he was.

SEND.

And back to spaceships and naked aliens…

Ding-buzz.

> Negative.
>
> Dips and chips or disps and crisps.
>
> 19:00
>
> Come alone and tell no one!
>
> And wear a hat.
>
> Secret password is "Fumplebuttocks"!

The boy was an idiot.

She stuck two fingers up to the screen and took her book through to the living room instead, leaving her phone behind.

That would teach him.

Kurgannoor the Great unleashed her multitudinous breasts and faced the betentacled Princess Gravestreech of the Octillian Clan, feeling the familiar warmth spreading deep within as the princess slithered from her glistening underslip and said, *'Oh for goodness sake, not* again*!'*

'Gffffnnnaaagh…!' Roberta surfaced on the living room's comfiest couch, arms and legs flailing as the antique golf club went in for another poke. 'Gerroff… 'Wake. 'mwake…' Blinking in the golden, early-evening light.

Susan perpetrated poke number three. 'Have you been hitting the Glenfeòrag again?' She was wearing her work suit, Genghis Khat scampering around her slippered feet – still attached to his lead – while Naomi and Jasmine peered in through the open door.

Both were carrying a pair of flat, square, cardboard boxes, each about the size of a paving slab. Jasmine in her bookseller's black, while Pirate Naomi had developed an eyepatch. Which she pushed sideways to peer at them. 'Arrrrrrrr, me hearties, is Mummy Steel blootered on cheap grog and opium?'

'No.' Roberta sat upright and *The Eternal Fall Of Gravity's Children* tumbled to the floor. 'Fell asleep. Reading.' Launching into a jaw-cracker of a yawn that ended with a little shuddery stretch and a burp. 'Time is it?'

'Six. So you better get cleaned up.' Susan unclipped Genghis's lead and the wee lad charged over, tail going crazy, hunkering down in excitement. Then jumping into Roberta's lap, tongue out, ready to subject her to The Lickening. Which was *not* happening, because he spent *far* too much time cleaning his own undercarriage with it.

Susan slipped the ancient golf club back into its antique bag, then turned and bustled from the room. *'I picked up some tortilla chips and one of those four-different-dips things, and some hummus. Everyone loves hummus.'*

She bustled back in again, without her jacket. 'Come on: chop, chop! Don't want to be late.' Then bustled out once more. *'Honestly you're as bad as the kids!'*

Both of whom had disappeared.

Pfff…

Roberta fended off another assault from Genghis's tongue. 'Aye, all right, I love you too.' Popping him on the floor and grabbing the fallen book, before limping after Susan. 'Eh? What? Hummus? What?'

A drift of kids' boots and jackets were strewn about the hall, along with hessian shopping bags and wine carriers. The whole place smelling of hot onions-and-peppers.

Susan hung up Genghis's lead. 'I didn't know what they'd like, so I got you a Crémant De Loire – because I'm really *over* prosecco, aren't you? – and a Chenin Blanc just in case.' Clapping her hands, like a bossy schoolteacher. 'Come on: upstairs, change, back here in five for dinner.'

Naomi must've been earwigging, because her voice brayed down the stairs. *'Blisterin' barnacles! Hop to it, you salty seadogs: we's having pizza!'*

What?

Roberta stood there, blinking at the chaos. 'Am I still asleep or something?'

'Arrrrrrrrrrrrrrr…!'

'Oh, and Tufty called: said "Don't forget to wear a hat."'

Nope, that didn't help, either.

Susan rolled her eyes. 'You're going to his *game* tonight?' A tut. 'Honestly, you'd forget your own head if it didn't have a massive metal plate in it.' She gave Roberta a quick hug and a kiss on the cheek. 'I think it's *great* you're making the effort and meeting new friends!' Then wiped the lipstick mark off Roberta's skin with a thumb. 'Being cooped up in here all day isn't good for you: making you round-the-twisty.' A grimace buckled Susan's face. 'Oooh, now I really *must* go wee.'

And away she scuttled, leaving Roberta alone and adrift in the hallway.

They were all mad…

Naomi tore into a slice of ham-and-mushroom, chewing as she reached for the tomato sauce. 'And I've been promoted to Pirate Number Three, on account of Linda Fullerton getting tonsillitis!' Babbling away between mouthfuls.

Susan sat on the other side of the breakfast bar – toying with her Fiorentina, extra olives, and frowning at Roberta as if the pizzeria had added bogies instead. A big sigh. 'Oh, *Robbie…*'

'Don't care.' Giardiniera with prosciutto, all vegetably and delicious. 'I'm no' being guilt-tripped, manipulated, or tricked into playing make-believe with a bunch of pluke-faced pillocks.'

'But you need a *hobby*.'

'Aye, like another hole in the head.'

Jasmine polished off her second slice of Calabrian Feast. 'Did I tell you we're getting an author visit, Saturday? M.D. Harris. How cool is that?'

Another sigh. 'But, *Robbie…*'

'*Pirates of Penzance* is cooler.' Naomi Jackson Pollocked her pizza with ketchup, singing away:

> *'Here's your crowbar and your centrebit,*
> *Your thing-umy-whatsit – la, la, la-la, thing.'*

Valiantly carrying on, even though she clearly had sod-all idea what the actual words were.

Roberta helped herself to an un-ketchuped bit.

'Hey!'

'You snoozed, you losed.' Grinning at Susan. 'It'll be a cold day in Satan's Y-fronts, before I fanny about pretending to be a sodding wizard.' Holding a hand up to forestall further protests. 'Never going to happen.'

2.17

Friday: 0 days to go...

Roberta crunched through the last corner of breakfast. Just a slice of toast this morning, slathered in butter and lemon curd, saving plenty of room for a monstrous bacon butty or three later.

The sun had been up for nearly an hour, but it still hadn't risen over the surrounding houses yet, leaving the back garden blanketed in deep blue.

Ahhhhh...

Coffee and toast and a nice *quiet* kitchen. No anarchy, no pandemonium, no bedlam, just Roberta and Mr Rumpole quietly enjoying the stillness of a Friday morning.

She checked her hair in the patio doors – part mirrored by the kitchen lights. All Nice'N Easyed back to a lustrous shade of Fruit'N Nut. Most of the swanky 'do' had grown out over the last nine weeks, but a good going over with the curling tongs had done a decent job of wrestling it back into shape.

Shame the same couldn't be said of her uniform, which had shrunk about two sizes since the explosion. T-shirt was so tight you could see the stitching on New Faithful. Trousers had got even itchier too. But it was all pressed and polished and ready to...

Hold on.

Roberta straightened her left epaulette.

That was better.

Quick glance at the kitchen clock: just gone half six.

Time to get moving.

Big day today.

'Mmmmmmmnnnmph.' Susan shambled into the room, wearing her happy-kittens nightshirt. Yawning and bleary, hair all rumpled, rubbing the heel of one hand into her eye. 'Urgh…'

'Hey, sleepy.' Roberta drained the last swig of coffee and dumped her mug in the sink. 'What you doing up?'

Susan held her arms out, then Frankenstein-shuffled closer to wrap Roberta in a big hug. Burying her head in Roberta's neck. 'Wanted to see my big brave girl off on her last day.'

Yeah…

The HAIRY PUSSY OF THE MONTH calendar glared down from the wall: Friday the fifteenth – all ringed around and marked with arrows and a new flurry of gold stars.

Roberta pulled her chin up. 'I'll be fine.'

'I'm so *proud* of you.' Brushing a stray hair from Roberta's forehead. 'How you feeling?'

'I'll be *fine*.' Another glance at the clock. 'Got to go.'

Susan kissed her. 'Don't get too drunk! And call me when you need picked up.' She turned and shambled away down the hall, making for the front door.

Right.

Tucking her peaked cap under her arm – death to the patriarchy – Roberta plucked her walking stick from the kitchen counter and hobbled after her wife.

Admired herself in the hall mirror on the way past.

Susan opened the door and held it for her.

Early-morning sunlight gilded the roofs and the tops of the trees as Roberta stepped outside to a twittering of weenie birds.

She nodded at the patrol car idling by the kerb.

Rennie, in uniform black, nodded back.

One last smooch for Susan, then Roberta hurpled over there and thumped down into the passenger seat.

At least it was cleaner than the Rennie Family Council-Tipmobile. But that wasn't hard.

He had the radio on – one of those news-and-comment shows where the presenters were fundamentally posh and up themselves.

A nasal public-school accent: '*…tensions in the Middle East, we really have to ask what the current US administration is thinking.*'

A flat American Midwest drawl: '*I'm sad to say that it isn't. This regime – and I refuse to dignify it with the term "administration" – reacts to world events like a drunken toddler in a soiled nappy, armed with a box of firecrackers, and stuck in front of a wasps' nest.*'

Susan cupped her hands either side of her mouth, making an improvised loudhailer. 'And no getting blown-up today! Remember: *c'est verboten*!'

'*Thank you, professor. And you can hear that whole interview on our podcast.*'

Rennie flashed a Cheshire-Cat grin across the car, then donned those ridiculous oversized sunglasses of his. And normally she'd rip the piss out of him … but today something weirdly nostalgic and *indulgent* was squatting inside her ribs, so she didn't even call him a twat.

A well-spoken north-of-England voice: '*Now, you might expect any fledgling political party to have* some *teething problems, but UK New Horizons have had to suspend a* second *by-election candidate after it emerged she'd been involved in a seven-million-pound* fraud…'

Rennie stuck the car in gear. 'You ready?'

'We did ask party chairman, Graeme Anderson, for comment *– apparently no one was available – but his office* did *send us this statement...'*

She took a deep breath. 'Nope. But here we go anyway.'

The muster room had that strange digestive-biscuity smell that crowds of police officers always exuded.

Every single member of dayshift had squeezed in, all facing the front, where Detective Superintendent Young led Morning Prayers: handing out the assignments, briefing the assembled congregation on what happened overnight, and what was likely to happen today.

Roberta stood near the back of the room, surrounded by her Queen Street Irregulars – Tufty, Harmsworth, Lund, and Barrett – in their stabproofs and utility belts, all fresh-faced and innocent. They had their whole careers ahead of them: plenty of time to become twisted and cynical.

Jammy sods.

Young was still droning away. No idea what he was banging on about, though, because today was for soaking up the atmosphere. Letting the whole *being-here* thing wash over her for the very last time. Wallowing in the—

Lund's elbow poked into Roberta's ribs, eyebrows jiggling, head jerking towards the front.

Roberta blinked Morning Prayers back into focus, and there was Young, pointing at her.

'...and only: Acting Detective Inspector Roberta Steel!'

A round of applause rippled around the muster room, though you'd think most of the buggers here would be glad to see the back of her.

Young let the clapping fizzle out. 'We'll be kicking off at

Wobbly John's, then on to the Prince of Wales, Ma Cameron's, the Old School House, and Slains. Kebab stop for anyone who *doesn't* think "eatin's cheatin'" and thence to Secret Service.'

The whole dayshift gave a pantomime, 'Oooooooooooh!'

'Who say "Folding money only!" You can buy Stripper-Quids at the bar, but no putting pound coins in the young ladies' pants! It's not hygienic. And makes them go all … bulgy.' Young cleared his throat. 'Or so I'm told.' He gathered his notes. 'All right, let's get out there and make a difference!'

And with that, Morning Prayers were over.

Everyone headed off to their assigned duties. Some even patted Roberta on the back on their way past – maybe for luck? – until only she and Detective Superintendent Young were left.

Young stuck his scarred paws in his pockets. 'Big day.'

'Aye.' Sniff. 'How'd we get on with our druggy-bonk-buddies: Babydoll and Y-Fronts?'

He ambled towards the door, taking it slow as she limped along beside him. 'Campbell Brown was a complete waste of time. Boy's thick as my granny's mince. Even if he *knew* anything, he's besotted with Charlotte MacNeal, so there's no way he'd dob her in.'

Young shoved through the double doors, into the stairwell. '*MacNeal's* altogether more slippery. Confirmed her name and address, then it was "no comment" all the way. Even offered her a deal if she gave us the supply chain, but nothing. Like interviewing an over-sexed postbox.' Wandering up the stairs. Taking his time, which meant she didn't have to struggle to keep up. Because he wasn't such a bad bastard, really. 'Remanded without bail. Both of them.'

Roberta followed him around the landing. 'I'll take Tufty and head out. Got a couple leads I want to chase down, and—'

'Oh, no, no, no. I have *strict* instructions that you are confined to barracks till the final whistle today.'

Sod that.

'But I've—'

'It's a three-line-whip: "Do not let that bloody woman cause any more trouble till she's out the door and someone else's problem." Unquote.'

And there was only one person in the whole of NE Division who could give Young a direct order like that: bloody Chief Superintendent Pine.

What the hell crawled up *her* bum and laid eggs?

How was this fair?

Young must've noticed that Roberta had fallen behind, because he stopped and turned to frown down at her. 'No point giving me the Little-Orphan-Annie eyes. If it was *my* choice, you'd be free to roam, but *it's* not, so *you're* not.'

Scowl. 'This is because I always tease Perky Pine about her bum, isn't it.'

'Hmmm….' Young headed up the stairs again, leaving Roberta behind. 'Couldn't possibly comment.'

Sod.

Roberta dipped into her desk drawer again and came out with a two-hole punch. Dumped it into the archive box sitting on the scuffed carpet tiles. Where it joined two multi-packs of Post-its, umpteen pens, a pair of rulers, and three staplers.

Blue-walled cubicles turned the large room into a maze, where each desk was decorated with a cheap-looking monitor, cheap-looking keyboard, cheap-looking mouse, and cheap-looking desktop computer.

But unlike Roberta's corner desk, none of them played home to dozens of floaty mylar balloons, streamers, and bunting. Or the banner pinned to the wall above her monitor:

'HAPPY RETIREMENT ROBERT!!!' Not sure if that was supposed to be a joke, or if they'd just got a particularly dense PC to buy it. God knew there were enough of them to choose from.

Top drawer emptied, she moved on to the next one down.

About a dozen knackered vapes of assorted sizes went into the box, followed by an unopened set-of-three novelty 'sexy' USB drives – last Christmas's secret-Santa present: a boob; an erect willy; and a pair of buttocks, complete with bumhole – then a bunch of notebooks, and two evidence bags containing a rainbow-selection of monstrous dildos. Another stapler. And all the other stationery she'd nicked over the years and forgotten to take home.

She thumped the drawer shut and slumped in her office chair.

Surveyed the collection of empty plastic cups that littered her desk, because it was a *long* morning when you weren't allowed to *do* anything.

Should've been out there catching crooks, not stuck in here, drinking endless cups of crap coffee, weeing, and reading the paper.

So far, the only productive thing she'd managed to achieve was clarting every single photo in that morning's *Aberdeen Examiner* with graffiti.

The paper lay open at 'TAYSIDE RIPPER LEAVES TWISTED NOTE FOR COPS' with a regurgitated picture of Mills Observatory in Balgay Park, featuring a big blue Scenes marquee that was almost invisible beneath the weight of biro genitalia. The thing was more willies than tent, now.

A miserable voice slumped over her cubicle wall. *'Hey, Guv.'*

She looked up from her Tayside Todgerfest and there was Tufty, with a quartet of folders tucked under his arm. Bottom lip poking out, like the sulky wee shite that he was.

Wonder if it was worth raiding the supply cupboard for more notepads and desk jotters?

His pout got even poutier. 'We'd been expecting you and *everything*. Colin – he's the party's bard – wrote a special song of welcome. It had hi-diddle-dee-dees in it and we did *all* learned the chorus!'

'Aye, it's a tough world, right enough.'

Better empty the last drawer before pilfering more stationery.

She pulled out a spindle of blank CDs and stuffed it in the box. Next up: a bunch of pods for the fancy coffee machine in Chief Superintendent Pine's office. Which served the spiteful, vindictive, ungrateful cow right.

Tufty pulled his shoulders in. 'And even though you're a rotten *snudge*head, the offer still stands.' He extracted one of the folders from beneath his oxter, and plopped it down on her desk.

She narrowed her eyes. 'What's this? And it better no' be work!'

'Post-mortem report on Operation Demogorgon.'

Nope. No idea.

'Our Body-In-The-Bin case? You wanted to see it, remember? And because you is back at work, I can officially gives it to you without getting into the troubles.'

'Now *that's* more like it!' She dumped an armful of empty plastic cups into the bin, clearing a bit of space, and dug into the folder. Lots of photos – first the deposition scene, with its wheelie bins and lay-by and railway tracks; then the post mortem, where they'd laid all the bones out on a cutting table to build a full skeleton. Or as much of it as they could, given the missing bits.

The report that went with all this was much smaller than normal, probably due to the lack of soft tissue.

Tufty pointed. 'Toxicology's at the back.'

She flipped through. 'Anything?'

'Don't want to spoil the surprise.' He plonked down the next folder from his Armpit of Investigative Delights. 'Everything we have on Operation Troglodyte, AKA: the stabbing of Billie Nesbit.'

That one was *much* thicker. No doubt full of interview notes and transcript summaries and witness statements and the like.

'And this ...' he balanced a much thinner folder on top of it, 'am the online trawl you asked for: Noel Sherman, Rory Hatton, Charlotte MacNeal, and Jeremy Yarrow. Who reposts lots of cute animal videos, so can't be all bad.'

Roberta sat back and surveyed her new files.

Had to admit, the wee loon really *had* put the effort in.

And she'd treated him like something you had to scoop up in a plastic bag when taking Genghis Khat for a walk...

Which was kind of shameful, when you thought about it.

Downright unreasonable, really.

Bloody hell: she was going soft, wasn't she. Last day at work and here she was, turning into some great-big squishy lump.

'Thanks. That's...' She gave him a nod. 'You did good, Tufty.'

Which made his face transform from pout to beaming smile. 'And lastest but by much the bestest:' He placed the final folder onto the pile, as if it were made of gold-leaf and nipples. It was the thinnest of them all and had 'THE GREAT EBERTO ALTERS, LOBSTER EATER ~ WIZARD OF RESETTLEBORA!' on it in sparkly pink gel pen, because *apparently* he was a six-year-old girl.

She shrank back a little. 'Yeah... That's ... very.'

'Coolio.' Tufty did a little hoppity-kick dance step. 'The last two you can keeps, but the *first* two must to go back in the filing cabinet by end of shift. Or is *illegal*, and terrible will be the spankings!'

Pfff…

A lot to get through by four o'clock.

She put the folders in order – wheelie-bin, then stabbing. Better get reading.

2.18

Roberta licked a finger, then dabbed it about the silvery foil interior of her eviscerated crisp packet. Gathering up the final prawn-cocktail crumbs – the rest of her Markie's meal-deal already wolfed and consigned to the bin.

Feet up on the desk, she frowned her way through the post-mortem report on those skeletal remains for the third time in a row, because there must be *something* Beattie and his crew of malodorous morons had missed.

No idea what it was, though.

Ding-buzz.

LOGAN:

> How's your last day going?
>
> Sorry I can't be there. I really wanted to (just to make sure you were actually gone) but I'm stuck in Dundee.

Cheeky sod.

Tick, tick, tic-tic-tic-tic-tick:

> I am desperately offended and will never forgive you.

SEND.

Actually:

> And you'd be home by now if you'd manned up and asked ME for help catching your Tayside tosspot!

That'd teach him.

SEND.

And back to the post mortem.

The trouble with skeletonised remains was that lots of things just didn't show up on them. You could slice someone's belly open and let them bleed out – long as you didn't damage the bones, who'd know? Could get away with drownings, suffocation, maybe electrocution? Hypothermia, heat stroke, hypoxia… Not to mention several poisons that wouldn't leave a trace once the flesh was gone.

And the toxicology report wasn't a hell of a lot of use. After all that time, fermenting away in the hot sun, everything was too degraded to help.

Meaning their victim was every bit as anonymous as she'd been two months ago.

Roberta stuffed the photos and reports back in their folder and tossed it into her 'OUT' tray.

Sagged. Rubbed her face with her hands. Grimaced at the ceiling. Picked up her phone, thumbs *tic-tick*ing away:

> Getting nowhere here, Laz.
>
> Pine's having a strop-fest, so I'm confined to barracks till end of shift.
>
> Starting to think her bum's not all it's cracked up to be.

SEND.

Roberta dug into the Operation Troglodyte folder instead – Billie Nesbit's stabbing – making separate piles for each set of interview notes: Inturds on one side, Polo-shits on the other.

Then there were the incident reports.

Every attending officer had filled one out … well, everyone except Roberta. But then she'd been a *bit* busy trying not to die with a dirty-big hole in her skull. But the wee loon had taken a brief statement from her while she was laid up in hospital, whacked on morphine, and under the watchful beady eyes of Doctors Blue, Pink, and Green.

The reports went in a pile of their own, along with one from the paramedics who'd wheeched Billie Nesbit away for emergency surgery.

Ding-buzz.

Logan:

> Maybe Pine just wants to keep you close because she LOVES you! (hahahahaha)
>
> Our boy's started sending notes now.

As if she hadn't already read about that in the paper. Then drew willies all over it.

There wasn't any point making a pile for witness statements, because there was only one – from Captain Rainbow-Tie, AKA: Emma Dornoch's camp campaign manager, Frank Abercrombie.

It was barely two sides of A4, and not a massive help.

Oh, I was *so* overwhelmed by the situation and all the thugs. I didn't see the knife. I heard Billie scream. Rushed to her aid. Got shouted at by a 'short, rude, angry policewoman'.

Better not have been talking about *her*.

And who the hell was he calling 'short'?

And she wasn't 'rude', he was just a big sodding Jessie.

The file also contained a whole bunch of photos: the rioters, the scene, the knife, the wound... Then there was a sort of ante-mortem report compiled by the surgeons at Aberdeen Royal Infirmary who'd plugged the holes in Billie's innards.

Had to give them points for effort on that one, but it wasn't exactly revelatory, given everyone already knew she'd been stabbed.

Roberta scoofed back the last mouthful from a tin of Irn-Bru, and frowned at her piles.

Was going to take a while to get through this lot.

She checked the clock hanging on the office wall. The big hand was at ten and the small hand at four. Which was bugger-all use.

According to her phone, it was twenty to two.

And Logan's text still sat there, unanswered.

OK:

> See? This is what happens when you don't ask the Great Roberta Steel to help with your sharny serial-killer cases!
>
> What kind of notes?
>
> And are you sure it's him, not some squirrel shit?

SEND.

Glancing up at the dead clock again.

OK: twenty to two. Shift ended at four. Which meant just over two hours to read all this, digest it, and get everything back to the wee loon.

No *way* that was enough time.

Of course, she *could* go and photocopy the lot…

If she had any idea how to work the photocopier. That kind of job was what you had constables for.

Besides, it'd take ages, and the chances of getting caught doing it weren't exactly slim.

Be nice to finish her final shift without having to sit through yet another bollocking…

Ding-buzz.

LOGAN:

> If it's a squirrel, the fluffy wee bastard knows things we haven't released to the press.

Locations of the bodies, which bits were missing, etc.

See, now *that* was interesting.

Tick, tick, tic-tic-tick:

Could be someone on the investigation?

Rogue cop turns cannibal serial killer!

SEND.

But didn't help with her dilemma.

Mind you, if paper copies were too risky, maybe electronic was the way to go? Have a wee dig through the office servers and winkle out the files. And yes, that kind of computery thing was usually the wee loon's area, but he'd just bitch and whinge and moan if she asked him. *'Ooh, Chief Superintendent Pine wouldn't like it! Ooh, you'll get me into trouble! Ooh, it's illegal!'*

Blah, blah, wankity wank.

Just have to find them herself – how hard could it be?

Question was: *then* what?

Couldn't email the files to her home address, because it'd leave a paper … well, *digital* trail. Which might make things a bit sticky if the Rubber Heelers ever tried to do her for unauthorised retention of police documents.

But there *might* be another way.

Roberta burrowed through her cardboard box for those novelty-shaped USB drives – hacking the plastic blister-pack open with a pair of stolen scissors. Then popped the boob free.

The thing was silicone, about the size of a squash ball, with a perky nipple. And it made squeaky noises when she squeezed it. Which was fun. *Squeak, squeak, squeakity-squeak.*

Anyway.

She plugged it into the USB port on her computer and the thing *vibrated.*

OK...

Took a bit of searching to find all the Billie Nesbit stabbing files, but Roberta copied the whole lot onto her jiggly boob. Then tried the same with Operation Demogorgon.

Only her boob wasn't big enough to hold all the data on *both* cases, so the overspill would have to go onto the USPenis.

When she inserted it into her USB port it sort of ... *wriggled.*

Don't know who Santa was, but no surprise he wanted to remain anonymous. Pervert.

Soon as the files were copied over, she unplugged the writhing willy and stuck it in her pocket, along with the jiggly boob.

Quick check left and right to make sure no one had seen any of that *highly* illegal—

Ding-buzz.

Roberta flinched. Because, you know...

LOGAN:

> Don't think I haven't considered it.
>
> I suspect everyone!
>
> Especially Sgt. O'Grady because he's a devious little squit who doesn't like rowies...

Deep breath.

> Aye, that's a red flag, right enough.
>
> ALMOST AS BIG AS MISSING MY RETIREMENT SODDING PUB CRAWL!

SEND.

That'd teach him for giving her a fright.

She clonked her phone onto her desk and leaned back in her chair, pulling an evil smile and steepling her fingers. All she needed was Mr Rumpole, a scar, a secret volcano lair, and she could give it the full Bond villain.

Now she had the files, she could review them whenever she liked.

Hmmm…

Wonder if there were any *other* investigations worth industrial espionageing while she had the opportunity? Cos it wouldn't come around again.

Roberta dug the bum from the blister-pack and slotted it into her USB port. Staring as the thing *throbbed.*

Wow.

Right.

She copied everything from Operation Basilisk onto it. Then filled her bum with Operation Firedrake, cramming the files in there till there was no space left.

Nothing left to do but kill time till four, then head off for a well-deserved hedonistic roister to celebrate thirty years protecting the public as a police officer.

And no one would *ever* know.

BWAHAHAHAHAHAHAHAHAHAHAHAHAHA…

2.19

Roberta hauled open the heavy wooden door and limped into Wobbly John's.

It was a subterranean affair, with a central bar and various levels leading off. Apparently, being underground wasn't gloomy enough, so they'd painted the rough walls in shades of blackcurrant jam and stained all the wood dark mahogany – lit by flickering fake candles.

But it was always quiet at this time of day, only a brief stagger from Divisional Headquarters, and the booze was cheap. So it could be as dark and burrowy as it liked.

No sign of anyone in the main bit.

She limp-clomped up the short flight of stairs to the upper bar, then through into the snug.

No one there, either.

And the lower bar was completely clear of off-duty police officers as well. Or anyone else for that matter. Other than a hipster barman, slouched over a novel with his tattooed forearms on show, Roberta was all alone.

She checked her phone: half four.

Shift ended thirty minutes ago.

And if *she'd* had time to get a lift home, dump her haul of purloined stationery and misappropriated files, change into her going-out-fit – jeans, boots, splot-free purple silk shirt, vintage leather jacket – and get back here, surely *someone* would've made the two-minute walk from DHQ to Wobbly John's by now.

Calling up her texts didn't help – no message about having already moved on to Pub Number Two. Besides, Detective Superintendent Young wouldn't just *abandon* her. He'd leave a PC behind to wheech her off to the Prince of Wales.

Maybe something was up?

Or maybe the buggers were just slow.

Whatever the reason, as first officer on the scene, it was her duty to secure the locus and nab the biggest corner table in the main bar – there to hold court till it was time to head on to the next boozer: 'Things I Have Learned In My Thirty Years On The Force', by Roberta Steel. Like the whole stupid *renaming* thing. First it's Grampian Police; then Police Scotland lands like a sack of jobbies, and Grampian gets split into A Division and B Division; and *that's* a cocking mess, so it's all smooshed back together into one big A Division, only it's also pronounced 'North East Division', but you've got to be careful not to confuse it with N Division or E Division, and A/NE Division's the same bloody shape and size as Grampian Police was in the first sodding place. So what was the *snidging* point of changing it?

Anyway...

Suppose she *could* just take over the upper snug, but no way that would be big enough for everyone.

Yup – this was going to be *quite* a night...

Pfff...

Still no one.

Roberta sat at her commandeered table, preloading a double-gin-and-tonic and a packet of dry roasted. Because it was always wise to put a wee lining on your stomach before embarking on a mammoth sesh.

She woke her phone up. Twenty to five, and Wobbly John's was just as dead as before.

That would change at five, when the council offices emptied out and the lure of a Friday-evening-post-work pint became irresistible. But now?

She sipped her gin.

Ate her nuts.

Chewed on her cheek.

Maybe something *had* happened?

Come on, it wasn't as if they were going to forget about her retirement bash, was it. Not after thirty sodding years.

Nah.

Bet some idiot got confused and told everyone kick-off was at five, instead of four.

Just need to be patient, that's all…

She checked her phone. *Again.*

Three minutes past five, and there were already half a dozen suits peppered around the bar. Each one sitting on their own, lanyards tucked away, ties loosened or handbags on the seat beside them. Pints and nips for some, big glasses of wine for others. One prick, with spots and glasses, even had a negroni – trying to kid herself she was out for a sophisticated after-work cocktail, even though she must've sprinted here in her knee-high boots soon as the office clock hit five.

Roberta polished off the second double-gin-and-tonic. Then thunked her glass down on the table, setting the ice cubes rattling.

Still no buggers from work.

You'd think someone would at least have texted her. Oh, sorry we're late! Running behind! Be there soon! LOL!

She squinted at the phone's screen. Which was all blurry, because electronic geeks were tossers who couldn't design a decent user interface to save themselves. And she wasn't wearing her glasses.

She held the thing out at arm's length, till it wobbled into focus.

Buggering hell.

No wonder – no reception.

Of course. Wobbly John's wasn't just a couple of steps down from the street, it was halfway to sodding Australia.

That's why she hadn't got any calls or messages.

Bet if she went outside, right now, her phone would light up like Bonfire Night.

Roberta tied her empty nut packet into a silvery knot, dumped it in her glass, and limped across to the exit. Lumbering up the stairs.

Took a while, but she finally shoved out through the double doors at the top and onto Broad Street, opposite the old council building. Breathing hard, because that was *far* too many steps.

The sky had dulled from this morning's shiny blue to something more like freshly poured concrete. A thin smirr of drizzle misted down, turning the pavement into shimmering slabs of slippery slate.

Ding-buzz.

Finally!

Sheltering beneath the pub's portico, she dug her phone out.

LOGAN:

> Good luck for tonight!
>
> Drink responsibly and don't forget to pace yourself!
>
> Stay hydrated!

Have a get-home buddy!

And eatin' is NOT cheatin!

;)

No messages from Tufty or anyone else…

A whole bunch of missed calls, though: 'YOUNG', 'TUFTY', 'TUFTY', 'TUFTY', 'TUFTY', 'LUND', and 'YOUNG' again.

And it looked as if they'd all left voicemails. She poked the button and an electronic voice buzzed out of her phone:

'YOU HAVE … SIX … NEW MESSAGES, AND … TWO … SAVED MESSAGES. NEW MESSAGE … ONE.'

Young: *'Steel? It's me. Look we're going to be a little late. Something's come up, but I'm hoping it—'*

DELETE.

Because, let's face it, this was clearly some sort of self-serving distractionary waffle.

'MESSAGE DELETED. NEW MESSAGE … TWO.'

Tufty: *'Flipping plurch! Guv, we was nearly out the door, but we're all getting called back in for a green shift, and—'*

'MESSAGE DELETED. NEW MESSAGE … THREE.'

It was Tufty again, but he was barely audible over the howl of a patrol car's siren. Going somewhere at speed. *'We does has an situation development! That car bomb? You'll never guess whose house it went off outside!'*

Car bomb? No one said anything about a car bomb.

That's what she got for deleting things without listening all the way through.

She hung up on her voicemail and called Young back instead. Might as well go straight to the organ grinder.

It rang. And rang.

A woman hurried up Broad Street, not really dressed for the weather in stiletto heels, a pencil skirt and matching jacket

– both in a lurid shade of terracotta, but getting darker in the drizzle. She was clutching a paper bag from Lush, held over her head as a makeshift umbrella.

Superintendent Young's voice growled in Roberta's ear. *'Wondered how long it'd take you.'*

The woman's left heel slipped on the slick pavement and that was it: gravity mugged her. Arms windmilling, then legs in the air and *THUMP*! Flat on her back, lying there like a squashed starfish.

Roberta tightened her grip on the phone. 'Where the hell is everyone? Meant to be getting blootered, here.'

'Just north of Bridge of Don. Looks like a car bomb went off outside your best friend's house.'

Eh?

'Best…? Do I know someone in—'

'Graeme Anderson, MP. The man who rescued you when that business park in Westhill blew up? Looks as if he might've been right all along – it really wasn't *an accident.'*

The paper bag from Lush must've ruptured in the crash, because now various, brightly coloured fizzy things frothed away to themselves on the pavement, like rabid tennis balls, as the woman lay there groaning.

Car bomb.

Roberta hobbled out into the rain. 'I'll get a patrol car and meet you there soon as I can. We—'

'Nope.'

'Blah, blah, doctor's orders.' Making for DHQ. 'Don't worry: I'm no' going to *drive* the thing. I'll get a PC to—'

*'There is no "*we*" anymore, Roberta: you retired, remember? You are an ex-cop. You have slipped away to join the ranks of the ancients. Gone to your eternal rest. You've permanently shuffled off the duty roster. On a full pension.'*

She stopped, halfway down the path. 'But—'

'And now you'll have to leave this stuff to those of us who still work for a living.' Young's voice went all muffled. *'Better block the road from the junction to at least three hundred yards that way. … OK. … Thanks.'* Back to full volume. *'I'm sorry about the retirement bash. We'll do it properly next week, OK? It's… Hold on…'* A scrunching noise – probably sticking one of those huge paws over his phone's microphone – was followed by an exchange too faint to make out. Then, *'Look, I've got to go.'*

The line went dead.

He was gone.

Leaving Roberta standing there as the drizzle turned into proper rain. Getting heavier and heavier.

The sprawled and soggy terracotta businesswoman struggled to her feet with a muttering growl of foul language that got ever louder as she gathered up her various fizzing mounds – using the paper bag as if it were a pooper scooper and there was something *seriously* wrong with her dog.

Shoulders slumped, Roberta poked at her contacts again and waited for Susan to pick up.

A bus rumbled past.

Then a taxi.

The woman rammed her fizzing bag in the nearest bin and limped away, swearing.

And the phone kept on ringing, because the world—

'Hey, you. How's the boozeathon? Are you behaving yourself, or is it all wine-and-nipples at the erotic—'

'I'm ready to come home now.' Sounding like a small child who'd just been forced to eat a fistful of worms. 'Can I get a lift?'

'Oh, Robbie. Has something…?' Deep breath. *'I'll be right there.'*

'Thanks.' Roberta hung up, put her phone away, and drooped a little more in the bucketing rain.

Thirty years.

Thirty *sodding* years, and never mind a gold watch, she hadn't even got a *free pint* out of it.

Talk about a policeman's lot…

just before the wheels come off

3.01

The bedside clock flickered from 08:01 to 08:02, glowing away in the thin grey light that seeped around the closed curtains.

Roberta huffed out a breath and went back to frowning up at the ceiling. It hadn't changed any in the last hour. Or the hour before that.

Normally, after a monster leaving do, everyone should be comatose till *at least* eleven. Not lying here, examining every lump and bump between the cornices, as the miserable day miserabled away…

Susan was curled up on her side, sleeping mask slightly squint, earplugs in.

A *bang* then a *thump* vibrated through the ceiling, because Jasmine and Naomi were half-delicate-young-ladies, half-elephant.

Even through earplugs it was loud enough to make Susan snork, twitch, then fumble her sleeping mask up. Blinking at the gloomy morning. She popped her earplugs out. Then a smile bloomed across her face as she rolled over to snuggle into Roberta. 'Mmmmmmmmmmmm…'

'What?'

'Got you *all* to myself, now.'

Which was true. No more Police Scotland politics to play; no more murders, robberies, rapes, assaults, or burglaries to solve; no more drug rings to bust up…

Should've been dancing naked in the street, whooping for joy.

So why was it like lying at the bottom of an open grave?

Waiting for them to shovel the earth back in.

Roberta took a deep breath. 'It's going to be fine.'

Wasn't it?

'Course it is.' Susan snuggled in deeper. 'And we don't have to figure everything out in one go. We've got alllllll the time in the world.'

The rest of Roberta's life…

'Retirement. God, I'm so *jealous*!' Susan gave her a big hug and a grin. 'Got something for you.' Then sat up and rummaged in her bedside cabinet.

Ahoy-hoy.

Roberta raised an eyebrow. 'It's no' handcuffs, is it? Silk rope and some lubricant? Jar of—'

'Surprise!'

It wasn't any of those things. Instead, a shower of leaflets fluttered down on Roberta. No two alike. Ranging from colourful and professional to crooked black-and-white photocopies.

Eh?

She picked one up and held it at arm's length, squinting. 'Stained-glass making?'

'Or this one:' rifling through the drift for a photocopied flier with a naked-lady sketch on it. 'Life-drawing classes. Painting people in the nude. You'd like that.'

Roberta sat up. 'What the buggering snudge is—'

'Evening classes, part-time community college courses. Or you could enrol at Aberdeen University, or Robert Gordon's – do a degree! History, English literature, poetry, pottery. Maybe try a creative writing class and work on your memoirs? "Batons, Butties, and Burglaries" brackets "my exciting life as a police officer in Aberdeen"!'

'But—'

'Mortimer said you should train as a magistrate, can you *imagine*? The man's senior partner at a law firm and doesn't know we don't *have* magistrates in Scotland?' Frown. 'Starting to think he's three or four marbles short of a Kerplunk. But you could be a Justice of the Peace? And I bet you've got *loads* of transferrable skills Citizens Advice would love.' Susan gave her a wide-eyed look. 'You could even start over and build a *completely new career*!' Then a poke. 'But only if it's nine-to-five with weekends off.'

Oh God…

Roberta sagged back into the pillows. 'But—'

'Like I say: you don't have to decide right now.' Susan snuggled in again. 'Got your whole life ahead of you.'

Why did those words echo around the room, like a dark bell's toll?

Outside, little and not-so-little feet thundered down the stairs.

Jasmine: *'Mu-uuuum! Can't be late today, got that author visit, remember?'*

Naomi launched into song, bellowing it out like a war cry:

'WITH CAT-LIKE TREAD,
UPON OUR PREY WE STEAL!'

'Nooo…' Susan covered her face with her hands. 'Maybe we can sell them for medical experiments? Or pet food.'

'IN SILENCE DREAD,
OUR CAUTIOUS WAY WE FEEL!'

Maybe Susan was right? – about the fresh start, not the medical experiments – after all, wasn't as if anyone at Police Scotland gave a toss about Roberta's retirement.

Thirty sodding years…

'NO SOUND AT ALL,
WE NEVER SPEAK A WORD!'

Maybe she *should* broaden her horizons a bit?

And painting people in the nip might be fun.

Long as they weren't horrible munters.

'A FLY'S FOOT-FALL,
WOULD BE DISTIIIIIIIIIINCTLY HEARD!'

'Mu-uuuum! We're out of orange juice!'

Actually, Susan was probably right about the medical experiments too.

Somehow Naomi managed to get even louder:

'TARANTARA, TARANTARAAAAAAAAAAA!'

'Oh, in the name of…' Grumbling, Susan rolled out of bed and reached for her dressing gown. 'Flipping kids…'

'SO STEALTHILY THE PIRATE CREEPS,
WHILE ALL THE HOUSEHOLD SOUNDLY
SLEEPS!'

Yeah.

Life was full of possibilities now.

Why not grab it by the testicles and *squeeze* till they pop?

Roberta lumbered into the spare room, carrying that stupid cardboard archive box. Which wasn't easy without her walking stick. But both hands were full, so lumbering was the only option.

The room was nice enough, if a bit … plain.

Unlike the mistress bedroom, it was at the front of the house, overlooking the street – where Susan was busy shepherding their unruly children into the Big Car. Jasmine: dressed for selling books, Naomi: dressed for pillaging galleons on the Spanish Main.

Roberta dumped the box on the carpet and watched as they all clambered into the car, seatbelts on. Some laughter, glimpsed through the Volvo's windows.

Maybe being a stay-at-home mum wouldn't be *too* bad?

Even if it gave her the total shudders.

The Big Car pulled away, and off went Susan and the kids.

So, Roberta returned to her box – still full of filched stationery, appropriated coffee pods, rude USB sticks, and the dildos that somehow never did make it back into evidence.

You know what? If Police Scotland didn't give a toss about *her*, then why should *she* give a toss about *it*?

All those years, slogging her guts out, trying to keep the various arseholes and assorted tossers of Aberdeen from killing each other, for what? A cancelled pub-crawl?

Sod them.

She put her slippered foot against the box and shoved it under the spare bed. Stuck two fingers up at the thing, Police Scotland, and all who sailed in her. Then shoogled the valance about till her pilfered stuff was completely hidden within the dusty depths. Where it could sodding well stay.

After all: this was the first day of the rest of her life. And she was going to *do* something with it.

Yes, she'd probably wobble a bit, and feel kind of lost from time to time, but she'd muddle through.

Always had.

Always would.

One thing was certain, though – no matter *how* bad things got, no matter how *bored* she became – there was no way in Satan's *sharny* bumhole that she'd *ever* join Tufty's stupid role-playing game.

Five Weeks Later

3.02

Roberta paused, one hand on the door through to Tufty's living room, earwigging on the conversation inside as the toilet cistern's *gurgle-roar* slowly faded.

A woman's voice, flat and nasal: *'I mind we were taking Sticky Paul in after he peed all over that charity shop on Union Street. And Christ knows what he'd been drinking, cos he absolutely drenched two racks of jackets and a dirty-big box of Dan Browns.'* That would be PC Loraine 'The Horn' Foggerty.

'Give me druggies over piss-heads any day. At least they dinna barf chunks a' ower your patrol car.' Sounded like … PC Colin 'Baddy' Goodman? Or maybe it was Constable Vernon 'Outie' McInnes? Difficult to tell. They both had that same teuchter drawl.

You'd think, after four weeks, it'd be easy enough to tell them apart.

'Aye, if you're lucky.*'* No, *that* was Outie. *'Cos if you're* un*lucky it's going all over the back of your heid.* And *down inside your stabproof!'*

Roberta turned the handle and hobbled inside.

It was maybe half the size of her living room back home, but then she and Susan didn't live in a two-bedroom flat, on the sixth floor of a twelve-storey tower block.

It was almost completely lined with shelves – crammed full of books and DVDs and figurines of monsters and cartoon characters and spacemen and robots – leaving just enough empty wall to mount a shiny elf-sword thing and a sort of oversized Star Trek Batarang, either side of a life-sized, cardboard cutout of Jean-Luc Picard.

The couch was pushed to one side, making room for a folding dining table and six folding chairs, five of which were occupied.

Tufty sat at the head of the table, dressed in a long hooded robe that made him look like a shortarsed monk from a horror movie. Lurking behind a leather screen that came midway up his chest, hiding his rule books, dice, and assorted paperwork.

Next was Outie – late twenties, looking nervous and hairy, with simian arms, and fur poking out the neck of his T-shirt. Wearing a purple-and-gold bishop's mitre with a big pentagram embroidered on it.

Then The Horn, with her squarish face and the kind of stubby fingers that could dig through concrete. Glasses, no make-up. Shoulder-length brown hair trapped beneath a long muted-red-and-green sock-type hat with a fedora brim. Freddy Krueger meets the Elf on The Shelf.

Then Tufty's bidie-in, PC Kate MacKintosh – dishwater-blonde hair held back in a ponytail, glasses, quirky smile, cute in a short-and-spanky-chase-me fashion, sporting a leather tricorn hat – à la Dick Turpin – that had dangly bits on one side and a plume of magpie feathers at the back.

Which just left Baddy, who actually had a *proper* haircut, instead of a shorn-to-the-bone DIY home-clippers job. Oval head, NHS glasses, and a chin that barely needed shaving once a month. The only brown face in the party, in a 'MOS EISLEY HOLOGRAPHIC CHESS CLUB' T-shirt and a scarlet Robin Hood cap. It had an oversized leather coxcomb tucked into the brim, like a prolapse. 'Aye, aye,' he grinned, as Roberta hurpled over to the last remaining seat, '*the Beast* returns.'

Roberta thumped down into place. 'Flipping heck, Outie, what did you put in that salsa? Goes straight through you like Toilet Duck.'

Another grin. 'Scotch bonnet.' Outie's hairy hand came up to point right at her. 'Haaaaaaat!'

Then the rest of them were at it: 'Haaaaaat! Haaaaaat! Haaaaaaaaaaaaaaaaaat!' until she picked hers off the table and stuck it on her head. A big pointy one in dark burgundy, with a wide saggy brim, and 'WIZZARD' across the front in gold sequins.

'Right.' Tufty rolled some dice in secret, behind his screen, then reached over to point at the big map that sat in the middle of the table. It was a burnt-out, medieval city centre, featuring a bunch of painted miniatures, cowped-over and scattered around the shattered streets.

Only five were still standing: by far the fanciest figurines, each one wearing fantasy outfits and the same hats as the people gathered around the table. Well, except for Tufty – who wasn't there.

The wee loon raised his arms. 'The first snows of winter begin to fall, drifting down from an ashen sky. Melting where they hit the stones that are still hot to the touch. Settling on the dead bodies.' Dramatic pause. 'The scrape-marks and blood you've been following disappear under the door to the local tavern. One of the few buildings still standing: "The Boar and Griffin".' Tapping the map with an extendible pointer, so they all knew where he was talking about.

Baddy put on his character's Terry-Thomas voice: all posh, English, and lispy. 'I rap on the inn door with a pleasing rat-a-tat-tat rhythm.'

Another secretive dice roll. 'The tavern door creaks open, and there stands a hideous half-troll in a stained leather apron, holding a mop in one hand and a severed human arm in the other.' Then Tufty dropped into a gruff, 'What you want? We'z *closed*!'

Kate went all pirate. 'I uses me Thief's Eye to see if there's anything worth stealing in the room beyond. *And* gets me a squint at what the 'eck's going on.' She rolled non-secret dice of her own. 'Thirteen.'

'OK...' Tufty consulted the inside of his screen. 'Between the half-troll's hairy legs you can make out a pleasing hostelry, with an open fireplace, wooden tables and chairs. It also contains a pile of crumpled bodies – some of who are missing various bits – and what looks like a Goblin, in chef's not-so-whites. She's using a pair of pliers to pull the teeth from a dead barbarian, singing away to herself.' He put on a creepy voice:

'Tooth pie, tooth pie,
We'll fry their gizzards and pickle their thighs,
Wrap it in pastry and stuff it with eyes...'

Baddy grimaced. 'Remind me not to eat here.' Then back to being Terry-Thomas: 'Hey nonny, nonny, and well met, jolly Innkeep. Allow me to introduce myself, *I* am Linda Mooncog, Bard par excellence, renowned throughout the nine kingdoms, and these are my companions.' A pointy finger went around the table, starting at Kate. 'Skink Moatcheat, logistics; the Venerable Cleric Rennin Omens, spiritual guidance; Ariglyn Rooftree of the Woodland Realm, security; and The Great Eberto Alters, Wizard of Resettlebora, spells, enchantments, and magical whatnots.'

Roberta gave Tufty/the Innkeeper a cheery wave, and because everyone else was doing funny voices, launched into an unflattering impersonation of Chief Superintendent Pine: 'Aye, braw tae meet ya, wee man!'

'Indeed.' Baddy leaned forwards. 'My companions and I were wondering: what happened to your *lovely* town?'

Tufty rolled. 'He sniffs. Chews. Then spits at your feet. It looks like mashed spiders.'

'Urgh!' The Horn shuddered. 'Too graphic.'

Tufty part-trolled it up again: 'What 'appened to our "lovely town?" What's it look like? Now sod off, we don't open till dinnertime. Chef's still workin' on the menu.' Miming pulling teeth. 'Then he slams the door in your faces.'

Hmm…

Roberta sat forward. 'Can I do some sort of time-window spell, so we can see into the past?'

'Check your spell book.'

Not so much a book as two sides of A4 with her character's stats on it. And only six spells: Tasha's Hideous Laughter, Chaos Bolt, Burning Hands, Magic Missile, and Detect Magic. None of which looked time-windowy. 'Bollocks.'

Outie raised a hairy hand. 'If we can find a victim of the attack, who's not *too* smashed up, I can cast Speak with Dead?'

'Arrrr…' Kate winked. 'Well, mateys: looks like we best rummage ourselves up some nice fresh corpses for the padre here…'

Baddy waved a tortilla chip about, generously loaded with Toilet-Duck dip. '…so *I* said, "Either you put your trousers back on, or I'm dragging you down the station like that." And you know what he did? He—'

'Whipped off his pants and ran around whirling his willy about like an aeroplane propeller.' The Horn rolled her eyes. 'You tell this story *every* time.'

The sound of busy rustling came through from the galley

kitchen – the door lying open so Kate could still be part of things as she clattered a whole bag of oven chips onto a tray, ready for cooking – while everyone else lounged about the table, out of character, but still wearing their hats.

Well, everyone except Outie: off for a fag on the wee concrete balcony.

Roberta scooped up some hummus on a cheese-and-onion crisp. Turned out crisps-and-disps were remarkably similar to chips-and-dips. 'Aye, we've all had helicopter willy wavers.'

'You know,' The Horn crunched a carrot stick, 'it's *so* nice we can talk shop again. Our last wizard was a civilian and you can't, can you. Too risky.' Going in for some cheese dip. 'And I know, *officially* you're not Job anymore—'

'Nah.' Baddy shook his head. 'Once Job, *always* Job.'

Tufty tried the taramasalata. 'I has been wondering though, guys, maybe Roberta does wants an break from all the police gossip? *Maybe* it does has being a sore point, and all that.'

Which was just sodding weird. Hearing the wee loon use her real name, instead of calling her Sarge, or Guv, or Your Royal Scariness. Could see him wriggling when he said it too. As if it was just *wrong*.

Suppose that's just what happened when you retired…

'Nah, I don't mind.' She shrugged. Frowned. Disped another crisp. 'Kind of soothing, to be honest.' Chewing on the thought. 'Not that I *miss* running about after stots and scumbags. I used to, but now?'

Tufty nodded. 'Good for you.'

'Did a mindfulness course at North East College. Got me to recognise my patterns of "learned obsession" and develop tools to deal with "obtrusive cognitive patterns".' Scrunching on a pickled-onion finger. 'Oh aye: my Police Scotlanding days are *over*.'

The Horn drooped. 'Wish mine were. You know what I

spent *my* day doing? Standing around like a pickled fart, guarding the burnt-out remains of a noodle van.' Making explanatory hand gestures at Baddy. 'Like a burger van, only for noodles.' Back to normal. 'Someone dragged the owner out and battered the living crap out of her with a cricket bat, nicked her takings and most of her ingredients-slash-kit, then set fire to her van, and *off* they buggered.'

'Ouch.' Tufty grimaced. 'Which noodle van was this?'

'Dunno... Something alliterative that rhymes. Somethingy Something, Noodley Doodley?'

'Oh noes! Not *Hungry Helen's Noodle Doodle*?'

She snapped her fingers. 'That's the one!'

'Thrice times arrrgh...' Bereft and saggy. 'Now I does *never* get to taste her spring rolls, Har Gow dumplings, chicken-and-mushroom chow mein...' Pouting. 'We got blowed-up last time, before I could eat anything.'

Baddy got stuck in to the Toilet Duck again. Boy must have a cast-iron stomach. 'That Operation Firedrake?'

A nod. 'Second time this month.'

Hard to tell which was nicer with the hummus – cheese-and-onion ridges, or spicy-beef maize hoops. So Roberta went for the double. Keeping her voice all casual. 'Any noise on our Body-In-The-Bin?'

At which, Tufty's eyes narrowed. 'Thought you didn't care?'

'Don't really. Habit more than anything.' Crunch, munch, scrunch. Not bad... 'See when I got back home from that aborted retirement party? I stuck my box-o'-shite under the bed in the spare room and forgot *all* about it. Haven't touched the thing since.' Big smile. 'You're looking at a changed woman.'

'Yeah...' Tufty stared at her with one eyebrow raised, as if he didn't believe her and was *desperately* in need of a slap.

But Roberta let it go, because she was a changed woman.

Plus, being Dungeon Master, the wee squit could make The Great Eberto Alters' life miserable. And you had to watch that kind of thing, because playing a first-level wizard was hard enough…

Chapter Three-point-Zero-Three

The front door bumped open and Susan swept into the hall, all bundled-up in her winter wear, because it was flipping *perishing* out there. She dumped her bags-for-life on the mat and pulled off her leather gloves, then unbuttoned her black ankle-length coat – which toned perfectly with the long grey heavy skirt, knee-high boots, pale-grey jumper, bright-orange scarf, and matching beret. Some might argue that staying monotone would be more stylish, but it was fun to throw in a little colourful nod to September's russet plumage.

She performed that famous small-dog ballet: *Danse Avec Le Petit Crétin* – swapping Genghis Khat's lead from one hand to the other as she corkscrewed her way out of her coat and hung it up. A *pas de deux*, for excitable Yorkshire terrier and *slightly* cuddly lawyer.

'Robbie?' She clunked the front door closed. Picked up her bags and bustled into the dining room to place them on the covered table. Raised her voice a little louder. 'Robbie?'

Then stood there, with her head cocked, listening.

But the only reply was Genghis Khat, whining.

'Sorry, little man.'

She unclipped his lead and he did a happy trio of catherine-wheel turns, then scampered off, yapping. As weenie dogs were wont to do.

Dear old Genghis Khat…

He was a twit, but that's what happened when you let your children name a family pet. Mind you, it was *still* better than Robbie's suggestion. Because there was no way Susan was standing in the middle of Duthie Park shouting, 'AGAMEMNON!'

Never live it down.

Susan pulled a box from one of her bags – a Lego Bonsai Tree. And yes, officially the kit was for ages eighteen-and-up, but kids grew up so *fast* these days.

Now: where were her wrapping things?

Susan located the correct plastic crate, then laid a dark-navy roll of paper on the table, followed by the special long scissors, Sellotape dispenser, gift tags, bows, and…

What happened to her scarlet ribbons?

Going back to the crate for another rummage.

And still not finding any.

Hmmm…

Maybe she'd filed them in the kitchen by mistake?

Out in the hall, she swapped her chic boots for a pair of fuzzy green slippers, hung up her beret, and took a deep breath. 'ROBBIE? I'M PUTTING THE KETTLE ON: YOU WANT TEA?'

No answer was the loud reply.

Strange.

Robbie didn't *say* anything about going out.

'ROBBIE!'

Honestly, the woman was a law unto herself. One of those forces-of-nature people Mother warned you about.

Susan raised her voice again. 'I SNEAKED OUT EARLY, BECAUSE NAOMI'S GOT THAT FRIEND'S BIRTHDAY PARTY TONIGHT AND *LORD FORBID* SHE SHOULD BUY HER *OWN* PRESENT FOR WHATEVER *SPOILED BRAT*'S INVITED HER.'

Scuffing through into the kitchen.

Which was nice and tidy. No breakfast or lunch things lying about. So, Robbie must have been busy. Before she disappeared.

'I GOT HER A LEGO TREE DOODAH! THIRTY QUID: SURELY THAT'S ENOUGH FOR A TEN-YEAR-OLD?' And it would've been over forty, if it hadn't been on sale.

She filled the kettle and set it to boil. 'I WAS GOING TO GET YOU A CUTE LITTLE ITALIAN RIVIERA THING TO BUILD, BUT YOU WOULDN'T *BELIEVE* HOW EXPENSIVE THE BIG SETS ARE! MAYBE FOR YOUR BIRTHDAY…?'

The only sound in the whole house was the kettle, pinging and gurgling.

While it did its business, Susan went through the kitchen drawers. But those flipping scarlet ribbons remained elusive.

The kettle rattled to a halt.

Two mugs, teabag in each, freshly boiled water. Stir-stir, squish-squish.

'I WAS THINKING: CAULIFLOWER CHEESE FOR TEA! MAYBE WITH CHIPS IF YOU'VE BEEN NAUGHTY?'

Without the kettle's song, the silence *throbbed.*

For goodness' sake.

Time to go searching.

Susan poked her head around the living-room door: no one.

Mistress bedroom: no one.

Spare room: the valance was all rumpled, and it needed a dust – because no one had stayed over for ages – but it was still devoid of Robertas. So, Susan straightened the valance and tried the dressing room, bathroom, box room, then up the stairs to Naomi's octopus's garden/pigsty: no one.

There *was* someone in Jasmine's room, but he was a

cardboard cutout of that author she'd been swooning over the month before – holding his latest blockbuster and smiling like a fat, middle-aged balding lothario. Signed in gold Sharpie.

But. Still. No. Roberta.

Susan even opened the attic door, flicking on the light to expose four generations' worth of dust, packing cases, and an infinite number of spiders. Closed it again with a shudder.

Back downstairs, she checked the utility room.

'Robbie?'

Nope.

'Unbelievable.' Taking a sip of what was now tepid tea. 'Poof – into thin air.'

Maybe a biscuit would help?

In the kitchen, she helped herself to a Wagon Wheel, leaning on the worktop to eat it, looking out over the back garden.

That lawn needed mowing again.

The apple tree was heavily pregnant with fruit, the branches bowed beneath the weight of scarlet temptations. And there was Mr Rumpole lurking between the yellowing leaves like a snake, out of the wind.

Susan rumbled open the patio door. 'Come in, you hairy lump!'

But Mr Rumpole just stared back at her with his ineffable amber eyes. Tail twitching.

Really: *men*.

Stepping out onto the patio, Susan clapped her palms against her thighs a few times. 'Mr Rummmmmmmmmmpole! Come see Mummy!'

It wasn't *that* bad out here, sheltered by the high garden walls, and their big granite house. Still a bit nippy, though. *Clap, clap, clap*. 'Come on, dafty!'

But he wasn't budging.

Perhaps she should put her wellies on and go get the silly muffin? Because he wasn't as young as he used to—

A … *something* moved, snagged the corner of her eye, and Susan turned hard right peering at the little line of outbuildings that ran along one side of the garden wall.

Oh no.

There was a light on in one of them – seeping out beneath the door.

'Robbie?'

She shuffled across the too-long lawn with its thick damp grass, to the door. It still had their silly sign screwed to the wood: 'THE POLICE SCOTLAND MEMORIAL RETIREMENT SAUNA'. No Boyz Allowed.

Susan reached for the handle … and froze.

What if it *wasn't* Robbie?

What if *someone* had broken into the house?

What if they were *lurking* in there, *right now*, waiting for a chance to pounce and murder them all in their beds?

Well, they were messing with the *wrong* lawyer!

A garden spade rested against the cancelled-sauna wall – even though she'd asked Roberta to lay it by at least a dozen times – Susan grabbed it.

Nice and heavy.

Bet the blade would do some damage too.

OK.

Raising her weapon like a Viking's axe, she hauled in a breath and threw the door open. 'YOU BETTER RUN, *MOTHERFUCKER*, COS I'M GONNA BASH YOUR BRAINS OUT!'

'Aye…' Robbie blinked back at her. 'Been there, tried that. And it's no' as much fun as you'd think.'

3.04

Ah… Roberta rustled up a nice, disarming smile as Susan stepped into the brand-new incident room. 'It's not what it looks like.'

Though it *definitely* was.

Susan did a slow three-sixty, staring.

Probably taking in all the changes Roberta had made to their no-longer-sauna over the last couple of days, when no one was looking. Like clarting the bare walls in cheap cork-boards, then clarting *those* in reports, statements, maps, and photos – all churned out on the old inkjet printer, that now lurked in the corner of the room – and then clarting those with hand-scrawled notes on pilfered Post-its.

She'd set up separate areas for each of the five cases, with signs at the top: 'OPERATION DEMOGORGON', 'OPERATION TROGLODYTE', 'OPERATION BASILISK', and 'OPERATION FIREDRAKE'. And unlike *Davey's* amateur-hour garage, she'd threaded scarlet ribbons through it all, connecting the important parts to each other. Like a weird routemap, or a drunken blood spider…

The office furniture left something to be desired, though: just a folding lawn chair and a makeshift coffee table – featuring a bunch of scribbled notes and a scummy mug of cold tea.

Susan sank into the seat. 'Oh, *Robbie*…'

'No' like I'm *hurting* anyone. And I'm still doing the evening classes, aren't I? Teacher says I can take my first stained-glass panel home next week! I just...' Gesturing at the walls. 'Sorry?'

A great-big sigh. 'Suppose I should be amazed you lasted five weeks.'

'You always say I need a hobby.'

'Yes, but I meant needlepoint, or Scottish country dancing!' She levered herself out of the chair and stepped in close, cupping Roberta's face in her hands. 'Robbie, Robbie, Robbie...' A squeeze. 'Your problem is: you've *finally* escaped the rat race, but you're still a *rat*.'

Roberta curled her hands into paws, exposing her two front teeth. 'Eeek, eeek?'

'You're impossible, you know that, don't you.' Looking around the room again. 'I *suppose* you'll need a sidekick. Well, you can't drive yourself about: doctor's orders.'

Ahoy-hoy. Things were looking up.

'You volunteering?'

'No, I am *not*. You listen to me, Roberta Alexander Steel: I'm *indulging* you here, not encouraging you. Besides, some of us still have full-time jobs.' Waving a hand at the maps and ribbons and printouts. 'There must be other sad, lonely, retired police officers you can play with. Maybe one of *them* can drive you?'

What, like Detective Sergeant Davey Greasy Two-Faced, Quisling-Wee-Bastard McLeod?

No sodding thank you.

Roberta shrugged. 'Can't think of anyone, no.'

'Then you're going to have a very short career as a consulting detective.'

Roberta slouched in her lawn chair – Boris Johnson's head clutched in one hand, phone in the other. Frowning up at the wall-o'crimes as she squeezed.

Pkongk-glonk. Pkongk-glonk.

Shame the stuff she downloaded on Operation Basilisk was incomplete. Not because *she'd* screwed up, but because whatever lazy bastard Young had put in charge of transcribing the interviews with Charlotte 'Babydoll' MacNeal and Campbell 'Y-Fronts' Brown hadn't bothered their arses to get it done before Roberta's leaving do. So now there was a hole in her case file, where details on drug-filled Lithuanian teddy bears should've been.

Suppose it didn't really matter, what with Charlotte no-commenting and Campbell being thick as mince, but still…

PC Whoever-It-Was hadn't even uploaded the interview footage. Because the world was full of idiots.

And speaking of idiots:

'*Yeah …*' Tufty hummed and hawed, '*but I—*'

'Look on this as a once-in-a-lifetime opportunity to ingratiate yourself with the high heedyins. Solving crimes on your *day off*? That's like catnip to those snidgers.'

A full-on whine came down the phone. '*But I don't* want *to! I has stuff to do. With Kate. Kate-and-Tufty stuff.*'

Bet it was naked stuff too. The dirty wee sod.

Roberta tutted. 'Are you telling me that playing Hide The Truncheon all day is more important than keeping the people of our fair city safe?' Channelling Susan for a full-on theatrical sigh that oozed disappointment. 'Oh, *Tufty…*'

'*Can't Rennie do it?*'

'He's got an early shift tomorrow. But *you've* got a rest day.'

Pkongk-glonk. Pkongk-glonk.

'*But… But what about Barrett, or Lund, or Harmsworth?*'

Roberta laid it on, nice and thick: 'I've always seen you

as the *lynchpin* of my Queen Street Irregulars, Tufty. My *Number-One*, *Main-Man*, *Go-To-Guy* when I need someone *smart* and *resourceful* to rely on.'

Pkonnnnnnnnnnnnnnnnnnnnnngk…

'Urgh!' Could hear him sagging on the other end. *'Gah!'* Probably holding his head. *'And thrice times "arrgh"!'* Because he knew she'd won.

Glonk.

'Good boy.' There was no need to rub it in, so she kept the evil smile from her voice. 'Tomorrow morning: nine o'clock sharp. And if you're well behaved, I shall buy you a nice bacon butty.'

'Make it a Neptune's delight. With two *fried eggs.'* Probably thought he was driving a hard bargain.

But Roberta nodded anyway. 'Done.'

And he certainly had been.

3.05

Roberta limped outside, clunked the front door shut and locked it.

Where the hell *was* he?

She checked her watch: eight fifty-seven.

The kitchen rush-hour had been and gone, Mr Rumpole was off doing whatever it was Mr Rumpole did of a morning, Susan and Genghis would be at work by now, Jasmine and Naomi at school. The dishwasher: humming. The washing machine: whirling. And now there was nothing to do but hang around on a miserable overcast Friday morning, waiting for the daft wee loon to show his daft wee face.

And as if by magic, a rusty old Fiat Panda growled up the street, trailing smoke signals from its leprous exhaust.

It pulled up outside the house, pinging and rattling and ticking away. Christ knew how many rolls of silver duct tape had been deployed to keep various bits and bobs from falling off the thing, but the whole car looked as if it were about to collapse at any moment.

Basically: if Davey's rattletrap lowered the tone, Tufty's *buried* it.

She hobbled over there, walking stick clunking on the leaf-strewn path. Hauled open the door.

He had the radio on, something poppy, buzzing away through the ancient speakers:

'When did you get so pretty,
When did you get so fine,
Why are you so smart and witty,
Cos I wanna make you mine!'

She thumped into the passenger seat. 'How did this thing pass its MOT? Did you cast Animate Dead?'

He stroked the dashboard. 'Don't you listen to the nasty lady, Betsy, she's just a snidgehead.' He'd gone all casual in a Xena Warrior Princess T-shirt, with a brown Puffa jacket over the top. That made him look a bit like the poop emoji.

Unlike her stylish stripy-top-and-hiking-jacket combo.

'It's a wonder; you're so wonderful,
It's a wonder; you're so wonderful,
Wonder, wonder, wonder, wonder,
Wo-on, wo-on, wonnnnnderfu-ul!'

She grimaced at the radio. 'What *is* this pish?'

Mercifully, 'this pish' faded out. Unfortunately, a machine-gun-voiced tosser took its place: *'Wooooooeee! There's a popalicious* stonker *to end on, A B Forty-Two Asterisk – are we supposed to pronounce the asterisk? – and "Wonderful You".* I've *been Kenny Mair,* this *was* Mair Banging Tunes, *and* you've *been wonderfullllllll! Murray MacDuff's up next, but right now it's nine o'clock and here's Damon with the news.'*

Tufty sniffed. '*Good morning*, lovely Tufty. Thank you so kindly for coming to pick me up, *on your day off*, like the twinkly star of delight you are.'

'Thanks, Kenny. … A further six people are known to have died, following yesterday's terrorist attack on—'

Roberta clicked the radio off. 'Hardly hear myself *think*.' Seatbelt on. 'Right: you've got two options. That way …' she pointed a finger over her left shoulder, 'or,' the finger swung around to point across the bonnet and down the road, 'that way.'

'Hmmm…' Tufty peered in both directions. 'Does it make a difference? Which is more fun?'

Time to pull on a reassuring *innocent* smile. 'One's a nice *relaxing* walk in the woods, the other's a lovely chat with a young man and the chance to see some boaties!'

He shrank away from her. 'Why do I get the feeling there's something you're not telling me?'

Because if she'd told him that today's plan was to screw over Beardy Beattie *and* ex-DS Davey McLeod, the wee twit probably wouldn't have come.

She dipped into her pocket for a wee pyramid-shaped plastic dice. 'Let's make it interesting. Why don't we roll a D4? Odd: east, even: west.' Bowling it gently across the dashboard. Three. 'East it is.'

Tufty smiled like a proud dad. 'See? I *told* you you'd like *D&D* if you just gave it a go!'

Yeah…

She *really* needed to get out more.

'Guv?'

A hand shoogled her shoulder.

'Guv, we're here. I mean, Roberta? We has an arrived.'

She gave a wee snork, surfacing from a weird dream about zombies running a brain-burger restaurant in the city centre. 'WrmI?'

Blinking as she took in the road, and fields, and trees.

Tufty pointed up ahead, then turned his rancid old Fiat Panda into the lay-by, because it wasn't coned-off anymore.

Nor was it a toenail clipping of potholes and scarred tarmac. Instead, Aberdeenshire Council had transformed it into a curve of perfect black.

He pulled up, just past the bins, and killed the engine. Or tried to. The thing kept running for a count of six – even though he'd removed the keys – then the cough-and-splutter gave way to *tick*s and *ping*s and a long slow *wheeeeeeeeeze*.

Roberta puffed out her cheeks. 'Aye, no offence, but this thing needs—'

'Shhhh…! You'll upset her.' Patting the dashboard. 'Who's a good girl? You are. You're *such* a good girl!'

Daft as a bag of ferrets.

Grabbing her walking stick, Roberta climbed out.

That overcast sky had darkened to an ominous lid of battleship grey. Going to rain at some point. But hopefully not *yet*.

The lay-by wasn't the only thing that had changed since last time. The field opposite had gone from mist-shrouded green to pale-beige stubble, littered with big round bales of straw. And the riot of rosebay willowherb had lost its bright-magenta flowers, swapping them for seed-pod fluff. Battling the nettles for dominance along the fence that separated the lay-by from the railway tracks.

Tufty locked 'Betsy' – as if anyone was going to steal that hunk of junk – and joined Roberta over by the bins. 'You've got to be nice to my lovely automobile-of-delight. The garage wanted to "send her off to live on a farm", last MOT.'

'Aye, and—'

'Still don't see why we couldn't take *your* car. Poor thing probably needs a good run after sitting there for months.'

Actually: that was a good point.

Could've got him to give it a wash too.

He nodded, agreeing with himself. 'Plus it'd be *your* petrol. I'm putting in for expenses, *comprende*?'

'Blah, blah, blah.' She checked her watch: nine fifty-one. Bags of time. 'Come on, then.'

'Wait, what now?'

Roberta limped off, towards the weed-choked fence. Whacking a path through the nettles with her walking stick. 'Last train through here was three-quarters of an hour ago. Next one's not for forty-seven minutes.'

'Oh, no, no, no, no, no.' He backed away, hands up. 'Nice boys do *not* play on the railway lines! What if there's a goods train or a maintenance thingy wheeching by, ready to turn unsuspecting young Tuftys into squished-people pâté?'

'You were quite happy trotting across when we were here before!'

'I was on duty! Police officers take risks all the time for the greater good. Is part of the price we pays for the sexy black uniform.' He pointed at his Xena T-shirt. '*Off* duty.'

'Don't be so damp.' Whack, whack, whack.

That was probably enough. She shuffled through the broken weeds to the fence and had a bash at slinging one leg over the top – which wasn't easy when you were a bit wobbly on your pins. 'Little help for a *poor*, *disabled*, *maiden* in *distress*?'

He glowered, muttering away to himself as if she couldn't hear him. '"Maiden" my perky bumhole.' Then Tufty slumped. 'Urgh…' Gave a big sigh. And finally took her arm, holding on tight as she struggled her way to the other side of the fence.

Roberta gave him a saucy wink. 'Never thought you'd help me get my leg over.'

'Urgharama!'

'You should be so lucky.' She clambered up the wee slope to the railway lines, then paused – taking a good look left and right. Because while Tufty was an idiot ninety-nine-point-nine percent of the time, he was right about this.

No sign of any train. And the tracks weren't making that *twiiiing-twonnng-pwanggg* noise, so it was *probably* safe. But, just in case, she lumbered across as fast as her gammy legs would carry her, then up into the woods. Pausing beneath the thick canopy of pines and beech. 'You coming or no'?'

Tufty groaned, slumping back to make miserable faces at the threatening clouds. 'In the name of the Elder Gods…'

A deep breath, and he scrambled over the fence.

The woods looked sort of … *different* to last time. As if someone had rearranged the trees. Thick whorls of bracken curled beneath the heavy canopy, which should've kept it dry, but the bloody stuff was still wet enough to soak through Roberta's jeans.

And either Tufty had wet himself, or he was having the same problem. He shoogled one leg, like a disgruntled cat. 'I know *that*, but why are *we* doing it? Why not tell Beattie and get *him* to search the woods again?'

She kept going. 'Would you trust Beattie to look after your cardboard Picard?'

A snort. 'No chance.'

'Then why the hell would I trust him with *my* murder?'

'Because you've retired!' Tufty pulled out his phone and scowled at the screen. 'And it's ten o'clock. Time for tenses. I was lured here with promise of an delicious butty. Better not've been false pretences!'

Ah, *there* it was.

Knew it had to be lurking in here somewhere.

The tree with the broken bough – where Harmsworth had crashed through on his way down – its cracked limb poking up through the bracken below, leaving a jagged stump behind.

Roberta patted the trunk. 'Up you go.'

'Urgh… But we already *searched* this one. And in case you didn't notice: *we does not has no sausages*!'

'Aha!' She reached into her inside pocket and produced a zip-lock sandwich bag with a quartet of Cumberland's finest trapped inside. Leftover from breakfast. 'Now: up.'

Pout. 'I should roll a saving throw against your evil magic.' But he took his poop-jacket off, hung it on the broken stump, and scrambled up onto the lowest branch. Unreachable three months ago, but now weighed down with new growth and cones.

He perched there, a wee forest gremlin in soggy jeans. 'You're joining me, right?'

'I can barely *walk*. You think climbing trees is a good idea?'

Shrug. 'What's the worst that can happen?'

A scream-filled vertiginous plummet with a sudden crunching stop at the end.

Flipping heck…

This was bad enough the first time around, and she hadn't been blown-up, then.

Roberta struggled from branch to branch, breathing like a … sex-pest running a marathon.

Pfff…

Of course, the wee loon had scampered up, no problem, because the little sod was three-quarters monkey and both of his legs still worked properly.

He'd come to rest three or four feet below the nest, lurking there. Presumably trying not to tip-or-piss-off the crows inside.

Roberta crackled, snapped, grunted, and hauled herself

level with him. Then hung there, forehead pressed against the bark, puffing and panting while sweat trickled down her spine and soaked into New Faithful. 'Sodding … sodding … *fudge*.' Pech, heech, wheeze, huff, groan. She pointed at the nest's underside. 'Are … are they…?'

'About to find out.' He orangutaned up the last few feet, poking his head above nest-height.

She stayed where she was.

Because if anyone was getting attacked by angry crows, it *wasn't* going to be her.

But there was no screaming or swearing or cawing or flapping-of-angry-wings. Instead, Tufty ducked down and grinned at her. 'Is safe! We has an corvid-free zone.'

She grappled her way through the branches, to see for herself.

The nest was empty. Maybe abandoned. Difficult to tell.

Had to admit, the view wasn't bad. Hard to appreciate it last time – what with all the dive-bombing, sharp beaks, and threat of being shat on – but looking out across the treetops revealed a pastoral panorama: down the hill and across the stubbled fields to the River Urie, with Logie Country House on the other side.

Tufty snapped on a pair of blue nitriles. 'Is examination time.'

The wee loon went much slower than last time, more methodically too. A proper search, rather than a quick rummage. Amazing what not being attacked by angry crows could do.

While he picked his way through the nest, Roberta dug a stolen evidence bag from her sausage pocket. Holding it open for anything findable. 'It was your Goblin chef gave me the idea: tooth pie.'

He made the icky face. 'We're not baking a pie, are we?'

'Just cos it *sounds* horrible, doesn't mean it's not someone's idea of a tasty crunchy treat. And just cos something wasn't here when we searched *first time*, doesn't mean the crows didn't nick it from the avalanche of sludge and bone. And who knows *what* little morsels might've rolled away into the weeds, or been secreted away for later.' Looking back towards the lay-by. 'Give you odds-on the black feathery wee sods' beaks are better at finding tasty treats than any police search team.'

'Here we go.' Tufty popped something into her evidence bag. 'Bottle cap.' Then another, dropping them in one-by-one: 'Bottle cap. Ringpull. Plastic bag. Condom wrapper. Bottle cap. Weird tubey thing – think that's part of a vape? Oooh. And what do we have here?' He held it up, turning the thing in his blue nitrile fingers. It was a small bone, about an inch – inch and a half? – and flared at both ends. 'What does you think: rabbit, or finger?'

'Ice Queen will know for sure.'

It went in the bag.

Followed by: 'Bottle cap. Clump of wool. Plastic comb. Bottle cap. They really *does* like bottle caps, doesn't they? Pound coin…' He was getting to the bottom of the nest now, pushing through downy feathers and bits of grass. Then froze, eyebrows up. 'Maybe we *can* makes a pie after all?' Offering her his cupped palm. A white molar sat in the middle. 'Could be a deer, though.'

'Oh *aye*. I'll bet there's *hundreds* of deer running around Aberdeenshire with NHS fillings in their back teeth.'

'Ooooh…' He placed it into the evidence bag as if it were the most delicate thing in the world. Then had one last dig through the nest. 'That's it.'

She sealed the bag. Gave him a smug smile. 'Told you.'

Oh yeah.

Phase One of Operation Screw-Beardy-Beattie-Over was complete.

Roberta Steel, Consulting Detective to the Stars, strikes again.

3.06

Roberta slouched in Betsy's passenger seat, vaping away with the window down.

Marischal College's façade might've been a spiky display of gothic frippery, but around the back it looked more like a Victorian prison, with lumpy blockwork and mean windows, devoid of fancy flourishes.

The car park featured a couple of mobile CCTV vans though, a speed-camera unit, and a trio of police Transits, five or six manky pool cars, and one lonely patrol car with a cracked windscreen.

A cluster of far swankier vehicles sat at the far end – BMWs and Audis and Range Rovers – because *senior* officers couldn't be expected to struggle for parking on side streets like the lesser ranks.

Meaning Tufty had no business abandoning his fusty old rattletrap here. But sod them.

Roberta sent another *whoomph* of raspberry out into the cold grey world, and reread Logan's latest text from sinful Dundee:

> Bloody papers are just making everything worse.
>
> Bunch of bastards!
>
> You see the Scottish Daily Post today?

Nope.

But then she and Susan were a *P&J/Aberdeen Examiner* household. None of your right-wing tabloid shite here, thank you very much. Even if the *Examiner* was heading that way fast.

And yeah, she *could* buy a copy to see what Logan was moaning about, or look it up online, but there was an easier way.

She thumbed out a text to Tufty:

> While you're there, go nick a copy of the Sharny Dick Plop for me, there's a good boy.
>
> TODAY'S!

Because Divisional Headquarters got copies of all the major papers. And nicking theirs would serve the buggers right.

And speaking of buggers: Chief Superintendent Pine's 'Executive' Mercedes was parked in the far corner. It had two spaces to itself, separated from the other cars by a pair of traffic cones. All kept safe and snug.

Be a shame if something happened to it…

Roberta *crunk*ed open her door and wriggled out, making a big show of leaning on her walking stick as she cast a furtive eye about.

No witnesses, but just in case: 'Oh deary me. I am so stiff and sore after spending *all* that time in this rather crap car, what with my traumatic head injury and everything. I had better stretch my poor legs.'

That should do it.

Roberta hurpled up the middle of the car park, between the cars and vans. Taking her time. Nothing suspicious to see here, nope, nope, nope.

Ding-buzz.

SUSAN:

Are you having fun playing consulting detective with Tufty?

Playing? *Playing*?

Roberta wasn't '*playing*', she was making breakthroughs, cracking cases.

Playing!

She stopped in front of Pine's Merc – all black and shiny and *desperate* for a house key to be dragged across the paintwork. Maybe all down one side? Or a nice rude word gouged deep into the bonnet?

Quick glance left and right, to make sure no one's watching.

Keys out. And—

'Guv?'

Shite...

Hiding her keys, Roberta turned. Pulling on a fake smile. 'Victoria. What a lovely surprise.'

Lund was in full uniform black, but without the stabproof, high-vis, and belt. 'Bumped into the wee loon in the mortuary. Said you were out here.' She squinted, head on one side. 'You OK? Only you're looking shiftier than normal.'

'*Shifty?* Cheeky sod. I'm a paragon of sodding virtue, me. Just stretching my legs. You know, after getting blown-up.' Hobbling back towards Betsy. 'What you working on now?'

'Operation Firedrake.' Falling into step beside her. 'Which is doing nothing for my diet. Can you believe we've got enough food vans in Aberdeen to have a turf war? You'd think one greasy burger would be much like another, but these deep-fried scumbags are at each other's throats like rabid weasels.'

'I heard: Hungry Helen's Noodle Doodle.'

'Urgh... Poor cow'll be lucky to walk again, after that.' Lund sighed. 'They're just *burger vans* – somewhere cheap to grab an unhealthy lunch – how can that *possibly* be worth crippling someone over?'

'She say who did it?'

'Can't: broken jaw.'

'Aye, it's a cruel, cruel world, right enough.' Roberta leaned back against Tufty's decrepit Panda, fiddling with a loose bit of duct tape. Keeping her voice all innocent and casual. 'Don't suppose you've heard anything about those arrests I made on my last day?'

'Who was that?'

'Charlotte MacNeal and Campbell Brown.'

Blank look.

'Operation Basilisk? Lithuanian teddy bears, stuffed full of class A drugs? Honestly, do you no' keep up with—'

'Not my case. It's…' Lund's eyes narrowed. 'Wait a minute, we were warned about—'

'You know, Veronica, I've always seen you as the *lynchpin* of my Queen Street Irregulars.' Putting an arm around her shoulders. 'My Number-One, Main-Woman, Go-To-Girl when I need someone *smart* and *resourceful* I can *really* rely on…'

Sounded as if Betsy's exhaust was more holes than muffler as the rusty old Fiat Panda splutter-growled its way across Danestone. Shambling through the warren of commuter cul-de-sacs, past copy-paste houses with hatchbacks parked outside and a lifetime's supply of wheelie bins.

A gurgling *snarl* popped and hissed – only that wasn't the moribund engine, it was Tufty's stomach. He rubbed his belly with one hand, steering with the other as he peered across the car at Roberta. 'No, seriously, where *did* you get that?'

'Hmmmm?' She turned the page on her brand-new file.

'Only, cos it looks like an official Police Scotland document-thing and you is *definitely* not allowed to has those no more.'

Not surprised it looked official. Because it was. Interview transcripts and interview notes on the drug-dealing underwearing bonk-buddies: Charlotte MacNeal and Campbell Brown. All freshly photocopied.

Roberta looked up. 'When did Creepy Sheila say she'd get the DNA results back?'

'*If* there's any DNA to find.' He puffed out a long breath. 'Just cos we found a tooth, doesn't mean it belongs to our victim. And if they've had a root canal on that molar, there'll be no tooth pulp to sample. So we're snidged.' Tufty's face scrunched for a moment. 'Hey! No changing the subject. Where did you get...' And his belly howled again.

She poked him. 'See: *this* is why Charlie Sausage-Fingers never invites you to his garden parties.'

'You promised me butties for tenses! And now it's *noon* and where is my butties – question mark, exclamation mark!'

True.

'Aye, you're right. That was very remiss of me. Soon as we're finished here it's butty time.' Pointing at the junction up ahead. 'Take a left.'

Tufty released a whiny groan, but did as he was told, turning into a dead-end road with weird little blocks of flats on either side.

The blocks were paired up – connected by a narrower, set-back bit – each the mirror image of the other. Three-storeys high, with a redbrick front and grey-harled gables. Dutch barn roofs in pantile grey, sprouting satellite dishes like mushrooms.

Tufty followed the road to a car park tucked behind the

buildings. Where Betsy was no longer the oldest and mankiest vehicle in all of Christendom.

An ancient, necrotic Daihatsu Fourtrak was parked by another brigade of wheelie bins, its bodywork more filler than metal. Rust blistered the hand-painted bonnet – and you could tell it was hand-painted, because the brushstrokes were clearly visible in the matt finish. The rear bumper: tied on with string…

He stuck Betsy in the furthest away space, as if frightened the Fourtrak might be contagious.

'OK.' Roberta dumped her new transcripts on the back seat, and pulled out the digital-deep-dive folder Tufty had given her on her last day. Featuring the three people Wee Davey McLeod snapped outside Noel Sherman's joinery workshop.

And the boy Sherman himself, of course.

She flicked through to the section on Jeremy Yarrow, with his prior conviction for prostitution and manky Daihatsu Fourtrak.

Tufty had dug up, and printed out, a bunch of Jeremy's tweets, updates, and posts, along with half a dozen photos.

Jeremy was one of those all-cheekbones-and-smouldering-eyes types. The kind of guy who thought it was OK to Blue Steel his way through every selfie. Thin, bordering on unhealthy, and sort of *waif*-like. Androgenous. Slightly pointy ears. A nose that had definitely seen the wrong end of someone's fist.

There wasn't a single photo of him with his top off – even splashing about at Balmedie beach in his budgie smugglers required a long-sleeved top. So, either he was covering something up, or trying to avoid hypothermia. Could go either way when you were swimming in the North Sea…

Going by his posts, Jeremy didn't have an 'isn't my life so shiny and great' approach to social media. Everything was about how *hard* his life was, and how his cat/dog/parrot –

depending on what day it was and what account he was publishing from – was in urgent need of veterinarian treatment, but he couldn't afford it, and they were going to die without some expensive surgery, and if they died he didn't know what he'd do with himself, because he couldn't face going on alone, and he'd been thinking about throwing himself in the river and just putting an end to all his *suffering*. But then, if he did, who would look after his poor ill pets?

And each one of these tales of woe came with a link marked 'DONATE TO ME', connected to a different fund-raising website.

Tufty pulled the keys, and Betsy's engine went into its running-on ping-and-click routine again.

Roberta sniffed. 'You know it's not meant to do that, right?'

'Still don't know why we're here.'

'So we can talk to Jeremy Yarrow.'

'No, I know *that*. That's not "why", that's "what". *Why* are we talking to him?'

'Because, my dear idiot friend, although I am celebrated as a paragon of fairness and generosity, if you cross me I can be a right vindictive bastard.' And with phase one of Operation Screw-Beardy-Beattie-Over complete, it was time to embark upon Operation Screw-Davey-McLeod-Over instead.

She flashed Tufty an evil grin. 'Shall we?' Then battled her way out of his half-dead car.

The blocks of flats weren't just symmetrical side-to-side, they were front-to-back too. Looked like twelve flats per building, where each set of six had its own front door.

Seemed weird, but that was developers for you.

Roberta hobbled for the nearest block, leaving Tufty to lock his fusty rattletrap and scurry after her.

'Just so we is clear,' catching up, 'I'm *not* the one you're vindictiving against?'

'No' this time.' The door wasn't locked, so she dragged it open and stepped inside.

According to her bloodstained PNC printout, Jeremy Yarrow lived in Flat K. Which meant the top floor. And lots of stairs.

Because God hated her.

'So who *are* we vindictimising?'

She lumbered up the first flight of steps, leaning on the handrail and her stick. 'You ask a lot of questions for someone who wants an extra fried egg.' Already starting to breathe hard.

'*And* a large tea.' He followed her up, hands in his pockets as if climbing stairs was something people did every day. 'But first I has to make a informed decision about vindictificating someone.'

Urgh.

Around the landing on the first floor, still climbing.

'It's a divorce case, OK? Joiner's wife thinks hubby dearest is playing *Hide The Hammer* with one or more persons. I find out who: I claim victory, and the guy who's *meant* to be investigating it gets fired.'

'Ah... So we're interviewing these suspected extramarital bonkists for *commercial gain.* That represents a change to our terms of reference and requires a renegotiation of my comestible remuneration.'

'I'll renegotiate ... your bumhole ... with my boot ... in a minute.' Leaning more heavily on her stick with every step, as the ache spread out from her knees.

'Ho no, no. Our butty-based agreement was for *tenses*. Union regulations say I is now due lunch as well.' Rubbing at his gurgling tummy. 'Possibly in the form of a nice fish supper?'

At ... top of stairs. ... Lungs ablaze. ... Breath rattle. ... Heart thump. ... Urgh...

Roberta collapsed against the handrail, too knackered to do anything but scowl at the greedy wee tit.

The landing was tiny, just a patch of lino in front of the two, side-by-side doors. The one on the right had a nice little sign, with a laminated kid's drawing of a happy dinosaur on it, a brass 'L', and a plaque with the name 'SAUNDERS'.

The one on the left had nothing but the 'K' and a bunch of stickers, peeled off supermarket fruit, arranged into a Christian cross. Because who could forget Jesus's sermon on eating your five-a-day?

She pointed at the bell. And wheezed.

Tufty poked the button, making it *trrrrrrrrrrrrrrring*. 'While we're renegotiating, I think a couple of pickled onions would be a nice gesture on your part. What with us using all my petrol.'

She flipped him the Vs.

'And I *assume* you'd like me to keep our little crows'-nest-rummaging trip a secret from Acting DCI Beattie? What with it being his case and everything?' Frown. 'Mind you, the man's a thirdwit, so you can probably have that one complimentary like.' *Trrrrrrrrrrrrrrring*. 'They've got a poster about you in the muster room, you know: "Do Not Engage With This Woman!" in big block capitals, with your photo and a bit about how you're a hazard to any ongoing investigation and an all-round general menace.'

There was a *clunk*, a *click*, and the door cracked open just far enough to let a watery pink eye peer out. Then a sniff. And a muffled, 'What?' Wiping the tears away.

Tufty smiled like a haunted ventriloquist's dummy. 'Mr Yarrow? Mr *Jeremy* Yarrow?'

Whoever answered the door whimpered, then thunked their head against the wood. 'Well, that's just … great.'

Jeremy led them into a living room, painted entirely black. It looked … *infectious*. One wall was coombed – part of the building's Dutch-barn roof, with three Velux windows set into it. All of which needed washing. The couch was stitched together with more duct tape than Tufty's car, while a collection of battered paperbacks filled a DIY shelf made of bricks and old chipboard. Lots of half-melted candles, but no TV. Instead, a three-foot crucifix dominated the wall, above a broken electric fire.

Then there was the *smell*. Funky. Stuffy. As if the room hadn't been aired in years. And exclusively inhabited by sweaty socks and feral underpants.

A pair of half doors lay open, exposing a kitchen that Typhoid Mary would've *loved*.

Jeremy kissed his fingertips and pressed them to the tortured Jesus on his way past, before collapsing onto the Frankencouch. Sagging there in his joggy-bottoms and long-sleeved top. The soles of his feet as black as the walls.

Tufty pulled his chin in, blinking. 'Wow…' No doubt enjoying the exciting odours.

Roberta stuck one hand in her pocket, leaning on her cane in a jaunty manner. Like a sexy Poirot. 'Just so you know, and to keep everything nice and legal – I'm no' a cop anymore. But I was one for *thirty years*.' Giving Jeremy a long hard stare. 'That means I can spot a lie the size of a sparrow's fart from orbit.'

He shrugged. 'Whatever it is, I didn't do it, OK?' Gazing up at his not-yet-risen lord. 'Found Jesus, didn't I.'

'Good for you.' A cold smile. 'I thought we could have a *nice* wee chat about a mate of yours: Mr Noel Sherman. Coillewood Development and Resolution Specialists Limited?'

The pause that followed was long enough for a fat bluebottle to do two circuits of the living room.

Jeremy licked his lips. 'Never heard of him.'

'*Really?* How weird. Cos we've got *photos*.'

Jeremy's mouth made a perfect horrified 'O', staring up at her with those soggy pink eyes. 'It…' He buried his face in his hands. 'I wasn't… It isn't…'

A *clunk* came from the hall, outside, then a razor-thin man appeared in the doorway. Tattoos snaked around his throat, covering the back of his hands where they poked out of a crisp white shirt. Slicked-back hair, parted on one side. So buttoned up he positively *thrummed* with the effort of holding it all in. Black trousers, tie, and a scuffed pair of trainers. As if he was on his way to a funeral at a brisk jog. 'Thought I heard voices.'

Jeremy waved a hand at Tufty and Roberta. 'This is—'

'Bloody hell!' Roberta stared. 'Gonorrhoea Bob, as I live and breathe! Thought you were *dead*.'

Pink rushed up the newcomer's cheeks. 'I don't—'

'Ha!' She turned to Tufty. 'Mr Cockburn here used to be a rabid ultra-nationalist racist dickbag, didn't you, Bobby?'

'That… Please, I…' Deep breath. 'That version of me *did* die. I buried him the day I accepted our Lord and Saviour into my heart.'

She beamed. 'Glad to hear it, cos you were a *right* prick.' Stepping in front of him. 'So how come you know Jezzer here?'

The blush deepened. 'I…'

Jeremy sat up. 'He was sent by God in my time of need and helped me find the light.' Running a hand up one sleeve-hidden arm. 'He ministered to me, when I was lost in the darkness.'

'Bet he did. Saucy minx.' Roberta winked. 'Now, perhaps my friend here,' giving Tufty a gentle thump, 'can help Bob minister up a lovely cup of tea for us all, while you and I have that chat. Hmmmm?'

Jeremy buried his head in his hands again. 'Oh God…'

3.07

A murmur of strained conversation filtered through the closed kitchen doors, underpinned by the *clink*-and-*rattle* of tea being made. With any luck, Tufty had insisted on boiling the mugs in bleach first, because that was the only way Roberta would even *consider* drinking anything that came out of Gonorrhoea Bob's Cholera Kitchen.

In here, Jeremy was huddled up on the couch, filthy bare feet on the seat, knees up to his chest, arms wrapped around them to turn himself into a little fortress. Avoiding eye contact.

Roberta remained standing though, for basic hygiene reasons. 'You still turning tricks, Jezzer?'

'Why can't you just leave me alone?'

'Cos Jesus might forgive all your sins, but Police Scotland makes you pay for them.' Leaving a sinister pause. 'Now: Noel Sherman. And don't lie. "Thou shall not bear false witness", remember? You think HMP Grampian's bad? It's got *nothing* on Hell.'

He pressed his forehead into his knees. 'You've got the photos.'

'Aye, but I want *you* to tell me about them. Think of this like a confessional.'

The bluebottle made another couple of circuits.

Jeremy took a deep breath. 'It was…' Cleared his throat. 'In the beginning, I'd got behind on my payments. Borrowed money.

Might've robbed somebody's stuff… But Mr Sherman "kindly" came up with a way I could repay my debt to him.' One shoulder raised, then fell again. 'And, you know, I was doing it for cash *anyway* – in pub toilets and dark alleyways – so why not? After you've sucked enough of them, one cock's very like another.'

Even the fly fell silent for that.

'Only…' Jeremy wiped his eyes. 'Only the interest keeps *growing*, doesn't it. And before you know it, you've been paying off your debt for *twelve months* and you still owe much more than you did to start with.'

'So go to the cops.'

A bitter little laugh. 'And say what? They banged me up for four months last time.'

She leaned closer. 'You want to hurt him? Sherman? Cos I know a way.'

'He's the kind of man who doesn't *get* hurt. He's the kind who does the hurting.'

'Except his wife wants a divorce: messier the better. And if she had *you* on her—'

'No!' Jeremy's head snapped up. 'No way in the Satan-buggering *fuck* am I testifying against Noel Sherman!' Eyes drifting to the closed kitchen doors. 'He wouldn't just hurt *me*.'

Yeah…

Bastards like that seldom did.

'OK.' Time to ask the obvious question: 'This debt of yours, what's it for?'

Jeremy bit his bottom lip, then looked away – hugging his knees even closer. 'What do you think.'

Roberta leaned on the concrete railings that separated the pavement from the pebbly expanse of Stonehaven beach.

A slate-coloured North Sea stretched away beneath the granite sky – heavy and threatening. Grey, grey, grey…

The headland curled around to the right, cupping the bay, but petered out in the other direction – letting a brisk northerly wind whistle along the promenade. Wheeching the seagulls sideways past the little collection of cafes and restaurants that fronted onto the crashing waves.

In a more Mediterranean part of the world, this bit would've been paved and dotted with palm trees, fancy lampposts, and alfresco dining tables, where chic couples would share chic conversations over chic dishes and chic cocktails. But this was northeast Scotland in September, so instead the road was split in two by a scabby line of shin-high red-and-white interlocking barriers – cordoning off a potholed stretch of mangey tarmac, so a pair of masochists in waterproofs could huddle together on a picnic bench and shiver their way through matching ice creams.

Morons.

Roberta checked her phone again.

Still nothing back from Young.

Logan:

> Oh HA, HA! Very funny. :(
>
> We had a visitation from the bloody Crime Campus this morning. Pointing fingers and poking noses.

Susan:

> Going to be late tonight.
>
> Have asked Gabby to drop Naomi off from school.
>
> Jasmine can take bus.
>
> Can you feed them fish fingers?

Possibly. Kind of depended on when Young got in touch.

Tufty appeared beside her at the railings, bearing two bundles wrapped in paper. 'Here we does goes: num-num-num-num-num!' He handed her one, warm and tempting. 'Got us both an seafood-platter supper, tartare sauce, and a thing of onion rings to share. *Plus* a portion of peas *à la* mush.'

'Where's my change, you thieving snidge?'

'Came to thirty-five pounds and twenty pence. You owe me a fiver. And twenty pence.'

'What?' She unwrapped her lunch, and the scent of crispy batter and sizzled potatoes wafted out like the nectar of the very gods themselves. Because what true Scotswoman *didn't* have deep-fried tatties and battered fish flowing through her veins? Plus, the seafood platter wasn't just a bit of haddock, you got a fishcake and a wee pile of scampi too. She popped one in her gob. Hot. Salty. Vinegary. Mmmm… 'Whatever happened with that car bomb?'

Tufty looked at her for a bit, then his lone brain cell must've fired, because you could see the lights come on in that hollow little head of his. 'Oh the *car* bomb. Yeah. Big scandal.' Chomping into a pickled onion. 'Graeme Anderson – brackets, MP, close brackets – points the finger at "gangs bringing in illegal migrants" because "they know the UK New Horizons Party will—" Ow!'

She flexed her thumping hand. 'I know *that* bit, you twizzle stick. I retired from the force; didn't give up reading the sodding papers. *Or* watching the news.' Onion rings were good too. 'What happened with the *investigation*.' Threatening him with an angry chip. 'And I mean the *real* details, no' that "inquiries are continuing", "exploring multiple leads", "leave no stone unturned" bollocks Media Liaison churn out.'

That brain cell of his got a workout as he munched on his fish. 'We got everything *started*, then the Mob Squad swooped in and said it all needed some very specialised forensic techniques to investigate *properly* and our local Smurfs weren't trained or experienced enough – only he word-saladed it up in fancy language – so he brought in a team from down south. And then *we* got to do all the *exciting* jobs: like Staying Out Of The Way, Guarding The Perimeter, and Not Touching Anything.'

Interesting…

More chips. 'These Mob Squad tossers: a pointy-nosed posh git, needs a haircut? And pug-faced baldy gorilla?'

A fishy grin. 'The very men!'

'Hmmmph…' Scowling out at the churning grey water and scudding seagulls. 'Detective Superintendent Rifkind and DI Matthew Prissy Stick-Up-The-Bum Kensington. Organised Crime and Counter Terrorism. Visited me in hospital.' She crunched through batter to the meaty flaky haddock within. 'They find anything?'

Tufty leaned in, voice low and sneaky. '*I* heard the bombers used locally sourced ammonium nitrate and Calor gas canisters and whatnot, but the fuse was …' his shifty eyes swept the promenade, searching for spies, 'of *foreign* origin. What they call a "Kremlin Kaboom" in spook circles.'

Ding-buzz.

She sooked the fingers on one hand clean, wiped them on the chippy paper, then dug out her phone.

Finally.

SUPT. YOUNG:

> We have a warrant.
>
> Going in hot: this afternoon: 16:00 soon as I've got the team together and done the briefing.

If you promise to behave you can watch FROM A SAFE DISTANCE (distance non-negotiable).

A smile spread across her greasy lips. 'We're on.'

Pfff…

No wonder Logan was pissed off.

Roberta sat in the passenger seat, frowning at that morning's *Scottish Daily Post*, liberated from DHQ by Tufty. Front-page splash: '"ARROGANT" COPS "IGNORING KEY EVIDENCE"' above a photo of some redbrick railway arches – the south side of the Tay Bridge, according to the article. A patrol car blocked the road that went beneath the nearest arch, with a PC standing behind a cordon of blue-and-white tape.

The paper had printed a grid of portraits beneath it – some formal, some casual snaps, one for each of the Tayside Ripper's victims. So far…

The subheading pretty much summed up the *Sharny Dick Plop*'s approach to quality journalism: 'Psychic Sue Snubbed By Struggling Investigation: "I Know Where Next Victim Will Die!"'

Sodding Psychic Sodding Sue.

Bloody woman couldn't keep her nose out.

As if catching a serial killer wasn't hard enough without some middle-aged, tie-dyed, incense-and-patchouli-scented *moron* making shite up.

Something *cawwwwww*ed, and Roberta looked up from her stolen paper.

A crow swooped up on top of the fencepost beside the car and peered in through the passenger window at her. Judging.

No doubt wondering what a magnificent sexy beast like Roberta was doing sharing a manky Fiat Panda with a penguin-nosed wee snudge like Tufty – parked behind a line of police vehicles, on a back road, not-quite-the-middle-of-nowhere, about four miles north of Stonehaven.

Normally, the muster point would be much closer to the dunt, but once you factored in the slip road and the A92, and the fact it was basically a one-way system, this was the nearest viable point not visible from the dual carriageway. Because sometimes it was fun to maintain the element of surprise when bashing in a drug kingpin's door.

The crow cocked its head and did some more peering. Then gave another *cawwwwwww*!

Probably hungry…

Ooh, there was a solution for that.

Roberta dug into her jacket pocket and produced the zip-lock-bag-o'sausages that'd been in there all morning. Armpit warmed.

She rolled down the window, liberated a snorker, and tossed it in the crow's direction.

Her sausage bounced off the top line of barbed wire and tumbled down into the grass below. Lying there, as if the Castration Fairy had just flown by.

The crow stared at it, then at Roberta, with a what-the-hell-is-*wrong*-with-you? tilt to its beak.

Ungrateful feathery bastard.

Roberta gave it a 'Hmmph!' and went back to her paper.

The *Sharny Dick Plop* was *really* sticking the boot in: making the murders as salacious as possible, and portraying Logan's investigation as a cavalcade of unprofessional morons and halfwits. Which was rich, given the whole article was based around the opinion of Psychic Sodding Sue. 'Buncha shites.'

Tufty didn't look up from his novel. 'Pound in the swear jar.'

'I'm *retired*. There is no swear jar.'

'Is in *this* car.' He put the book down. 'Look, standards matter. You can't let yourself go just because you're "economically inactive" now.'

She snorted at him. 'I am *not* "economically..."' Wait a minute. 'Oh Christ: I'm a *pensioner*! Bath slippers and furry chairs. Next thing you know I'll be getting fitted for a beige cardigan and hearing aid!' She scrunched the newspaper up, and stuffed her head into it. Which did sod-all to muffle her scream.

Then sagged back.

A pensioner.

An OAP.

A coffin-dodger.

No wonder that crow was judging her.

Up at the front of the parked-up convoy, a PC climbed out of his patrol car – a lopsided, baggy-eyed, half-chewed-pencil of a man, who seemed to have forgotten his chin somewhere. He made his way down the line, past the Operational Support Unit's Transit van, and the Dog Unit's tiny van, before stopping beside Tufty's rustbucket.

He knocked on the car roof, then stood there, hands behind his back as Tufty wound the window down.

'Are you *bothering* this young lady, sir? I do believe I heard a scream.' He peered into the car, like the crow's unhealthy, older brother. 'I do hope it wasn't one of sexual ecstasy: this is a public road.'

A wave from the wee loon. 'Hey, Sporky.'

'Boss wanted you to have this, as a wee token of his esteem.' Passing over an Airwave handset. 'Give it back, though. No keepsies.'

Roberta leaned across the car. 'Are we going yet or no'? Supposed to be roaded at four.'

Sporky stepped back, eyes wide, one hand against his chest. 'Goodness me! As I live and breathe, who is this *vision* of loveliness? For it is as if *Scarlett Johansson* and *Audrey Hepburn* had a lesbian lovechild that surpassed even *their* ethereal beauty.'

Hard not to smile at that. 'You're a lying bastard, but I'll take it.'

He winked. 'Next five to ten, is what I hear; soon as the Boss gets here.' A wee salute. 'In the meantime: try to keep the sounds of passionate lovemaking to a bare minimum, eh? This is a respectable neighbourhood.' Then Sporky turned on his heel and shambled off.

Tufty checked the Airwave handset was on.

Placed it on the dashboard.

Then they settled back to wait…

3.08

The dashboard clock ticked over to quarter-past four. Which made it the only thing on this rustbucket that still worked properly.

Tufty puffed out his cheeks. Drummed his fingertips against Betsy's taped-up steering wheel. Wriggled in his seat.

'Will you sit *still*?'

'Can't believe they is letting us snooch along on the dunt.' A frown. 'Well, not *me*, cos I still has a *being an police officer*, but you? Not so much.'

'We're here because Detective Superintendent Young isn't as big a prick as he pretends. And he knows there wouldn't even *be* a dunt if I hadn't made the—'

Their borrowed Airwave squawked into life: *'Well, don't just sit there: bums in gear, people! We've got a joiner's workshop to raid.'*

Exhaust plumed out of the vehicles ahead, then they pulled forward, leaving Steel and Tufty behind as Betsy went *yididi-dididididididdd…*

Roberta thumped the wee loon. '*Today* would be good!'

Tufty cranked the key again: *yididididididididiiddd…* Grimacing. *Yidididididididididdddddd-did-did-did…* Then the exhaust back-fired like a faulty shotgun and Betsy's engine phlegmed into life. 'Good girl!' Patting the dashboard. 'You is the *bestest* girl!'

'Everyone will obey the rules and follow the plan. No exceptions. By the book. This Op goes nice and clean, people!'

The mouldy Fiat Panda lurched and sputtered after the departing convoy.

In the wing mirror, that crow finally hopped down from its fencepost and ripped into the fallen sausage.

A grin from Tufty. 'Is so exciting!' Bouncing in his seat as they caught up with the Dog Unit.

'You've been on dunts before.'

'Yes. But this one's *different*.' Pointing at her, then himself. '*We* did this!'

He paused for the 'Give Way' sign at the end of the lane, before following the others onto a curve of road that separated the wee clump of houses from the A92, like an oversized lay-by.

'Aye, I've been thinking about that... See when they're busy shining our bumholes for being investigative geniuses? I think *you* should take the credit.'

A bus stop sat near the junction with the dual carriageway, where a pair of Goths paused mid-snog – black-and-white make-up smeared to a mooshy grey – disentangling their tongues for long enough to watch the procession of police vehicles pass.

Tufty stopped at the junction, letting an artic lorry thunder past while he stared at her. 'Really? You want *me* to take the credit?' Narrowing his eyes. '*Why?*'

'No skin off mine: retired, remember? Wouldn't do your career any harm to have a nice big win under your belt.' And the more people who owed her favours the better.

'Oh.' Nodding. 'Cool.' He nipped across the dual carriageway, heading south, towards Stonehaven.

Off to the left, the North Sea was little more than a thin smear on the horizon as a darkening veil of drizzle drifted along the coast. Blurring the convoy's flickering blue lights.

'Oooh, oooh, oooh!' Sitting up straighter. 'I could even has an *promotion*! Would be all like *Sergeant* Tufty!'

God help us.

Now they were on the A92, the police vehicles put their feet down, pulling away from Betsy.

'Did you forget to wind the elastic band this morning?'

He rocked back and forward, as if that was going to make this rusty heap go any faster. 'Come on, Daddy's brave little girl, you can does it!'

Just maybe not before they all died of old age.

By the time they'd reached the Stonehaven slip road, the North Sea had grown from a thin smear to a massive chunk, with only a narrow wedge of headland to keep its heavy grey mass at bay.

The main railway line south sat in a deep cutting on the other side of an agricultural shed – about the size of a large drive-through, with 'Coillewood Development & Resolution Specialists Ltd' mounted on the corrugated cladding. Its triangular yard secured behind an eight-foot high chain-link fence, topped with barbed wire, keeping the stacked pallets of wood safe from a vicious-looking flock of sheep.

First through the workshop gates was the OSU Transit, followed by the Dog Unit and the patrol car. Then an unmarked pool car. Leaving Betsy to putter in at the tail end.

The vanful of Thugs screeched to a halt, and out piled five *huge* officers in full Method of Entry kit, complete with crash helmets, pads, and riot shields. A lumbering giant made it a round half-dozen, clutching a scarlet mini-battering-ram in her huge hands, ready to smash her way into Noel Sherman's office.

She must've been disappointed when the lead Thug turned the handle and the door just swung open: no need for the Big Red Door Key after all.

In they thundered.

Soon as Betsy was tucked inside the yard, Tufty leapt out, snapping on a pair of nitrile gloves as he sprinted back to the gates.

Roberta extricated herself from the passenger seat and stood there, leaning on her door, enjoying everybody doing some *work* for a change.

Down in the cutting, a train clattered past, engines howling, leaving a haze of blue-diesel behind as it headed south to Stonehaven, on its way to Edinburgh Waverly.

Detective Superintendent Young appeared from the pool car, Airwave in one hand, pointing at people and things with the other. 'I WANT THAT PERIMETER SECURED!'

Off a PC scampered.

But Tufty was already doing it, swinging both sides of the gate shut with a rattling *clang*.

PC MacLauchlan clambered out of the Dog Unit's manky wee van. A shambolic collection of body parts – in black cargo pants and a Police Scotland baseball cap – he had a sort of goblin-cannibal hybrid look. Not helped by his loping gait as he hurried around to the rear doors and liberated Police Dog Branston: a Godzilla-sized Alsatian in black-and-brown, straining at her leash, barking and scrabbling, towing her handler towards the workshop. No doubt keen to sink her teeth into a criminal or three, while MacLauchlan held on like a waterskier being hauled behind a hairy speedboat. That loved to bite people.

A trio of voices boomed out inside the workshop:

'DROP THE TOOLS! DROP THEM!'

'EVERYONE ON THE FLOOR! NOW! MOVE IT!'

'OH NO YOU BLOODY DON'T!'

Followed by scuffing, thumps, a collection of clanging noises and a scream, all interspersed with PD Branston's howitzer barks.

Tufty shot the bolt on the gates, rattling a chain into place, holding both sides together.

The train's engine howled into the distance.

Traffic thundered past on the A92 barely two hundred feet away.

Another scream.

BARK! BARK! BARK! BARK!

'I SAID, "ON THE BLOODY FLOOR"!'

Roberta let loose a happy sigh. 'I do *miss* these relaxing days out.'

Four of Noel Sherman's crew were marched out through the workshop's big up-and-over door, limping and scuffed, in overalls and handcuffs. All men. Two in their mid-twenties, two middle-aged. *Glowering* in the rain.

The only woman was sixty-something, wearing a Sex Pistol's T-shirt and tartan miniskirt – which did nothing for her Chesterfield thighs – greying hair dyed pink on one side and neatly shaved on the other. Purple DMs.

Somehow, she'd escaped being handcuffed, but then it was the Big-Red-Door-Key-wielding behemoth who frogmarched her across the yard towards Young's pool car. So that probably wasn't an issue.

Tufty shuffled his feet, shoulders hunched as drizzle turned into something far rainier. Inching closer to Roberta, as if she was going to let him in under her umbrella.

Silly sod should've looked at the forecast this morning and packed one of his own.

Which is why *she* was a consulting detective, and he was an idiot.

Soon as Granny Punk had been delivered to the pool

car, the door opened and Detective Superintendent Young climbed out.

Officer Door-Key shoved her forward. 'Mrs Irene Ashton.'

Young loomed. 'I'm only going to ask this once: where's Noel Sherman?'

Mrs Ashton stuck her chin in the air. 'Eat me, you Neanderthal prick!' Her left boot slammed into his groin, making Young's eyes bug as he folded like a deckchair, clutching his bits.

She spun around on those purple Doc Martens, far faster than someone her age should, fist flying. Catching PC Door-Key right in the throat.

More bugged eyes and crumpled knees. Gasping and going red.

Oh for God's sake.

'Tufty!' Roberta set out at a hurple, with the wee loon hurrying after her.

Mrs Ashton, meanwhile, hauled in a deep breath: 'NOEL! NOW!'

A door banged open, somewhere on the North-Sea-side of the workshop, followed by a clatter of falling wood, and Noel Sherman appeared. Like his crew, he was dressed in overalls and safety boots, but he had something they didn't – a large, heavy backpack. Hauling it on as he lumbered away.

'HEY, FASCISTS!' Mrs Ashton grabbed a big chunk of two-by-four from the nearest pallet, swinging it broadsword-style as the OSU team and PCs closed in. 'ANY ONE OF YOU *PIG-FUCKERS* MOVE, I'LL TAKE YOUR FUCKING HEADS OFF!'

Which was everyone's cue to rush her. Only to be beaten back by a wheeching great-big dod of wood.

Giving Noel Sherman a clean stagger at the nearest segment of fence.

Roberta pointed. 'Fetch!'

And off Tufty sprinted, leaving her to shamble after him as fast as she could with two dodgy legs and a walking stick.

Instead of clambering over the fence, like a normal human being, Sherman lowered his shoulder and charged at the chain-link. So he wasn't the brightest of fish in the swimming pool. He'd just bounce off and Tufty would arrest him and—

Son of a bitch.

There must've been a hidden gate there, because Sherman went straight through. Stopped on the other side. And turned to fiddle with the fence. Bet he was locking it behind him.

Tufty leapt a pile of offcuts. 'STOP, OFF-DUTY POLICE!'

The officers tried to charge Mrs Ashton again, but the two-by-four did another sweep, sending them jerking back to avoid getting walloped.

Now that he'd escaped the yard, Sherman couldn't make for the slip road, or the dual carriageway – they'd pick him up in minutes. Which meant there was only one way to go. And when he'd cleared the railway line, all he had to do was scramble down the cliffs to the boat he'd no-doubt planked there for this very eventuality, and sail off into the gloom.

The bastard was going to get away.

Mrs Ashton swung her club again, but this time, soon as the wood whistled past, the team charged. Forming one big scrum with an old age punk at the bottom. An OAP who knew some impressive swearwords.

Tufty scuffle-hopped to a halt in front of the hidden gate, just in time for Sherman to give him a grin and the finger.

Roberta clambered over the offcuts, arriving at the gate as Tufty grabbed the thing and rattled it.

A thick brass padlock held the gate firmly shut.

Sherman dangled a key in front of them, then hurled it away into the field of dangerous sheep. Flashed *both* middle fingers at Roberta. Then staggered off, taking his heavy backpack with him. Picking up a bit of momentum, till he could break into a jog. Crossing the narrow strip of field, scrambling over the drystane dyke at the bottom, and disappearing down the embankment.

'Flipping…' Tufty yanked on the gate again. But that padlock was going *nowhere*.

Then, a loud *'HONNNNNNNNNNNNNNNNNNNNNNNNNNNK! HONNNNNNNNNNNNNNNNNNNNNNNNNNNNNNNK!'* bellowed out. Followed by a horrible meaty *thunk* as the 15:58 Scotrail service from Montrose – calling at Laurencekirk, Stonehaven, Portlethen, and Aberdeen – battered through Noel Sherman like a sack of mince.

Followed by the metallic screech of railway brakes and a tortured howl of diesel engines.

The blue-grey belch of exhaust fumes was joined by a faint-pink mist and cloud of powdery white, drifting out towards the sea.

That would be the contents of Sherman's backpack.

So, there were going to be some *very* coked-up fish out there tonight.

Tufty stared at Roberta, then monkey-clattered his way up the inside of the fence, until he was high enough to peer out through the barbed wire. Probably getting himself a good view down into the railway cutting. 'Oh noes…' He rattled back to earth, mouth hanging open, eyes darting from her to the embankment and back again. 'I does not want the credit. I does *not* want the credit!'

3.09

Roberta slithered into Betsy's passenger seat, out of the rain. Whistling an innocent tune. Face the perfect model of virtuous piety as a teuchter voice battered out of the car radio: *'And it's time fir anither travel update. The main line sooth is still blockit, so yer no' goin' oanywhere by train the day, unless it's* north.' A sigh. *'Dear me, fit a sotter!'*

Tufty grimaced across the car at her.

His rusty Fiat Panda now slumped in the furthest corner of the yard, making room for a Scenes Transit in the usual shade of wash-me 'white', another patrol car, and the police van Young's search team had arrived in. Nearly a dozen bodies, now dressed in white SOC suits, picking their way back and forth across the field and down along the cutting. Gathering up all the lumps and chunks of Noel Sherman, before the crows and seagulls got their pointy little beaks into him.

'Mind you, a' the main routes in and oot o' the city are nae bad, *but there's a wee loon brokit doon in the ootside lane, northbound on* Denburn Road, *so the middle o' Aiberdeen's a' snarled up.'*

Chief Superintendent Pine's Mercedes was parked out of the way too, in a stay-away-from-my-expensive-motor-car, you-lowlife-ruffians! kind of way. Passenger side close to the fence, leaving as much space on the other three sides as possible. Because God forbid someone should accidentally brush against that shiny black paintwork.

Tufty pulled his chin in. 'No, but … what've you been up to?'

'Tell you whit, why don't we play the loon a wee tune tae keep his spirits up till the brack-doon mannie gets there?'

'Me?' She wiped her fingers clean on a leftover napkin from lunchtime. Because sausage grease was hard to shift. Especially if it'd been festering away in your armpit all day. 'Nothing. Sat here with you the whole time.'

'And if yer drivin' doon Denburn Road, be sure tae gie him a wee wave*! Here's Crimson Summer and an auld favourite: "The Midnight Rose".'*

'Nooo…' Tufty folded over, hands covering his face as the music swelled. 'Are things not bad enough?'

The yard's gates were open again, but a line of blue-and-white 'POLICE' tape cordoned off the entrance, guarded by a uniformed PC in a high-vis jacket – drooping and dripping in the pattering rain.

A bunch of journos had congregated in the field opposite Coillewood Development and Resolution Specialists Ltd, squeezed between the A92 and the slip road. Looking soggy, and miserable, and bored.

'Seriously,' Tufty peered through his fingers at her, 'what did you *do*?'

The workshop door opened and Pine stepped out, followed by her loyal guard dog, Sergeant Brookminster, with Superintendent Young bringing up the rear. Pine looked around the yard, face hardening as she spotted Betsy. Then marched towards them.

OK.

Roberta wiped a sausage-free hand across her face, clearing away any rain. Straightening her hair. Cranking up the innocent look. 'I haven't done *anything*, Constable Quirrel. I've been here *all the time*, remember?'

The vocals kicked in on the radio, a nasal transatlantic voice, but he'd barely sung two words before Tufty switched the thing off. Whimpered. Went 'Oh noes…' And clambered out into the rain. Standing to attention.

Pine glowered at him. 'I *told* you to stay in that car!'

'Eeek…' He scrambled back into the driver's seat.

The Chief Superintendent planted herself at the passenger window, arms folded, staring in and down at Roberta.

Probably not best pleased that Roberta just sat there, pretending to read the *Scottish Daily Post* Tufty stole from DHQ. Completely ignoring her.

Tufty kept his voice to a strangled whisper. 'Guv? I mean, *Roberta*: there's a chief superintendent standing right outside the car!'

'Is there?' She lowered the paper and checked. 'So there is!' Winding her window down. 'Afternoon. We'll have a Bacon Double Cheeseburger, Chicken Royale, two fries, medium Sprite and a chocolate shake.' Because the oldies were the goodies.

'WHAT THE HELL WERE YOU THINKING?'

Roberta frowned. 'Aye, you're right: chocolate shake doesn't go with *fries*. Have you got any Irn-Bru?'

'GET OUT OF THAT BLOODY CAR!' Face getting redder and redder.

Young held up a hand. 'Now, Boss, maybe we should all—'

'OUT! NOW!'

'Meh, why not.' Roberta chucked the paper to Tufty, then opened her door and struggled out. Making a big show of how *difficult* it was with a walking stick and traumatic head injury. Then gave Pine a nice bland smile. 'Roslyn. That foundation's doing nothing for you – makes you look like a squeezed pluke.'

Pine's eyes bulged. 'WOULD YOU CARE TO EXPLAIN WHY I HAVE A DEAD LOCAL BUSINESS OWNER

SPREAD OVER HALF A MILE OF SODDING *TRAIN TRACKS*?'

A tut. A sigh. Then Roberta adopted Susan's disappointed tone. 'And are we going to be shouting *all* the way through this interaction, or shall we try acting like *grown-ups* instead?'

'"*GROWN-UPS*"?' Trembling, spittle flying. 'GROWN-UPS!'

'Cos you might no've noticed, but I retired six weeks ago – so I don't have to listen to your …' swirling a finger in Pine's direction, 'whatever *this* is meant to be.'

'How *dare* you—'

'Fuck me!' A wee laugh. 'I've been bollocked by bigger and better tossers than *you* in my time. And I had to stand there and "Yes, sir!", "No, sir!", "Three bags sodding full!" But no' anymore.'

Young stepped in. 'All right, this has all got far too heated. I need everyone involved to take a step back and a deep breath.'

Pine opened her mouth, but Young got there first: 'Everyone!'

The Chief Superintendent clamped her jaw shut and trembled a bit more. Then hauled in a deep breath and stepped back. Ever the rebel.

Steel slouched against Betsy. 'You want to know why Noel Sherman died? Because he's … *was* an idiot. We gave him plenty opportunities to surrender himself, instead of which he grabbed as much gear as he could carry and legged it. Into the path of an oncoming train.' She pointed a finger at Young. 'Have Scenes done a presumptive test on the white powder in that backpack yet?'

He nodded. 'Cocaine. Estimates about one-point-seven *million* pounds, street value. About half of which has drifted off into the wild blue yonder. The crabs and seagulls will be off their tits on sniff for a week.'

'So, our poor "local business owner" was probably the

biggest distributor of class A drugs north of Dundee. Plus, you'll *never* guess who was a regular visitor to his place of work.' Roberta produced her phone and scrolled through the photo gallery to those surveillance shots Davey took – quickly deleting any featuring Jeremy Yarrow, because the poor bugger had seen enough grief for one lifetime – then held the screen out for Young and Pine. 'Why, bugger me if it isn't Charlotte MacNeal and her lime-green Toyota Yaris.'

Young raised an eyebrow. 'Operation Basilisk...' He turned to Pine. 'We'd assumed the drugs were coming in from Lithuania, already concealed in the teddy bears. But what if Sherman was just buying the *bears* in bulk, cheap from a Lithuanian supplier, and filling them with "product" here?' Staring out through the fence, at the Scenes Smurfs in their ghostly white SOC suits. 'Shame he's dead. Could've found out how he got the drugs into the country – shut down the whole supply chain.'

'Hmmm...' Roberta pulled a big thinky face, tapping a finger to her forehead. 'Yeah, I *wonder* how he could've done that?' She swiped through more shots on her phone, bringing up the sequence from Stonehaven Harbour: *The Nippy Partan*, buggering off around the breakwater. 'Rory Hatton. *Also* a frequenter of Coillewood Development And Resolution Specialists Limited. Who has, *coincidentally enough*, bought himself a dirty-big, brand-new Jaguar four-by-four. How *ever* did he afford that by selling the odd lobster and crab?'

At which point Young turned away, already on his Airwave as he marched off: 'Porter? It's me. I need you to get another warrant...'

Which left Roberta, Pine, and Brookminster – who looked about ready to crawl away and hide, the tips of his ears glowing pink.

Pine cleared her throat. 'Yes... Well...'

Roberta tipped her a wink. 'Oh, I'm stappit fu of surprises, me.'

'Perhaps … under the circumstances … I may have been … a touch … *hasty* … in my condemnation of your actions.' Every word sounding as if she was squeezing a hedgehog out of her arse. The wrong way around. 'I *apologise* for any offence I may have *inadvertently* caused.'

Hmmm…

'Ah, what the hell.' Roberta stuck her hand out, but when Pine went to shake it, she pulled it back, swirled her fingers around, and gave the Chief Superintendent of NE Division the same one-fingered salute that Noel Sherman gave Tufty.

'I see.' Pine sniffed, stuck her nose in the air, and marched back towards the workshop. Abandoning Brookminster.

He shuffled his feet. 'Oh, dear…'

A grin. 'AND YOUR ARSE IS MEDIOCRE, SQUARE, AND FLAT!'

Pine froze for a second. Then kept going. Spine ramrod straight.

Brookminster sagged. 'I wish you hadn't done that.'

'Aye: into every life some shite must splatter.'

'Yes, but *I'm* the one who has to clear it up…' A big sigh, then he turned on his heel and stalked after his flat-arsed boss.

Ha!

Roberta clambered into Betsy's passenger seat and *thunk*ed the door shut. Pulled on her seatbelt. 'Better get this rusty old heap on the road, Tufters. There's a storm brewing and I want to be *far* away from here when it hits.'

'Oh … poop.' He turned the key – making the engine *yiddddddiddidid-yiddddddiddididid-yididididididididididididid* till it spluttered into life – then performed a gear-crunching five-point turn, heading for the workshop gates.

The PC on guard raised the blue-and-white tape, and they puttered beneath it.

Roberta scootched down in her seat, keeping the yard in her wing mirror, getting a lovely view of the seagulls. A whole *riot* of the buggers, staging a turf war on top of the Chief Superintendent's --Mercedes.

Because what web-footed feathery bastard could resist armpity sausages?

The assembled members of the soggy press snapped off a few half-hearted photos as Tufty headed past them and down the slip road. Heading for Stonehaven, with his face like a spanked arse. 'Are we running away cos of what you did?'

She grinned at him. 'Didn't do anything, remember? I was with *you* the whole time.'

'Oh, God.' He put his foot down.

Because he wasn't as daft as he looked.

3.10

Rain shivered the leaves overhead, as Tufty navigated his crumbling rattletrap through the genteel, tree-lined, and waterlogged streets of Rubislaw. Face pulled out and down, as if someone had just introduced his bumhole to an unbuttered pineapple.

Which was daft. He should be living in the moment. Enjoying the small pleasures, like Roberta did.

She grinned, which only made him wince harder.

Shame they couldn't have been there when Chief Superintendent Pine found out what'd happened to her precious Mercedes. But sometimes you just had to run away *before* the explosion happened.

Learned that one the hard way.

Roberta whistled a happy tune, composing a text to Susan:

> What say we get Jasmine to babysit Naomi tonight, then you and me can go somewhere nice for tea?
>
> Bit of a celebration, because *I* am a HIGHLY SUCCESSFUL RAT.

Tufty turned Betsy onto Roberta's street. And the pineapple was joined by a globe artichoke. 'But did you *have* to criticise her bum?'

'Course I did.' Holding up a finger. 'One: it was a *massive* heap of fun.' Next finger. 'Two: this way all her rage is focussed on *me*, and no' *you*.' Another finger joined the party. 'And three: no bugger shouts at *Roberta Steel*, like I'm some wheezy Jack Russell terrier who's just peed on the living-room rug again.'

He gave a little sobbing moan. 'But I has to go back to *work* on Sunday! Night shift's bad enough without unexploded Chief Superintendents!'

'Where you can tell them how that nasty old Roberta Steel bullied you and made you do all those naughty things.' A sniff. 'By then Perky Pine will've forgotten all about it anyway.' Or more likely, she'll have spent the whole weekend working herself up into a flat-arsed tizzy. Planning revenge. But the wee loon didn't need to know that – bad for morale. 'I still say you should take the credit for ID'ing Noel Sherman, Drug Kingpin of Aberdeenshire South.'

'Who's now *jam*.' Tufty shuddered. 'To be honest, I've been kinda waiting for that to happen since we started... Which is why nice boys do *not* play on the railway lines.'

He pulled up outside Roberta's house, right in front of her poor abandoned MX-5 – all covered in *sticky* and leaves and bits of tree and bird poop and lumpy-dirty stuff. Definitely need to get that washed.

After all, if she was stuck with being chauffeured around for the foreseeable future, why not do it in style? Maybe bribe the kids to—

Oh, for goodness' sake.

Jasmine and Naomi.

The pair of them were huddled by the front door, beneath a scant overhang of scarlet rambling roses – nowhere near as voluminous and porch-like as the one outside traitorous Davey's miniature bungalow.

They were both drenched.

Silly sods.

Roberta opened her door, popped her brolly, and hauled herself out into the rain. Then turned to lean back into the car. Putting on her Eberto Alters wizard voice: 'You did good today, wee man. Pure dead brilliant, so you were.'

He looked at her, then pink rushed up his cheeks, bringing a stammer with it. 'I… I don't…' He cleared his throat. 'Sorry. Only you've never been properly *nice* to me before.' Then Tufty's eyes widened. 'Are you *dying*?'

'I take it back, you're a knob.' She thunked the door shut, then hobbled up the garden path to her sodden children. Shaking her head. Taking in the drookit pair of twits. '*Why?*'

Jasmine pulled a face. 'Forgot my keys.'

Naomi glowered, shivering. 'She's a s-s-s-silly s-s-s-soggy ars-s-s-se-biscuit!'

True.

'And what about *your* keys?'

Naomi shrank into her school blazer. '*Non parlo Inglese, S-s-s-signora.*'

'Yeah, I bet you don't.' Roberta unlocked the door. 'Come on. But you better no' tell Mummy Susan about this or somehow it'll end up being *my* fault.'

The squelchy idiots barged inside, wreaking a thump-and-rattle barrage of wet shoes and jackets – cast off and dumped on the hall floor as they scurried away.

Because she and Susan had raised messy, lazy, *feral* little monsters.

Roberta turned to close the door, and there was Betsy, sitting at the kerb, engine idling like a demonic bowl of Rice Crispies, while Tufty grinned at her from the driver's seat. Still chuffed with himself. Waving.

Urgh…

That's what she got for being nice.

3.11

Had to admit, it looked good on her incident-room wall.

Roberta straightened the brand-new framed front page from Saturday's *Aberdeen Examiner*: 'TRAIN TRAGEDY AS EX-COP CRACKS CASE'. The photo was an overhead shot of Noel Sherman's workshop, probably taken via drone, with multiple police vehicles in the fenced-off yard and the railway line just visible at the top of the shot – where a big blue marquee covered *most* of Noel Sherman's body parts. There was an inset pic of the man himself, and one of Roberta. Though it must've been taken a while ago, because she wasn't sporting her swanky new hairdo.

Subheading: 'Drug Kingpin Dies In Raid On Stonehaven Business As Plucky Roberta Stops Crime Spree'. Which sort of made it sound as if *she* was the one who'd been on the spree.

Had to admit, the *Examiner* had gone downhill a bit since that shortarsed Weegie knob-hat, Colin Miller, took over as editor. But the article said all the right things about how brilliant *she* was and how crap Chief Superintendent *Pine* was, so what the hell.

Roberta stepped back from the frame and smiled.

Her very first case as a consulting detective was *officially* a massive, resounding, unqualified success.

She had a slurp of tea, and thumbed out a text:

> You're a silly sod, Tufty.
>
> Should've taken the credit like I told you.

SEND.

And then, for poops and giggles, she opened Logan's message for the umpteenth time since receiving it on Saturday.

LOGAN:

> I'm assuming this was your handiwork?

He'd attached a short video file, no more than a couple of seconds long, lifted from *Reporting Scotland.*

She hit play and a damp PC raised the tape cordon, letting Chief Superintendent Pine's Mercedes pull out of Noel Sherman's yard. That glossy black paintwork was scuffed and bespattered with seagull crap. But the *best* bit was just before it turned to head down the slip road towards Stonehaven, when the passenger side was on full display. And yes, Sergeant Brookminster had parked it right up against the chain-link fence to keep it safe from harm, but that hadn't stopped some *naughty* individual from sneaking up and scratching the word 'WANK!' deep into the paint, across both doors.

Roberta burst out laughing again, because that shite would never *not* be funny.

Logan's follow-up text took the shine off it a little, though:

> You had to go too far didn't you.
>
> Now she's going to take it out on Tufty!
>
> And everyone else at DHQ.

Yeah, well Pishy Pine better not, because Roberta had a lot more where *that* came from.

Didn't make Logan's text any less of a buzzkill, though.

She deleted it, then poked out a revenge reply:

> Have you still not caught your killer pervert yet? Lazy sod!
>
> You need to hire a decent Consulting Detective.
>
> I solved Operation Basilisk in ONE DAY!

Well, technically *forty-four* days, if you included the five weeks between arresting Charlotte MacNeal and Friday's raid on Noel Sherman's gaff. But those weeks didn't count, because Roberta wasn't *actually* working the case, then – she'd been doing life drawings, learning how to craft stained-glass windows, perfecting homemade custard, and being a wizard hunting dragons, and stuff.

So there.

SEND.

As a reward for all this industriousness, Roberta played the video of Pine's scratched-and-crap-spattered Mercedes again. And again. And again… Laughing like a drunken magpie every time.

Ahhh… Happy days.

Right.

Might as well tidy away Operation Basilisk, now that she'd solved it.

Roberta unwrapped the red ribbons first, then unpinned the notes, transcripts, maps, paperwork, and photos and stuck them in a binder – because what was the point of nicking a two-hole punch from work if you didn't use it? Popped it on her new bookshelf. Then settled into the folding chair to sip tea, munch on a chocolate digestive, and ponder which case to tackle next: Operation Demogorgon, or Troglodyte.

Cos with a wheelie-bin murder and a stabbing to choose from, who could get excited about Operation Firedrake and its food van turf war? Talk about small baked potatoes.

Ding-buzz.

Sadly, it wasn't Logan with a job offer.

TUFTY:

> Flipping plip-plop! Stop
>
> Chief Supt. Pine going ballistic after what you did. Stop
>
> All shouty and ranty. Stop
>
> Says your a bad influence. Stop
>
> Says anyone caught helping you is for the chop. Stop
>
> STOP!!!

Honestly, wee loons today.

She texted him back:

> *you're

SEND.

Idiot.

Then had another go:

> And I didn't do anything = I was with you the whole time, REMEMBER?!?!

SEND.

Ding-buzz.

TUFTY:

> Thought I'd be safe on nightshift till Wed, but she was waiting for me when I got off work this morning!
>
> That wim is MONSTER SCARY BISCUITS!!!

Sodding hell.

You know, it *really* didn't help that Logan had been right about Pine picking on the wee loon.

I TOLD you to take credit for the raid!

The rotten cow wouldn't be picking on you if you had.

Roberta scowled at the room's bare lightbulb for a moment.

And stop calling women 'wims'!

It's disrespectful, you parsnip-faced wee shite.

Because picking on Tufty was *her* job.

SEND.

Bet Pine was planning on driving a wedge between Roberta and her Queen Street Irregulars. Divide and conquer. Which would be a pain in the arse, long-term – hard to be a consulting detective without sidekicks who could run PNC checks, call for backup, and arrest people.

Maybe it wouldn't hurt to give the troops a wee carrot instead of the stick for a change?

Or even a small baked potato...

Roberta scrolled through her contacts, giving Boris Johnson's head a good squeeze as Lund's phone rang. He was looking decidedly unwell now, as if his thyroid was acting up, a sad wheezy edge to the *pkongk* and *glonk*.

Took a while, but eventually Lund's voice battered out of the handset, brittle with forced cheer. *'Kevin! Much though I'd* love *to talk, I'm kind of in the middle of something. I'll call you back, OK?'*

Eh?

'Someone spike your morning coffee, Veronica? It's me.'

'I know *that, Kevin, but I'm* in *a* meeting.*'* It went all muffled, as if she'd put her hand over the phone. *'Sorry, Guv, it's the plumber. He's fixing the washing machine.'*

'Sounds like the start of a Seventies porn film. Take it I'm persona non grata at DHQ?'

'That's right. Now, I have to go.'

'Only I *might* have a wee something that's to your advantage. If you're interested…?'

Silence.

Roberta levered herself out of the chair and limped over to Operation Firedrake – with its surveillance photos of burger vans and chip vans and noodle vans and tattie-and-taco vans… Then the pictures of battered faces and burnt-out vehicles.

Pkongk-glonk. Pkongk-glonk. Pkongk-glonk. Pkongk-glonk.

'I'm listening.'

'See, I think I know why your turf war's raging. And you were right: a greasy burger's no' worth crippling someone for.' Milking the moment, drawing it out. 'But do you know what *is*…?'

Lund's end went all scrunched and muffled again. *'Sorry, Guv, I need to … just step outside for a,* really *brief second.'* Shuffle, clunk, then the echoing click of footsteps in a corridor. *'Have you any idea how much trouble you've caused? Pine's flipping livid!'*

Oh dear, how sad.

Beaming like a Cheshire Cat. 'You want the fruits of my wisdom or no'?'

A sigh. *'Fine. Give me your wisdom fruits.'*

'Charlotte MacNeal – the scummy mummy I arrested – she's got a burger van, right? Know what else she has? Teddy bears stuffed with cocaine, heroin, and fentanyl. Aye, no' all together, mind.' *Pkongk-glonk.* 'So what if Operation Firedrake is *actually* an offshoot of Operation Basilisk? And they're no' fighting over where they can sell their deep-fried shiteburgers – they're carving up the Northeast's drug market.'

'I see. … Yes. … And that helps us how?'

A fair question.

'We just took out one of the biggest players in the northeast supply chain. Which means your turf war…?'

One: two, three, four.

Two: two, three, four.

Three: two, three, four.

'Oh for the name of sod.' A deep breath was hissed in and rattled out again. *'If one side's lost its command structure, it's going to be a bloodbath. Urgh…'*

Bingo.

'So *maybe* it *might* be an idea to get yourselves a bunch of search warrants and go through everyone who's been targeted? Lockups, houses, garages. See what illicit treats they've got stashed away with the tomato ketchup.' Roberta dropped a sneaky conspiratorial edge into her voice. 'And if I were you, I'd do it *fast*, before Superintendent Young twigs, swoops in, and steals all the glory.'

And just like that, Lund was all sweetness and light. *'Thanks, Sarge! I mean,* Guv. *I mean … feels a bit weird calling you "Roberta".'*

'We live in weird times.' *Pkonnnnnnnnnnnnnnnnnnnnk…* 'And now that I've done *you* a huge favour, maybe you could do me a *tiny* one in return?'

You'd think the view from the sixth floor of a twelve-storey tower block would've had a bit more glamour to it, but the lobby outside Tufty's flat could only muster up two small windows, both of which looked out on the branches of unhappy trees.

Not so much as a squirrel.

The floor was that knobbly-grey-plastic stuff they had in the heavy-wear sections of Aberdeen Royal Infirmary, and the walls were tiled like a Victorian toilet, but for some strange reason they'd put pine cladding on the ceiling. Like the world's worst sauna.

Which was still kind of a sore point.

Someone had decorated the lift doors up here with big stickers that had 'BEWARE OF' on one side and 'THE LEOPARD' on the other. Because people were weird.

Roberta pressed Tufty's 'bell' again.

The other three flats on this floor had normal-looking doors, with the occasional pot plant to enliven the squirrel-free space.

Not Tufty, though.

No, he'd painted *his* to look like the TARDIS, and stuck a stupid Star Trek TNG fake computer panel beside it – like an oversized iPad – all interconnected boxes and lines in cheery shades of orange, yellow, and blue, with stupid Star Trek things written on them, beneath a big sign: 'USS VALLEY FORGE'.

A brass plaque sat in the middle of the door, with the White Tree of Gondor on it, wrapped around with Elvish script.

And to top it all off, the 'doorbell' was built into the display panel, and you had to press the blue block marked 'BRIDGE' to make it ring. Only it *didn't* ring, it played the 'Imperial March' from *Star Wars*.

Because nothing screamed 'Massive Sodding Nerd!' like mixing your fandoms.

Soon as the tune finished playing, she set it going again. And again, until the door finally opened and a bleary Tufty peered out at her.

'Wht? M'sleep. G'way...' He was wearing a pair of jammies, printed to look like Chewbacca – all brown and hairy, with a bandolier – but he was so short it made him look more Ewok than Wookie.

Which was a reference that made her bum itch, because she was far too cool to know crap like that.

Or at least she *had* been.

Forcing a smile, Roberta patted the wee twit on the

shoulder. 'Tufty, my most excellent friend: good news! I have an opportunity for you that you're going to *love*.'

A pink-eyed scowl. 'No I'm not. Because I'm going back to bed.'

'How can you sleep on a *beautiful* day like—'

'Because I'm on nights! And it's raining. And Chief Superintendent Pine says you're a bad influence and if I play with you, she's going to decapitate my "happy truncheon" with a pair of scissors.' He shivered. 'Only not in so many words.'

'Oh…' Roberta's forced bonhomie sagged right out of her. 'That bad, eh?'

'Worse.' Then he grimaced at the grey day lurking beyond the sad trees. '*Please* leave me alone, I have to be on-shift at eight!'

'That's no' for *ages* yet.' Reaching down, she plucked the hessian bag-for-life from the floor. Held it up. 'And look: I've brought you a bribe! That girly fruity cider you like and a big bag of crispy pickled-onion rings.'

'Away with you. Go.' Making shooing gestures. 'You shall not pass!'

'But—'

He thumped the door shut, leaving her in the lobby.

'Tufty?'

She put her bag down, then pressed 'BRIDGE' again. Only instead of 'The Imperial March' the thing just made a wee chirrupy error noise.

'Tufty!' *Knock*, *knock*, *knock*. 'Don't make me instigate Plan B!'

Silence.

'Tufty?'

She tried the policeman's thump: three loud, hard raps on the TARDIS doors. 'Tufty!'

Nothing.

Not even a squeak.

The wee shite wasn't coming back.

'Crap.' Roberta slumped, groaned, and grimaced up at the wooden ceiling. 'I *hate* Plan B.'

3.12

Harmsworth had plumped for a Volvo too. Only where Susan's was a swanky new hybrid model, his was a poop-brown estate car from the last century, that looked as if a jobbie had sex with a hearse.

Its tan leather interior sported a number of suspicious stains, and a driver's seat with one of those bead-curtain covers. A Hawaiian hula girl hanging from the rear-view mirror, who twerked every time they went over a pothole. Despite all the boot space, the only thing the car seemed full of was a fusty infected-foot-type smell.

Its driver had dressed-up for an episode of *The Sweeney*, in a grey shirt and a brown tie, Chinos, and slip-on leather shoes that matched the upholstery.

He drove along Straik Road in Westhill, the straggly trees of Denman Park on the right, the industrial estate where Roberta got blown-up on the left.

Couldn't see the explosion site from here, though – hidden away behind business units and a Premier Inn – but even after three-and-a-half months it still radiated menace. Throbbing away like a tumour.

Roberta went back to her printouts, skimming the reports from Operation Troglodyte – peeled from her incident room's walls. Doing her best to ignore Harmsworth as he droned on and on and on…

'...of course I always *knew* I was the lynchpin of the team – any fool could see that it was me holding everything together – but it's so nice to hear it *said*. Out loud. To be appreciated. Properly.' Waving one hand about as if he were a maiden aunt. '*Acknowledged.*'

Suppose it wouldn't hurt to inflate his already massive ego a little. While he was being useful, anyway. But she wasn't going to put any effort into it. 'Of course you're appreciated, Owen. You're my Number-One, Main-Man, Go-To-Guy when I need someone smart and resourceful to rely on.' All delivered in a tired monotone.

But Harmsworth lapped it up, anyway. Preening. 'Of course. Of course. The others probably don't realise it, but I'm a bit like a father figure to them. A guiding hand, keeping their more idiotic impulses in check and *directing* them back on the right path.' So pleased with himself you'd think he'd just invented wanking.

'Yup.'

The trouble with Operation Troglodyte was that it featured over a dozen witnesses, and not one of them *saw* anything.

Didn't see the knife.

Didn't see Billie Nesbit get stabbed.

Fourteen clueless bloody idiots.

Fifteen if you included Emma Dornoch's campaign manager: Frank Abercrombie. Which Roberta did.

At least the Inturds had cooperated when they were interviewed – *tried* to be helpful, unlocked their phones and shared any footage of the mini-riot. Billie was their friend, after all. Even if their sleazy lawyer, Elgin Woodburn, made them shut up any time anything even *vaguely* self-incriminating came out of their mouths.

The Polo-shits, on the other hand, said bugger-all. Beattie barely got them to confirm their names and addresses before their swanky solicitor from Edinburgh locked everything down. No unlocked phones, no footage, no comment…

But then Beattie was an idiot.

The next time Roberta looked up from her file, Westhill had long disappeared from the rear-view mirror. Now Harmsworth's poopy Volvo wound its way out along the A944, past fields of soggy barley and barely upright wheat. All getting gently rained on this miserable Monday morning.

Little northeast farmhouses huddled into the landscape, sitting back from the road, sinister granite-and-slate lumps. Narrow windows watching them drive by with suspicious eyes.

And *still* Harmsworth wanked his ego ragged: '…of course, not everyone would've noticed that, but I kept my head and I said to myself, I said, "Owen, what kind of—"'

'Thing is: why would anyone want to stab a pretty wee thing like Billie Nesbit?'

He blinked at her for a moment, mouth moving, but nothing came out. Derailed mid-wank. 'Sorry, who now?'

Roberta tapped her file. 'See, it's a *weeny* riot, a skirmish between political factions: bleeding-heart liberals on one side, fascist cock-spanners on the other. You could stab *any* of the blokes there – Christ knows there's enough to go around – but you try killing the sexy redhead instead?'

The road curled around the Loch of Skene, its dark waters flickering between the trees. Distant hills visible for a moment, before the rain swallowed them.

'Ah.' Harmsworth nodded. 'OK. I see…' Chewing on that for a bit. '*Suppose* it's a kind of *penetration*, isn't it? Stabbing?'

Roberta stared at him.

A shrug. 'You did ask.'

The loch disappeared behind a clump of trees, leaving only fields, woods, drookit stirks, and sharny dubs behind.

Harmsworth held up a finger. 'Or *maybe* our stabber is the kind of tosser who just likes hurting women.'

'But in *public*? With all those witnesses? Bit risky, isn't it?'

He puffed out his cheeks. 'Apparently not.'

Hate to admit it, but the useless snudge had a point.

She went back to her file.

Dunecht was a quaint wee planned village, spread along one side of the A944 – a sort of waypoint between Aberdeen and Alford, Banchory and Kintore.

They drifted past the village shop and the garage; then a row of quaint little cottage-style semis, with bowling-green lawns; then the estate offices; a school; a *minute* housing estate; and out the other side. Sneeze and you'll miss it.

Roberta checked the map on her phone for Corskieford Croft, then pointed off to the right. 'There.'

A gravelled track stretched away between two fields, lined with hawthorn and jagged gorse.

Harmsworth took the turn, face a pained rictus as chuckies *ping*-and-*clank*ed in the Volvo's wheel arches. Slowing to a crawl, they made their way down the corridor of green, towards a squat mean-fronted farmhouse with a row of steadings off to one side.

Would've been quicker getting out and *walking*.

But still Harmsworth crept along, all the way to a sparse parking area, part overgrown with grass and dandelions.

The steadings had probably been a cow byre at some point, but an enterprising and grippy farmer/developer had turned them into a row of small holiday lets – going by the key-boxes next to four of the five front doors.

The only one *without* a key box had a Land Rover Discovery parked outside. And there were no other vehicles here, so maybe tourists weren't exactly flocking to northeast Scotland on a manky Monday in late-September?

Harmsworth parked his funereal jobbie. 'This us?'

She slipped her file back in its folder and struggled out of the car. Opening her brolly, before lumbering towards the not-for-let house. It even had a name, mounted above the door: 'DUNLOBBYIN'.

The view wasn't exactly killing it – flat as a concrete slab, in various shades of green and brown, leached of all joy by the never-ending sodding rain.

But a nice toasty baking smell came from somewhere nearby. Sweet and buttery.

There was a bell, but what was the point of keeping a Harmsworth and ringing it herself?

He extricated himself from his poop-coloured car and sauntered over. No brolly for him. Instead, he'd pulled on a retro brown leather jacket, with matching leather flat cap, rounding out his *Sweeney* ensemble. With the shirt and tie, white socks and slip-ons, he looked like a right tit.

Harmsworth squared his shoulders. 'What's the plan, Guv?'

'Ring the doorbell. Question the witness. Hopefully get a cuppa and a non-crap biscuit.'

'Sweet.' He rang the bell, then popped his oversized retro collar. Which just made him look even *more* titlike.

She suppressed a smile, pointing. 'This is a good look for you. Very manly: intimidating.'

He gave her an aw-shucks shrug. 'Thanks, Guv.'

Because he was a complete and utter, massive—

The house door opened, and there was Frank Abercrombie

in a floury apron. He'd ditched the shirt and rainbow tie for jeans and a purple sweatshirt, but his combforward had come adrift a bit, exposing even more shiny forehead. White powder on his heavy moustache. Wobbling slightly as he held onto the doorframe for support. So he'd either been snorting cocaine, or the big-old glass of rosé in his other hand wasn't his first this morning. 'Can I help you? Only I'm in the middle of a big bake, and…' His bleary eyes narrowed as they fixed on Roberta. 'It's *you*, isn't it!' Knocking back a glug. 'God, when I saw that photo in the papers – him carrying you out of the explosion – I knew we were *completely* F. U. C. K. E. D. You don't come back from a visual like that.'

Which was *not* her fault.

'Can we come in, only it's raining out here and, you know…' She wiggled her walking stick, hamming up being lopsided and limpy.

'Oh, God, yes, sorry, please, I was just…' Abercrombie threw the door wide, stepped back out of the way, scoofed another mouthful. 'If you can take off your shoes that would be *super* helpful.'

Dunlobbyin's kitchen was compact and cosy. Just big enough for a rectangular wooden table – that matched the units – and a big fake range cooker, whirring away to itself and filling the air with the crispy golden scent of baking biscuits.

Roberta and Harmsworth sat at the table, drinking tea and munching their way through a plate of homemade shortbread, while Frank Abercrombie rolled out a slab of cheese-scone dough. Pausing every now and then to guzzle more wine:

'So then I said, "Go away you thugs; I've called the police!" And they *didn't*, of course. And then… Erm…' Brow furrowing as he cut out perfect little discs and arranged them on a baking tray. 'I think it was something like, "Get back! You're not allowed to harass people!"'

Roberta checked to make sure Harmsworth was writing all of this down. Because being a consulting detective was no reason to lower standards.

The leftover dough got smooged into a lopsided nugget, and joined its mates. 'And *that* didn't work either, because these … far-right fascist types always think they're above the law, don't they?' Forking up an eggy wash. 'Then Billie *screamed* and I rushed to her side, but she was already falling – that knife…' He shuddered, the colour fading from his cheeks. 'Sorry. It's just…' *Big* gulp of wine. 'God, I thought she was going to *die*.'

Roberta helped herself to another shortbread petticoat tail. 'Did you see who did it, Frank?'

A blank look. Then he shook himself. 'Right. Who did it. I … he had a polo-shirt on. And a shaved head? Or maybe it wasn't shaved, maybe he was just going bald? Or *was* bald?' Another frown. 'It…' Abercrombie wiped a floury hand across his eyes. 'I'm sorry. I've lain awake, night after night, running through it in my mind, but … it just gets fuzzier.'

The oven pinged and clicked.

'I'm *sure* I saw his face. *Properly*, saw the thug who stabbed Billie. But I close my eyes and it could be anyone. Just … another angry white man, taking his impotent rage out on an innocent woman.'

Abercrombie huffed out a ragged breath, then sprinkled parmesan and cheddar over his sticky scones. Downed the last of his wine. Grabbed a fresh bottle from the fridge. Cricked off the top. Poured himself a hefty measure. Pausing with the glass halfway to his lips. 'Sorry. Certain you don't want one?'

The microwave clock glowed 11:52.

'Aye, what the hell.' Roberta pushed her mug away. 'Nearly lunchtime. And it's no' like I'm on duty anymore.'

'Good, good. Excellent.' He fetched another glass from the cupboard and filled it – which took nearly a quarter of the bottle – then handed the thing *carefully* to Roberta.

'Cheers.' She raised her almost overflowing glass and took a sip. Not bad. Nice and fruity, without being sweet. Unlike Tufty's cloying cider.

'Then everything happened so *fast*, and Billie was on the ground and I was trying to get the knife out of her stomach and you shouted at me, because – I know, I know – it was a *stupid* thing to do, and there was blood everywhere...' Abercrombie clunked the oven door open, slid his scones inside, clunked the oven door shut again. Set a timer. Each movement *constrained* and *controlled*, as if trying desperately hard not to lose it.

Scones in to bake, he turned his back on the table, ripped a sheet of kitchen paper from the dispenser and dabbed at his eyes. 'I'm sorry. I'm *useless*.'

Big swig of wine. Then another.

Yeah...

Might as well let him wallow for a bit, while Roberta sipped her rosé and polished off another shortbread.

Probably time to lead Frank away on a wee diversion, then circle back to the stabbing from a different angle. Sometimes that jogged people's memories.

'What you up to these days, Frank? Can't be easy now Emma Dornoch's Westminster bid is up the crapper.'

He leaned on the worktop, shoulders rounding. 'We've got a few years till the next general election. Time to work on campaign messaging and getting her face out there.' A laugh. 'Never easy launching a *new* candidate, but now we've got a bit of brand recognition and something to run *against*, right?

Graeme Anderson and his brownshirt bastards.' The tips of Abercrombie's ears flushed bright pink. 'If you'll pardon my language. Sorry. They just make me so … they make me so *angry*.'

Oh aye, bet he was a proper hamster-in-a-china-shop when roused.

'Plus, I'm still working on *Claire's* campaign.' He turned to face them again. 'You know: Lady Fordyce?' Toasting his employer, then drinking to that. 'And the *Scottish* elections will be here before you know it. Assuming we can keep the wheels on – touch wood.' Tapping two fingertips against the tabletop. Swigging down more wine.

'And are the wheels *likely* to come off?'

This time the laugh was *far* more bitter. 'Oh, you have no *idea* how much can—'

A *binglety-bong* noise rang out in the kitchen, accompanied by an angry-vibrator *buzzzzzzzz*.

Abercrombie grimaced, then plucked a mobile phone from the windowsill. 'Sorry.' His face curdled even further as he read and drank. 'Oh, for Christ's hairy…' A big dramatic sigh. 'It would be nice, if just *once*, people would make my life easier instead of more sodding difficult! I mean, what do I have to do here? Staple his bloody flies shut?'

The wine glass went on the counter as he jabbed out a text with his thumbs, mouth a thin pinched line. Then he stared at what he'd written. Closed his eyes. Sighed. Deleted it. And composed his message again. Slowly this time. Before sending it off with a *pop-ding*.

He shook his head. 'Don't get me wrong, I love Claire to bits, I really do, but if I have to shuffle *one* more young intern hottie off to someone else's campaign…'

Interesting.

Roberta sat back, contemplating him over the rim of her

wine glass. 'Now you come to mention it, I had noticed some of your staff were … no' exactly munters? Vivian Staybridge, Billie Nesbit?'

'Don't forget Sophia Mitchell.' A swig of rosé. 'Amelia Wilson, Megan Lockheart, Violet Erving… People have *no* idea how challenging it is to keep that kind of thing out the public eye.' Topping up his glass again. 'Press finds out a sitting MSP's husband is a randy octopus? How am I supposed to spin that?'

Abercrombie stared deep into his wine. Took a deep breath. Cleared his throat. 'I'm sorry, that's really unprofessional of me. Just…' Rubbing at his bloodshot eyes. 'Please. Ignore me. I'm… It's been a long six months.' He bit his bottom lip. Looked away. 'Ewan always *said* I was a drama queen. Sorry.' One last swig, and he clinked his glass down on the draining board. Took off his apron. 'Think I'm going to lie down.'

And off he lurched, legs rigid at the knee, torso lagging a bit behind his lower half. But then two or three bottles of rosé before noon will do that to some people.

Harmsworth opened his mouth, then shut it again, both eyebrows raised. 'Are we…?'

'Aye.' Roberta stood, downed the last of her wine, because why waste good booze? And there was nothing wrong with a wee pre-lunch buzz. Then limped over to the oven and switched the thing off. No point burning the poor sod's scones. Or his house down.

Pocketing a couple of shortbread petticoat tails, she leaned through the kitchen door, voice raised nice and loud: 'We'll see ourselves out!'

No reply.

So Roberta shrugged, and did just that.

3.13

Westhill was every bit as exciting on the trip back, followed by a thrilling stretch of dual carriageway and then a roundabout that was half lump-of-grass-with-some-half-arsed-trees-on-it and half support-pillar-for-the-bypass. Would the delight *never* end?

Harmsworth's Volvo puttered around it, heading for the Aberdeen Western Peripheral Route.

Unlike Tufty, he wasn't keen on the radio. Presumably because it got in the way of his dreary monologues about complete and utter boring bollocking shite.

'…so Barrett said, "No, I don't think so." But, of course he was wrong, because—'

'Let's see your notebook.'

Harmsworth kept his eyes on the road, mirror-signal-manoeuvring before accelerating up the hill. Already indicating to join the flow of traffic at the top. 'Jacket pocket,' jerking his chin at the rear-view mirror, 'in the back.'

Pfff…

She squirmed around in her seat, reaching for it, hand flapping about until her fingers finally latched onto that retro leather.

By the time she'd dragged it through to the front, he'd merged with the inside lane, doing a sedate sixty while lorries and caravans thundered past – the illegal speeding bastards.

She rifled through the pockets, found the notebook, then

tossed the jacket over her shoulder and into the rear footwell.

It wasn't an official *police* notebook, because for all his multitude of faults, Harmsworth wasn't a complete idiot. And leaving evidence of sneaky unauthorised investigations got you hauled up by the Rubber Heelers.

Instead, it was a cheap ring-bound job, that seemed to mostly consist of shopping-and-to-do lists. She flipped through them to the last entry: their interview with Frank Abercrombie.

Harmsworth risked a peek. 'What you after?'

'Names of the pretty ladies old Frankie-boy had to find new homes for, after Sir Slick-Dick had his sticky way with them.'

'Now, he never said there was any hint of *impropriety*.'

'Course he bloody did. You don't shuffle sexy bits of stuff off your campaign team unless your boss's husband's shagging them.'

'Or *maybe* his wife's the jealous type? Doesn't like competition hanging round her old man.' Glancing across the car. 'You know what older women are…' His mouth clicked shut and he faced front again. 'Never mind.'

Sexist satchel-faced prick.

Roberta treated him to a testicle-withering glower for a good count of ten, then went back to the notebook.

The names were on the final page.

She dug out her phone, texting one-handed:

> Tufty – need you to run another deep dive.
>
> Sophia Mitchell, Amelia Wilson, Megan Lockheart, & Violet Erving.
>
> All worked on Claire Fordyce / Emma Dornoch's campaign.
>
> Quick as you like.

SEND.

Harmsworth wriggled. 'Yes, but *why* do you want to know their names?' Frowning at her in the mirror. 'Is something going on?'

'Something's *always* going on, Owen, the key is figuring out what.' Tapping her forehead. 'An enquiring mind is a police officer's deadliest weapon. Well, except for an extendible baton. Taser. PAVA spray. And a good old-fashioned kick in the balls.'

Which seemed to shut Harmsworth up for a bit.

Thank God.

Outside, a bunch of hills and trees slouched by, drooping beneath the rain's onslaught.

An eighteen-wheeler overtook – howling past in the outside lane, kicking up a thick fog of filthy road-spray.

A lone horse sagged in a field.

And on they drove…

Ding-buzz.

That was quick – Tufty must've got up for a piddle or something and saw her text. Because he wasn't a bad wee spud, really.

Only it wasn't Tufty, with a nice wodge of background info on Sir Norman's peccadillos, it was Lund:

> Update on YKW:
>
> DNA is AOK.
>
> No match in DB.

What?

Roberta poked out a reply:

> What the hell does any of that mean?

SEND.

Ding-buzz.

LUND:

> I was trying to be subtle!
>
> They got a good DNA sample from the tooth pulp cavity but it doesn't match anything in the database.

Oh for God's sake:

> THEN WHY NOT JUST SAY THAT IN THE FIRST PLACE?

Whole team had gone to buggery without her supervising the bejesus out of—

Ding-buzz.

LUND:

> Well excuse me for doing you a favour!

Roberta jammed the phone back in her pocket, folded her arms, and seethed all the way to Portlethen.

The rain had declared a ceasefire by the time they'd reached Thistle Crescent, but going by the dark blue-grey clouds, it wouldn't be long before it violated that.

The little road wasn't far from McIntosh Donald, and even though the abattoir was hidden behind a high leylandii hedge a couple of streets over, it was hard not to imagine that the damp air had a sort of delicious *beefy* tint to it.

The houses here were all grey, semidetached, two-storey, flat-fronted lumps, with lichened pantiles. Each pair was made up of one small house bolted onto another twice its size. Which must've galled the weeny-house people, being lorded over by their larger next-door neighbours.

The trees were quite nice, though.

Number six was much smaller than its conjoined twin, but the garden was tidy, with an enthusiastic pampas grass growing in the middle of the lawn – and everyone knew what *that* meant – while a couple of Beefeater gnomes stood guard.

A sign dominated one upstairs window: 'UK New Horizons ~ For A Better Britain!' Adding a touch of gammon to the general meatiness.

Harmsworth held up the printout, reading aloud. 'Clive MacGregor, forty-eight. Lost his licence for speeding in 2013, got it back, lost it again in 2019. Other than that, his nose is clean.'

'Let's give him a rattle, then.' Roberta limped through the garden gate, past the Swinger's Bat-Signal, and on to the front door.

Harmsworth rang the bell. 'Think this MacGregor will talk to us? Because his interview is one long "no comment".'

'Aye, but that was *Beattie*, making an arse of things after I got blown-up.' She poked her own chest with a thumb. 'See how a *real* detective handles this knuckle-dragging bacony tosser. He'll be Play-Doh in my hands.'

A ginger tabby wandered across the neatly manicured lawn.

A big dog barked somewhere behind the house.

A strange eggy smell tainted the beefy air – but that was probably Harmsworth.

Then, just as Sir Fartsalot was reaching for the bell again, the door opened and there was Clive MacGregor, in all his unsmoked-gammony glory.

He'd swapped his protester's chinos-and-polo-shirt for a Union Flag hoodie, a pair of knee-length shorts, and flip-flops. Still bald and ugly, though. He looked them up and down, a sneer curling his lip. 'You Jehovah's Witnesses? Cos we're Methodist and don't hold with that shite.'

Roberta smiled. 'Surprised you don't recognise me, Clive. I arrested you when that wee girl got stabbed.'

He pulled his double chin in, tripling it. 'I'm not speaking to any cops without my lawyer present!'

'Then it's your lucky day! Cos I retired. And I need to talk to you about who did the stabbing.'

The chin went quadruple. 'Wait, you're *not* a cop?'

She spread her hands. 'Sadly no'.'

'Then I don't have to talk to you anyway. Feel free to fuck off. And take Disco Stu with you.' Then Clive MacGregor slammed the door in their faces.

Harmsworth shrugged. 'Maybe we'll have more luck next time?'

Yeah.

Bound to.

47 Caiesdykes Court, Kincorth (12:56)

It was a short row of terraced housing. Bland, two-up-two-down blocky slabs of beige harling with paved-over lawns where dilapidated cars were parked.

Stan Hendrickson glowered down at them from his top step – a stodgy middle-aged man, balding from all sides, in a 'SEND THEM BACK!' T-shirt. 'Fuck off.' He stepped inside and slammed the door.

That would be a no, then.

32 Mansefield Avenue, Torry (13:18)

The whole street looked like the same kid's drawing of a house, photocopied over and over and over again. Identical buildings lined the next street over. And the one after that. And the one after that. Like some creepy *Twilight Zone* episode.

Liam Ramsey had cunningly decided to hide his male-pattern baldness by shaving his head, but a seven o'clock shadow just drew attention to the problem. A big lad, with a barrel chest and piggy eyes. Tattoos.

He sniffed. 'Aye: no comment.'

Roberta tried a disarming smile. 'You don't have to say, "no comment", this is just you and me having a—'

And he slammed the door.

14 Kettlehills Place, Northfield (13:48)

Wind snarled up the street, bringing a hissing *crackle* of rain with it that sparked off Harmsworth's ridiculous jacket. Every gust yanking at Roberta's umbrella – threatening to Mary Poppins her at any moment. The houses here formed a narrow, sloped terrace of four homes, where each building was a *slightly* more depressing shade of sputum than the one next to it.

Toby 'Jug' Forbes must've been planning on doing a fascism later, because he was wearing his polo-shirt-and-chinos outfit. Bet if you looked-up 'Angry Gammon Bastard' on Wikipedia, it'd be his photo they used to illustrate it.

He bared his teeth, stuck two fingers up at Steel, then slammed the door. Leaving them standing there, like pricks, in the rain.

Roberta puffed out her cheeks. 'You know, I'm starting to take this personally.'

Harmsworth checked his list. 'One more to go.' His stomach gurgled like an angry frog. 'Then, I believe Tufty said something about you taking him for a *fish supper*...?'

Greedy sod.

18 Perwinnes Lane, Bridge of Don (14:15)

Mansefield Avenue might've been *Twilight Zone* creepy, but it had nothing on Perwinnes Lane. It was as if the whole street had been made of Monopoly houses, so new that the lawns hadn't bedded in yet. Brown lines between the strips of turf.

Jack MacCowan was only twenty-seven, so Christ knew how he could afford a brand-new home on the edge of town.

Even a sinister, plastic one like this. He scowled out at them, in his blue jeans and brown shirt. With a jutting jaw and a lazy eye.

Roberta tried again: 'Come on, Jack, we just want to—'

And he slammed the door, making it five for five.

Harmsworth raised both eyebrows. 'So … chips?'

She rolled her eyes and limped back to the Turdmobile. 'Chips.'

Traffic crawled along King Street, with Harmsworth's jobbie Volvo stuck right in the middle of it.

Roberta had her window down, letting the grumble of cars and buses wash in from the rainy afternoon as she puffed out clouds of rhubarb-and-custard vape.

The Bobbin drifted slowly by, where a bunch of students had escaped their afternoon studies to drink themselves into a sloppy coma and each other's beds. One group were all in knitted pink T-shirts, going baggy in the rain, belting out a medley of showtunes from *Sawney Bean*, in a manner that implied they were either rugby players or a *really* crap musical society:

'Some people say a stranger is a friend you've never met,
Well Sawney says a stranger's just a meal you 'aven't et!'

And on the Volvo crawled.

A set of temporary traffic lights loomed through the rain ahead, marking off a chunk of road outside the Esso petrol station. Where a yellow council digger was gleefully mangling its way through the tarmac and into the substrate beneath.

Which explained the hold-up.

Roberta took another long sook on her vape. Blowing it out as the knitted students got to the chorus:

'Sawney Bean, the cannibal king,
All of his family cause a calamity,
Sawney Bean, from the gallows he'll swing,
All of his family feast on humanity,
All of his family wracked with insanity,
All of them cannibals, breeding like animals!'

The lights changed, and the traffic sped up a little, leaving the 'singers' behind. But it all ground to a halt again as, two cars in front, a blue hatchback stopped to let someone out of the petrol station.

And that someone was driving a rattletrap Daihatsu Fourtrak in a slightly less dysentery-shade of brown than Harmsworth's Volvo…

Hard to be one hundred percent sure – because she'd deleted all the photos of Jeremy Yarrow from her phone, so Young and Pine wouldn't see them – but it definitely *looked* like his manky old truck, right down to the rear bumper held on with hairy string.

The Fourtrak growled off down King Street, dragging a smog of diesel fumes behind it, and the traffic got moving again.

Both cars ahead of them made it through the contraflow, but soon as it was Harmsworth's Volvo's turn, the lights changed to amber.

He coasted to a halt and reached for the handbrake.

'What are you *doing*?' Roberta thumped him. 'Go! Go! Follow that crapmobile!'

Harmsworth sort of vibrated in place for a moment, eyes wide, going, 'Em, em, em, em…' hands clutching and unclutching, then self-preservation kicked in and he did what he was told, juddering the car forward as the lights turned red. Kangarooing along in warm pursuit. 'Why are we following… Who… *What* are we following?'

She pointed at the Fourtrak. '*That* one, sharny boxy-wee-truck thing with all the rust.'

'But *why*?'

'Because police officers are naturally nosy animals. And mine is twitching.'

He pulled a face, but followed the manky Daihatsu anyway – to the next junction, where it turned left onto Linksfield Road.

Old granite tenements faced off against insipid blocks of flats, across a minefield of speed humps.

The Volvo lump-and-bumped over them.

'Hang on…' Harmsworth frowned at her. 'Is this you trying to get out of providing lunch?'

'Don't be such a greedy whinge.'

Harmsworth harrumphed, still following the Fourtrak's diesel wake. '*Typical.* Tufty gets fish-and-chips, and what does poor Owen get? Nothing.'

Down at the end of the road, past more beige flats and dull semis, a swathe of green appeared: Kings Links Golf Course. And the closer they got, the worse the wind and rain became.

He scrunched his shoulders together. 'But then why would *Owen* deserve anything? It's not as if *he's* giving up his free time to ferry people around, who haven't even *offered* him *petrol money*. Why would *he* get chips?'

The Fourtrak took a right at the end of the road, skirting the Links.

Still moaning away, Harmsworth gave chase.

Hard to believe, but a handful of daft bastards were out

playing golf in the snarling rain. Without Aberdeen's streets acting as a windbreak, the storm *raged*. Now, the only things between them and the North Sea were the eighteen-hole course, a steep embankment with a road on top, and the beach.

Harmsworth stuck his nose in the air. 'Oh, yes, poor Owen can just—'

'For God's sake: I'll buy you chips! I *said* I'd buy you chips, didn't I?'

They trailed the Fourtrak past the redbrick hulk of Pittodrie Stadium, then left, down a narrow road, towards the embankment.

'I'm just making sure you're not backing out of the deal, because—'

'When have I ever welched on a deal?'

'You bilk people all the time!'

'I do *not*!'

'Do so. Remember Sergeant Willis?'

Ah…

She squirmed in her seat. 'That's *different.* That was "shrewd negotiation to obtain a competitive advantage".'

'You sold him a case of Bulgarian "whisky" that tasted like boiled frog rectums!'

'No' *my* fault he didn't read the small print.'

The road took a sharp left, heading up this side of the embankment.

'You *bilked* him.'

'Gave him an important life lesson, more like! Never drink anything that dissolves varnish on contact. Or is made from smoked amphibians.'

At the top of the hill, the Fourtrak turned right, onto the Esplanade.

Harmsworth hung back a little, before pulling his Volvo up the final stretch and into the storm's teeth. It bit down on the poop-brown estate car, shaking it from side to side as rain fizzed against the bodywork like fireworks. The sky: murderous black.

An extra-wide pavement ran along the seaward side of the road, with benches spaced out along its length so you could rest your bum while catching pneumonia – overlooking Aberdeen Beach and a wrathful North Sea.

Waves crashed and roared against the colourless sand.

A converted Transit van was parked about a hundred yards down the road. They'd painted it fluorescent orange, with black tiger stripes, and bolted an illuminated sign to the roof proclaiming 'RAJ AGAINST THE MACHINE' between two Labrador-sized fibreglass elephants.

Presumably, on a less stormy day, its serving hatch would've been on the seaward side, so punters could line up safely along the promenade. Today it was the other way around, parked nose towards town, shielding the hatch from the wind and rain. But it wasn't as if the Esplanade had a lot of traffic at twenty to three on a foul Monday afternoon, so they were probably safe enough.

The Fourtrak drove past, then pulled in just in front of it.

Roberta pointed. 'Park this side.' Which would keep the food van between them and their rusty quarry.

Harmsworth did as instructed, sitting there with the engine running, blowers howling in counterpoint to the stormy afternoon. Frowning at the van's back doors. 'But—'

'No fish supper for *you* the day, Owen. You've just been upgraded to a *curry*!'

3.14

A veritable feast of Indo-Scottish fusion stretched along the Volvo's dashboard in a collection of takeaway containers: macaroni-cheese pakora, stovies samosas, mince-and-tattie jalfrezi, and a haggis vindaloo, served with plain rice and two peshwari rowies. Filling the car with delicious aromas and the tempting nip of spicy delight.

Harmsworth chewed, waving the other half of his samosa at the misting-up windscreen. 'What now?'

Good question.

Roberta munched on a pakora – crispy and cheesy with more than a hint of fiery green chilli. 'That's all the protesters done. Well, except for the ringleader: Arch Twat Lewis Kelman.' Crunch, munch, crunch. 'Suppose he's next.'

'I meant with the "follow that truck".'

The Fourtrak hadn't moved from its spot behind the tiger-striped Transit. But so far: no sign of Jeremy Yarrow getting out to order any food. Or Gonorrhoea Bob. Or anyone else, come to that. Assuming it was even Jeremy's car. Which it might not be.

Pfff…

'Don't know.' She helped herself to a samosa. 'Like I said: just being nosy.'

And at least they'd got a tasty lunch out of it.

She chewed, looking out of the window, across the wide

promenade and down the steep slope of grass to the walkway below. Then a big angled swathe of concrete blocks, and finally the beach – being pummelled by angry waves.

So, Jeremy probably wasn't here for a swim.

Not unless he was planning on doing a Reginald Perrin...

And with Noel Sherman reduced to a train-smeared paste, Jeremy's debt would be null-and-void, so why bother faking your own death?

Maybe he was just getting a nice romantic lunch for himself and Gonorrhoea Bob?

Harmsworth popped a whole pakora in his gob, masticating the words. 'Think he'll tell us to go stick it up our crudge-holes?'

Eh?

'What, Jeremy Yarrow?'

'*No*: Lewis Kelman.' Throwing in a deep sigh, as if *she* was the idiot.

Roberta gave him a dose of the evil eye, till he pulled his knees together and his cheeks pinked.

'Sorry.'

'Should think so too.' Munch, crunch, munch. 'And yeah: probably. Kelman's going to be about as much help as barbed-wire loo roll.' She had a wee sag in her seat. 'Ever wonder why we bother, Owen?'

'*Normally*, because it's our job.' Another pakora disappeared, as if he was trying to scoff the lot before she noticed. 'And yes, some of us do it better than others, but in the end, if we weren't getting paid, do you think we'd put up with *half* the crudge we do?' Then a samosa. Chewing away with a frown. 'Let's be honest: no *sane* person would police Aberdeen for free.' Giving her a food-flecked smile. 'Except for you of course, cos you're not weird at all.'

'Cheeky bugger.' Polishing off the last pakora, before Greedy

Guts struck again. 'I do it because I get an *obscene* amount of pleasure from proving twunts like *Chief Superintendent Pine* wrong. And in this life you need to—'

Deep in Roberta's pocket, 'Take Your Mama' discoed into life.

She sooked her fingers clean, wiping them on a napkin, before checking her phone: 'SKETCHY DAVEY'.

Hmmph…

Probably calling to apologise for being a traitorous prick back at Charlotte MacNeal's house – about sodding time too.

Roberta hit the green button. 'Well, well, well: look who comes grovelling back. I suppose you saw my *massive* triumph at Noel—'

'Thank you.' Wouldn't have thought anyone could get so much clipped, trembly anger into those two words, but Davey managed. *'Thank you very* fucking *much!'*

'Oh don't whinge. You could've been there when I took his empire down, but you—'

'His bloody wife *won't pay my bill now, because every penny they've got is subject to a Proceeds of Crime order!'*

And that was Roberta's fault, how?

'Well, she can hardly—'

'Doesn't matter what she gets awarded in the divorce, bloody Crown's confiscating it all! She'll probably lose the house!'

Now wait a minute.

Roberta sat up, teeth bared, more than happy to bite back. 'Then she shouldn't've married a sodding drug—'

'AND I GET SCREWED!' Loud enough to make her wrench the phone from her ear and hold it at arm's length till Davey finished bellowing.

Soon as he had, she was back in there like a *knife*. 'Oh aye: I take Aberdeen's biggest drug-dealing-kingpin *scumbag* off the streets, and you're having a moan because you won't—'

'YOU JUST DESTROY EVERYTHING, DON'T YOU? YOU JUST BLOODY—'

Sod this.

She hung up.

Screw him.

Screw Wee Davey Wanky McLeod.

With a big fucking stick.

She brought up her contacts and renamed his from 'SKETCHY DAVEY' to 'SHITEHEAD!' And yes, she *could* just delete it, but then he'd go back to being an 'UNKNOWN NUMBER' – at least *this* way she'd know when the ungrateful bastard called. Which would suffice till she figured out how to block him. Or got Tufty to do it. Or Jasmine would know…

While she'd been busy with Shitehead, Harmsworth had wrestled his way into the haggis vindaloo, and was now stuffing his face with spicy vinegared offal.

Speaking with his mouth full. 'Your mate sounded happy.'

'Prick that he is.' She put her phone away. 'Tell you, Owen: some bastards don't know which side they're buttered.'

Which left the jalfrezi.

Roberta dug a spork into it, scooping out a bite of piquant mince-and-tattie delight. Even though buggering *Davey* had soured it a bit.

She chewed away, scowling as the wind raged, rain strafed, and waves crashed upon the shore.

A battered red hatchback emerged from the storm, wobbling with every gust as it parked between the Volvo and the tiger-striped Transit. Poor thing was all dents and scrapes, with one wing a completely different shade to the rest of it.

The driver's door cracked open and out climbed a woman in her late thirties who had *not* dressed for the weather. Instead of thick trousers and a padded waterproof, she sported a short skirt, knobbly knees, a crop-top, and blouson jacket. Hunching her way to the serving hatch on too-high heels, bleach-blonde hair streaming out sideways – turning mousy in the downpour.

Silly sod.

Harmsworth shovelled in more vindaloo. 'Know what I think?'

Roberta just sat there in sulky silence. Chewing.

'No.' He sniffed. 'No, Owen, please share with me the *unfettered* genius of your wisdom and insight.' Spearing a chunk of curried neep and holding it aloft. '*I* think they're all in on it: the UK New Horizons guys. Like a joint-enterprise, everyone's-a-killer deal.'

She grimaced. 'Been there, done that.'

'*That's* why they're all saying nothing. Keeping schtum for the good of the team.'

Sheltering beneath the Transit's open hatch, Little Miss Underdressed ordered her food, then huddled there, stomping her high heels on the damp tarmac. Lighting a cigarette with trembling fingers.

Not surprised she was shivering, given how much corpse-pale flesh she had on show. Must be *freezing*.

Harmsworth chewed his neep. 'Would explain why none of the interns can ID the culprit. How do they single out *one* individual when they're *all* responsible.' A frown. 'And I'm aware that's an orphaned pronoun, but you know what I mean.'

God, he didn't half talk some bollocks.

He gave her a condescending smile. 'It's when a pronoun – like "he" or "she" or "they" – is ambiguous because it's not entirely clear who's being referred to.'

'You want to *wear* that sodding curry, you patronising snudge?'

A harrumph. Sporking up some more vindaloo. 'That's what *I* think, anyway.'

Don't know what the woman ordered, but it was already being handed over in a blue plastic bag that bulged with take-away containers. She didn't sod off out of the rain, though. She stood there, shuffling her feet, one hand clutching her sallow throat. Face all contorted, as if she was wheedling and whining about something.

Not enough poppadoms?

Harmsworth shrugged. 'I suppose it's immaterial, really. Not as if we can prove anything if they all close ranks.'

Whatever the moaning was about, it must've worked, because another blue plastic bag appeared. Not full of rect-angular shapes like the first, but something lopsided and lumpy. Maybe a couple portions of keema rowies? The woman grabbed it, and a sickly grin spread across her pale face. Then she hurried back to the pock-marked hatchback. Clambering inside.

Could only see the back of her head and shoulders from here, but it looked as if she dumped one of her bags in the passenger footwell, then hugged the other. Reaching inside to pull out a teddy bear.

Oh for Jesus's hairy...

Roberta screwed her eyes shut.

Wait a minute.

She snapped them open again. Reached across the car and thumped Harmsworth. 'Seat back.'

He stared at her. 'Eh?'

'Put your sodding seat back!' Roberta reclined hers as far as it would go, then whipped out her phone – fumbling through the camera settings to put it in video mode. Holding the thing up like a periscope, peeking over the dashboard and through the rain-flecked windscreen.

Filming as the woman turned her new teddy bear face down, bum in the air.

Harmsworth ratchetted his seat back. 'Why are we lying down?' A slight hint of panic in his voice. 'Is this some sort of … *sexual* thing?'

'Shhhhhhhhhhhhhhhh…!' Zooming the phone in.

The woman looked around, furtive, sneaky. Then a flick-knife clacked open in her other hand. She stabbed the bear in the head, sawing her way down its spine, splitting the seam. Dug her fingers into the kapok. And pulled out a handful of little plastic baggies.

She dropped the bear and cradled her find instead, rocking back and forth, spare hand covering her mouth as her shoulders shook.

Then the hatchback's running lights clicked on, a whoomph of exhaust stuttered out into the downpour, and away she drove – while Roberta got a full-screen shot of her number plate.

'You wee dancer.'

'OK…' Harmsworth frowned at Roberta from his supine position. 'You going to tell me what we're doing?'

'Gathering evidence. Like a sodding pro.' Her finger reached for the red button to stop recording, but the zoomed-in picture framed a perfect view of the Fourtrak's driver's door popping open. And out climbed Jeremy Yarrow.

He hunched against the wind – one hand up to shield his eyes from the clamouring rain as he looked up and down the Esplanade.

But she and Harmsworth were reclined out of view, so, from his perspective, the place must've looked deserted.

Clearly satisfied that no one was watching, Jeremy hurried around to the Fourtrak's boot and hauled the door open, struggling to hold on as the wind yanked at it like a rusty sail. He pulled out a large cardboard box. And forced the rear door shut again, before ducking his head to one side and hurrying over to the Transit's serving hatch. Out of the rain. Giving himself a shake, like a soggy whippet.

Roberta followed him with her phone.

He didn't order anything – didn't even speak – just hefted his box onto the counter. Waited for it to be pulled inside. Then accepted a wad of notes, counting them before stuffing the whole lot in his pocket. Gave his benefactor a nod. Then scurried back to his truck.

The Fourtrak's headlights snapped on, then flickered for a bit. A bang of blue-grey smoke erupted from the exhaust and was shredded by the squall. Then the manky wee truck juddered its way through a U-turn, heading back the way it came, straight past Roberta and Harmsworth.

Yarrow didn't even *glance* at their 'empty' Volvo.

She waited for him to take the turning down the embankment before she stopped recording. A long, disappointed sigh seeped out. 'Bastard...'

Even lying down, Harmsworth managed to spork-in the vindaloo. 'I *still* don't know what we're—'

'Never do anyone a favour, Owen.' Scrolling through her contacts to Lund's number. 'It'll only come back and sink its teeth in your arse.'

When Lund answered, it was hushed and whispery. *'I already* gave *you the DNA results! Go away; leave me alone. I'm in enough trouble as it is.'*

'Get your backside down the Beach Esplanade, near the Accommodation Road junction: pronto. You've got a drug bust to take credit for.'

Harmsworth folded his arms, yet again, and huffed out another sulky *harrumph.*

The storm shoved and jostled his poop-brown Volvo, rain pinging like ball bearings against the bodywork. Only ten past three, and it was already dark enough to make streetlights bloom across the city, glittering bravely in defiance of the North Sea's churning, dark, ominous mass.

Since Yarrow sodded off, Raj Against The Machine hadn't had a single customer for its curried delights.

Roberta shook her head. 'Suppose it was obvious, really. No bugger's setting up shop out here, in the middle of a sodding gale. How much passing trade are you going to get?'

Speak of the wingwang – a pair of headlights appeared in the rear-view mirror, then a manky Vauxhall drove past. Pulling in, between Harmsworth's Volvo and the tiger-striped Transit.

A bundled-up figure emerged from the driver's seat, bending into the wind, one hand holding the hood down on their waterproof as they lurched towards the serving hatch. Leaving their passenger behind in the warm and dry.

Harmsworth unfolded his arms, but only so he could fold them again with another petulant grunt. Just in case she'd missed it the first two dozen times.

A second manky Vauxhall appeared from the other direction, parking on the far side. This time the driver *and* the passenger made for the hatch. Queueing up for tasty treats.

While the Currymeister was busy taking orders, the passenger from the first car slipped out into the storm – crouch-running along the promenade to the Transit's driver's door. Hunkering down to fiddle with it.

Captain Grouchy gave a big, *martyred* sigh.

Roberta rolled her eyes. 'Do you have to?'

'I just don't see why you're handing the credit to *Lund*. I was right here! *I* could take the credit if you don't want it. As recompense for all the petrol money I'm not getting!'

Children.

'Owen, you're not thinking this through. Say I give you the glory—'

'Chance would be a fine thing.'

'Then you've got to explain to the Boss and *all* her little minions why you were conducting an *unauthorised* covert surveillance operation, on a food truck, without any official sanction or oversight.'

Another set of headlights appeared in the rear-view as a third Vauxhall pulled out of the junction and came their way.

'Well, *clearly* I had—'

'What: a tip off? You've got an unapproved Chis feeding you info? And instead of passing it on to a superior officer, you decided to play Sam Spade?'

His cheeks darkened in the gloom. 'Well … maybe—'

'*All* Covert Human Intelligence Sources must be authorised and managed by the Intel team. Any idea how much *trouble* you'd be in?'

'It… I could … have had a hunch?'

'Aye, like bloody Igor.'

The third Vauxhall didn't pull in to the kerb, instead it made to drive past, then slammed on its brakes as it drew level with the food van.

The driver and passenger jumped out, wearing thick gloves, shin-knee-and-elbow pads over their fighting suits. Hauling on MOE crash helmets and flicking out extendable batons as they charged.

The passenger from Vauxhall Number One wrenched open the Transit's door and yanked the keys from the ignition.

Two of the queueing customers produced their warrant cards:

'YOU: DROP THE KNIFE!'

'ON THE DECK, NOW! NOW!'

While the remaining customer headed for the back door.

All nice and orderly and—

Crap.

The Transit's rear door burst open, catching Customer Number Three full in the face.

He hit the ground as a young-ish woman leapt out into the storm. Late twenties, wearing a white chef's jacket and red joggy-bottoms. Black trainers. Blue nitrile gloves. Blue hairnet on over curly brown hair. Big glasses, long nose, black eye.

She might've been a size eighteen, but she couldn't half run. Sprinting along the pavement. Right towards Harmsworth's Volvo.

'Time to show these *amateurs* how it's done.' He opened the door and struggled out, nipping around the bonnet to block her way – knees bent, arms out. Goalkeeper style.

Her eyes widened behind the glasses. 'Shite!' And she clattered straight into him.

They crumpled to the ground, tumbling over one another, off the tarmac promenade and onto the grass. Over the edge … and down the steep slope towards the beach. Plummeting in a jumbled octopus of flailing limbs and swearing.

Then disappeared from view.

Roberta slapped a hand over her face. 'In the name of Stalin's hairy bumhole…' And climbed out into the storm.

3.15

The howling wind yanked and tugged at Roberta's shoulders as she limped towards the spot where Harmsworth and Chef Chunky had disappeared.

'STOP! POLICE!' The two idiots in the crash helmets and MOE gear hammered past, waving their truncheons. Wheeching over the embankment's edge.

Roberta hobbled off the promenade and onto the grass. Peering after them, squinting into the rain.

Yeah…

Good job they *were* wearing crash helmets, because it looked as if the steep slope had caught them by surprise, and now the MOE Twins were sprawled across the walkway below in a twisted heap.

Between them and the beach lay a metal handrail, the breakwater – like cubes from a packet of concrete jelly – then the anaemic sands of Aberdeen beach. Beaten by the relentless waves.

The scarpering chef was legging it along the high-tide mark, while Harmsworth hurple-jogged after her – falling behind.

Roberta waved her walking stick at the tumbled officers and offered some words of encouragement and support: 'GET AFTER HER, YOU USELESS JOBBIES!'

No idea if they heard that over the wind, but they struggled to their feet anyway, and chased after the escaping cook.

Lund appeared at Roberta's shoulder – all bundled up to play the part of Customer Number One. Voice raised in competition with the storm. 'What the hell happened?'

And Roberta raised her stick to indicate the scene below.

The Chuckle Brothers were sprinting down the walkway, pausing only to vault the handrail – mountain-goating across the lumpy breakwater, and out onto the beach. Where the going was much softer, cutting their speed.

But at least Harmsworth had backup now.

Just as well, cos the lazy sod was getting slower and slower and slower…

A voice, just audible through the tempest: 'COME BACK HERE!' as the Crash Helmets closed the gap.

The pair of them were *almost* in place to cut the cantering caterer off, when she did an abrupt about-face – probably thought her chances were better with Harmsworth. Who had staggered to a halt, like the useless lump he was.

Crash Helmet Number One tried a sudden course correction of his own, and ended up skiteing flat on his back in the wet sand. Where an incoming wave promptly crashed right over him. Leaving him flailing and spluttering.

Lund covered her face. 'Oh … for buggering … *wank*!'

Crash Helmet Number Two *nearly* ended up the same way, but righted himself at the last moment. Arms and legs pumping as he hammered after the chef.

Roberta hooked her walking stick over one arm and made a loudhailer with her hands. 'DON'T JUST STAND THERE, YOU HOPELESS TOSSER: GET HER!'

The idiot Harmsworth did his overweight-goalie routine again. Blocking the cook's way. Because that had worked *so* well last time.

Seeing him, she swerved back the way she'd just come. Only Crash Helmet Number Two was *much* closer this time.

The chef jinked into an even tighter U-turn, only to run slam-bang right into Harmsworth's open arms.

Crash, and they both hit the sand. Legs waving in the air, grappling with each other. Wrestling for supremacy.

Harmsworth's cry flittered up from the beach, tattered by the wind: 'OW! NO BITING! NO BITING!'

Then Crash Helmet Number Two dived on top of them – joining the fray.

Down at the water's edge, Number One struggled to his squelchy feet and stood there, arms out like a droopy scarecrow, water pouring off him as waves crashed around his ankles.

'Aye…' Roberta sniffed. 'Police Scotland's really gone downhill since I retired.'

Lund pulled her shoulders up. 'Oh, come on. It wasn't *that* bad.'

Even with Harmsworth and Crash Helmet Number Two pinning her to the sand, somehow the chef managed to break free. Springing upright with a set of handcuffs dangling from one wrist.

She leapt away, making another bid for freedom, but Harmsworth's arm snapped out and grabbed her ankle.

So down she went again.

And the mini-scrum rolled over her.

Struggle. Struggle. Struggle. Struggle.

'OW! OW! STOP IT! I SAID, "NO BITING!"'

Roberta looked at Lund. Then sighed and shook her head. 'Really?'

'Yeah…' A cough, a blush, and a shuffle. 'Maybe not our *finest* hour.'

Not by a long bloody way.

Roberta heaved the Volvo's passenger door open and thumped down into her seat, bringing two paper bags of tasty treats with her. Letting the howling wind slam the door.

They'd moved about a mile down the beach – opposite the cluster of shops, restaurants, and cafes, a nightclub, cinema, and funfair. Because who didn't love a thing of candyfloss to go with their frostbite?

Harmsworth had the engine running, blowers cranked up full, but the windows remained opaque and misty. And the air was ripe with the unmistakable funky fug of wet constable.

Probably best not to mention that, though, because he had enough of a gob on as it was: being soaked through and crusted in sand. Sitting there with his arms crossed and his forehead creased up like dreels of tatties. Time for Roberta to work her motivational magic.

Removing a wax-paper mug from one of her bags, Roberta handed it across the car. 'Fly cup and a fancy piece from the Inversnecky. Never say I don't spoil you.' Dipping in again, she produced a rectangle of millionaire's shortbread, thick with chocolate and sticky caramel. She popped it on the dashboard. 'You're no' *still* sulking, are you?'

'I want to go home.' Raising his arms then dropping them again. With a squelch. 'I'm *cold*. I'm *wet*. I've got sand in my … areas. And bite-marks on everything else!'

'That's your own fault for being so tasty.' She emptied out her other bag: tea and a slab of lemon drizzle. Slurping the former, and getting crumbs all down herself as she munched on the latter. 'Look on the bright side – last time I went on a dunt, someone got smeared along a mile of railway track.' Good cake. Nice and sharp. 'You got off with a bit of light nibbling.'

He indulged in some performative sighing, then shrugged one shoulder and tried his fancy piece. 'Still want to go home.'

'Come on, Owen, you're my *Go-To-Guy*, remember?' Giving

him a nudge. 'We've only got a couple more people to interrogate, then you can go hoover Aberdeen beach out your Y-fronts.'

That got her a scowl.

'And look what we *achieved*! Drug dealer off the streets, lovely curry for lunch, and Lund says she'll give you cover for being there *and* a bit of the credit too.'

Probably.

Or she would once Roberta had a go at her.

Another nudge. 'We made a good team, didn't we? Just like old times.'

He munched, then huffed out a big long biscuity breath. A smug expression spread across his saggy-satchel face. 'I suppose I *am* the lynchpin.'

Talk about *gullible*…

Grey terraced buildings turned this bit of George Street into a granite canyon. Some were two-storeys tall with attic conversions, others: three. All with dormers poking out of their slate roofs. The ground floor of nearly every building was given over to shops. Big shops, small shops, colourful shops, dull shops, takeaways and betting shops, off-licences and nail salons, tanning parlours and solicitors'…

'MOCHIE HOUSE' was a three-floor job: nine flats sitting above a Turkish takeaway, a pawn shop, and a tattoo studio. A scuffed door was wedged in at the far end, with an intercom that had a button for every upstairs flat, but no numbers, and all the nameplates were faded and illegible. Which meant Harmsworth was spoiled for choice. Ringing them one after the other, then sighing every time nobody answered. Which was really starting to grate, because nobody ever bloody did.

Roberta frowned up at the place, with its weedy guttering

and flaking window frames. 'This no' seem a bit ... down-market for Graeme Anderson's right-hand man?'

Harmsworth poked his way through the buttons again, setting the intercom gurgling. Hauling his damp trousers out of his undercarriage. 'Maybe this is some sort of lying-low, man-of-the-people thing?'

'Even that lazy-eyed wee snodge in Bridge of Don had a house. And he's barely out of nappies.'

'True.' Another trip to Button Town, another dig at the crotch. 'But *maybe—*'

'What?' A voice crackled out of the intercom's speaker. *'What you want? What?'*

Harmsworth leaned in. 'Is Mr Lewis Kelman in?'

'What about him? Why? ... Know what: don't care.' The speaker cracked and fizzled. *'He at work. Go away.'*

'Where's he working?'

A bus growled by.

Then a hatchback, with the windows vibrating to the *dmmm-tsssh-dmmm-tsssh-dmmm-tsssh* of bloody awful music.

A seagull got into a swearing match with one of its neighbours...

And then, finally: *'Back of building.'*

An angry-wasp buzz sounded, then the door lock *click*ed.

'Tell him we out of milk!'

Harmsworth took his finger off the button and pushed through into a manky narrow hallway.

Roberta limped in after him.

Gloomy in here, with cracked plaster on the walls. They'd probably been painted an exciting shade of magnolia once, back in the LongAgo, but it had faded over the years to tooth-enamel grey. Stone stairs wound up to the first and second floors, letting the unmistakable twin scents of cannabis and frying garlic waft down from above.

The space between the stairs and the wall was barely wide enough to accommodate Harmsworth's shoulders as he squelched towards the back door, following the long, ragged gouge marks that ran all the way down the hall.

A mechanical *screeeech* rattled around the tight space, getting louder the closer they got to the featureless door at the end.

Roberta gave the nod and Harmsworth opened it.

The screech turned into a howl.

She stepped out into a murky well at the back of the building, lined on all four sides with granite walls – three-storeys high. Dank and dark and claustrophobic. Creepy too, with all those grubby windows looking down at her.

This place must've been left to rot for *years*.

Trees and bushes cracked their way through the concrete floor, weeds choking the one patch of earth. The walls were a mess of loose guttering and dripping downpipes. Algae growing up the blockwork, turning it slimy and green.

A petrol-powered woodchipper sat in the middle of a cleared area, shrieking away as Lewis Kelman fed a branch into it.

He'd swapped the Toad-of-Turd-Hall outfit for a grubby pair of overalls, work boots, work gloves, eye protectors, and a hard hat with a built-in face screen and ear defenders.

That was a lot of Health-and-Safety for a right-wing, death-to-the-nanny-state tosspot.

As the branch disappeared into the machine a fountain of damp chips spattered out of the nozzle, into an already-full half-tonne builder's bag. Three more were lined up against the far wall, stuffed with shredded undergrowth. A scuffed orange chainsaw lurked in the gloom – along with a billhook. Curved, glinting, and deadly…

Kelman had been busy.

He didn't look up as Roberta and Harmsworth entered his domain.

Harmsworth waved his arms about. 'Mr Kelman?'

As if the bugger was going to hear *that* over all this racket.

So Roberta stuck two fingers in her gob and let loose a shrill whistle. Then: 'HOY! LOUIE!'

Kelman's head snapped up, staring at them as if they'd just broken into his bedroom and crapped on the pillows.

The woodchipper devoured its branch, leaves and all, then Kelman hit the off switch. The machine whined down, spinning and rattling to a halt.

He swivelled his ear defenders up. 'Wondered when you'd get here.' Took off his hard hat and hung it on a stunted tree.

Roberta made a show of looking around, top lip curled. 'Bit *humiliating*, isn't it? A man of *your* calibre: manual labour?'

'I hear you're retired.'

'No' to mention living in a manky wee flat. We seen some of your mates, and they've all got *houses*.' Kicking at a loose twig. 'Would've thought your multimillionaire mate would've seen you right. Trouble in paradise?'

'Hmmmph.' He picked up the billhook, weighing it in his hand. It was the kind of thing you could do some serious damage with – a ten-inch blade with a hook on the end. 'People like you: you see somewhere like this and you think, "Manky, manky, manky."' He hacked at a twisted beech, trimming off the smaller branches, grunting out a word with every swing: 'People … like … me … see … luxury … apartments … with … easy … access … to … the … city … centre.'

She turned again, taking in the algae-greened walls, knackered guttering, and rotting window frames. 'Part of Graeme Anderson's property portfolio.'

Kelman stopped hacking. 'It's *mine*.' Pointing at her with the billhook. 'Everyone else told you to fuck off, what makes you think I won't too?'

'Someone stabbed a wee girl, Lewis. Thought you "alpha males" were against that kind of thing?'

He slashed away at the tree again. 'I didn't stab anyone.'

'Aye, you were too busy getting the mob all whipped-up with your loudhailer, weren't you.' Folding her arms, head on one side, acting puzzled. 'Or… Nah. I can't believe a fine upstanding gentleman like you *authorised* the knife attack on Billie Nesbit…?'

'Course I sodding didn't.' He whacked his blade into the tree trunk, sticking it there. Gathered up a double-armful of trimmings, and dragged them over to the pile by the chipper.

'So, what: one of your crew thought, "Sod what this prick Kelman says, I'm stabbing her anyway!" You losing your grip on the foot soldiers, Louie?'

He hauled the overflowing half-tonne bag over to join the other three. Yeah… Lewis Kelman might *look* like a weedy streak of frog piss, but there was some power there. Wasn't even breathing hard. 'What makes you think it was one of *my* boys?'

'Oh, fuck *right* off.'

Kelman unfolded a new bag, propping it into place beneath the woodchipper's spout. 'Think about it. We're there flying the flag for common sense and decency, you think it works in our favour to kill a photogenic young woman? Think that plays well in the press?'

'Two people saw one of your—'

'Then why don't you *arrest* the bastard?' Kelman barked out a laugh. 'One of my boys stabs a woman in the guts, and *somehow* doesn't get a drop of her blood on him? Please.'

Roberta tightened her fists. 'Lots of broken noses and split lips that day. Samples get corrupted.'

'You're so *ungrateful*.' Looking her up and down like a piece of rancid meat. 'You should be on your knees, singing

Graeme's praises. Saved your bloody life; putting a bill through Parliament with your *name* on it; and you've not so much as said "thank you"!' Kelman sniffed, then spat on the ground at her feet. 'Should be ashamed of yourself.'

Wee shite.

She turned to Harmsworth. 'Ever notice how these right-wing tits play the hardman the whole time, Owen? Beating their chests and shouting the odds, but they never stop *whining* cos they're scared of *everything*. Women, foreigners, vaccines, gay people, trans people,' giving Kelman a withering look, 'personal hygiene.'

Harmsworth tugged at her sleeve, voice low and warning. 'Guv?'

Kelman stuck his chest out. 'Typical bloody "tolerant left". Can't say anything without you snowflakes taking offence and running home to mummy with your thumbs up your arses. *We* get things done!'

'Yes.' Harmsworth nodded. 'Well, it was nice talking to you, Mr Kelman.' Tugging Roberta towards the exit. 'We should be going, Guv.'

No chance.

'Guv?'

She thunked her walking stick against the weedy concrete. 'Aye, and we all know what you knuckle-dragging hate-filled freak-of-nature *shite*-mongers "get done".'

'Guv!'

Kelman stepped forward. Teeth bared. 'Hey, *I'm* not the one with a six-inch steel plate in my head. *You're* the freak.'

'It's *titanium*!' Chin up. 'And it's no' six inches, it's *three*. And that's still twice the size of your micro-dick!'

They glared at each other in crackling silence.

Up on the rooftop, that seagull was back, *scrawk*ing as its nemesis went *kyeeick-keeyick-keeyick*.

Somewhere in the distance, an ambulance siren wailed.

Out on George Street, a drunken idiot launched into an a capella rendition of a deeply silly song about how his milk-shakes brought all the boys to the yard.

Kelman put the hard hat back on. 'Graeme should've let you bleed-out on the tarmac.' Jerking a thumb at the exit. 'Now bugger off: I've got work to do.'

He was halfway through getting his ear defenders into place when Roberta held up a finger. Giving it her best Columbo. 'Just one more thing.'

Kelman glared. 'Oh for… *What?*'

'You're out of milk.'

Maybe not the *coolest* of lines to finish on, but it made him stare at her as if she'd just turned into an octopus and spewed ink everywhere.

So she turned on her heel and limped off, with Harmsworth scuttling ahead.

The woodchipper was screeching before she'd even reached the door.

3.16

Roberta snorked, flinching awake as something weird vibrated against her left boob.

Where the buggering hell was…?

Harmsworth's plop-brown Volvo. Passenger seat.

He bloody better not have interfered with her!

Know what *men* are like.

But both his hands were on the wheel as they tootled their way through sleepy, rain-drenched Newmachar – past the Co-op, heading north.

The Volvo's windscreen wipers *screeeeek-scroonk*ed across the glass, just out of time with the miserable buggers moaning away on the radio.

'And they drove the darkness to our hearts,
Sang midnight's song, and screamed inside,
They built a pyre, made fire an art,
And lied and lied and lied and lied…'

Harmsworth wriggled in his seat, which can't have been good for his unmentionables. What with all the sand. He glanced across the car at her. 'Your phone made a noise.'

She rubbed her eyes, sitting up. 'What the hell is this Goth shite?'

'We tried … to sing,
We tried … to fly,'

'Dunno. It's just the radio. You were asleep.'

'It's *called* a "power nap".' Plus it'd been a long day, what with all the running about and fresh air and everything.

'We tried … to sing,
We tried … to cry,'

'How is this music?' Grimacing at the radio as the band chuntered on.

'We tried … to cry,
We tried … to cry,'

'Whatever happened to *proper* rock stars – with skin-tight leather trousers, frilly shirts, too much make-up, and manly bouffant hair? Groupies and wrecking hotel rooms. Album covers clarted in big-breasted bikini babes.' Pulling her phone out. 'This lot sound like they lactate smudged mascara.'

TUFTY:

> Had weird dream.
>
> ALL BIRDS ARE OPERATED BY REMOTE CONTROL!
>
> CHEESE LIES TO US!
>
> SO DOES BADGERS!
>
> Now eating Weetabix.
>
> Will do DDD after Weetabix eated.

The wee loon was off his rocker.

And an inconsiderate funtnugget. Sending buzzy texts when people were asleep. What kind of behaviour was that?

On the plus side, there was no more singing from the radio, just a whole lot of gloomy-flailing-away on acoustic guitar and piano.

Outside the car windows, Newmachar went from an old-fashioned Scottish village to a commuter town – swapping granite for harling and brick, with snaking rows of plastic semis, lock-block driveways, and yet more bloody hatchbacks.

The song ached to a halt, followed by a long exhale, then a full-on teuchter voice. *'Oh, me, fit a* miserable *song! If I kent it wiz* that *bleak I wouldn't've played it. Let's hiv summit a bittie mair* cheery, *shall we?'*

Roberta stuck two fingers up at the radio. 'Shut up, you pish-headed cock-lump.' Then switched it off. Yawned. Stretched. Let out a wet raspberry and sagged, smacking her lips. 'Thirsty.'

'Maybe Graeme Anderson will offer us a nice cup of tea and a biscuit?' More wriggling. 'And somewhere I can dig half of Aberdeen beach out of my pork scratchings.'

'Urgh!' A shudder rampaged down her spine. 'Don't you *dare* ruin pork scratchings for me.'

The Volvo drifted past yet more new-ish-build housing estates, where all the homes were crammed in like battery hens.

Harmsworth pulled his chin up. 'I've been thinking.'

'Oh, God…'

'No, listen: about what Lewis Kelman said. Who you really shouldn't have antagonised, by the way, even if he *is* a tit. But he's right.'

She snorted. 'He's a *twat*.'

'OK, a tit *and* a twat.' Frown. 'But what *have* the ASDG

got to gain from stabbing Billie Nesbit? They know everyone'll point the finger at them, right? And what does it achieve?'

'That's the thing about the far right, Owen – they don't do joined-up thinking. And I'll antagonise anyone I want. What's he going to do, clype on me to the Rubber Heelers?' She grinned. 'Professional Standards can kiss my pert and succulent buttocks. Creepy snudgers can't touch me, now I'm retired.'

'Do you mind? I'm lynchpinning here.'

Roberta rolled her eyes. 'Pfff...'

'*Thank* you. If Kelman's goons didn't do it, then Occam's razor implies it must be someone from the *other* side.'

She stared at him. '"Occam's razor"?'

A smug, know-it-all smile burst across his chubby face. He opened his mouth, but she got there first:

'I know what it is, so if you try mansplaining it I *will* punch you right in the pork scratchings.'

His mouth clacked shut again.

They puttered through the last gasps of Newmachar and out the other side, into a landscape of fields and pylons and wind-battered barley. Sheets of rain thundering down from an angry sky.

Clearly suffering from a case of mansplainus-interruptus, Harmsworth drove on in silence for a bit. Pouting as they passed waterlogged sheep and mini-lochans and great swathes of mud. 'It's just, if we're looking for the *simplest* explanation, it's got to be one of the counter-protesters who stabbed her.' Preening away in the driver's seat, like a self-satisfied twunt. Gosh, Owen: you're such a *genius*. 'So, who had motive? Jilted boyfriend? Jealous rival? Or maybe it's a money thing?'

Hmmm...

He might've been a satchel-faced idiot, with Y-fronts full of sand, but he had a point.

Roberta reached behind her, into the rear footwell, fumbling for her tote bag. Pulling out the Operation Troglodyte file. Then flipped through the witness statements – searching for Paddington 'Paddy' MacInver's. Because let's face it, she'd read them all often enough to know what she was looking for.

'*This* guy said Billie and Vivian Staybridge had some sort of feud going.' Paddy's statement went on the dashboard. Next: 'Erm… Here: Ethan Rattray gushed about how great Billie was. Which is exactly what you'd do if you wanted to deflect away from the fact that you stabbed her.' That went next to Paddington's. 'Vivian says Billie was jealous of her being promoted to campaign media liaison.' Dashboard. 'And Declan Tinworth says Todd Pherson-Weir's dick was all out of joint because Billie rejected his advances and wouldn't shag him.' Closing the file. 'That's about it for motive.'

Smugness radiated off her driver. '*See?* Three perfectly viable suspects, right there.'

Nothing worse than a total bumwank who was actually *right* for a change. But yeah: it was worth exploring.

Harmsworth took a left, onto a single-track road that wound through an avenue of trees. 'Smart *and* resourceful, remember?'

He swanked all the way down the avenue, self-satisfied lump of arseholes that he was. Then turned right, onto a short section of road that led to a pair of stone gateposts – topped by what were probably supposed to be roaring lions, but looked more like Labradors who'd just stepped on a bit of Lego.

Between them stretched a set of black iron gates.

Closed.

Which explained the intercom, fixed to a post, on the driver's side of the road.

Harmsworth pulled up beside it.

A pair of security cameras were mounted high up in the trees, glaring down at them with glittering eyes.

Which was interesting.

Roberta turned in her seat, peering out at the woods on either side of the road. 'Back up a bit.'

He looked puzzled, but did what he was told.

Very interesting indeed.

She pointed. 'This "car bomb" that went off – how come there's no sign of any damage? No broken trees, no burnt bits, no scorched tarmac, no buckled metalwork?'

'Maybe Anderson had all the damaged stuff replaced?'

'He got the *trees* replaced?'

'Oh.'

Exactly.

'Ring the doorbell, there's a good lynchpin.'

Harmsworth pulled forward again, wound his window down, and poked the intercom till it made a strangled electronic squeak. 'Anderson's probably not even here. He'll be down in Westminster, won't he? Snuffling in the trough, like all the other—'

A young man's voice buzzed out of the speaker, riding on a prissy Central Belt accent. *'Hello?'*

One of the security cameras turned – zooming in on the Volvo's occupants. The other stayed where it was, probably focussed on their number plate.

'Yes.' Harmsworth leaned out of his window, one arm up to shield his receding hairline from the rain. 'We'd like to speak to Mr Anderson, if he's in?'

Roberta thumped her idiot driver. 'Course he's in – checked before we left this morning. "On constituency business" according to his website.'

'Hello-oh?'

Harmsworth tried again. 'We'd like to—'

'You have to hold the button down, if you want to talk!'

'Oh for…' Doing as he was told. 'Hello, we'd like to talk to Mr Anderson, please.'

'He's busy.'

Roberta gave Harmsworth another thump. 'Tell your man, "The person Anderson named a *law* after wants a word."'

Harmsworth pressed the button. 'The person he named a—'

'I heard.' Which meant the voice had been screwing with them the whole time. *'Hold on.'*

The gates gave an almighty *buzzzzzzzzzzz*, a *clang*, then juddered open.

'Come on up.'

So they did.

Anderson's conservatory was huge, featuring lots of wicker furniture and bright cushions. Pot plants. A small dining table. Three walls of floor-to-ceiling glass – two of which looked out over the fields surrounding his house; while the third provided a view of the driveway, parking area, and paved bit around the front door. Perfect, if you wanted to monitor everyone's comings and goings.

And given the plethora of security cameras mounted all over the place, Anderson *did.*

Roberta took a sip of tea – slightly bitter, but that probably had something to do with the ASDG-branded mug it'd been served in, with 'No Thank EU!' on it. The plate of mixed chocolate biscuits helped, though.

She munched, watching one of those robot mowers valiantly battling in the rain, keeping the huge sweep of front lawn in check. Circling the pollarded sycamores, to head out on another sweep.

Couldn't be good for it, getting soaked like that...

Hector cleared his throat. 'I'm sure Mr Anderson won't be long.' The voice from the intercom turned out to be a fey young man with a whole heap of tattoos *just* visible through his crisp white shirt. They didn't really go with the smart tweed waistcoat and shiny shoes. A short-back-and-sides blond, sporting a stupid wee goatee and glasses. 'In the meantime, please make yourselves comfortable.'

Then away he went, taking his tea tray with him.

Harmsworth helped himself to another Jaffa Cake. 'How the other half live, eh?' Slurping from 'STOP THE BOATS!'

'Oh, Graeme Anderson's no' the "other half", Owen, he's the One Percent.' She wandered the conservatory, sipping Eurosceptic tea and chomping on a dark-chocolate ginger. A three-hole golf course was tucked behind the house, along with a tennis court, and right at the bottom of the garden: a pair of mammoth Alsatians stared back at Roberta from the fenced-off kennels.

And the buggers looked hungry.

She popped the last chunk of biscuit in her gob and pulled out her phone. Dropping Tufty a subtle reminder:

> Were those Weetabix too much for you?
>
> Where's my digital deep dive!?!
>
> And see if you can find me pics of that car bomb at Graeme Anderson's hovel.

Pocketing her phone, Roberta sauntered over to the door that led back through to the house. Acting all calm-and-casual-like.

Harmsworth wolfed down a chocolate-coated jammy dodger. 'What are we actually *doing* here, though? If we accept the perfectly plausible hypothesis that it was one of Emma Dornoch's campaign staff who stabbed—'

'Now, now, now:' Roberta tapped her forehead, 'enquiring mind, remember?' Then slipped out through the door, like a sleekit jobbie, into a hallway that looked more mid-market hotel than private home. Magnolia-and-beige, with an oatmeal carpet, a handful of watercolours depicting Aberdeenshire landmarks.

Four doors off.

Couldn't see any internal security cameras – which didn't mean there *weren't* any, you could hide a spy-cam in pretty much anything these days – but nothing ventured…

She tiptoed down the corridor, taking her tea with her.

Door Number One opened on a living room, about three times the size of hers. It was cold and lifeless, though. Decorated in the same Holiday Inn chic as the hall.

Door Number Two: a cupboard full of cleaning things.

Door Number Three: a loo, with sparkling tiles on the floor and walls.

Door Number Four led to a spotless boot room, with a partially-glazed UPVC door down the far end. Spotless coir matting on a spotless tiled floor. A spotless bench seat with spotless wellies underneath it, and spotless waxed jackets above. A special peg for the dogs' leads. A rack of fishing rods, another for loose golf clubs, and one for croquet mallets – wha-wha-wha, don'cha know, Old Sport.

And unlike all the other rooms, a vague muffle of voices was just audible – coming from somewhere nearby.

Which made this the perfect spot for a touch of light eavesdropping.

Roberta snuck inside.

An internal door sat opposite the bench – couldn't see it before, because of the fishing rods. She stuck her ear to the panelled wood, but no voices.

A quick peek revealed a wet room: sparkling clean, with

white marble tiles; gold taps and matching shower; a black toilet, sink, and bidet. Bet you could take a *very* swanky crap in there.

That left the back door.

She eased it open a fraction and a woman's voice lumbered in through the gap, dark and growling – as if the speaker lived on cigarettes and rough vodka:

«А потом я сказала: „Сначала я выебу её в жопу, а ты будешь смотреть. А потом я трахну тебя туда же." У него, реально, встало. Да я ему руки отбила, для понимания.»

Not a bloody clue what any of *that* was about, but a laugh followed it. Sharp and cruel.

«Ну ... Да. ... Ублюдки должны научится делать что им велено, и расплачиваться за долги.»

Roberta edged the door wider, just far enough to squint out through the gap.

A stocky, stumpy lump of a woman paced back and forth outside the house, smoking a black cigarette that stank like burning rubber. She had broad shoulders to go with her spade-shaped forehead – currently creased as she listened to whoever was on the other end of the phone.

And she looked *really* familiar…

Course she did: it was the woman from Silvermoss Business Centre. The one Graeme Anderson had a conflab with outside the UK.EPF headquarters. Right before the explosion that almost killed everyone.

«Нет… Тебе лучше его прикончить. Долбоёбам нельзя давать спуску, а то остальные прикинут что ты слабак. Это—»

Then another voice, right behind Roberta, starched and Central-Belty: '*What are you doing?*' Hector The Detector

She pulled on a big smile and turned, hamming-up the Doric. 'The very man! Far's the crapper? Gotta take a dump the size o' a *caravan*.' Handing him her mug. 'Cheap tea aye goes straight through me.' Then opened the wet-room door. 'Aha! This'll do *fine*.'

Roberta hobbled inside, and shut the door in Hector The Disinfector's face.

3.17

Roberta sat on the ink-black toilet, having a swanky wee – because might as well, since she was here anyway. After all, it helped kill a bit of time, and with any luck Hector The Infector might have got bored and sodded off by the time she'd finished.

Then she could get back to snooping.

Meantime, she checked her phone.

TUFTY:

> Why do I have to do all the finding of stuff?
>
> Does your phone not have Google?
>
> Arrrrgh!
>
> Here:

He'd added four attachments.

She poked the first one, getting a photo for her trouble. Only it wasn't an official police crime-scene snap, it was a shot of the gate outside Graeme Anderson's house, with a patrol car blocking access and a fire engine just visible through the trees behind it. A caption was superimposed across the bottom: 'EMERGENCY SERVICES RUSHED TO THE SCENE, NEAR NEWMACHAR © *Aberdeen Examiner*'. The next photo was much the same, only from the *Press And Journal.* The third came courtesy of the *Scottish Daily*

Post. Only the *Sharny Dick Plop* didn't give a toss about privacy, so they'd sent a drone in over the wall – giving an aerial view of the house, with the conservatory off to one side. And the lawn with its brave little robotic soldier. And the smouldering, burnt-out wreck of a vehicle, about halfway down the drive. No idea what brand or make the car was, but the roof had been peeled off in the blast. The grass on either side of the road was seared and blackened in a huge teardrop shape.

Must've been quite an explosion...

A handful of figures in white SOC suits picked through the debris. That would be the Mob Squad's special forensic team.

'DID SICKO JIHADIS BOMB BRAVE ANDERSON?'

The fourth attachment was an article from the *Aberdeen Examiner*, which was light on detail and heavy on speculation. But it *did* say the car in question used to be a Fiat Uno, stolen from a housing estate in Northfield, and packed with DIY explosives. They'd done a mini-interview with the woman who'd owned it, as if getting your car nicked gave you an insight into acts of terrorism.

Waste of sodding time.

Roberta poked away at her phone:

> Where's my crime reports on the car bomb?
>
> Forensics?
>
> Photos?
>
> Finger out, you lazy wee snidge!

SEND.

She was fiddling with the loo roll when the reply came in. TUFTY:

> Oh noes! Not sharing confidential stuff! Public domain only!

Tufty does like being an Police Officer!

NO GETTING HIM FIRED!!!!!!!!

Wee shite.

Mind you, given Chief Superintendent Pine was on the rampage, he was probably right.

OK, give it another five minutes and Hector The Inspector should've buggered off. Which could mean only one thing: another game of Hedgehog Hodgepodge…

By the time Roberta eased open the wet-room door to sneak a peek, her bum was well and truly numb. That was the problem with toilet seats, even swanky ones.

Right, no sign of Hector The Objector, which meant—

'Ex-Detective Inspector Steel.'

Little sod had been lurking behind those fishing rods. Standing there with his arms crossed. Waiting.

She slipped through the door, closing it behind her. 'Aye, I'd leave that a minute if I was you.'

Silence.

Roberta pulled on her 'innocent' smile. 'Don't let me keep you. Sure you've got loads of things need doing about the place.'

'I'll escort you back to the conservatory. In case you get "lost" again.'

Crap.

Horrible Hector The Roberta Collector stood guard by the conservatory door, radiating disapproval. Probably worrying about the alleged massive poop she'd allegedly clogged the wet-room toilet with. Allegedly.

Because if you couldn't screw with prissy wee racist pricks, what was the point?

Harmsworth fiddled with his phone.

Roberta slumped all the way back on the couch, legs dangling over the arm, wearing a doily on her forehead. Making a game of trying to blow it off. Which lacked the bells, whistle, and flashing lights of Hedgehog Hodgepodge, but Doily Blow was harder than it looked.

Pfffffffff…

Nope.

Pffffffffffffff…

Finally, the door opened and in strode the man himself: Graeme Anderson. At long sodding last. Rolling his sleeves up as if he was about to fight them all.

A patronising smile. 'Sorry to keep you waiting. I've been on a Zoom call with the US.'

As if that was supposed to impress anyone.

Harmsworth scrambled to his feet. Standing to attention as he hid his phone away and dug out his notebook. Pen poised.

Meh.

Roberta stayed where she was, still having no luck moving that doily. 'While we were waiting, I may or may not have blocked your wet-room toilet.' Nothing like doubling down on a lie.

Pffffffffffffffff…

Pffffff… Pfffffff… Pffffffffffffffff…

Nope. This doily wasn't for moving.

She peered at him, between the lacy bits. 'You seem to be *very* popular with the blowing-things-up crowd, Graeme. Getting to be a habit.'

He did that 'caring' face he always faked for the TV cameras. 'Are you feeling better? I was going to visit you in hospital, but you wouldn't believe what the first few months are like when you're elected to Parliament.'

Pffffffffffffff...

'Aye: first the industrial estate goes boom, then a Fiat Uno, right outside your palatial gaff?'

His lips went as stiff as his starched shirt. Probably getting a touch peeved at the lack of forelock-tugging. Poor baby. 'Can you *not* lie on my sofa; I've just had it cleaned.' Checking his big, fancy watch. 'Is there a reason for this visit? Only I've got Beijing at ten past. Perhaps you came here to say, "thank you" – for me saving your life?'

'Aye, but the dreaded Industrial-Estate Bomber wasn't targeting *me*, though, was he. He was after *you*.'

Pffffffffffffffffffff...

Pffffffft...

She shrugged, which was weird lying down. 'So, if you think about it, it's *your* fault I got blown-up in the first place.'

And yes, that was the same line she'd given Billie Nesbit in hospital, but it was still true.

Plus it seemed to have hit a nerve.

Pink flushed across Anderson's cheeks, making him that bit more gammony. 'That's not the point. Look, will you sit up when I'm talking to you?'

Nope.

'I've been speaking to your wee friends, Graeme. Great bunch of lads; lovely tattoos; nearly all their own teeth.'

Pffffffffffffffffffffffff...

She raised a finger. 'One of them said something that got me thinking.'

Pffffffffffffffffffffffffffffffffffffffffffffffffffffffffff...

Anderson marched over and snatched the doily from her forehead. Scrunched it in his fist. 'I saved your *life*.'

Roberta didn't get up. 'See that Fiat Uno?' Pointing in the

vague direction of the front lawn. 'How come it went *BANG*! halfway up the drive?'

'This is ridiculous. Clearly that blow to your head damaged something inside.'

'*How come* it wasn't stopped at the gates, like we were?'

Hector The Interjector scowled down his nose at her. 'The gates had been stuck open for a couple of months. Took ages to get the parts in from Belgium.'

'Ah, Brexit – the gift that keeps on giving.' Throwing the wee loon a wink. 'So, why detonate the bomb all the way down there? Why no' drive up to the house? Much better chance of *killing* someone. Instead: what did they take out – few blades of grass and a couple of moles?' Letting the words hang in silence for a breath or two. 'That no' seem *odd* to you?'

Anderson stuffed the crumpled doily in his pocket. 'I'm willing to make allowances, because of your injury, but there are limits, *Ex*-Detective Inspector.'

'You're no' going all domestic violency on me, are you? Thought you were a changed man. Pillar of the community!'

A glare. 'I actually thought you'd come here to say "*thank you*", but you're just like all the others, aren't you?'

Roberta grinned at him. 'Oh no, no, no – I'm quite ... *unique*. Aren't I, Owen?'

Harmsworth grimaced. 'And then some.'

A knock at the door, and who should poke her head in, but Little Miss Stocky McSquare-Forehead – with a fancy cordless phone pressed against her rectangular boobs. Only instead of the expected Eastern European accent, when she spoke it was pure Mockney. 'Boss? Got Radio Four on the blower – you wanna do the *Today* programme tomorra?'

Anderson blinked, turned. 'Who else is on? What about?'

'"Migrants ate my baby." I dunno, do I – some EU trade bollocks. With a Tory prick and some Labour wanker.'

His face scrunched. 'Fine. Yes. As long as it's not Angela Rayner. Bloody woman's like a beartrap.'

The newcomer jerked her chin at Roberta. 'Speaking of wankers…?'

Roberta gave her a little wave. 'We were just asking your employer about Billie Nesbit getting stabbed.'

Anderson's chin retreated. 'What?'

Ever slow on the uptake.

'Didn't see you at the protest.'

McForehead seemed puzzled by that, so Roberta frowned at Anderson instead.

Gave him a disappointed sigh. Then: 'Tut, tut, tut, Graeme. I thought *Wee Louie Kelman* was your right-hand man. Person. *Creature*. Does he know you're two-timing him with Dick Van Dyke, here?'

Van Dyke curled her free hand into a fist. 'Eh?'

'Stephanie is my *PA*. Running a parliamentary office takes a lot of organisation.' Another ostentatious glance at his ostentatious watch. 'And I have a meeting with the Chinese government to prepare for.' Pointing at Stephanie. 'See them out.' Then Anderson swept from the room. Not so much as a tatty-bye-bye.

Soon as the door clunked shut, Stephanie McSquare-Bits was on the phone. 'You still there? Yeah, he'll do it. Send us the details.' She hung up. Jerked a thumb over her shoulder, glowering at Roberta. 'You: on your feet. You're leavin'.'

Aye, right.

Roberta stayed where she was, swinging her legs, kicking her heels against the side of the couch. 'So, are you more a Bernard Woolley or a Humphrey Appleby type of character, Steph? When you're wheeling and dealing in Westminster.'

Which seemed to go completely over Stephanie's rectangular head. 'Don't fink I won't drag you out by the ankles.'

Suppose people just didn't appreciate classic TV shows anymore. Which was sad.

Or maybe Roberta was just getting old.

Which was sadder.

A sigh. 'Ah, what the hell.' She swivelled her legs off the couch and stood, making a *big* show of yawning and stretching. 'Thanks for the tea, Hector. Take care of yourself, eh? Things around Graeme Anderson have a habit of exploding.' Then threw a wee salute to Stephanie. '*Do svidaniya*, Comrade.'

Which seemed to completely fluster Stephanie, leaving her staring with her gob hanging open, showing off lots of dark metal fillings.

Good.

Roberta swaggered from the room.

Behind her, Stephanie's voice growled out. '*You too, Lard Boy.*'

Cruel, but fair.

Harmsworth's face was crumpled and sour as they headed down the driveway, blowers on, radio off.

Roberta scootched down in her seat, watching as Graeme Anderson's swanky home retreated in the rear-view mirror.

And there she was: the mysterious Stephanie, standing outside the conservatory in the pouring rain, scowling after the Volvo.

Really tempted to wind down the window and give her a cheery wave goodbye. But it wasn't worth getting wet for.

A snort from the driver's seat. 'What was the point of coming all the way out here, just to rile the guy up?'

'Because *sometimes* – and pin back your lugs here, Owen,

I'm about to lay some Wisdom Of The Ancients on you – you've got to shake the tree to see what falls out.'

His face darkened. 'She called me "Lard Boy"!'

'Stop here.'

'What?' Looking around. 'Why? Why am I— Ow!'

She hit him again, and the Volvo came to an emergency stop on a section of tarmac that was a good three shades darker than the road on either side. No sign of any scorch marks in the grass, though. Already grown in, green and lush…

Roberta sat upright again, frowning out at the lawn. 'Why stop *here*? Makes bugger-all sense.'

'Cos you told me to!' Rubbing his battered arm.

'Don't be dense, Owen.' She turned in her seat and peered back at the house.

Stephanie hadn't moved. Probably wondering what they'd stopped for.

'Oh…' Harmsworth's eyes widened. 'You mean, the *bomber*!' Engaging that four-watt brain of his. 'Maybe it was just a warning?'

'Then stick a severed pig's head in the bugger's bed. Or send him a shoebox full of dog shit. Or an unlubed dildo studded with nails…' Drumming her fingers on the dashboard. 'Why *here*?'

Didn't make any sense.

'Can we go home now?'

'Unless you *wanted* to cause as little harm as possible?' She pointed at the patched tarmac and reseeded turf. 'Too far away to damage the house or burn down the woods.'

'*Exactly!*' Giving himself a smug wee nod. 'That's what I *said*: sending a message.'

'Aye… But who to?'

The wee robot mower wobbled past through the downpour, making sod-all difference to the soggy grass.

Harmsworth wriggled in his seat again, foostering about with his sandpapered unmentionables. Accompanied by a woe-is-me sigh.

She rolled her eyes. 'Go on, then.'

And away they drove…

3.18

Dear. *Snidging*. God. Why. Did. He. *Never*. Shut. Up?

'Of course, then you come to the mince itself. And that's *another* barrel of worms.' Harmsworth pulled a face, as if this was one of the greatest scandals of our time.

Twenty past six and the sky was a solid lid of slate and burnt toast, with a line of fire on the horizon. The headlights on the other carriageway glowed, misty and blurred in the rain, as the ancient Volvo followed an Aberdeenshire Council van along the bypass: its load bay stuffed full of orange cones – probably off to enlighten someone's morning commute with a surprise contraflow – rear tyres kicking up a dirty wash of road-spray, lit blood red by its taillights.

Roberta pressed her head against the passenger window, doing lots of sighing as rain streaked the glass.

And Harmsworth *still* wouldn't take the hint.

'...because you can't make decent mince-and-tatties with low-fat mince! You just can't. It needs to be twenty percent minimum.'

She rolled her eyes so hard they nearly fell out her arse. 'Uh-huh.'

The Volvo's windscreen wipers *screek-scronnnnk*ed greasy arcs through the road-spray and fizzing rain.

'Now *some* people will tell you to fry off your onions and carrots first, but you're never going to get a proper *sear* on your mince that way.'

Ding-buzz.

Oh, thank Christ for that: a distraction.

TUFTY:

> Have emailed you the DDD!
>
> @~@
>
> Flipping Wingwangs of Spon! Young people today don't 1/2 post a load of corrugated snidge!
>
> I can feels IQ points withering away as I does read them!!!

Oh, the irony.

Anyway, it was about sodding time.

Lazy little sod.

Bet he'd been getting wriggly with his tasty wee bidie-in, when he should've been working.

Roberta opened her emails.

Meanwhile, on wanged Harmsworth: 'And you have to *really* sear it. Till it's all gnarly and crackling in the pan. Cos that's all flavour, flavour, flavour, flavour.'

Spam, spam, spam, spam…

But between the threats to cancel antivirus software she didn't subscribe to, offers of free solar panels, and discount Viagra, lay Tufty's digital deep dives on Sophia Mitchell, Amelia Wilson, Megan Lockheart, and Violet Erving.

Each came with a brief summary and links to at least three social media accounts – Vivian Staybridge topped the league with six – followed by contact details and a decent head-and-shoulders shot of the four young women.

'Of course the *key* to perfect mince is in the onions. Lots and lots of onions. Cooked down until they *melt* into your gravy. Now—'

'Bloody hell.' Roberta sat up.

Abercrombie wasn't joking: they were all *raging* hotties.

Sophia Mitchell was hydraulically blonde, with a dainty wee upturned nose and electric blue eyes; Amelia Wilson was a full-on Bollywood sex kitten; Violet Erving had bee-sting lips and the kind of smouldering gaze that could strip the pants off a grown woman at thirty paces; while Megan Lockheart…

Hang on.

Roberta zoomed the picture.

Long black hair in a central parting, pouty lips, Disney eyes, teeny dimple in her chin. Familiar. In a déjà vu kind of way.

Harmsworth harrumphed. 'As I was *saying*: I like to roughly chop, then microwave two large onions while the mince browns. And before you say anything, a microwave is a *perfectly acceptable* method of softening onions without colour.'

Roberta *stared…*

Then scrolled through the lot of them again.

Hotties, hotties, hotties, hotties…

Had to wonder – did Sir Norman Fordyce have a pop at Billie Nesbit and Vivian Staybridge too?

Bet he did. Dirty, randy, *jammy* old bugger that he was.

Now, where was that sodding file?

Roberta flailed a hand about in the rear footwell, until it latched onto her bag-for-life, pulling out Operation Troglodyte. Then the photos of Billie Nesbit and Vivian Staybridge. Peering at them in the light of her phone's torch.

Yeah.

Line all six of them up, and the pattern was clear – Sir Norman Fordyce liked his wife's interns *young* and he liked them *pretty*, with small noses and sexy eyes. They were just bonkable variations on the same theme.

'You add your softened onions to the now *crispy* mince with a splash of soy sauce and enough beef stock to properly cover. Then let it simmer for *at least* twenty minutes.'

But that still didn't explain why Megan Lockheart looked so familiar, with her long dark hair and rosy cheeks and big eyelashes…

Of *course* she looked familiar – seen her before. Megan was one of Davey McLeod's missing persons, with her poster up in his office/garage.

'Then you've got the vexed question of peas or carrots? And I mean *in* the mince, not *with* the mince.'

That's why Megan had seemed so strangely familiar at the time. Didn't matter that Roberta had never actually *seen* her before, she'd recognised the same *thing* about her that Sir Norman found so attractive in all the others.

Megan had that Billie-and-Vivian-iness about her.

Harmsworth sniffed. 'Some people don't put either in. Can you believe that? I favour both, but then I've always been a great epicurean gourmet.'

Roberta followed the links in Tufty's email, digging into Megan's social media posts.

'But *not* cut into rounds. No one should be eating rounds of carrots, they're a crime against humanity. Little random chunks are what you need.'

She'd put out loads of posts about world hunger; and Putin's murderous war in Ukraine; and the mass slaughter of Palestinian civilians in Gaza; and the Trump regime's chaos, incompetence, and cruelty…

And it all came to a sudden halt on Saturday the third of May.

After that: not a single post on Bluesky, Instagram, TikTok, Bindle, or Pinterest.

Something nasty crawled its way up Roberta's spine.

'And down south, they put garlic and tomato puree in it! I mean, what are you even *eating* at that point?' Harmsworth indicated right, slowing as the sign appeared for the Kingswells South Junction. Preparing to leave the ring road. 'That's not *mince*, that's a half-arsed bolognese!'

Third of May.

Digging back into Operation Troglodyte, Roberta ferreted out Frank Abercrombie's statement. Couldn't care less what he'd said about Billie's stabbing, but his contact details were printed at the top of the form.

She poked Abercrombie's number into her phone. Set it ringing.

'So, twenty minutes have passed, and only *now* do you add in your random nuggets of carrot. And another chopped onion. Because—'

'Shut up a minute, OK? I'm on the—'

'Urgh…' A muffle-mumble voice gravelled down the line. Thick and sticky with a rosé hangover. *'Who is this?'*

'Aye, we met this morning. You were baking scones?'

'What? God… Urgh…' There was a clinking noise in the background, followed by the kind of *glug-glug-glug* that implied someone was filling a large wine glass with Chateau Hair-Of-The-Dog.

'Need to ask you about Megan Lockheart.'

No reply.

'Frank? Mr Abercrombie? You there?'

A long shuddery exhale – as if he'd just chugged the whole glass in one. *'Sorry. Who?'*

'Megan Lockheart.'

'What about her?'

Dear Jesus…

'What *happened* to her?'

Another silence, another sigh. *'In what way?'*

That six-bottles-a-day wine habit had clearly pickled his brain cells.

'You had to find some other campaign for her to go work on? Because Sir Norman Fiddly Fordyce couldn't keep it in his pants? Kept "polling the electorate"? "Stuffing her ballot box"?'

Glug-glug-glug…

'Please! There's no need to be so crude. *And I'm sure I never said anything as indiscreet as that. Sir Norman is a patron of the arts, a proud supporter of women's issues,* and *happily married.'*

Why did everything have to be such a sodding struggle?

'Whose. Campaign. Did. You. Move. Her. To?'

Could hear him swigging. *'Does it matter? Why does it matter?'*

Roberta massaged her forehead. 'Frankie: I switched your oven off, so you didn't burn your house down. Give us a break, here.'

He made a little groaning noise. Then drank some more. *'Look, between you and me, sometimes young women's heads are turned by a dashing older gentleman with silver hair, a flash car, lots of money, and a knighthood. It falls on me to ensure they don't confuse their infatuation for some sort of … mutual* feelings *on his part.'* A little snort. *'Because he hasn't* got *any. Trust me.'*

One more go: 'So where, in the name of all that's sodding holy, did you send her?'

'Oh.' Drink. *'Hold on, I'll check my little red book.'* Followed by some *clunk*ing and *thunk*ing and rattling, then the bang of a drawer being shut. *'Here we go. There was a councillor in Edinburgh, got caught with one hand in the till and the other in his assistant's frilly knickers. Which put a seat in play, so Megan went to help our preferred candidate win it.'*

At least now they were getting somewhere.

'And did she?'

'He. And no, it went Labour instead.'

'When was this?'

'Erm… Says here I told her on Thursday about the change – first of May – played it as a promotion to "Campaign Coordinator", starting Monday in Edinburgh. She was going to stay with a friend in Portobello, I think?'

Thursday the first, Friday the second, Saturday the third, and Megan Lockheart never posts on social media ever again.

'So what happened to her?'

Another groan. *'How do* I *know. I can't keep track of every delusional hormone-addled teenager that flounces through the place.'* Swigging back more wine. *'Now, are we done? I've got important work to do.'*

Aye, involving a corkscrew and rosé-tinted glasses.

Roberta put a bit of steel in her voice. 'We're no' done till you tell me who the candidate was. Name, address, phone number, the whole doodah. Right *now*.'

Streetlights trembled in the wind, rain turning into sparks as it fell through their fever-yellow glow. Hazlehead grumbled by the Volvo's windows, drenched and dreich, the tower blocks off to one side of Queen's Road like shimmering checkerboards of fireflies through the gloom and whipping branches.

One of those would be Tufty's, where he was probably getting ready for work. Roberta didn't wave though: busy.

A posh Edinburgh accent hummed and hawed in her ear. Then, *'Well,* quite. *But, I thought you'd retired?'*

'Come on, Plocky, I'm no' asking you to throw a suspect down the stairs, just make a couple of calls.'

No reply as they drifted along, Harmsworth taking one

hand off the wheel to rearrange his itchy, sand-filled bits as he wriggled in the driver's seat. Having a moderate-level sulk, because his 'masterclass' on mince-and-tatties was on hold while Roberta wheedled away at Chief Inspector Irene 'Plocky' Whitelaw.

'That really would be highly *irregular.'*

Time to bring out the big guns: 'Who held your hair back when you went Mr Creosote on tequila-and-blackcurrant? And who stopped you booty-calling your ex-husband after the Police Pizza-and-Prosecco Pyjama Party? And who—'

'All right, all right; we don't need a trip down Embarrassment Lane. I'll make the calls.'

A smile broke across Roberta's face, like the dawn. 'Thanks, Plocky!'

'I'm a fool to myself, I really am…'

Plocky hung up, and Roberta had a happy wee stretch. Because sometimes it was nice to talk old friends into doing *slightly* sketchy things.

Harmsworth took a deep breath. 'Which brings us to accompaniments. Let's face it, doughboys are all very well and good, but a decent *skirlie* is where it's at. So—'

'Aye, that's fascinating.' She pointed. 'See the roundabout? Do a one-eighty and back the way we came. There's a knight of the realm needs a visit.'

His face sagged even further. 'But I thought we were going *home*!'

'Look at it this way: all the more time for you to tell me your *desperately* interesting and *informative* facts about cooking mince.'

The hamster wheel in his head creaked around a few times, followed by a nod. 'And we haven't even got to the tatties yet!'

Oh God…

'...nope. Complete no-show. I checked the friend she was meant to be staying with too. Says Megan Lockheart never turned up.'

Roberta scowled out the car window. 'Sodding shite-trumpets.'

Muchalls scowled back.

It was a tiny wee village on the coast, about halfway between Portlethen and Stonehaven, little more than a handful of streets. The Volvo crept along a narrow lane, lined with squat terraced houses – single storey with a miser-thin pavement out front and gardens so small a single step would take you from your front door onto the road. Homes that were hunkered down, with mean little windows. Built to keep wind and storms at bay.

Plocky sighed. *'Sorry it's not better news.'*

'Thanks for looking.' Even if it was a disaster. 'Next time you're up for a night of drunken debauchery, give me a shout. They do a peekaboo night at the Whip and Corset you're gonna *love*.'

A filthy laugh rattled in Roberta's ear. *'And in the meantime, I have to go kick a certain detective sergeant's arse for him. TTFN.'* Then Plocky hung up, because she was never one for goodbyes...

Harmsworth squeezed them past a red hatchback, parked up on the teeny pavement, leaving *just* enough space. 'And the secret is not to peel your potatoes. Scrub and cut out any gritty bits, or eyes, that kind of thing, and then scarify the skins with a julienne peeler.'

That thing was crawling up Roberta's spine again.

If Megan never made it as far as Edinburgh, where was she?

Because none of the options were good.

Unless she'd eloped with a lucky boy/girlfriend?

Only, kind of got the feeling she hadn't. Cos even an idiot like Davey could've solved *that* one.

The Volvo emerged from the far end of the street, leaving its huddled shelter – rocking as the wind shoved and barged, howling straight in off the North Sea.

'You see, that way you get the extra *flavour*, but you don't get the peel hanging around like … big scabs of skin. And *nobody* wants to eat scabs.'

Had to wonder how many people were getting away with murder every year.

Bet it was loads.

Long as you didn't leave the scene clarted in blood and forensics – and everyone thought your victim had run away from home – you could kill *dozens* of people before anyone found out.

Assuming they ever did.

'And when you've boiled them, for goodness' sake, *pour* them and leave them to steam *completely* dry in the warm pot *before* you mash them. Otherwise you're in for watery tatties.'

They left the protective glow of Muchalls behind, heading out into the storm-tossed gloom, with only the Volvo's headlights to lead the way.

'Then add your cold milk and butter to the pan and bring it up to a simmer, before mashing your tatties with lots of white pepper.'

Of course, the *real* question was: how long would it take Chief Superintendent Pine and her Brigade of Morons to figure out Roberta was the one who'd murdered Detective Constable Owen Harmsworth for never shutting up about bloody mince?

Mind you, they'd probably give her a medal…

3.19

'You see, what a lot of people don't understand is: you can't properly *thicken* your mince if you've got doughboys floating in it.'

The single-track road wound along the coast for about half a mile, drystane dykes offering no cover from the hammering rain and angry squalls. Off to the right, the North Sea was a huge black mass beneath the coal-scuttle sky, while the western horizon glowed as if Scotland was ablaze.

The last gasp of a dying sun.

Up ahead, the road disappeared between chest-high stone walls, embracing a phalanx of twisted trees and creepy old rhododendron bushes.

A ravine stretched out to either side, lined with gorse – in full bloom, so the whole gully *burned* as one final burst of sunlight seared across it.

'And what's the point of watery mince?' Harmsworth drove through the open gates. 'Mince has to be *thick*. After all, the expression is "thick as mince", isn't it – not "Oh, catch the boy, Tufty, he's thin as mince." Doesn't even make sense.'

Fordyce House lay at the end of a twisted, gravel driveway: an eighteenth-century pink-granite lump that not even an estate agent could call 'charming'. Blocky, with bay windows, a single turret, and a slate roof.

Ivy crawled up the walls, like mould on a corpse. All glowing in the jaundiced glare of a dozen spotlights.

No sign of Sir Norman's fancy-pants electric BMW – so it was either in the large garage, or he wasn't home.

'If you can't stand a spoon up in it, your mince is too thin. And that's why Bisto is your friend.' Harmsworth's Hearsejobbie grumbled to a halt, right in front of the Fordyce family pile. 'And that's how you make the perfect mince-and-tatties.'

Oh thank Christ for that.

Roberta escaped into the rain. Popping her umbrella. Breathing *deep* the air of freedom.

Didn't really notice it when Harmsworth was just one voice, vying for attention with the rest of the team, but on his own?

Holy *crap* that man could bore for Scotland.

She limped her way to the front door – a heavy blue slab, with a brass lion's-head knocker in the middle. Didn't wait for Captain Tedious, just whacked the thing herself. Like an animal.

The Duke of Dull locked his Volvo, flipped up his retro collar, and hurried over. Sheltering beneath an overhang of shuddering ivy. 'Next up: stovies.'

No sodding chance.

She warded him off with a hand. 'Let's leave that for next time, eh? Something to look forward to.' Like scrofula.

Because otherwise they'd be finding bits of his body for *months*.

'Oh. OK.'

Roberta knocked again, only this time a salvo of barks rattled out inside the house. Not big scary gunshot ones, more high-pitched and yippy. Something Genghis-sized.

Then a posh woman's voice bellowed out on the other side of the door. *'Waldorf! Statler! Quiet down, you pair of twits.'* A clunk, a rumble, and the door opened all the way, revealing Lady Fordyce in a huge baggy green jumper and tartan leggings. Clogs on her feet. What looked like a gin-and-tonic in her free hand – with cucumber and ice, to show how classy she was. Sounding a little buzzed as she smiled at Roberta. 'Can I help you?'

'Aye, *course* you can. Is your—'

A pair of terrifying hell hounds rushed forwards to protect their mistress. Well, maybe in their own eyes. But only if Hades had swapped out Cerberus for a wrinkly dachshund and a lopsided corgi. Barking and barking and barking and—

Roberta pointed at them. 'Wheesht.'

And lo, they did wheesht.

Lady Fordyce *stared*. 'Good grief. You found their off switch! Wish I could do that.' Blink. 'Sorry, yes, where were we?'

'Can we come in and have a chat? It's about your campaign staff.'

And the happy look disappeared, replaced by a pained grimace. 'What have they done *now*?'

The kitchen was a mix of old-fashioned and brand-spanking new, with lots of fancy appliances and shiny copper pots on hooks – glinting away in the spotlights as Lady Fordyce filled a teapot from a freshly boiled kettle. '…so I don't know if he'll be back tonight. Business, business, business. You know what men are like.'

'Thankfully: no.' Roberta hunched in her seat, fussing over Statler and Waldorf. The pair of them beamed up at her with adoring eyes, as if they'd never seen a lesbian sex-goddess before.

Lady Fordyce snorted. 'Lucky you.' Then placed the pot on the kitchen table. 'So, who's done what to whom, this time?'

Roberta gave the dachshund's ears one last shoogle then straightened up, cos that sounded interesting. '"This time"?'

Over by the fridge-freezer, Harmsworth stood – notepad ready, pen poised.

'Bless their little hearts.' Her Ladyship handed out matching campaign mugs. 'We like to give as many jobs to young people as we can. Means the next generation are a bit more energised and excited to enter politics. There's enough ancient duffers in the House and Upper Chamber as it is.' She pursed her lips. 'Sometimes the kids have … a little *growing up* to do. Tempers fray, office romances bloom and wither. Jealousy's a big one.' A shrug. 'Much though I love young people, they can be a *bit* challenging.' She surveyed the table. 'Would you like a biscuit? The Police Investigations and Review Commissioner wouldn't consider that to be a bribe?'

Roberta threw her arms wide. 'I'm retired, so feel free to bribe away.'

'Oh.' Lady Fordyce pulled her chin in. 'I thought this was an *official* visit.' Pointing at them both. 'Aren't you—'

'Aye: I got blown-up. And now I'm retired. And I need to ask you about Megan Lockheart.'

Pink flushed the tips of her ears, but Lady Fordyce's face remained poker still. That was politicians for you. 'Megan…?'

'You can play cutesy me-no-wemember games, or we can *actually* help a family find its missing wee girl.'

The poker face changed to a frown, and she sat. 'Megan's *missing*?'

'Nearly five months.'

Lady Fordyce's eyes closed, and she stayed there. Silent. Not moving.

Roberta poured the tea. Then motioned to Harmsworth – who got the milk from the fridge and plonked the plastic carton on the table. Heathen.

Lady Fordyce gave herself a wee shake. 'How *awful* for her mum and dad. That's…' Down the far end of the kitchen, a plastic rendition of the '1812 Overture' rang out. She rose halfway out of her seat, looking at one of those BT hub-handset things with the built-in answerphone… Then sank back again, letting the machine take care of it. 'Sorry.' Sitting forwards. 'As I was saying, they've—'

'Claire?' Frank Abercrombie's voice buzzed out of the speaker, all wobbly and slurred. *'Claire, hi. … Hi, it's me … Frank.'*

She stood. 'Sorry. I'd better get this.' Moving down the kitchen as Frank kept on talking:

'Listen. Listen. No, listen… I had… The police have been to see me … about … about Sir Norman*! … They know about … about his little … peccadildos. Dillos. … Don't know … who told them, but don't worry! I'll … I'll take care of every—'*

She snatched the handset from its base unit, her plummy tones going clipped and cold. 'Yes, *thank you*, Frank – they're here now.' Giving Roberta and Harmsworth the side-eye. 'I'll talk to you tomorrow. When you're *sober*.' Wrinkles furrowed her brow, and her voice got even sharper. 'No, Frank, I think it's time we had "the talk". … That's *exactly* what I mean. … *Goodbye*.'

Her thumb stabbed a button on the handset, and she scowled at it for a bit. Before taking a deep breath and returning the thing to its base. Pulled on that practised, politicians' porcelain smile and took her seat again. Spread her hands upon the table. 'Right…' Licking her lips. 'You have to understand that … sometimes … it's very *difficult*. Living in the public eye. Married to someone who…'

Lady Fordyce dipped her head, cleared her throat. 'Young women are often attracted to older men.' Eyes flicking to Harmsworth. 'Not bald, fat ones. Older men like Norman: rich, successful, charming. *Powerful*.' Pushing her mug of tea to one side and going back to her gin. 'And there were times in the past when he felt the need to *bask* in that attention. Encourage it even.' Harmsworth got another glance. 'You know what *men* are like. They hit middle age and suddenly it's crisis time: sports cars, ponytails, and … younger women.'

Waldorf rolled over on his back to expose his long sausage-dog tummy. Roberta gave it a wee rub, setting his tail wagging.

'Norman swore it was just a phase, and he needed to work through some things, and he still loved me, but "*everyone* strays from time to time".'

'I used to: till I met my wife.' Roberta shrugged. 'Turns out, when you love someone – properly, deep down in your bones – you don't need to cheat.'

Lady Fordyce gritted her teeth and looked away. No doubt wishing she was a member of the sapphic sisterhood with Romantic Roberta for a partner, instead of the crappy shag-happy Sir Norman of the Wandering Cock.

Took a moment, but she got it together. 'And every time another *pretty young thing* came to work for me, there was Norman. Buying pizza and wine for the team. "Mentoring" them. And me? I was just being "paranoid" and "silly" and "jealousy isn't becoming in a woman *your age*, Claire"…' A bitter laugh. 'Then the shine would wear off his latest gaudy bauble, and he'd tire of them, and I'd have to get Frank to palm them off on someone else's campaign.'

'And Megan was one of "them".'

Statler, clearly jealous of all the tummy rubbing, tried to muscle in on the act. Grinning up at Roberta with his tongue hanging out. After all, she had *two* hands, didn't she?

'By then Norman was obsessed with Billie Nesbit. So…' Lady Fordyce mimed a little goodbye wave. 'And *now* it's "Isn't Vivian Staybridge *capable* and *hard-working* and *clever* and we should really *promote* her to Media Liaison." As if I can't *see* what he's doing…'

Rubbity, rub, rub.

'So divorce the bastard. He's worth millions, right? Take him for every penny.'

'It's not that easy when you're a sitting MSP.' The bitter edge soured even more. 'And a woman. And the right-wing press hates you. And your husband is screwing *twenty-one-year-olds*!' She weighed the glass in her hand – no gin left, just a rattle of ice cubes, then hurled it into the sink with a shattering crash. 'SHE'S YOUNG ENOUGH TO BE HIS BLOODY GRANDDAUGHTER!'

Waldorf and Statler leapt to their feet, scampering across the kitchen tiles to whine up at their mum with big button eyes and swishing tails. Cute and pathetic.

Steel sat back and sipped her tea.

Took a while, but eventually Lady Fordyce's breathing slowed and her shoulders drooped. 'Sorry. That was…' Hands spread out on the table again. 'The only bright side is that he's never managed to accidentally *impregnate* one of his stupid little girls. Can you imagine if the press got hold of *that*?'

Yeah…

Actually, it wasn't hard to imagine something much, *much* worse.

Lady Fordyce didn't come to the front door and wave them a cheery goodbye. Instead, Harmsworth's Volvo had barely pulled away before the house spotlights clanked off, leaving nothing but headlights to illuminate the thrashing trees and driving rain.

Harmsworth sooked in a breath through clenched teeth. 'Frank Abercrombie's getting fired tomorrow, isn't he.'

'Oh aye.'

Because rich, posh gits were *always* happiest when they could blame the hired help for their own cock-ups…

The Volvo grumbled around the bypass, swaying about in the wind's push-and-shove. Rain snarling against the windscreen as the wipers' *screek-scronk* did its best to clear the view. But the car was still only doing forty, with Harmsworth hunched over the steering wheel like a saggy old man. Peering out into the storm.

Making for the Kingswells South Junction.

Roberta slouched in her seat, frowning down at her phone.

LOGAN:

> So either our boy's not killed anyone since the 15th, or he's decided to start hiding the bodies instead of just leaving them lying about where he ripped them.

Hmmm…

She leaned her forehead against the passenger window's cool glass.

Headlights crawled past in the opposite direction as the Volvo staggered onto the slip road.

Ding-buzz.

LOGAN:

> And the notes the bastard leaves are no sodding use.
>
> Got ourselves a forensic psychologist who couldn't analyse Beardy Beattie for Restless Moron Syndrome.
>
> You'd think the top brass WANT us to fail!

Moan, moan, moan.

Her thumbs *tick-tick-tick*ed across the cracked screen:

Tell you what: I'll do you a favour.

You send me your Ripper's notes and I'll see what I can deduce. I've dealt with enough sick-and-twisted tosspots to know my way around an offender profile.

Mates rates?!?!

How could anyone say no to an offer like that?

SEND.

The lights of Westhill sparkled off to the right, rising up the hill like a knot of depressing fairy lights through the downpour.

Well, Roberta and Harmsworth were about to make them even more miserable…

She hunched her back against the wind and rain, hands out to receive the hairbrush in its clear plastic sandwich bag.

Mr Lockheart hesitated. 'And you're *sure* they'll give it back?' He can't have been a day over forty-five, but he looked mid-sixties – what with the bald-shaved head and the big tuft of grey in his spade-sized beard. Wearing an 'EMMA DORNOCH ~ BETTER FOR SCOTLAND!' T-shirt, with a grey hoodie on top. Bags under his pinched eyes.

Roberta nodded. 'Oh aye. Bound to.'

The family home wasn't even vaguely Scottish. Instead, the whole street had been clad in faux-sandstone blocks, making it look as if the builders had meant to stick all this up in the Cotswolds somewhere and got hopelessly lost. Identikit foreign houses, thumped down en masse on the edge of Westhill, with tiny gardens, UPVC windows-and-doors, and no privacy. Adding yet more new-build sprawl to a commuter town, five miles from Aberdeen, that'd spent the last forty years spreading across the countryside like a growth.

Megan's dad sniffed. 'Only it's her favourite brush, so she's gonna want it when she gets home.'

Poor sod.

Roberta faked a reassuring smile. 'I'll make sure they get their finger out.'

He frowned on that for a moment, then placed the bag in her hands.

Lucky Megan didn't clean her favourite brush very often, because the thing was like a mammal-on-a-stick, tangled with long brown hair.

Roberta produced a Sharpie and marked the bag with time, date, location, her name and Mr Lockheart's. Getting him to sign it, as a chain of evidence. 'Thanks. We'll be in touch.' She turned to hobble back to the rain-lashed Volvo.

'It's been nearly five months.' His voice caught on the words, as if each one was made of broken glass: 'Just tell Megan we want her to come home and we're sorry for whatever it is we did to make her leave…'

What the hell were you supposed to say to that?

So Roberta gave him a nod and a wee wave with her walking stick. Then limped away.

3.20

The Volvo's windscreen wipers mourned back and forth across the glass as rain clattered against the bonnet.

'I know, I know, but just cool your bum.' Roberta switched the phone to her other ear – putting it between her and Harmsworth. Not because he was earwigging, just so she wouldn't have to look at his droopy face, drooping even further as they drifted down King's Gate in the dark.

He was even *more* hunched-over now, squinting through the gloom and spray and haze from oncoming headlights, the bags under his eyes swollen to industrial sacks.

Doing *far* too much sighing too.

But at least he wasn't banging on about *mince*.

Roberta glanced out the passenger window, checking their progress.

Streetlights swayed in the storm, their wan glow guttering through the thrashing tree branches.

Not even at the Atholl Hotel, yet.

'We'll be there in … two minutes? Tops.' Which was a lie.

Tufty groaned in her earhole. *'But I have* proper *work to do! I am a dedicated officer of the law, and I cannot afford to take time away from my allotted duties for* frivolous *activities.'* Which sounded weird, even for him.

Beginning to get the feeling the wee loon wasn't right in the head.

'Three, four minutes and you'll be on your way. Snidging about to your bizarre little heart's content.'

'Urgh…' Deep breath. *'Honestly, this is like when Admiral Ackbar led the assault on the second Death Star. In* Return of the Jedi*?'*

What?

The boy was an idiot.

King's Gate turned into Beechgrove Terrace with yet more big granite houses.

'And while we're at it, where's my triple-D on Sir Norman Wingwang Fordyce?'

He sighed. *'You really need to learn how to use Google. I cannot always be there to hold your hand during these activities.'*

'Stop slacking and get it done!'

'It is like dropping out of hyperspace, near the forest moon of Endor, only to find there are dozens *of Star Destroyers waiting for us!'*

A genuine card-carrying, chrome-plated idiot.

'Blah, blah, blah. Are you my team lynchpin or aren't you?'

Harmsworth stiffened in the driver's seat.

'OK.' Another sigh, bigger this time, pained. Resigned. *'Remember: I tried.'*

'Good boy.' One more look out the window. 'Five or six minutes. Tops.' She hung up. Shook her head. 'Swear to God, he's getting odder by the day.'

They tootled along in silence. Past terraces of neat grey homes, then BBC Scotland's Beechgrove Studios, then a bunch of—

'You said *I* was the team lynchpin!' Harmsworth glared across the car at her.

Ah…

Right.

She shifted in her seat. 'Aye, well … *obviously* I have to tell

Tufty he's the lynchpin, cos the wee sod's so insecure! Always needing his ego stroked.' Yeah, that would work. She threw in a reassuring smile. 'Wouldn't do a *lick* of work otherwise. No' like *you*, Owen.' Adding a twirly hand gesture to really sell it. 'With the boy it's just *shameless flattery*, with *you* it's the truth.'

Silence.

The lights turned green ahead as Harmsworth chewed on that one, and they wheeched straight across the junction outside the Co-op.

'Hmmm…' He nodded, liking the taste. 'I see. Yes.' A smile. 'That *does* make sense.'

Sometimes you really had to worry about the state of police recruitment in Scotland.

Harmsworth pulled up outside the Nelson Street labs. A ragged pine tree drooped on one side of the double gates, and a big yellow bin for grit on the other.

For a main entrance it wasn't very swanky – looked more like the arse-end of the building than the front – with a large yard all wrapped around in spiky metal fencing. None of your easy-to-climb chain-link here. This was the kind of stuff that left puncture wounds.

Security lights blazed down inside, illuminating a collection of police vans, patrol cars, and support vehicles, where Mobile Command Units rubbed shoulders with trailers, forensic Transits, and seized vehicles.

The building itself wasn't much better: a magnificently depressing lump of grey, with two dirty-terracotta vertical stripes on each side, and a band of dirty-terracotta around the top. It was probably meant to make the place look jaunty, but really it was more like a manky ribbon on the world's most miserable Christmas present.

Tufty shuffled his feet by the grit bin, standing beneath one of those spotlights – making his high-vis jacket *glow* as rain thundered down. Bouncing off his wee peaked cap.

Yeah…

Maybe it was a *bit* cruel to leave him standing out here for ages. But hey-ho.

Roberta wound down her window, but he didn't move from his post.

Even waving at him made no difference – he just stood there. Lazy wee shite that he was.

Oh for God's sake…

She grabbed her umbrella and hobbled out into the downpour. Popping the canopy.

Rain drummed on the taut fabric.

Tufty didn't even meet her halfway, she had to limp and hurple all the way over there.

'OK, so we're a *couple* minutes late. Is your sulk worth us *both* getting wet?'

He drooped. 'I'm sorry.'

'So you fridging should be. Just dried out from last time. Here:' She produced the makeshift evidence bag, with Megan's brush inside. 'Need this tested for DNA. And get them to sharpish it. None of that "backlog" bollocks: ASAFWP.'

He took the bag and drooped even further. 'I tried to warn you, I really did.'

'Tried to…' She narrowed her eyes. 'What?'

'Well, well, well…' A man's voice, behind her.

Roberta turned and there was *Acting* Detective Chief Inspector Beardy Bloody Beattie, emerging from behind the tree. So not a *man's* voice: a wee prick's. He'd got himself a high-vis too, but it was one of the long ones and about three sizes too big, dwarfing his dumpy frame. Pot-bellied, slouchy, and useless, with a supply-teacher beard and hooded eyes. The kind of copper whose fighting suit had never seen a fight.

He curled his lip. 'If it isn't the late, great, *ex*-Detective Sergeant Roberta Steel.'

She squared her shoulders. 'Ex-Detective *Inspector*, you pube-faced dick-wobble.'

'Hmph... *I'll* take that.' Snatching the sandwich bag from Tufty's hands. 'Do you have any *idea* how much trouble officer Quirrel would be in if he gave this to the labs?'

Roberta went to snatch it back, but Beattie wheeched the bag away, stuffing it into an inside pocket.

'DNA tests cost *money*. And that money comes out of *my* budget. And you have *no* authority to spend it!'

'Give me back that bloody...'

'No.' Beattie danced away from her, around the back of Tufty, using him as a human shield. 'And there'll be no more of this "Queen Street Irregulars" nonsense! You're not a member of the force anymore, and you will *not* interfere with ongoing investigations! And any serving officer found helping you will face disciplinary action.' He gave Tufty a shove. 'Is that clear: *Constable* Quirrel.'

The wee loon's voice was flat as a week-old balloon. 'Yes, Acting DCI Beattie.'

A grin. Then Beattie pointed at Roberta. 'You think you're so *clever*, don't you? Trying to take over my cases. Well, *you're* not a police officer! *I* am.' Thumping a hand down on Tufty's shoulder. 'And unless you want to ruin your whole team's careers, you'll sod off, play crown bowls, and crochet toilet-roll holders – or whatever it is you OAPs do – and leave *policing* to the *professionals*!'

She glanced back at the Volvo for backup, but Harmsworth was sinking down in his seat, trying to disappear his lumpy self behind the dashboard. Out the line of fire.

Nose in the air and oozing triumph, Beattie buzzed himself through the smaller, officer-sized gate in the fence. And flounced away across the car park.

Roberta scowled after him, then turned and thumped Tufty. 'What the buggering hell were you playing at? You set me up!'

'I *tried* to warn you! Admiral Ackbar: "It's a trap!" How could you not know that? It's his only famous line in the whole— Ow!' Retreating out of hitting range.

'Next time just *say* it's a trap!'

'He was standing right there, when you called!' Jabbing a finger at the pavement next to himself. 'I put on a weird voice and everything. What was I supposed to do? And there won't *be* a next time. You heard him: "disciplinary action".' The finger came up to point at his own chest. '*Does not want* disciplinary action!'

They stood there, the only noise: the gallows drum of rain on her umbrella.

Then Tufty shook his head, sighed, and made for the gate.

'Fine. I'll ...' Roberta waved a hand about, 'see you Wednesday. The kids have sequined some arcane runes on my wizard hat.'

He paused, one hand on the keypad, sounding as if he'd just buried a beloved pet. 'Maybe it'd be best if you don't come round for a while.'

Bzzzzzzzzzzzzzzzzz.

Then slipped through the gate and scuffed off into the spotlit gloom.

Leaving her standing there in the rain, all on her own.

She sagged. 'Tufty?'

But he just kept going.

The drive home wasn't exactly full of happy chitter-chat. Instead, they sat in bleak silence as Harmsworth drew up to the kerb outside Roberta's home.

She forced a bit of fake cheer into her voice. 'Bloody Beardy Beattie, eh? Thinks he can throw his weight about. Lardy lump of poop that he is.' Giving Harmsworth's arm a playful punch. 'Like he's going to intimidate *you* guys! Ha!'

Harmsworth shifted in his seat, and for once it probably had nothing to do with the sand in his undergarments. Not saying anything.

'Right, Owen?'

'Riiiiiiight...' Looking down at his fingers.

'Cool.' She climbed from the passenger seat, grabbing her bag and brolly, because it was still dinging down. Looking back into the car. 'Same time tomorrow?'

He scrunched his shoulders, picking at the steering wheel. 'I can't tomorrow, I'm... I've got a *thing*. You know. Last minute ... thing.'

'Oh.' She puffed out her cheeks. 'Right.'

'Yeah.' Deep breath. 'OK. Well, I'd better be... You know.' Trying for the same faux cheeriness. 'Got to get this sand out my pork scratchings! Ha, ha, ha...'

Silence.

A hollow weight sank through Roberta's chest.

She nodded. 'Thanks for all your help today.' Then stepped back and closed the door.

Stood there in the rain as the Volvo pulled away.

Didn't even bother unfurling her brolly.

Just watched Harmsworth's scarlet taillights disappear into the night.

A deep sigh.

Then Roberta turned her back on the world and limped up the path. Let herself in and slumped against the door.

Dark in here.

Flipping the switch sent light blooming through the hallway, glinting off the framed photos. 'HELLO? SUSAN? MONSTERS?'

No reply.

'MR RUMMMMMMMPOLE? GENNNNNGHIS?'

But no wife, kids, cat, or dog came scampering up to greet her.

Half eight.

Where the hell *was* everybody?

The bag-for-life went on the sideboard, the umbrella in the stand by the front door, her jacket on its hook. Then she booted off her boots and slipped on her slippers.

Sagged there like a rag doll, grimacing at the ceiling.

They had to be *somewhere.*

Roberta scuffed through to the kitchen, turned the lights on, and scowled at the soggy apparition reflected in the patio doors – looking like a wet weekend in Rhynie.

No jumble of plates and mugs in here, but there *was* a note, sitting on the countertop:

Dear Robbie,

We've gone to Waterstones for that Book Event with JC Williams.

Jazz has scored us an invite to dinner with JC & her editor & publicist!

Got you a microwave lasagne – in fridge.

♥♥♥♥

Susan

Great.

A ready meal.

While *they* were off partying with publishing types, eating prawns and steak, and drinking buckets and buckets of wine…

Urgh.

She checked her phone, but instead of a slew of grovelling texts – apologising for grassing her up to Beattie – there was nothing from Tufty. Nothing from Harmsworth, either. Or Logan.

Nobody wanted or needed her…

Well, there was only one thing for it:

Roberta got out the whisky.

because things can always get
much, *much* worse…

4.01

The bedside clock glowed a gloomy 08:10 at Roberta, lying there like a big lump in the bed, buried beneath the duvet.

A thin sliver of grey seeped around the closed curtains, but it was still nearly dark in here. Not dark enough, though. So she pulled both of Susan's vacated pillows over her head, blocking it all out.

Could still hear the rain scrabbling against the window like rats.

The bedroom door creaked, then a soft voice cushioned its way across the room. *'Robbie? Are you awake?'* Susan.

'No.'

The mattress shifted as Susan sat on it, and a hand explored beneath the pillow fort, warm and gentle against Roberta's forehead. *'You still upset?'* A hmmph… *'Which is a silly question* – obviously *you're still upset, or you wouldn't be sulking in here with the curtains shut.'*

'I'm no' sulking. I'm … *tired.*'

'Oh, Robbie.' A long, sad sigh. *'I'm sure they didn't—'*

'Don't you *dare* defend those traitorous bastards!'

'I wasn't going to.' Could hear the smile in her voice now. *'I've been putting up with your sulks for* two decades, *Roberta Alexander Steel* – and *your hangovers – I know how they work.'* The hand moved down to cup Roberta's face. *'There's plenty of stinky cheese in the fridge and pickled onions in the pantry. If*

you're going to make a bacon butty, there's a pack of streaky that's near its sell-by date, use that.'

There was a lot to be said for marrying a good woman.

'Is it smoked?'

'Of course *it's smoked. We're not animals.'* The hand disappeared, and Susan's weight lifted from the mattress. *'I can't take Genghis today, so make sure he gets a good walk, OK? OK.'* The bedroom door creaked again. *'Love you.'*

Buried beneath her pillowy grave, Roberta grimaced. 'Glad somebody does…'

The wind had died down a bit, but it looked as if that rain was settling in for the day.

Standing at the patio doors, Roberta took another bite of her overstuffed butty – all smoky and savoury and salty and buttery and sweet and spicy. Because the trick to defeating a hangover was mixing a good dollop of hot sauce in with your ketchup. And using a whole packet of streaky bacon didn't hurt.

Genghis Khat sat at her beslippered feet, staring up in rapt adoration – hoping for a piggy windfall.

No sign of Mr Rumpole, but then he wasn't a dafty, *or* a mooch, so he'd probably be curled up somewhere warm and dry.

Couldn't blame him.

Roberta swirled the last dregs of coffee, then necked it. Third mug since getting up twenty minutes ago, so everything was beginning to vibrate. Didn't help with the overwhelming crush of ennui, though…

And Genghis still gazed at her as if she were some sort of bacon-dispensing goddess.

'They all turn on you in the end, little man. Every last one of the ungrateful *bastards* will line up to stab you in the back. And the front. And the sides too, if they can get away with it.'

She put on her patented Genghis voice: growly, but high-pitched – like a strangled weasel. 'They're a bunch of womble-funting spudge-nuggets right enough. You're the *best*, Mummy Steel, and they should all snadge off and *die*!'

A bite. A chew. Then back to being Roberta again. 'That's a little harsh, Genghis. But I think you're right: we *should* kill them all.'

All growly: 'Before we go on our murderous rampage, can I have some bacon?'

Normal: 'How could I say no to that angelic wee face?'

Crunch, crunch, crunch...

'...it is as we feared, Inspector: the Whitechapel Werewolf has indeed, once more, struck!'

Roberta slouched on the couch, with Genghis curled up beside her, noodling about on her phone as the TV wanged away to itself in the background.

Sitting there, sending texts out into the aether. Even though, as Genghis said, they were all a bunch of womble-funting spudge-nuggets:

> Come on, Veronica, don't tell me you're scared of a wanky bum-lump like Beattie!
>
> The man has the intellectual capacity of a tumble drier's lint trap.

SEND.

'This foe we face is a man possessed of an all-consuming rage, Meadowcroft, so how is it that he so readily escapes our grasp?'

So far, not one of the buggers had replied.

She scrolled through her outgoing messages.

> Hi Barrett, haven't heard from you for ages. How are you getting on without me? They make you a full sergeant yet?

'Perhaps, Inspector, it is because he is aided and abetted by some third party as yet unknown?'

Next:

> I think you're wise to keep your head down, Owen. Make that halfwit, hairy-faced titwank think he's won, when we all know he's just a massive tosser.

'Someone for whom the death of these poor souls is neither a tragedy nor an inconvenience, but an outright boon?'

And right at the bottom:

> What the hell were you thinking, clyping on me to bloody Beattie?!?
>
> That farching twunt's had it in for me for years.
>
> HOW COULD YOU HELP HIM!?!
>
> You two-faced, quisling, traitorous, wee dick!

Yeah... Maybe that last one to Tufty had been a bit harsh. Even if he *did* deserve it.

'You may be right, Meadowcroft, but who in this benighted maze of filth and horror could benefit from crimes as grotesque as these?'

She shut her phone and harrumphed. 'Starting to think you're on to something, Genghis: we *should* embark on a murderous rampage, and...'

Oh no.

Roberta coughed, spluttering as the smell truly hit – as if a slurry tanker had just collided with a ruptured septic tank – peeling the wallpaper, making the rug curl, blistering the leather sofas, burning the hair in her nostrils as the air fizzed…

Genghis grinned up at her, tail thumping against the cushions.

'Gaaaaahhhh…' She pulled the neck of her top up over her nose and mouth, flailing both hands about trying to waft the stench away. 'No more bacon for you, you stinky wee monster!'

Five to five, and *still* no reply to any of her texts.

So Roberta stood in her barely furnished incident room, scowling at the murderboard for Operation Demogorgon. Squeezing Boris Johnson's head.

He was looking a bit worse-for-wear now, like an undead Marty Feldman.

Pkongk-glonk.

Tempting to tear it all down. And the other cases too. Rip the whole lot off the walls and stick it in the recycling. After all, now she was *officially* frozen out of everything, what was the point?

Pkongk-glonk.

With Genghis banished to the back garden – where his stinky bum-farts could cause the least damage to human health – Mr Rumpole had appeared, commandeering the room's only chair. Doing cat yoga as he had a bit of a wash. Keeping half an eye on proceedings.

Pkongk-glonk.

'See, Mr Rumpole, trouble is: none of the buggers at Divisional Headquarters have a *clue* what they're doing. Without me to lead the way, they're gonna screw the whole thing up.'

She put on her cat voice, sleek and refined. 'You're probably correct, Mother, but *what* can you do if none of the aforementioned idiots will talk to you?'

True.

Roberta frowned at the collection of photos and notes and lines of red ribbon.

Pkongk-glonk. Pkongk-glonk. Pkongk-glonk.

Normal: 'It would help if we knew who the victim is. Was.'

Mr Rumpole: 'But you *know* who she is. That's why you wanted Megan Lockheart's hairbrush tested for DNA.'

Normal: 'That's not "*knowing*", that's suspecting. Different thing.'

Mr Rumpole: 'Well, for the purposes of this thought experiment, let's assume our Body-In-The-Bin *is* Megan Lockheart.'

Normal: 'All right, Mr Rumpole, we'll do it your way.'

Pkongk-glonk. Pkongk-glonk. Pkongk-glonk. Pkongk-glonk.

She narrowed her eyes, head on one side. 'The *obvious* suspect is Sir Norman Wandering-Hands Fordyce. He has his greasy way with her, she gets pregnant.'

High-pitched, breathless, girly voice: 'Oh, Sir Norman, isn't it *wonderful*? Our love has been *blessed* with a *miracle* child!'

Mr Rumpole: 'But there's no way he can accept that. If his wife finds out, she'll sue for divorce, and he'll lose half his fortune. Just for fornicating with some *stupid* little girl who should've been on the pill in the first place? She'll have to get an abortion.'

Girly: 'But I couldn't *possibly* kill *our baby*, Sir Norman!'

Mr Rumpole: 'Then she's left him no option. She simply *has* to die.'

Hmm…

Roberta moved closer to the wall, till the photo of their victim's skeletal remains filled the world. 'Bit *dark*, isn't it? Killing Megan and her unborn—'

Ding-buzz.

Roberta dropped Boris Johnson's head and lunged for her phone.

But it wasn't Lund, or Harmsworth, or Barrett, or even Traitorous Tufty.

LOGAN:

> I heard about Beattie.
>
> You OK?
>
> The man sucks lumpy farts from Satan's hairy bumhole.

Her shoulders sank a bit.

But at least *someone* was still speaking to her.

She poked out a reply:

> Course I'm OK.
>
> It's not like I'm going to let some halfwit like Beattie ruin my day, is it?
>
> Screw him. I'm retired anyway.

SEND.

And her shoulders drooped a little more.

Mr Rumpole: 'You should tell him, Mother.'

Roberta gave herself a shake. 'Don't be daft. I'm supposed to be the strong one, remember?'

Mr Rumpole: 'You *do* realise you had a conversation with that halfwit *stinky* Yorkshire terrier this morning, don't you?'

'Oh ... shut up.' Thumbs working on another text:

> How you getting on with your Ripper?
>
> Going to send me those notes he wrote?
>
> My Consulting Detective genius is still available at very reasonable rates...?

It was worth a try, anyway.

SEND.

Mr Rumpole jumped down from the seat, stretched, then sauntered over to scratch at the door. 'If you're going to be *rude* I shall take my leave of you, and see if I can't find some *mice* to torture and consume instead.' A sniff. 'If you're lucky I shall bring you the head and gallbladder.'

She bent down and stroked his beautiful fuzzy head. 'Mummy's little serial killer.' Then opened the door.

He trotted off – fluffy tail in the air, waving like a plume of smoke.

At least it'd stopped raining.

Ding-buzz.

With any luck, that would be an invitation to join the investigation in Dundee – and Detective Inspector Beardy Beattie could go stuff a pie up his bunghole.

It wasn't Roberta's day, though.

SUSAN:

> Heading home soon.
>
> What a day!!!
>
> Did you remember to walk Genghis?

Sod.

Erm...

> Of course I did. Paragon of virtue, me!

SEND.

Right, better grab the wee stinker's lead, and get it done before Susan got back.

Flipping heck...

Roberta hobbled along the pavement, moving tortoise-slow and getting slower. Because this heavy-arsed bag-for-life was killing her, and Genghis kept pulling at his lead – eager to get home now he'd piddled on nearly every lamppost, tree, and car tyre between home, Fountainhall Road, and back.

To be honest, tottering all the way to the off-licence had probably not been the *best* of ideas.

And yes, it would probably be easier if her walking stick, the lead, and clinking bag weren't all in the same hand, but she needed the other one free to hold her phone.

Logan's voice worried in her ear. *'Far as we can tell, the latest one isn't.'*

'Isn't … isn't … what?' Limp, shamble, pech, heech.

'A real Ripper victim. The MO's all different.'

Why did her sodding street have to be so *long*? House was still miles away.

'Are you sure you're OK? You're breathing like a sex offender.'

Lumber, lurch, puff, pant. 'Fit as … as a fiddle, … me.'

A fiddle on the brink of a frunking heart attack.

A weird whooshing noise had started about two streets ago, pulsing and whumping, not quite in time with her steps.

'I mean, how screwed-up does someone have to be to look at a string of horrific *murders and think, "Yeah, I fancy having a go at that!"'*

'Uh-huh…'

Strange little black dots followed the noise – swirling around the edges of the road and houses. *Whoosh, whump.*

Logan sighed. *'Starting to think we're never going to catch this bastard.'*

And on she slogged, sweat dribbling between her shoulder blades to soak into her bra.

Whoosh, whump.

At least she could see the end of the road now.

Like a sodding mirage between the dripping trees.

Calling to her.

Whoosh, whump.

A final resting place to lay her knackered bones.

They could bury her between Stalin and Old Faithful.

Whoosh, whump, whoosh, whump, whoosh, whump.

'You still there?'

Barely.

'Uh-huh.'

'You should get yourself an exercise bike or something.'

'Feel free … to sod … off.'

Whoosh, Whump.

'Might do you some good: from one previously-blown-up person to another.' He huffed out a breath. *'Don't suppose there's any point telling you to go easy on Tufty? Poor wee loon was only doing his best.'*

'He's a … traitorous … wee … turd.'

'Yeah, thought as much. If they ever make "Being Thrawn" an Olympic sport, you're a shoo-in.' Another sigh. *'Anyway, got to go: briefing's in ten, and this new Superintendent they've inflicted on us is doing my balls in.'*

WHOOSH, Whump.

Someone must've tied breeze blocks to her ankles in the off-licence, cos no way her shoes weighed this much when she put them on. 'Uh-huh.'

'Catch you later, Beattie hater.' And Logan was gone.

WHOOSH, WHUMP.

Roberta stuck the phone in her pocket and collapsed against the nearest tree, forehead pressed into the bark.

WHOOSH, WHUMP. WHOOSH, WHUMP.

Wheezing and coughing.

WHOOSH, WHUMP. WHOOSH, WHUMP. WHOOSH, Whump. Whoosh, Whump. Whoosh, whump…

Staying there, until the world stopped swirling.

Maybe Logan was right about the exercise bike?

Had to be better than *this*, anyway.

Finally, the noises faded, and the twirling black dots withered away.

Pfff…

Come on: nearly there.

She straightened up and lumbered homeward.

Past the neighbours, and thence to Casa Steel-Wallace.

The Big Car was back, parked in front of her poor sticky old MX-5.

'Should've … called Susan … and got her … to give me … a sodding lift … *back*!' Wheeze, hiss, rattle, pant.

Strangled weasel voice: 'But … but Mummy Steel, … then it … wouldn't be … a nice … surprise!'

Cough. Gasp. Puff.

'Oh, cause … cause me having … a sodding … heart attack … will be a delightful … shock…'

Roberta struggled down the path to the front door. Unlocked it. And stumbled inside. Thunked the thing closed, and slumped against the wall. Eyes shut, lungs burning, legs aching, head throbbing, little dog whimpering…

She let him off his lead and away he scampered – making for the closed living-room door. Gazing up at it, then at her, then the door, then her, with his gob hanging open and tail wagging.

Roberta hung up her coat and got into her slippers, then dragged herself over there to open the door for him.

Only, as she reached for the handle, a burst of laughter came from inside, followed by voices. Too muffled to make out the actual words, but it didn't *sound* like the TV. It sounded like visitors.

Which was the last thing anyone needed with a sweaty bra.

Mind you, maybe it was Lund? Or Harmsworth? Or maybe even Barrett, come to see how she was getting on?

Course it was.

Or maybe *all three*: turned up with a few bottles of wine and a selection of fancy crisps, to show how much they'd missed her since she'd retired. And complain about everything going to hell. And Beattie being a tit. And Tufty being a greasy treacherous wee shite. And how Police Scotland simply couldn't cope without her…

Grinning in the hall mirror, Roberta wiped her shiny face. Straightened her collar. Then opened the door and followed the wee man as he scrambled into the living room.

And stopped dead.

Because it wasn't Lund and Harmsworth and Barrett. It was that sinister prick, Superintendent Rifkind, and his wardrobe-sized sidekick, DI Kensington, from Organised Crime and Counter Terrorism.

The Mob Squad.

4.02

The smile died on Roberta's lips.

Susan had taken the couch nearest the fire, sitting opposite Rifkind.

He was in a red tartan tie today and a black suit.

Kensington loomed by the fireplace, sporting the same outfit he'd worn when they'd visited the hospital. And like last time, all he was missing were the bolts through his neck…

Susan must've broken out the good tea set, because they all had delicate china cups and saucers. The matching pot, milk jug, and sugar bowl sat on the coffee table, alongside a plate stacked with chocolate biscuits.

Don't know what they'd been talking about, but Susan was chuckling away to herself.

And they all turned to smile at Roberta.

Except for Kensington, of course – grim-faced wank that he was.

Genghis scooted across the rug to Susan, yipping and bouncing and wagging. Got his ears rubbed for his trouble.

'Robbie: look who's here to see you.' Fussing away at Genghis. 'Who's Mummy's little man? You are. *Yes* you are!'

Rifkind stood. 'How's the head, Roberta? I must say you're looking *well*. Retirement suits you.'

Liar. Especially given how flushed and sweaty she was.

Roberta scowled at Susan. 'What are *they* doing here?'

'I was just telling your lovely wife about the Finnish Ambassador's penchant for "sauna diplomacy", and the American official who thought they were all getting naked for an *entirely* different reason.'

Susan giggled. 'Oh, Robbie, he'd taken *two* Viagra!'

Roberta pulled her shoulders back. 'You came all this way just to tell my wife dirty stories? And there was me thinking Organised Crime and Counter Terrorism had no sense of humour.'

A kind smile. 'Wonderful as the delightful Susan is, we're actually here to talk to *you*, Roberta.'

Shock fucking horror.

'On or off the record?'

Rifkind bent over to ply Susan with that auld-mannie charm. 'Susan, my darling, could I possibly bother you for a mashed banana on buttered toast? Sorry to be a nuisance, but I'm supposed to keep an eye on my blood sugar, and I've been a bit "headless chicken" today.' Wincing. 'I know it's a pain.'

'Oh, *of course*, not at all.' She popped Genghis back on the rug. 'We have a partner at the firm who's type-one. I'll just be a tick.' Then bustled off.

'You're *so* kind.' The smile widened. 'No hurry, take your time!' Then, as soon as the door closed, the charming old fart act disappeared – replaced by something far sharper. 'I understand you met someone interesting yesterday, Roberta.'

Keeping one eye on the lump by the mantelpiece, she thudded onto the couch, taking Susan's place. 'I meet lots of people.'

Kensington folded his arms. 'Don't play cute; answer the question.'

'This *particular* "someone interesting",' Rifkind settled back into his seat, 'would have been at Graeme Anderson's *pied-à-terre*. Near Newmachar? I believe you paid a visit, with one Detective Constable Owen Harmsworth.'

She scowled back. 'How do *you* know where I've been?'

'Hoy!' Kensington bared his teeth. 'Answer the question!'

Two could play the snarling game. Roberta stuck two fingers up for good measure. 'You think you scare me, Princess? I've flushed scarier shites than you.'

He opened his mouth to answer back, but Rifkind got there first:

'Now, now, Matthew: don't be rude to Roberta.' Tutting. 'In her own home too.'

The big lump glared at her, then sniffed and took a delicate sip from his bone-china cup – little finger extended.

Rifkind sat forward. 'Let's just say it's our job to know where certain pieces are on the chessboard. How they move; where they go.' He pursed his lips, as if choosing his next words with care. 'Now, I know you had a somewhat … *chequered* career at NE Division, but people tell me you actually care about what happens. Right versus wrong. Good versus evil. Justice may be an old-fashioned concept in this post-truth world, but *some of us* still believe in it.'

'Oh aye?'

'Which is why I think you'll do the right thing and help us.'

She snorted. 'And what's in it for me?'

That made the old bugger blink. '"In it"?'

'For *me*.' Letting that sink in for a couple of breaths. 'As a sandy-crotched lynchpin of mine once said: "Only a fool would police Aberdeenshire for free."'

'I see.' He raised an eyebrow. 'Well, it's highly irregular, but what would you *want*?'

'A favour.' Genghis leapt up beside her, burying his pointy head in her lap as she made herself comfortable. 'I'm guessing you don't mean Hector The Defector: Anderson's house-slash-rent-boy with the white-nationalist tattoos. Which leaves "Stephanie" – and a fiver says that's no' her real name. Mockney accent thick enough to tarmac drives with? Speaks … *Russian* – I'm guessing – like a native?'

Rifkin's other eyebrow joined the first.

Bingo.

Roberta smiled, stroking Genghis's scruffy fur – giving Rifkind and Kensington her best Ernst Stavro Blofeld. 'Which makes me wonder why you and Lurch here have such a stiffy for Graeme Anderson. Hmmm…' Stroke, stroke, stroke.

What was it Tufty said about the explosion?

Right: 'A wee birdie told me, the detonator on that car bomb was called a "Kremlin Kaboom".'

Wait a minute…

Her eyes narrowed. 'The little *bastards*!'

Rifkind applauded, beaming like a proud parent. 'I have to say how *refreshing* it is to see a police officer *actually* put all those disparate pieces together.'

Which should've sounded horribly patronising, but he looked so genuinely chuffed it came off as a compliment.

Didn't do anything to quench the fire growing in the back of Roberta's head, though. Spreading through her skull in scorching waves. 'It was *them*, wasn't it. Graeme Bloody Anderson bombed his own press conference, so he could pose as a hero and everyone would vote for him!'

Startled by all this, Genghis hopped down to the rug and spun around a few times, growling at his own bum.

She lurched to her feet, fists clenched. 'The fuckers blew me up!'

Pink flushed through Kensington's cheeks. 'Language!'

This time she only gave him the one finger. 'That's why the car bomb detonated so far away from Anderson's house: he didn't want to damage his bloody paintwork!'

Rifkind tilted his head to one side. 'Which means…?'

'He's working with the Russians. And those manky Kremlin *wankers* put a racist *prick* in Parliament. And I bet he's not the first. Probably with more pricks to follow.'

'I couldn't possibly comment.'

Which meant 'yes'.

Roberta banged her walking stick against the floor, setting Genghis growling. 'So *arrest* him!'

Rifkind poured himself a top-up of tea. Adding a splosh of milk, stirring it in with one of Susan's grandma's silver spoons. Taking his time. 'Some people think foreign interests have their sticky little fingers in every single one of our political parties. Russians, Israelis, Americans, Chinese… Even the French. Funnelling money, here – advice and social media campaigns, there. Bot networks. Influencers. Opposition research. And plain, good-old-fashioned *blackmail*.' A wink. 'You'd be surprised what you can achieve with a hidden video camera and two under-age girls in a Moscow hotel room.'

Kensington sniffed. 'Allegedly.'

'And then there's the *sabotage*, the arson, the hacking, abductions, assassinations. Polonium tea and Novichok on door handles.' Rifkind shrugged. 'You see, Roberta, what everyone fails to understand is that *we* are at *war*. We've been at war for years and years. Decades. We're all just too polite to talk about it.' A sip of non-radioactive Tetley. 'And in the interests of the war effort, I'm going to ask you *very nicely* to leave Graeme Anderson and his little friends to me.'

What?

'HE BLEW ME UP!' Flinging a hand in the direction of Aberdeen Royal Infirmary. 'I spent a month and a half in hospital! I've got a three-inch titanium plate in my fucking skull, because of him!'

Kensington stepped forwards. 'I *said*, watch your language!'

This time he got both middle fingers.

His jaw clenched.

Roberta's fists tightened.

Because if this massive lump of steamed shite thought he was too big to get her boot *right* up his—

The living-room door swung open, and Susan appeared, carrying a tray with a slice of buttered-and-banana'd toast – cut diagonally, to impress – on a nice serving dish, beside a small orange ramekin and a couple of napkins. 'Sorry that took so long.' She handed the tray to Rifkind. 'There's sea salt in the pinch pot, in case you don't like it too sweet.'

He beamed. 'Ah, lovely Susan, you are *too* kind.' He took the toast and sprinkled it with salt. Bit. Chewed. Eyes closed. 'Mmmmm... *Perfection.*'

'Oh, I'm *so*...' She frowned at Roberta. Then at Kensington. Then at Genghis, standing there with his hackles up. 'Is everything OK?'

Silence.

Rifkind took another bite. Dabbed at his mouth with a napkin. 'That rather remains to be seen. Doesn't it, Roberta?'

More silence.

'Aye, it does.'

4.03

Roberta lay flat on her back under the duvet, one hand massaging her forehead, while the other held the phone to her ear. Trying not to move too much, because the post-whisky malaise is a harsh mistress. And vomiting wasn't as much fun as young people thought. 'Of course I'm up and doing. Why would I no' be up and doing? It's…' She checked the alarm-clock-radio. 'Five past eleven on a lovely Wednesday morning.'

The useless curtains were still drawn, but that didn't stop the morning's miserable light from spilling in around the edges. Making the room grey and gloomy.

'Oh, Robbie.' Susan groaned in that *disappointed* way she had. *'You've been moping around the house for days! You need some fresh air. Go do something* fun *for a change.'*

'I have *no'* been moping. And it's only been one day.' Well, *two* if you counted today. Two days since Rifkind and his pet gorilla turned up to tell her that Graeme Anderson almost got her killed in a fake terrorist attack. 'And I'm no'—'

'How about I take tomorrow morning off, and we can have a lazy breakfast and play a round of golf? Your swing's getting so much better, *it's—'*

'I'm up and doing!'

A long-suffering sigh. *'Has Tufty been in touch?'*

'It's unethical to threaten people with golf. Against my European Convention on Human Whatnots.'

'Oh, Robbie – talk *to him! Apologise. Send him a muffin basket. Make this right!'*

'Apologise?' She dropped her hand and glared at the ceiling. '*He's* the one screwed *me* over!'

Susan broke out the disapproving tut. *'You put him in an impossible position. What's he supposed to do; he's only little.'*

Hard to hide the whine in her voice. '*I'm* only little.'

'No, you're not. You're big. Certainly bigger than him. So be the grown-up and say you're sorry. *Maybe he'll let you back into his role-playing thingy? You'd like that, wouldn't you?'*

Urgh…

Roberta pulled the pillows over her head again. 'Life was *much* better when I was ordering people about. Being retired sucks arse!'

Why was sewing such a fiddly sod of a thing?

Roberta sat at the dining-room table, surrounded by plastic boxes, tongue sticking out the side of her mouth as she poked the needle through the felt, then her wizard's hat, then back through the felt again.

Should've used superglue, or some bollocks like that. Be done by now.

But that would be cheating.

And the path to redemption was paved with fiddly bollocks…

She tied off the final stitch and sat back to admire her hard work.

The lobsters looked OK. A little wonky maybe, but that was because she'd made them herself, cut from a scrap of red felt with the big scissors you weren't supposed to run with.

At least Mr Rumpole seemed to approve – supervising

from the far end of the table, making schlurping noises as he washed his tummy.

Wonder if her hat needed more sequins? Or—

Her phone *buzzzzz*ed, skittering on the table's protective mat, then launched into 'Take Your Mama'.

That would be Tufty, calling to say that everything was forgiven and of course she should come to the game tonight, they'd be lost without her, and the whole party was looking forward to…

But it was Harmsworth's name, glowing in the middle of the screen.

Pish.

Hope this wasn't the Stovies Lecture.

She answered anyway. 'Hello?'

The sound of a busy room burbled from her phone – lots of voices in an echoey space. Then Harmsworth whispered over the top. Barely audible through the racket. *'You need to turn your TV on: BBC One.'*

Yeah, cos *that* didn't sound suspicious.

'Why?'

'Lynchpin, remember?'

OK…

Roberta plonked her wizard's hat on her head, stood, and limped through to the living room. Grabbed the remote and pointed it at the television.

It took a couple of moments for the set-top box to warm up, then a big bald TV chef appeared, wanging on about mixing suet through the mince for his burgers. Because Roberta hadn't had enough mince-talk for one week/lifetime.

She changed the channel. 'What's happened?'

BBC One filled the screen. A middle-aged bloke in a too-tight suit – buttoned up, so the centre of his chest looked like a bumhole – waved a hand at a map of the UK. '*…return of* *those unseasonably high temperatures across most of the country…'* Even though a thick band of rain covered all of Scotland and Northern Ireland.

She settled into the couch. 'And you're whispering *why*?'

'Because we're not supposed to talk to you, remember? The wee loon got cranked through the mangle yesterday, and even I *got a shouting at. Mind you, I didn't look like I was going to cry afterwards, but then I'm made of sterner stuff.'*

Still whispering, though.

Mr Bumhole-Suit turned his back on the map. *'…returning to normal by the end of the week. So don't put away your wellies and brollies just yet.'* Winsome smile. Chuckle. *'Back to you, Miriam.'*

The picture cut to a glamorous older woman, in a blue suit and modest cleavage. Sensible haircut. Standing in front of her generic studio backdrop. *'Thanks, Rob. That's all from us; now it's time for the news and weather, wherever you are.'*

The screen launched into the BBC News ident, in all its horrible pulsating scarlet glory. Like a colonoscopy-themed rave.

'How is he: Tufty?'

'Just off nightshift, when I got in this morning. Don't know what Pine and Beattie said to him, but you could grill toast on the poor wee sod's lugs.'

Yeah… Maybe Susan was right.

On screen, the Throbbing Colon of News gave way to a bland studio, featuring an attractive woman sitting behind a curved desk thing. She had shoulder-length dark hair, and a matching pair of beauty spots – one on each cheek. Heavyset, but just enough to ensure exciting jiggling at bedtime. A NRILF.

She smiled at the camera. *'Good afternoon. Here's the Scottish headlines.'* Pause for effect. *'Three people have been stabbed in what police are calling a "terror attack" on Glasgow's Sauchiehall Street.'*

Harmsworth hissed out a breath. *'Good job Tufty's off till the weekend now, cos he looks like someone drove over him with a threshing machine.'*

Yeah… Maybe Susan was right.

'The east-coast line remains shut following yesterday's storm, as crews battle to remove fallen trees and debris.' Another pause. *'Government minister denies shoplifting from Edinburgh sex shop.'* And again. *'But first: Aberdeen.'*

An inset graphic appeared – showing the lay-by on the A96, where they'd found the Body-In-The-Bin. Or what was left of her. A couple of patrol cars were parked up, along with the Scenes van, and a couple of characters in white SOC suits, picking their way along the railway tracks in the background. That would be Lund and Harmsworth, doing their fingertip search.

'Police have made a breakthrough in the murder of a young woman, as the victim's remains are identified after DNA testing. We go live *to Aberdeen.'*

The media briefing room at DHQ filled the screen. They'd set up a small stage – with a covered table, four seats, a bouquet of microphones, and one of those foldable exhibition-stand backings covered in little Police Scotland logos and adverts for Crimestoppers.

Mr Lockheart sat behind the table, on the outside left, blinking back tears in an ill-fitting suit. Beside him was an earth-mothery blonde, whose curly hair hung lank around her shell-shocked face. That would be Megan's mum. Next: the Arch Wank, Acting DCI Beardy Beattie, who couldn't seem to decide if he was looking grim or smug, today. And last, but definitely least, the Media Liaison Officer, AKA: PC Nigel Sweeny – a worried-looking bloke, with an outsized nose and massive chin, who was one hunch short of whacking a crocodile with a stick and screeching 'That's the way you do it!'

A pair of large flatscreen TVs flanked the stage, displaying yet more Police Scotland logos. In case anyone had confused this for a car boot sale.

Beattie shuffled his papers. *'Good afternoon.'*

A weird pre-echo came from Roberta's phone, which meant Harmsworth must've been at the briefing. That explained all the whispering.

'Earlier this morning we were finally able to identify the remains discovered in a lay-by off the A96 as missing twenty-one-year-old, Megan Lockheart, from Westhill.'

A portrait of Megan appeared on both monitors. It wasn't the one Tufty had plucked from the internet, or the one Davey printed on his missing-person poster, but a professional head-and-shoulder shot. And she was *painfully* pretty.

At which point, no amount of blinking would keep Mr Lockheart's tears in check. He wiped them away with a trembling hand.

Roberta sat back. 'Buggering hell…'

'You were right.'

'That's no sodding comfort, Owen.'

Beattie waited for the press to settle down. *'Megan was a popular young woman who had many friends and accomplishments, and our sympathies are with her family at this terrible time.'*

'Hold on.' Roberta hit 'RECORD' on the remote, followed by 'MUTE' – leaving Beattie flapping his gums in silence.

Harmsworth sniffed. *'Of course, according to Beattie,* he's *the one responsible for figuring all this out. Apparently, you and I had nothing to do with it.'* A bitter harrumph. *'With the risk of sounding like The Idiot Tufty: Beattie's a snudge-wadging snidge.'*

And then some.

'Doesn't really matter.' Roberta puffed her cheeks out, wincing as Mr Lockheart struggled his way through a short pre-written statement, wiping his eyes every couple of seconds while his poor wife sat there in some sort of horrified trance.

'What *matters* is they finally know what happened to their poor wee girl.'

'Yeah.' A sigh. *'Kinda leaves one big question hanging though, doesn't it: who killed her?'*

'*Two* questions, Owen: who killed her, and who got her pregnant. And are they the same person.'

'That's three questions.'

She frowned at the screen. 'And do you want to guess who's top of my suspect list?'

Mr Lockheart finally got to the end of his statement. He lowered his eyes, then his head, sagging there as if someone had just ... switched him off.

A barrage of flash photography was reflected in his bald head. Because nothing sold papers like raw agonising grief.

Beattie reached out and squeezed Mr Lockheart's shoulder.

Wasn't expecting a gesture of *humanity* from the bearded tit. Didn't think he had it in him.

Harmsworth cleared his throat. *'Yeah... About that...'*

Oh, for God's sake.

Roberta slumped back on the couch, free hand covering her eyes. 'Owen! What did you do?'

'Well, I had *to tell him, didn't I? It's a murder investigation.'*

On her TV: the Media Liaison Officer silently threw the briefing open for questions. On the phone: everyone shouted over one another. Barracking to get the first juicy soundbite.

Even Harmsworth had to raise his voice. *'We're mobbing out to Fordyce House later: just in time for the six o'clock news. A pair of OSU teams; Dog Units; flashing lights; a marquee; not one, but* two *forensic teams in the full Smurf get-up. Making a big dramatic thing out of it for the cameras.'* Snort. *'You'd think we were bringing down Pablo Escobar.'*

'Seriously?'

'I would've done it on the QT, myself, but what do I know? I'm

only the smartest person on the team. I'm sure Beattie *knows* much *better than* me.'

A major operation, organised by Acting Detective Chief Inspector Beardy Bollock-Face Beattie. No way *that* could be a complete and utter *cocking* disaster…

Bloody Beardy Bloody Beattie…

Roberta sploshed her sponge into the bucket of warm soapy water and hauled it out again. Slapped it onto the MX-5's sticky, filthy bonnet. Scrubbing and scowling.

How *dare* the fat hairy bastard ruin things.

Come between her and her Queen Street Irregulars?

Splosh. Slap. Sending a *froomph* of bubbles up into the chilly afternoon air.

Half an hour she'd been at this, and the car was just as manky as when she'd started. And she was soaked – all down her front and up to her elbows.

Scrub, scrub, scrub.

Picking on the wee loon!

Which was inex-sodding-cusable.

No one picked on Tufty but *her.*

Splosh. Slap. Scrub.

And she only did it to toughen him up and help him learn. So turd-snudgers like Beattie wouldn't take advantage of him.

She was like a *big sister* to that boy.

Beattie was lucky she didn't limp over there and punch him right on his big fat beardy nose.

Scrub, scrub, scrub, scrub-scrub-scrub.

Hauling in a deep breath and bellowing it out: 'AAAAAAA-AAAAAAAAAAAAARGH!'

On the other side of the road, one of the neighbours

averted his gaze and sped up – getting out of there before she popped.

Got a good sodding mind to do it.

She hurled her sponge into the bucket, sending up a *sploosh* of grubby water.

Yeah, why not?

What the hell did she have to lose?

Call a taxi, take a ride down to DHQ, call the greasy incompetent *twunt* out, and BANG! Right in the face. Break his bastarding nose.

Serve him right!

Roberta kicked the bucket over, turned, and hobble-stomped back into the house…

She limped down the stairs – showered, scrubbed, and suited. Because, if you were going to twat an acting detective chief inspector, you might as well look your best.

Roberta shot her cuffs, checking herself in the hall mirror.

Good enough.

'Let's do this.'

Her Genghis voice growled in agreement. 'That's the ticket, Mummy Steel! Let's go fuck that fucking fucker up!'

'Damn straight.'

Then Mr Rumpole chipped in, sleek and refined. 'What a *great* idea, Mother. Assaulting a police officer? There's *no way* that could lead to legal repercussions! Maybe you'll even get to pay Beattie damages? You'll like that, won't you: your hard-earned cash in his bearded little pocket, while he plays the martyr?'

She scowled at her reflection. 'Shut up.'

Genghis: 'Yeah! Shut up!' Bark-bark-barking at the mirror. 'Grrrrrrrrrrrrrrrrrrr!'

Mr Rumpole: 'There's a *reason* revenge isn't served hot.'

Silence settled in on the hall.

The Roberta in the mirror's shoulders drooped.

Then the real thing sagged back against the wall and grimaced at the ceiling. 'Starting to think Susan's right. Maybe being cooped up in here all day *is* making me round-the-twisty.'

Mr Rumpole: 'Well, *I* could've told you that.'

Which made her smile.

But it faded.

'Yeah… I've got to stop doing that.'

Didn't change the fact that her Mr Rumpole voice was right, though: punching Beattie wasn't going to fix anything. Fun though it might be.

Pfff…

And if Susan was right about the whole round-the-twisty thing, she was probably right about Tufty too.

The muffled blare of a car horn sounded outside, and when Roberta opened the front door, there was her taxi – ready to whisk her away to Divisional Headquarters and Beattie's oh-so-punchable face.

She locked up and limped down the path, opened the passenger door and leaned in.

Her driver looked as if someone had crossed an orangutan with a turnip, sitting there in a shirt and tie that seemed to be cutting off all the blood to his sideburns. A nod. 'Aye, aye. Polis station, is it?'

'Change of plan.' She slipped into the front seat. 'We've got a couple of stops to make.'

The taxi pulled up outside Martin House: twelve storeys of grey with added grey on top.

Each flat had its own wee balcony, but it was a miserly affair, not best suited to a dreich Aberdonian Wednesday in October. Unless you enjoyed chilblains and frostbite.

For some weird reason, the ground floor was smaller than all the others, so the whole structure seemed to perch, uncomfortably, on concrete box pillars. Onto which someone had spray painted a big hairy willy.

Roberta paid her extortionate fare – so much for the ex-cop discount – with a fair amount of bad grace and muttering, then hobbled in through the building's entrance, struggling under the weight of two bulging carrier bags.

Into the lift.

And up to the sixth floor.

Those pot plants needed a water.

She dumped her bags outside Tufty's flat, and pressed the 'BRIDGE' button. This time it was 'Flight Of The Sorcerer' that twanged out as she partially collapsed against the door, breathing hard. Because there'd been a *lot* of hurpling about in the last half hour, and those bags weighed a ton. And about £74.30.

No reply from inside, so she set the intercom banjoing again – sticking a finger over the door's spy hole, just in case the boy was going to be a dick about—

'I know it's you.'

She took her finger off. 'Then open … the door.'

'No. Go away: I'm asleep.'

Urgh…

He was going to make her do the full humble-pie spiel, wasn't he.

Roberta pressed her forehead against the White Tree of Gondor. 'I'm sorry, OK? … I didn't get … the Admiral Handbag reference. … I…' Shuffling her feet on the grey-bobbly flooring. 'I got all dressed up … to go to DHQ … so I could punch Beattie's lights out, ... cos he was mean to you. ... Booked a taxi and everything.'

There was a pause, then: *'Ackbar. Admiral Ackbar, not "Admiral Handbag".'*

'Well, I don't know, do I! New to all this nerdy-geek stuff.' She took a step back, so he could get a proper look through the spy hole at her best contrite face. 'I'm sorry I got you into trouble. Beattie's a dick. And I brought peace offerings.' She hefted one bag up into viewing range. It clinked. 'Really, really expensive ones.' Frown. 'And before you say anything, Susan wanted me to get you a muffin basket. I went for fancy-pants cheese, wine, crusty bread, pâté, and imported pickles.'

Silence.

'And did I mention that I'm sorry?'

The door popped open an inch and a wee rumpled face peered out. 'Were you *really* going to punch him?'

'Right on his fat beardy nose.' Indicating her last ever Police Scotland fighting suit. 'And I was going to do it in *style*, and everything.'

'Fair enough.' Tufty opened the door wide, revealing the rest of him – wearing Tribble slippers and pale-blue PJs, covered in little Daleks and TARDISs. His eyes narrowed, making wrinkles on his sleep-puffied face. 'But these better be *super*-nice cheeses.'

4.04

Tufty's living room looked much bigger without the folding dining table dominating the middle of it. Well, maybe not *much* bigger, but *slightly* bigger. Instead, the table was shrunk down and stuffed into one corner – doing double-duty as a shelf, with a big Lego Barad-dûr perched on top, along with a bunch of fist-thick hardback fantasy novels.

Making enough space for the coffee table, where Roberta had spread her bribery/apology feast: sourdough bread, four different cheeses, two pâtés, a jar of gherkins, one of pickled shallots, a tub of olives, a tub of artichoke hearts, a tub of sundried tomatoes, a pack of wholegrain crackers, and a bottle of dark-and-spicy Zinfandel. While the Chardonnay got a quick chill in the freezer.

Keen to be seen as a generous host, Tufty had contributed a tub of low-fat spread and a couple of wine glasses. Still sitting in his jammies as he spread a dollop of melty gorgonzola on a 'buttered' biscuit. 'A toast!' Raising his wine. 'To Acting DCI Beattie – may his bum fall off, and his bits burn in the eternal flames of Muspelheim.'

No idea.

But she clinked glasses anyway. 'I'll drink to that.'

Mmmm... Not a bad bit of Zinfandel. Should think so too, given how much it cost.

They got stuck into the cheese and pâté.

'You were right, by the way.' She helped herself to the tub of pickled artichokes.

'I was?' The wee loon shrank back on the couch. 'OK: who are you and what have you done with Ex-Detective Inspector Roberta Steel?'

'Oh ha. Ha. Ha-ha-ha. My poor sides.' Withering look. 'You can't always be there to do these DDDs for me, so I need to learn how to do them myself.'

His mouth pinched. 'Is this going to be like one of those things where I try to teach my dad how to work Facebook, and everyone ends up crying and throwing things?'

'Don't be a snudge.' Licking her fingers clean, then producing her phone. 'Take Sir Norman Fiddly Fordyce. I could've done a digital deep dive myself, right?'

'*Yeah*, but it'll be much quicker if I just do it.' Stuffing in some truffled brie. 'What do you want to know?' He whipped out his own phone.

'Well, it's too late *now*, isn't it. They're going to arrest the bastard in …' Roberta checked her watch, 'five minutes? Ish?'

'What, just in time for the news?' More brie, talking with his mouth full: 'Let me guess. Helicopters and SWAT teams? Camera crew following their every move? Cos *apparently* we has learned *nothing* from that Cliff Richard fiasco.'

She raised her glass again. 'Bingo!'

'Numpties. The world is full of *frudging* numpties.' Tufty poked at his phone's screen. 'Right: let's find Sir Norman Fordyce. Nor-man For-*dyce*. Norman. Normy. The Normster. Abnormal Norman the Mormon longshoreman…' A nod. 'I'm in.' Crunching on a gherkin. 'OK, we've got an official Bluesky, an official Twitter – cos we is *not* calling it "X" – a LinkedIn, and Facebook.' Skim, scroll, poke. Frown. 'Looks like they're all corporate wingwang stuff. Probably gets his comms team to post everything, cos it's obvs blandaraaaaaaaaaama.'

More poking and scrolling as Tufty sipped red wine and munched on an olive. Then cheese. Then pâté. Then a fancy pickled onion.

Until finally: 'Ooh! But we *does* has what looks like a *personal* Instagram account, what he do run *himself*.' Scroll, scroll, scroll. 'Which am mostly pictures of him and his lunch, and breakfast, and dinner, and "Totes amazeballs, doesn't I has a spanktastic life!"' Tufty handed the phone to Roberta. 'See, that's the *easy* bit of a triple-D.' Pointing as she worked her way through a huge, long reel of fancy-pants dishes in fancy-pants restaurants and hotels. 'You does search for their name, find a account that fits – keeping an clever eye out for catfishers, cos scammers is sneaky – and there's always links and co-promotional posts from their other accounts. Sometimes they do also list them in their bio, which makes it even easier.'

Bloody Sir Norman Dingley Bum-Lice was *obsessed* with food. The whole thing was nothing but plates and plates and plates of the stuff. Most of it was high-end cuisine, with the occasional state banquet and ambassadorial reception thrown in, rubber-chicken industry dinners rubbing shoulders with the odd 'dirty' street-food treat. And each picture was *always* accompanied by a wee chunk of self-indulgent blah: 'Oh My God, The Red Mullet With Cherries At La Pergola is to DIE For!'

Tufty scoffed some Mull Cheddar. 'As DDDs go, *this* am the equivalent of paddling about in the shallow end of the pool. With your armbands on.'

Next up were a bunch of shots from a tasting menu, taken at some swanky restaurant on a wee island off the west coast of Scotland. Then a mac-n'-cheese shack in Maine where everything came with lobster. Sushi in Melbourne. A South Africa braai of Antelope ribs and buffalo steak…

'The *real* challenge is finding the ones what am *unofficial.* The secret little Truth Social account for posting all that stuff you're not allowed to say without getting cancelled. Or the Twitter account you only use to sockpuppet your rivals, or call women who disagree with you whores.'

Fresh fish in the Norwegian Fjords. Escargots, steak tartare, and crème brûlée in Paris. Moules-frites in Brussels. Schnitzel and Kartoffelpuffer in Berlin…

She frowned at the screen. 'Why are there no boobs?' Scroll, scroll, scroll. 'Do you think he wanks-off to photos of crispy duck and pasta primavera?'

'And to swim in those *deeper* waters, you need custom algorithms and cross-platform pattern matching.'

She stopped scrolling at a series from Raffles in Singapore, featuring a whole suckling pig and a cornucopia of other delicious-looking things. Then a feast of crab in a fiery red sauce, from a shack by the coast. Then cocktails on an idyllic palm-treed beach. All with their own boastful little caption.

Hmmmm…

Tufty went in for another gherkin. 'Because people don't just have unique *fingerprints* – how we use *language* am also—'

'Aye, Tufters? See these photos on his food-fetish Instawhatsit? It says when they were posted, but is there any way to tell when they were *taken*?'

'Yuparoonie: in the image's metadata.'

The clock on Tufty's phone ticked over to 18:00.

She handed it back. 'Six o'clock. Want to watch the fireworks?'

'Suppose.' He pulled up his shoulders. 'I mean, might as well, right?' Rummaging down the back of the couch, he dug out the doofer and turned on the big-flatscreen-monster TV, which set the attached soundbar, speakers, and subwoofer buzzing into life.

Bet it was a real treat living downstairs when Tufty was watching Star Trek/Wars/Gate/Ship Troopers.

He poked away at the remote, until BBC news appeared onscreen, where a perky blonde newsreader – doable, in a curly-and-curvy weather-girl-who's-been-promoted kind of way – was already cranking through the headlines: '*...New Horizons insist the best way to deter small-boat crossings is for the Royal Navy to sink them.*' Pause. '*Economists predict a global downturn, as US Presid—*'

The mute icon appeared and the telly's sound disappeared.

Tufty speared a sundried tomato. 'Unless you *want* to know what the Clementine Cretin's done now? The Kafkaesque Kumquat. The Tangerine Taint. The—'

'All right, Oscar Wilde, we get the picture.'

They cheese-and-wined as the silent headlines passed, then a story about a member of the shadow cabinet being suspended for making AI porn of female MPs.

Then one about the collapse of a hedge-fund that wiped billions off pension funds.

And then the screen filled with an aerial shot of Fordyce House. It was Acting DCI Wanky-Beardy Arsehole-Beattie's time to shine.

Should've done the dunt for the lunchtime news instead, because the sun was already low in the sky, painting the trees and rhododendron bushes with fire and honey. But that was October for you: be dark before Reporting Scotland and the weather had finished.

Tufty waved the remote. 'Want me to turn it up?'

'Nah. It'll just be the same old frunch as usual.' Idle speculation, press-release bollocks, suspicions, and gossip. She pointed at his phone. 'Tell me about this metadata.'

A phalanx of police vehicles wheeched into shot – going single-file on the narrow road, lights flashing and flickering.

'Right.' He sooked his fingers clean and prodded his mobile back to life. 'Every electronic device what takes photos leaves a stamp on the image it does save. It's like: think of an invisible barcode, hidden in the file, and *some* devices leave heaps of info, and some leave not-so-heaps.'

The lead OSU van slithered to a halt on the gravel drive, and out scrambled a whole squad of thugs, followed by a second team from the other van.

And there were still patrol cars and Dog Units to come…

How could Pine sign off on Operation Impending Disaster? She must've been pissed as a shart to let Beattie talk her into deploying *this* many officers to arrest *one* man. On live TV. With the world watching.

Roberta shook her head and focussed on Tufty again. 'OK. Do your forensic-metadata thing on the Singapore photos. Here.' Taking his phone and scrolling through to those crispy suckling-pig pics, before handing it back.

'Erms… Okeydoodles…' Fiddle, fiddle, fiddle. 'And we open the image in the Scootchy app…' Fiddle, fiddle. 'What do you want to know?'

Why did no bugger ever *listen*?

'When was it taken?'

The first OSU team got into position, and their biggest thug lumbered up to the front door – carrying the Big Red Door Key – while the second team legged it around the back.

The camera drone swooped closer, getting a nice juicy close-up as whoever was in charge gave the nod, and Mrs Big Thug swung her mini-battering-ram, smashing the Fordyces' front door right off its hinges on the first go.

Which *wasn't* easy.

Tufty held his phone up, screen facing Roberta – as if she could read all that teeny writing from here, without her glasses. 'Second of May, this year.'

Everyone swarmed inside, followed by a couple of dirty-huge Alsatians, dragging their handlers through the front door.

Wonder if one of them was PD Branston.

Hope so.

She'd sink her teeth into Sir Norman Fordyce's buttocks quicker than you could say 'police brutality'.

Roberta squinted at the indecipherable text. 'What about the next one?'

'Erms… Also second of May.'

'Keep going.'

'Righty-bing-bongs.' Fiddle, fiddle, fiddle.

Now that half of NE Division had piled into Fordyce House, nothing much seemed to be happening. So, it was a safe bet that there would be some sort of pointless voiceover at this point, filling in time by repeating everything already in the public domain.

The chyron, scrolling across the bottom of the TV, went for 'LIVE: POLICE RAID MSP'S HOUSE IN MURDER INVESTIGATION'.

An inset graphic appeared of Megan Lockheart – looking stunning in a strappy top – putting her on display, so everyone could have a wee *thrill* to see another beautiful young woman murdered by a dickhead man.

'Here we does go. The first batch: brackets, piggy feastings, close brackets, are from the second of May; spicy-crab-fest is the third; and cocktails on the beach are the fourth.'

Roberta frowned at the telly. 'Of May?'

'Of, as they say, May.' Tufty reached for another cracker, then froze. Pulling the next word out and buttering it with suspicion: '*Whhhhhhhhhhhhhhy?*'

The drone circled the building, presumably to add a bit of visual interest to the whole heap of nothing going on at the scene.

A sleekit grin spread across Roberta's face. 'Just interested. Cos early May's when the Instawhatsit posts *say* they were taken.'

The wee loon threw his hands in the air. 'Then why did I waste my time looking at the metadata?'

Her grin grew wider and eviller as she unlocked her own phone and scrolled through the contacts.

'What?' Tufty shrank back again. 'What have I did?'

Onscreen, the whole heap of nothing came to a dramatic halt, as a trio of officers frogmarched Sir Norman from the house – hands cuffed behind his back. They bundled him into a patrol car and the chyron changed to 'LIVE: SIR NORMAN FORDYCE ARRESTED IN CONNECTION WITH MURDER OF MEGAN LOCKHEART (21).'

Perfect.

Roberta poked the call button and listened to it ring.

Took a while, but eventually Harmsworth picked up, with a curt, *'Not a good time.'*

'Owen! How's my favourite lynchpin? Listen, I need you to get your pork scratchings round to Tufty's, sharpish. The game's afoot.'

Could actually hear his gob opening and closing and opening and closing. *'Are you* insane*? Turn your TV on, we're in the middle of—'*

'I know, I'm watching it.' She waved at the telly. 'Can't you see me waving?'

'Then how *can I go anywhere?'*

'And bring Lund with you. Barrett too, if he's about. I'm getting the band back together.'

'And I repeat, once more, for the benefit of those no longer with us: I can't, *we're—'*

'Because the wheels are about to come off Operation Demogorgon, *big* style. And you can stay for the crash, like an idiot, or eject before things start exploding. Boom! Splatter! *Aaaargh!*' Making one hand into a claw and crushing an imaginary Boris Johnson's head.

Pkonnnnnnnnnnnnnnngk...

Could hear the wobble in Harmsworth's voice now. 'But it's—'

'Pretend you've got a tummy ache, or a knob ache, or the squits. Don't care. Just get your bits here *now*!' She hung up.

Glonk.

Tufty blinked at her. Grimaced. Put down his half-eaten biscuit. 'Oh noes...' Knees together. Slippers tippy-tapping on the carpet. 'This is all going to go *horribly* wrong, isn't it.'

She beamed back. 'Probably,' a wink, 'but when did that ever stop us?'

Twilight turned the sky from pale blue to inky violet as the Volvo headed out the A944, past trees and fields. Which was a real improvement on yesterday's wind and rain.

Harmsworth sat behind the wheel, face squinched and pinched, as if someone had jammed something spiky where angels feared to tread. He'd changed out of his uniform and into civvies, making him look like someone's uncle from the seventies. Roberta had the passenger seat, dressed to impress. Tufty was in the back, wearing jeans and a stripy top, like a trainee burglar. While Lund sat next to him: pink sweatshirt and blue joggies.

In hindsight, *probably* should've asked everyone to wear their fighting suits. But it was a bit late now.

Harmsworth fidgeted at the steering wheel. 'Are we sure this is wise? Only I was supposed to be on a green shift and if we're all getting fired, I'd really like paid for the extra hours I did.'

Lund lounged. 'Don't look at me, I clocked off at four, like a normal person. The buggers can't touch me for skipping work.'

Tufty put his hand up. 'Rest day.'

Roberta grinned. 'Retired.'

A long, semi-sobbed groan wrenched its way out of their driver. 'So just *me*, then.'

The fields gave way to a narrow band of trees, and there, on the other side, was Dunecht. In all its lopsided, little-village splendour.

Roberta rubbed at her aching leg. 'How do you think they're getting on, with Sir Norman Fiddly Fordyce?'

'Well,' Lund leaned through from the back, 'if they arrested him at … six? He's probably stewing in his cell waiting for his fancy solicitor to arrive.'

'Good. Cos I would hate it if he spoiled my surprise.' She produced her mobile, scrolled through the contacts to 'FLAT-ARSE!', and poked the button. Sticking it on speakerphone as it rang and rang and rang and rang. But eventually, Chief Superintendent Pine's carrion-crow voice *scrawk*ed out into the car: *'This better be good.'*

'Rosy!' Roberta held her phone out, so everyone could hear. 'How's my least favourite Chief Superintendent?'

'All right, I gave you a chance. I'm hanging up, right—'

'Before you do, let me ask you a quick question. Apropos: Sir Norman Fordyce.'

A sniff. *'We're not issuing any statements at the moment. You'll just have to wait for—'*

'What do Singapore chilli crab, a Singapore sling, and a suckling pig at the Raffles Hotel *in Singapore* have in common?'

'Goodbye, *ex-Detective—'*

'Fine, make a fool of yourself. See if I care. But can't say I didn't try to warn you…' Roberta hung up and winked at her team. 'Now we wait.'

Harmsworth groaned again. 'We're all getting fired, aren't we.'

Didn't have to wait long, though, because Roberta's mobile launched into 'Take Your Mama' before they were even halfway through Dunecht. And whose name glowed in the middle of the screen? Good old 'FLAT-ARSE!'.

Roberta bopped away in her seat for a bit, grooving to that disco beat, before answering. 'Rosy! What a coincidence.'

On speakerphone again.

'You have one *minute.'*

'See: what those things all have in common is one Sir Norman Fordyce. He posted *all* about them on his Instagram.'

'Fifty seconds.'

'Because he was there between the second and fourth of May, before heading to Australia for a week of meetings, scuba diving, and fine dining.'

'Forty seconds.'

Oh, this was just too easy.

'Come on, Rosy, engage that wee lump of gristle nestling between your lugs. When did Megan Lockheart go missing?'

'Hmmph. I don't see how that's relevant. She was last seen…'

Silence.

They passed the estate offices and the turnoff for Echt.

Took a while, but Pine finally twigged. *'Oh for the love of the bastarding…'* Her voice went all muffled – probably a hand-over-the-phone job. *'BROOKMINSTER! GET IN HERE!'*

'There we go! Knew you'd work it out eventually.' Roberta wriggled in her seat, like a happy Jack Russell. Really laying it on thick now: '*Good job* you didn't make a big show of *arresting him* in some sort of *elaborate circus* of lights and sirens and TV coverage, right?'

'BROOKMINSTER! WHERE'S BEATTIE? I WANT THAT HAIRY CRETIN IN MY OFFICE, NOW!'

Roberta didn't bother to press the mute button, just burst into a proper *rattling* bout of maniacal laughter.

4.05

An unmarked pool car was waiting for them at the turnoff to Corskieford Croft.

Well, not so much 'unmarked' as filthy, with 'WARNING: CONTAINS BACON!' scratched deep into the Vauxhall's paintwork, all across the boot and bonnet.

The last member of Roberta's Queen Street Irregulars was sitting behind the wheel – Acting Detective Sergeant David Barrett. With his oversized ears, snub nose, blond hair, and the kind of prominent overbite that gave him an unmistakable air of … *Watership Down*iness. A tall man, in a dark-grey fighting suit. So at least someone else looked the part.

Harmsworth made an 'after you' gesture through the windscreen, and Barrett turned his scrimshawed Vauxhall onto the track, leading the way. Headlights off, to maintain the element of surprise.

The Volvo followed at a safe-ish distance, gravel *ping-clang*ing in its wheel arches. Crawling along.

By the time they'd reached the converted steadings/holiday homes at the end of the track, Barrett had already blocked Frank Abercrombie's Range Rover in. And now he stood, leaning back against the Baconmobile, with his arms crossed in the gathering gloom. Watching as Harmsworth parked outside the holiday home next door.

Roberta climbed out, and Barrett gave her a wee salute:

'Guv.' He straightened up to his full six-foot-three. 'Before it's too late, I want to go on record saying this is a silly idea and we're all going to end up in a world of frudge.'

Which got him lots of agreeing nods.

Ungrateful sods.

'It's no' a "silly idea", it's the unfettered genius of Roberta Steel!' She pointed down the length of the steading. 'Lund, Harmsworth: round the back, in case Abercrombie does a runner.'

And off they trotted, disappearing behind the steadings. Like a good little boy and girl.

Her pointy finger found Tufty next. 'Quirrel: you guard the front. Last resort in case he gets past us.'

'Guv.'

The pointy finger turned into a poker – right in the middle of the wee loon's chest. 'And if this one ends up under a train, my boot is getting lodged in your small intestine, understand?'

'Eeek!' Snapping to attention. 'Guv! Yes, Guv!'

She jerked her head at Barrett. 'You're with me.' Then limped for 'DUNLOBBYIN'.

Barrett slouched along on his long, long legs, dropping his voice to a whisper. 'Do you think Tufty knows there isn't a railway line for, like, fifteen miles?'

'I won't tell him if you don't.'

A shrug. Then Barrett stuck his hands in his pockets, looking out at the landscape. 'So … are you planning on telling me why we're here, oh Great Unfettered Genius? Or is this meant to be some sort of blind-loyalty test?'

'Because, my dear Meadowcroft, I asked myself "who in this benighted maze of *filth* and *horror* could benefit from crimes as grotesque as these?"'

He frowned at her. 'Retirement's made you a bit weird, hasn't it.' Not waiting for an answer. 'We got a plan?'

'Same as usual: I rattle our scumbag's tree till all the squirrels fall out. You arrest him. Home in time for tea and medals.'

Barrett smiled. 'Good to have you back, Guv.' Then reached for the doorbell.

But she stopped him. 'Policeman's three, I think.'

'Fair enough.' He pounded on the door with his fist instead – hard and sharp. Ominous. The kind of noise that could awaken the dead. Or a pished campaign manager.

And sure enough, less than a minute later the outside light bloomed on, the door opened, and there was Frank Abercrombie. All rumpled and bleary, in creased jeans, a bright-yellow tank-top, and an un-ironed pink shirt.

Roberta gave him a big smile. 'Frankie-Boy! I think we need to talk, don't you?'

He stared at her for a moment. Then his bottom lip trembled. And he burst into tears.

'All right.' Her smile faded. 'Why don't we talk in—'

Frank slammed the door in her face.

Actually, properly *right* in her face, making her flinch back. 'Ow!' One hand over her stingy nose. 'Barrett!'

Barrett shoulder-charged the door, flinging it wide.

His rabbity bulk almost blocked the hallway, but there was just enough room to make out Abercrombie sprinting for a door at the far end – wrestling it open and buggering off into the great outdoors.

Barrett hammered after him, with Roberta limping along at the rear.

It was a fairly *bland* hallway. Nicely decorated, in a restrained kind of way, with a handful of photos of a happy couple on holiday, gracing the walls. Only one half of the happy couple didn't have a face anymore. Abercrombie had scrubbed the guy's features out with a biro, hard enough to chew through the glossy print all the way to the backing board beneath.

Kind of weird that he must've taken them out of the frames first, then returned them afterwards…

Harmsworth's voice blared like a foghorn, somewhere behind the steading: *'OH NO YOU— GHAHHHH! OW! OW! OW!'*

By which point Barrett had reached the end of the hall and was hurtling out after Abercrombie.

A bellow from Lund: *'COME BACK HERE!'*

Roberta lurched down the hall to the back door, which now lay wide to the world.

Hard to tell if the view was nice or not: the steading's security lights only reached as far as the drystane dyke at the end of the garden. On the other side lay a dark wodge of field – maybe grass for haylage? – then up a slight hill to a darker band of trees beyond.

Abercrombie was legging it for the far horizon, his tank-top and shirt standing out against the battered grass, with Lund and Barrett in hot pursuit.

But not Harmsworth, who lay flat on his back by the garden wall, thrashing about like an overturned turtle.

A wee pointy-nosed figure, dressed like a burglar, streaked into view. But while Barrett and Lund were chasing straight after Abercrombie, Tufty was on a curving intercept course. A stripy, shortarsed, scroat-seeking missile.

Had to admit, for a guy who must've been about eighty-percent fermented grape juice, Frank Abercrombie had a fair turn of speed on him.

Not quite fast enough, though.

Tufty slammed into his side and the pair of them disappeared into the long grass in a tumble of limbs and swearing. Lund and Barrett leapt on top, turning it into a proper piley-on.

Back in the garden, Harmsworth rolled onto his front and slowly struggled upright, breathing hard. One hand propping himself up against the stone wall, the other prodding away at the base of his spine. 'Ow, ow, ow, ow, ow…'

Roberta gave him a wee round of applause. 'Never mind, Owen: good effort.'

Out in the field, Barrett dragged Abercrombie to his feet.

They already had both hands cuffed behind his back. Proving that Police Scotland officers *could* actually catch fleeing suspects, when a proper Great Unfettered Genius was in charge.

Tufty mugged a grinning thumbs up.

Then Lund and Barrett marched their prisoner back towards the house.

4.06

With everyone squeezed into the kitchen it seemed much smaller than last time.

Abercrombie and Roberta sat at opposite ends of the table, while Lund and Barrett loomed. Owen winced – half bent over the work surface, rubbing at his back. And Tufty made a round of teas for everyone.

Roberta tapped a fingertip on the tabletop. 'Before we drag you back to the station, you want to tell us why you did it?'

'Did what?' Abercrombie gazed out the window, into the darkness, avoiding her gaze. He was a bit … *lopsided* in his seat, smeared with green stains; a welt on one cheek and bits of grass sticking out of his hair. They'd shifted his handcuffs around to the front.

Well, it made things cosier.

'She was *twenty-one*, Frank. Whole life ahead of her.' Tap, tap, tap. 'Megan's mum and dad've been worried sick, but *now*? Can you imagine what they're going through?'

His head drooped. He dragged in a ragged breath. And cried.

And cried.

And cried.

Tufty plonked a mug in front of Roberta, then placed one in front of Abercrombie, before handing out the others.

Her tea was lovely and hot, but not a wisp of steam rose

from Abercrombie's. Looked disturbingly milky too – so pale it was almost white. Because a scalding-hot beverage could be a formidable weapon in the wrong hands. And while the wee loon might be daft, he wasn't stupid.

Made a nice cuppa too.

Roberta took a sip, keeping her voice all calm and casual. 'Did she call you back? Lady Fordyce?'

The tears snivelled and sniffed to a stop.

A bland smile. 'Can't be easy, after all these years, Frank. Giving everything. Fixing their messes.'

'Oh, you don't know the *half* of it.' Scrubbing at his eyes – not easy in cuffs, but he managed.

'Messes like Megan Lockheart?'

Silence.

Everyone stared at him. Even Harmsworth.

Abercrombie gave a sour wee laugh. 'It was so *stupid.* He never wears protection. And I tried, OK? I *tried.*' More of those serrated breaths. 'But she wouldn't have an abortion. Wouldn't even *think* about it. And I told her, I told her: "He *always* does this. He doesn't love you. Because the only person Norman *Bloody* Fordyce loves is Norman *Bloody* Fordyce."' The tears welled up again. 'And we got into this big argument, and she just went ... *crazy*. Kept screaming about how I'm not allowed to kill her baby, and Sir Norman loves her, and he's going to leave Lady Fordyce, and they'll live on his yacht, sailing round the Mediterranean.' That laugh got sourer. 'So bloody naïve...' Abercrombie wiped the tears away, but more took their place. 'And I told her. I told her, "Megan: he's already *moved on.* He's sniffing round Billie Nesbit now!"' The campaign manager's voice jumped half an octave: '"No, he loves *me.* He doesn't love Billie. You're a liar!"' Then a shudder. 'And she's hitting and hitting me, and I'm trying to make her stop and...'

Wrinkles deepened across Abercrombie's brow.

His mouth fell open as he curled in on himself.

Pink surged through his face, darkening.

Eyes bugging.

Tears streaming.

No one moved.

Didn't even drink their tea.

Then Abercrombie's voice whispered out, small and scared. 'It was an accident. She slipped and fell and hit her head. And I ... panicked.' A tortured breath. 'I didn't mean to *hurt* anyone.'

A hush settled over the kitchen, like a thick, suffocating blanket.

And then Roberta leaned forward, reaching across the table to put a gentle, reassuring hand on Frank's arm. 'What a load of *utter* bollocks.'

He flinched back.

'You hacked her fingers off, Frank, and battered all her teeth out. With. A. Hammer.' Getting louder. 'Stripped her naked, drove her out to the middle of nowhere, and dumped her body in a sodding wheelie bin! If you hadn't cocked-up and missed one of Megan's wisdom teeth, we'd never have ID'd her. She'd be left to rot in a mortuary drawer for *decades*.'

Abercrombie's eyes darted left and right, muscles tensing...

'Don't.' Lund slapped a hand down on his shoulder. 'It *won't* end well.'

His body drooped again.

Roberta sat back in her chair and scowled at the nasty wee shite. 'Megan didn't "fall and hit her head", cos if she *had* we'd've found it in the post mortem. Cracked skull. Blood staining in the cranium. But there was none of that.' She curled her lip. 'So what did you do: poison? Or maybe you just stabbed her? Cos you like knives, don't you, Franky?'

No reply.

'And cos you got away with it once, why no' kill Billie Nesbit too? There she is, banging your boss's husband; it'll all go south anyway, right? Might as well nip it in the bud, before someone finds out.'

Abercrombie pulled his chin in, staring at her. 'But—'

'And *this* time you wouldn't even have to hide the body: could just blame it on those slack-jawed knuckle-dragging pricks from the Anglo-Saxon Defence Group. Two birds with one stone! Tie up a loose end *and* get yourself a bump in the polls.' Because why should Graeme Anderson have all the fun? 'That's why you were in there like a ferret when Billie was stabbed, trying to pull the knife out to "save her". Aye, making sure you had a nice wee alibi for why your fingerprints and DNA were all over the weapon, and the victim's blood on your hands.'

'What? No. No.' He shook his head. 'I never… No. I *didn't*!'

'Course no'.' Roberta snapped her fingers, then pointed at the murdering bastard. 'Get him out of my sight.'

Lund hauled him out of his chair. 'On your feet.'

As the only on-duty officer not currently crippled, Barrett did the honours. 'Francis Abercrombie: I am arresting you under Section One of the Criminal Justice, Scotland, Act 2016, for the murder of Megan Lockheart and the attempted murder of Billie Nesbit.'

'Get your hands off me!' Struggling, and getting nowhere.

'The reason for your arrest is—'

'I demand to speak to my lawyer! You can't *do* this to me! I know important people! THIS ISN'T FAIR!'

Yes it bloody well was.

4.07

'. . . absolutely no sodding idea what's happened to him.'

'Uh-huh.' Roberta scuffed in through the front door and thunked it closed behind her. Shutting out the streetlights and chilly air. Shifting her phone from one ear to the other as she locked-up and dumped her keys in the drawer.

All while Logan moaned on and on: *'I mean, the last victim was a month ago, and there's been no new bodies since. What kind of Ripper gives up when they're on a roll?'*

'Uh-huh.' Kicking off her fighting boots, she pulled on her cosying slippers.

'You know what I think? He was escalating, right? The gap between murders getting shorter? Serial killers don't just go to ground after that. Not voluntarily.'

'Uh-huh.'

Muffled television noises oozed through the closed living-room door. Some sort of canned-laughter panel show.

'I think he's either had some sort of accident – or a stroke, heart attack – and ended up in hospital. Maybe one of his victims fought back and he's dead in a ditch somewhere, and we won't find his body for years. He's been banged-up for some minor offence and this'll all start again when he gets out. Or he's killed himself.'

'Uh-huh.' She headed through, and there was Susan, snoozing away on the main couch, with Genghis and Mr Rumpole curled up beside her.

'You're not listening at all, are you.'

'Uh-huh.'

Mr Rumpole stretched as Roberta came in, but stayed where he was, while the wee lad hopped down and scampered around her legs – yipping away, gazing up as if she were the most wonderful thing ever to walk the earth.

Daft lovely little sod that he was.

'This is all because you caught your *killer, and I didn't catch* mine.'

'Yup.' Mind you, hard to know exactly what the appropriate response was: smug celebration, for solving the case; or soul-crushing depression at how horrible people were.

Maybe a bit of both.

'I'll give it two weeks, then put in for a transfer home.'

'Told you: should've hired the great Roberta Steel, Consulting Detective.' She picked Genghis up and the wee dog trembled with joy, tongue going like a slobbery pink thing. 'Would've got the guy ages ago.'

'Blah, blah, blah…'

On the couch, Susan snorked and sat up. 'What? Why?' Blink. Blink. '*Robbie.*' Sticking her arms out for a hug. 'Where have you *been*?'

'Got to go.' Roberta hung up, popped Genghis down, leaned in, and gave Susan a squeeze and a smooch. 'I've been having a *bloody* good day, thank you very much. Caught a murderer, ruined Beattie's career, and *seriously* antagonised Chief Superinfectant Pine.' Grin. 'Ah, it was glorious.'

A yawn. 'Been trying to call you for ages.'

'Had my phone off.' Disentangling herself, Roberta limped over to the drinks cabinet. 'You want?' Pointing at the booze.

Susan shook her head. 'Mint tea.'

'They let me watch from the observation suite while they did the initial interview. Thought Pine was going to have an aneurism from the strain of being nice to me. Ha!' Pouring herself a *mighty* whisky.

A yawn. 'I put your friend in the spare room.'

Got to love whisky. It tasted of smoke and fire and victory…

Hang on a minute.

Roberta lowered her glass. 'What "friend"?'

Maybe it was one of the Wednesday-Night-Dungeon-Crew? Outie, or The Horn, or Baddy? Couldn't be Tufty – he'd gone back to his love nest for rampant Nerdsex.

Susan frowned. 'David … Thingummy. I'm sorry, I didn't really catch his last name on account of Mr Rumpole yacking up this *huge* hairball on the rug. Your friend? The one you were private-eyeing with?'

Roberta's jaw *clenched*. 'Wee Davey McLeod?'

The two-faced, back-stabbing, shite-brained wee fuck was here? In *her* spare bloody room?

Well, he was in for a rude sodding—

'Oh, Robbie,' Susan put a hand to her chest, 'his wife, Jenny, just died.'

Oh…

Roberta placed her drink on the coffee table.

Ears going warm in the now too-hot room, even though all the fire had drained right out of her.

'That's…' Jesus. 'OK. Right.'

'He was lost, and alone, and a little bit drunk. Maybe you should take him a cup of coffee, or an Ovaltine, or something? Talk to him.'

She puffed out a lonnnnnnnnnng breath.

Dead.

Wow.

That kind of put everything into perspective, didn't it.

'Yes. I'll … Ovaltine.'

It wasn't easy, carrying a big porcelain mug of steaming-hot-malty-bedtime-drink *and* a large Bowmore, while in possession of a walking stick, but Roberta did her best. Didn't even spill any of it – well, none of the whisky, which was the important thing – all the way up the stairs, and down the hall to right outside the spare room.

For a bit of procrastinating.

Because, you know: dead...

At least Genghis had decided to keep her company. Just in case she had some bacon hidden about her person and might need a small obliging dog to dispose of it. Nice to have some moral support, though.

OK.

Roberta propped her stick against the wallpaper, and raised a hand to knock.

Deep breath.

Then rapped on the door.

Counted to ten.

She eased it open a fraction.

The lights were off, but the curtains open – letting in the stale-urine glow of corporation streetlights. But it did nothing to dispel the gloom.

She cleared her throat. 'Davey, you awake?'

No reply.

'I heard about Jenny. I'm sorry.'

Still nothing.

Poor sod was probably asleep.

'OK, I'll just leave you to rest.'

His voice wobbled out of the darkness. *'Forty-one years.'*

The words were a little mushy, softened around the edges with grief and alcohol. *'Forty-one years, we were married.'*

'Cancer sucks balls.'

'I never looked at another woman, all that time. Not even when she got sick.'

Roberta nodded.

What was it she'd told Lady Fordyce? Right: '"Turns out, when you love someone – properly, deep down in your bones – you don't need to cheat."'

'All I wanted was … to do one *nice thing for her, before she went. You know?* Something *that wasn't just washing her, or cleaning up after a visit. Something that wasn't about … her illness.'*

Poor sod.

Roberta hurpled into the room, leaving her walking stick behind. Davey's toasty-hot beverage in one hand, her tumbler of neat Bowmore in the other.

Dark in here, with just the vaguest of shapes visible. Genghis trotted ahead to investigate, tail going, because who knew when bacon would strike?

'I brought you some Ovaltine.' She looked down at the glass. 'Or a whisky, if you want?' Because, while she might've been many things, Roberta Steel was *not* a monster.

'It's not much to ask for, is it?' Davey's voice cracked. *'Just a little something?'*

A wee sob was all it took to locate his position – a slightly darker silhouette, in the chair beside the window. Turned, so the occupant would be spared the streetlight's pustulant glow.

Probably been crying.

Couldn't really blame him.

'Davey, I'm so sorry.' Moving closer, then stumbling over something hidden in the gloom – nearly going arse-over-beak – because trying to walk without her stick wasn't hard enough. Hot Ovaltine sloshed down the back of her hand.

'Buggering…' Roberta clamped her mouth shut, because a foul-mouthed tirade probably wasn't appropriate right now. 'Do you want to switch the light on? Dark as a superintendent's heart in here.'

He sniffed. *'Close the door? I… I don't want anyone else to see me like this.'*

Fair enough.

She pushed the door shut, and the hallway lights disappeared. Making the room even darker. Then a *click*, and the wee lamp on the table in the bay window bloomed into life, chasing away the gloom.

Revealing Davey, sitting there, fully dressed, holding a double-barrelled shotgun. That came up to point right at Roberta's chest.

4.08

Pish…

Now the light was on, the thing that Roberta tripped over was clearly visible: a nice big holdall. The sort of bag you could put clothes for a week in, or smuggle a firearm past someone's sweet, but unsuspecting, wife.

Lund *said* Davey had parking tickets and a shotgun licence.

Should've paid more attention to little details like that.

Roberta forced a smile. Voice all chummy. 'Davey. Let's not be—'

'Turns out, I have nothing to lose anymore. I'm broke. The bank's gonna take our *home*. And now Jenny's…' For a moment, it looked as if his whole face was about to burst. But he bit his lip and forced it down. 'The good news is: I'm going to join her!'

Which explained the gun.

Bit of a shitty thing to do in someone else's house, though. Spray your brains all over the walls and ceiling. Leaving them to clean up the sticky, gritty mess.

'Come on, Davey, that's not—'

'The *better* news is: you're coming with me.'

She stood up straight, chest out, teeth bared. Fists tightening on mug and tumbler. 'I swear to God, if you've hurt *any* of my family…'

'What?' He flinched back into the chair. 'No! I would *never* do something like that. If anything, I'm doing them a favour – getting rid of you, before you screw their lives up the way you screwed up mine.'

Genghis stopped his sniffing and scampered over to stand guard in front of Roberta. Hackles up. Even managed to muster a growl twice his size.

Good boy.

'*I* screwed...?' Roberta glowered at Davey. 'I'm no' the one who invested all my cash on the American market! I'm no' the one who couldn't find his arse with a search team and Dog Unit, never mind missing people!'

The shotgun raised, until she was looking straight down the barrels. His jaw tightened. 'Be *very* careful.'

'Why, what you gonna do: *shoot* me?' A snort. 'You were a crap detective sergeant and you're an even crapper private eye!'

Which was Genghis's cue to snarl and bark-bark-bark. Not exactly intimidating, but at this point Roberta would take any help she could get.

Davey clambered out of his seat, looming over the wee lad. 'Shut up you stupid—'

And Genghis launched himself at Davey's ankles, teeth snapping. A hairy wee piranha with the heart of a Dobermann.

'AAAAAAARGH! GET OFF! GET OFF!' Davey twirled in a tight circle, but Genghis kept at it. Till Davey swung a foot back, then booted it straight into Genghis's ribs, sending the poor lad tumbling.

Yelping and yipping and whining in pain.

'BASTARD!' Roberta launched herself at him, but the shotgun swung around and *roared*.

In the confined space of the spare room, it was like taking a hammer to her eardrums.

She battered into Davey – shoving him backwards, swinging that mug of Ovaltine.

It smashed against his cheek in a firework-burst of broken porcelain and freshly boiled malty-milk drink. Because a scalding-hot beverage could be a formidable weapon in the *right* hands.

Davey stumbled backwards, screaming, shoulders clattering into the bedroom window – bouncing off the double glazing.

As he ricocheted, the gun's barrels swung up and over, bashing down against his right shoulder.

She made a grab for the thing, fingers latching onto the wooden stock, but Davey yanked it away.

Must've tightened his grip on the trigger, because the shotgun *thundered* again – only this time the windowpane took the full brunt.

Glass exploded out into the night, sparkling and glittering like sharp cubes of snow, filling the air with the bitter-sharp stench of a thousand fireworks.

'GRAAAAAAAAAAAAAAAAAAAH!' Roberta swung her whisky tumbler like an axe, catching him bang in the face. The cut crystal shattered, spraying neat spirit into his eyes. Leaving razor-sharp edges that carved their way through Davey's cheek, across his nose, and out through the opposite eyebrow.

His scream went up an octave. Scalded on one side, slashed on the other, with forty percent alcohol searing in the wounds.

Eyes screwed shut, Davey reared backwards, trying to escape the pain. Only *now* there was no double glazing left to bounce off, so he went straight through the tattered window – wailing as he Hans Grubered his way to the ground, eighteen feet below.

Must've landed with quite a thud.

Difficult to tell after two short-range shotgun blasts. Everything was one high-pitched screech, ringing in Roberta's ears.

She leaned out through the shattered bedroom window

and stuck two fingers up at the crumpled body moaning and twitching in the rose bushes.

One of his legs looked a *very* funny shape.

Ha, ha, ha, ha…

Pretty sure knees weren't meant to bend that way. And arms were only supposed to have *one* elbow.

She made loudhailers with her hands, because his ears were probably ringing with tinnitus, like hers, and it would be a shame if he missed this: '*HASTA LA VISTA*, DAVEY!'

Then Roberta staggered back a couple of steps, turning as the door banged open.

And there was Susan – an antique golf club clutched in both hands like Thor's hammer, ready to wreak vengeance.

'WHERE'S GENGHIS?' Roberta half-fell against the newly-vacated chair. Eyes raking the spare room. 'GENGHIS?'

Susan's eyes went wide. 'Robbie? Oh God, Robbie, what happened? You're bleeding!'

Was she?

'GENNNNNNNNNNNNNNNNNNNNN-GHIS!' Then her wobbly legs gave out and down she went, bouncing off the spare bed, and *thunk*ing onto her knees.

From down here, it was easy to see the smear of scarlet that disappeared under the bed. 'Oh, my brave wee man…' Roberta lifted the valance.

Genghis lay on his side, in among the dust bunnies, still and silent – his hind legs a mess of torn fur and blood.

Roberta scooped him up in her arms and *howled.*

the graveside

5.01

It wasn't a good day for a funeral.

Funerals should be dreich, *wintery* affairs, full of rain and tumbling leaves. As if the whole world was mourning.

Instead, the sun beamed down from a clear blue sky – birds chirping and warbling in the trees and bushes that bordered the cemetery.

At least it had the decency to be a bit nippy…

The Kirkton of Skene graveyard had a good view too: green, undulating hills giving way to purple-sloped mountains. A newish cemetery, barely a third full, on the outer edge of a small village caught in Westhill's ever-expanding gravitational well. Waiting for the day the larger suburb swallowed it whole.

Roberta leaned on her walking stick, squinting against the inappropriate sunshine, dressed all in black. As were Tufty and Barrett, Lund, and even Harmsworth.

Her Queen Street Irregulars, hanging back a few rows from the graveside.

They weren't the only mourners here, though. Most of the crowd was distinctly younger – early-twenties, maybe – shuffling about the surrounding graves. Talking in shuttered whispers. Not quite knowing what to do next.

Probably the first time they'd ever buried a friend.

The minister wiped dirt from his hands, bowed his head,

and left the field of play. Sweeping out in his shroud of raven black.

The youngsters shuffled after him, heading off to the Red Star Inn for a funeral tea: little sandwiches, sausage rolls, and 'I can't believe she's really gone…'

With the kids out of the way, that left Mr and Mrs Lockheart, standing beside the dark hole they'd committed their daughter to for all eternity. Wrapped in each other's arms, heads bowed, shoulders quivering as the tears flowed.

No headstone yet – the grave would have to settle first – but there were *heaps* of floral tributes, and a display board with a huge photo of Megan on it. Looking impossibly sweet and innocent.

But then, those were the lies that got families through the darker days.

Lund grimaced. 'I *hate* these things. Not the showing-our-respects bit, the fact we've… You know.'

A shrug from Barrett. 'Can't prevent *every* death.'

'Look at it this way,' Harmsworth pointed, 'at least we stopped Abercrombie killing anyone else. That's something.'

Tufty shuffled his feet, in his black work boots and black fighting suit, even though this was officially a rest day. 'You guys going to the wake?'

'Can't.' Barrett hooked a thumb over his shoulder at the car park. 'Gotta get back to work.'

'Guv?'

Hard to imagine what it would be like losing a daughter. If Jasmine or Naomi just … didn't come home one day. What would hurt more: thinking they'd run away because they didn't love you anymore, or finding out some bastard had taken them from you? Dumped them in the bin like yesterday's rubbish.

And the Lockhearts got to suffer *both*.

'Guv? Hello? The wake?'

'Hmmm…?' Roberta blinked the world back into focus, and there was Tufty staring at her. 'Oh. Right. No. I think the family deserve some space *without* police officers hoovering up all the mini-Kievs.'

Through the scattering flock of funeral crows, a flash of bright-red hair stood out like a robin.

Roberta blinked again. ''Scuse me.' She hobbled off and left her team standing there. Making her way between the headstones, past the open grave, and over to where Billie Nesbit slouched, all on her own. Keeping a safe distance between herself and Megan's parents.

Her skin was ghost-pale, dark-purple bags slung beneath her eyes. Hunched and shrunken. As if she'd aged a decade in the last few months. But at least she was upright – no more tubes and machines and hospital beds.

Roberta nodded. 'You're looking better.'

'Am I?' The two words flat and grey as a granite slab.

Over in the car park, doors clunked shut, engines starting as the crows took flight.

Roberta leaned on her walking stick. 'Want to tell me the truth this time?'

Wrinkles deepened on that pale brow as Billie frowned at the open grave. 'You know, I look at her picture and all I feel is … sad. There was a time I'd have bashed her skull wide open, just to spend a *minute* with the illustrious *Sir* Norman Fordyce.'

Mr Lockheart sank to his knees, hands over his face. And Mrs Lockheart knelt beside him, holding him tight.

'And then, all of a sudden, Megan was gone. And I was *so* glad, because that meant he was all *mine*.' A small laugh slipped through those thin lips. 'Frank tried to tell me – "this is what Sir Norman's like with *all* the pretty girls" – but I thought I was special.' Her face tightened. 'Until *Vivian* came along.' Billie put a hand over her stomach, where the knife had been. 'I just wanted him to notice me again.'

Oh for God's sake…

Roberta groaned. 'Frank Abercrombie didn't stab you, did he.'

'Does it matter now? He killed Megan. He's going to prison for the rest of his life anyway.'

'You really are a *stupid* wee girl. You could've died! You nearly did!'

'Was only meant to be a *tiny* stab wound.' A sickly smile. 'Turns out, it's not as easy as it looks.'

'And you're going to let Abercrombie take the blame.' Roberta shook her head. 'Suppose it's up to you. Maybe *yours* is the kind of conscience that'll let you forget all about it: get on with your life. Or *maybe* it'll torture you every single day and night till there's nothing left but a hollow bitter shell, no one will ever love.' Roberta gave Billie's shoulder a wee pat. 'Something to think about, anyway.'

Then hurpled off.

And with any luck, Billie would be staring after her, lamenting every decision that ended with … *this*.

What was it with heterosexual women, mooning about over men? How self-destructive did someone have to be to *stab* themselves because of a bloody man? A married man. A grey-haired titting *wank* of a man, who chased after every bit of skirt that crossed his arrogant, misogynistic, lecherous path.

Tufty was waiting for her, outside the cemetery gates, leaning back against the shiny red bonnet of her freshly valeted MX-5. Top down, ready to roll. 'All good?'

A sniff. 'Depends on your definition of "good".'

Roberta opened the passenger door, and looked back across the headstones.

There was Billie, still standing where she'd left her.

Watching.

'Let's go home.'

5.02

Now that Susan and the monsters were off to work and school, peace and calm returned to the kitchen, leaving only a battlefield of abandoned plates, bowls, mugs, and cutlery behind.

Roberta limp-hobbled back and forth, filling the dishwasher with the aftermath of breakfast.

How did three people make so much sodding mess *every* morning?

The radio burbled away to itself in the background, because it was better than silence, as she tidied up.

'…and between you and me, he's been half-naked ever since.' A wee pause. *'But we've got a special guest for you the day: Graeme Anderson, who'll be answering a' your* questions. *So dinna be shy – you can email, text, or phone in, any time aifter ten.'*

Bloody Graeme Bloody Anderson.

She jammed a couple of knives in the cutlery bit. 'Here's a question for you: WHY ARE YOU SUCH A MASSIVE TWAT?'

Which didn't help anything, because he wasn't on-air for half an hour yet. No point shouting at the radio if the person wasn't even *there*.

Cereal bowls and spoons.

Mr Rumpole: 'You still have to do something about the bastard, Mother. After all, are you *really* going to let him get away with blowing up the great *Roberta Steel*?'

Not in this sodding lifetime.

'Now, how do ye fancy a bittie old-fashioned rocktastic *rocking rock? Here's The Unfettered, wi' "Burning Bones"!'*

Drums and electric guitars pounded and twanged.

Roberta scraped sticky crumbs from toast plates as a bloke roared and squeaked in true 1970s fashion.

'Down in the river, washing this clean,
Finding the places that lay in-between,
Can't stop, this mayhem machine,
Giving your life, guillotine gasoline,
To the guys on their thrones,
Throwing stones, burning bones!

The house phone launched into its rendition of *The South Bank Show* theme tune. Which *really* didn't go with the adenoidal screeching.

She turned the radio down then picked up the handset – disturbingly sticky and smelling of marmalade. 'I'm no' in.'

A man's voice, posh and Scottish, old and patriarchal: *'Good morning, lovely Roberta, I hope today finds you well?'* Rifkind.

The mugs went in the top bit. 'I was just thinking about you. *And* your Neanderthal friend.'

'How kind. Listen, I've been thinking about that favour of yours—'

'Too late for take-backsies – they already tested the hair-brush for DNA. Suspect is in custody, a confession has been beaten out of him, and the case is closed.'

'That's why I'm calling. You see, I can't help thinking: as your "favour" was essentially altruistic *– catching a killer, bringing closure to Megan Lockheart's family – you should probably get that one for free.'*

Roberta paused, scrambled-egg pot in hand. 'For *free*?'

'Call it a gesture of largesse. What with us having a deal *and all: you, leaving Graeme Anderson and his little Russian friends to me?'* Adopting the kind of 'chummy' tone that had an underlay of warning to it. *'You do* remember *that, don't you?'*

Eh?

She turned in place, looking up at the kitchen units and light fittings.

Did the bugger have a spy camera or microphone hidden in here? How did he *know*?

'You're no more from Organised Crime and Counter Terrorism than I am.'

Could hear the laugh in his voice. *'Aren't I?'*

'Aye.' The pot went in the sink. 'Thirty years on the Job: I can smell another cop a *mile* off, and you don't smell of cop – you smell of *spook*. MI5, or MI6, or SIS, or whatever the hell it is you're calling yourselves these days.'

'Nonsense. I'm just a simple, run-of-the-mill detective superintendent. Cor blimey, Guvnor, salt of the earth, etcetera.' Hard not to see him sitting forward, like a spider, ready to strike. *'And even if I* were *some sort of secret agent – which, I'm not, of course – wouldn't it be* nice *to have someone like that on* your *side, Roberta?'* A loaded silence. *'Hypothetically speaking, of course.'*

Which just made it sound even more like a not-so-veiled threat: *right now, you have a powerful friend. Don't turn him into a powerful enemy.*

Yeah…

Maybe screwing Rifkind over wouldn't be the best of ideas.

She put the butter back in the fridge. '*Hypothetically?* Aye.'

Still stuck in her gusset, though.

'Excellent!' Sounding genuinely pleased that he wouldn't need to have her killed. Yet. *'Take care of yourself, Roberta. We'll be in touch.'*

And with that, he was gone.

Hmmm…

On the bright side: she now had friends in high places, who still owed her a favour.

Which might come in handy.

She turned the radio up again, and the screeching broke free:

'Going in hard, we'll live till we die,
Cranked up to ten, the screams amplify,
Rattle the walls with our battle cry!'

Might not be a bad idea to get the wee loon round. See if he couldn't do some sort of sweep for bugs. Kid on it was just research, for work. Assuming he even knew how to do that.

Bet if he didn't, he'd look it up on the internet…

She popped a tablet into the dishwasher and whumped the door closed. Beep-beep-booped the controls in time with the song.

'It's time for the fire,
It's time: let it burn,
Let it burn, let it burn,
Let the flames all burn higher!'

Followed by an Epic Guitar Solo.

Roberta joined in on her walking stick, using it as a faux air guitar. 'Come on, Genghis, dance with Mummy!'

But Genghis had no intention of dancing with anyone.

Instead, he lay in a plush new bed – in the corner, by the radiator – wearing the cone of shame. The poor lad was wrapped in bandages from the shoulders down, looking very sorry for himself. Which was understandable, given he now had one fewer back leg than before.

But at least his tail still wagged.

She put on a bit of a show for him, giving it the full Middle-Aged-Jimi-Hendrix-In-The-Kitchen Experience – when the doorbell tolled its traditional *dinnnnnng-donnnnnng*.

Killing the radio, Roberta wiped her hands on a tea-towel, grabbed her walking stick, and limped out into the hall.

'Friends' or not, it couldn't hurt to do a *wee* bit of digging into Anderson and his dirty little Kremlin comrades, could it? On the quiet: lowdown, sneaky style.

A figure lurked on the other side of the frosted glass.

Better leave it a couple of weeks, though: let the trail go cold.

Maybe a month. Just to be sure.

After all, these spooks had fingers everywhere. Eyes in every pie…

She opened the door.

It was a woman: one of those mid-forties, hard-faced types, dressed like a sack of tatties against the nippy weather. Red nose, red ears, pink cheeks, multicoloured gloves and a Blackburn Rovers bobble hat.

Mrs Bobble-Hat pointed at the brand-new plaque, mounted beside Roberta's front door:

R. STEEL & ASSOCIATES
CONSULTING DETECTIVES
(FEATURING THE QUEEN STREET IRREGULARS)

A late retirement present from Tufty and the team. Because they weren't bad spuds, *really*.

The woman sniffed back a drip. 'This you?'

'Yup.'

A frown. 'Is the "R Steel" like in "*Remington Steel*"?' Wobbling one hand about in a seesaw gesture. 'Plucky young female private detective has to pretend a man's in charge so people will take her seriously?'

'No. It's my first name: Roberta.'

'Oh. Right, right. Mine's Stacey. Stacey Burrows.' Stacey had a scratch beneath her bobble hat. 'I'm looking for someone to find my sister, Ruby. She went missing from work: Kirkenwell Academy, she's a music teacher. Just drove out of the staff car park one day and we haven't seen or heard from her since.'

Which sounded kind of familiar…

'Oh aye?'

'I did hire a private detective, but he fell out a window.' That pink face scrunched into a frown. 'And now he's in prison, and won't give me my deposit back. And I read about you in the papers. And I just want *someone* to find my sister.'

Roberta pulled on a reassuring smile. 'Why don't you come in and tell me all about it?'

Because *maybe* being retired wouldn't be so bad after all?

With Thanks

A book is a vast wriggly beast, especially a book as big as this. It needs many people to wrangle it into shape, many of whom end up getting quite muddy in the process. And as we all limp away from its cage, battered and bruised, I owe thanks to those who have risked life, limb, and dignity to get this monster ready for you.

So, let's kick off with my lovely editor, Francesca Pathak, for all her help and support, aided and abetted by her excellent sidekick, Emily Sumner. Melissa Bond worked on fixing all my mistakes, while Holly Sheldrake saw the book through production; Anne O'Brien performed her copyediting magic, and Linda Joyce was my ever-constant proofreader. James Annal did the cover and art direction; Laura Sherlock and Kimberley Nyamhondera spanked the publicity; while Claire Bush and Zoe Coxon marketed up a storm, as have the digital team – Andy Joannou, and Alex Hamnet. On the sales front I have to thank Christine Jones, Stuart Dwyer, Ellie Kyrke Smith, Richard Green, Gillian Mackay, Charlotte Cross, and Julia Finegan in the UK, with Leanne Williams taking care of international, while Gordon Kemp and Becca Souster do the digital side. Becky Lloyd is my big noise in the Audio World. Then there's Kerry Pretty and Kirsty Barber in Ops, and the crack team at MDL: Amy Pitcher, Carys Williams, Carwyn Jones, Lianne Bailey, Kelly Patterson, Christian Davies, Julie

Pugh, and Theresa Morgan. And, of course, where would I be without the lovely Lucy Hale and Joanna Prior?

There are bound to be people at Pan Macmillan I've missed off this list, but I assure you it wasn't on purpose and you're still groovy!

More thanks go to Phil Patterson, and the team at Marjacq Scripts for agenting the heck out of me.

A hat-tip is required for the invaluable feedback I received from Allan Guthrie (nee Buchan); I raise a peaked cap to the excellent Chief Inspector Bruce Crawford, who answers all my daft questions about Police Scotland; and I doff my Ushanka to Ilona Chavasse for checking and fixing my Russian; and my bobble hat is off to Tricia Pathak, whose most *excellent* line about 'still being a rat' was perfect for this book.

Let's also give a HUGE THANK YOU to all the Booksellers and Librarians out there. In a world where some people now think it's cool to be thick, uninformed, cruel, and a shitty human being, we need books more than ever. And Booksellers and Librarians are the ones loading the literary cannons and giving these bastards a broadside, even as the tossers do their best to ban every book they disagree with.

Which brings us to *you*, the person reading this. While the tossers besiege the gates, READERS are the ones guarding the ramparts. Thank you for being the last line of defence between us and the darkness. I wouldn't be out here writing books without you.

And now I'll finish by asking Fiona, Gherkin, Onion, and Beetroot to take a bow. They've all helped-and-or-hindered to various degrees (though only one of them brings me tea and biscuits).

Speaking of which, I'm off for a cuppa.

Be good, have fun, and I'll see you in the next book…

'MacBride is a damned fine writer'
Peter James

Move over, Miss Marple...

The great and the not-so-good are gathered at Skirivour Castle Hotel, in the heart of the Highlands, for the wedding of the year – but they weren't expecting Detective Sergeant Roberta Steel to crash their party. And get horribly, *horribly* drunk.

The whole valley's been cut off by a massive thunderstorm and the phone lines are down, so when the father-of-the-bride's body is discovered – decoratively impaled on a stag's head in the hotel lobby – it's up to DS Steel to find out whodunit. Which isn't easy when you've got a monstrous hangover and only a world-weary sergeant and a halfwit police constable for backup.

With no witnesses and every wedding guest a suspect, Roberta will need to use every one of her little grey cells if she's going to catch the killer and get out of there alive.

Discover the world of Stuart MacBride
with *This House of Burning Bones...*

The Granite City is ready to burn
and all it takes is a single spark...

In the heat of a blistering summer, Aberdeen's police are struggling: half the force is off sick, leave has been cancelled, someone's firebombed a hotel full of migrants, and there's a massive protest march happening this Saturday.

With officers dropping like flies, Detective Inspector Logan McRae is forced to juggle cases and run a major murder investigation with a skeleton staff of misfits, idiots, and malingerers until the top brass can arrange backup from other divisions.

It doesn't help that the *Aberdeen Examiner* has just been bought by Natasha Agapova, a tabloid media tycoon hell-bent on blaming local police for everything. And she's *more* than happy to fan the flames.

But, as bad as everything seems,
it's all about to get much, much worse...